Liverpool Annie

MAUREEN LEE

An Orion paperback

First published in Great Britain in 1998
by Orion Books
This paperback edition published in 2017
by Orion Books,
an imprint of The Orion Publishing Group Ltd,
Carmelite House, 50 Victoria Embankment,
London EC4Y 0DZ

An Hachette UK company

1 3 5 7 9 10 8 6 4 2

A CIP catalogue record for this book
is available from the British Library.

ISBN 978 1 4091 7560 5

Printed and bound in Great Britain by Clays Ltd, St Ives plc

MIX
Paper from
responsible sources
FSC® C104740

www.orionbooks.co.uk

Maureen Lee was born in Bootle and now lives in Colchester, Essex. She is one of the best-loved saga writers around, and the author of many bestselling novels including *Mother of Pearl, Nothing Lasts Forever, Martha's Journey* and the three novels in the Pearl Street trilogy; *Lights out Liverpool, Put Out the Fires* and *Through the Storm*. Her novel *Dancing in the Dark* won the 2000 Parker Romantic Novel of the Year Award.

All of Maureen's novels are set in Liverpool and the world she evokes is always peopled with people you'll never forget. Her familiarity with Liverpool and its people bring the terraced streets and tight-knit communities vividly to life in her books. Maureen is a born storyteller and her many fans love her for her powerful tales of love and life, tragedy and joy in Liverpool.

To find out more, please visit Maureen's website,

www.maureenlee.co.uk

For all the Margarets I have known,
not forgetting Audrey and Evelyn

Orlando Street

I

Annie stopped running. Her breath was raw within her pounding chest, and her legs felt as if they were about to give way. She'd come to the stretch of sand where Auntie Dot used to bring them in the summer when they were little, and where she and Sylvia came on warm evenings to talk. Now, at half past ten on a bitter March night, Annie found herself drawn towards the dark isolation offered by the litter-strewn beach.

What had she done? What had possessed her to say those terrible things? She wandered, stiff-legged, towards the water. The texture of the sand beneath her feet changed from fine to moist and the heels of her flat school shoes sank into the mushy surface. The horror of what she'd just witnessed couldn't be true: she'd imagined it, or she'd wake up any minute and find it had been a bad dream, a nightmare.

'Please God, make it not be true!' she prayed aloud in a strange, cracked, high-pitched whisper.

Before her, the black, oily waters of the River Mersey glinted, rippling, reflecting the distant lights of Wallasey and New Brighton and a segment of orange moon which appeared from behind a veil of cloud.

Annie stared into the water which lapped busily at her feet, at the black seaweed which wrapped itself around her shoe, to be swept away when the tide rustled forward in a frill of dirty froth to reclaim it as its own. She was fifteen, nearly a woman, yet felt as if, from this night on, her life was over. She knelt on the sand and began to pray, but soon the prayers gave way to recollections: of her mam and dad, her sister Marie, of Sylvia, and of course, Auntie Dot . . .

She searched for her first memory, but could think of nothing in particular. Those early years living with the Gallaghers had been happy, full of fun, despite the fact the war was on. She remembered it was the day Dot threw the cup at the wall that caused things to change. The cup had been a catalyst. Afterwards nothing was ever the same again.

Auntie Dot was still in the same house in Bootle: small and terraced, outwardly the same as the one in Orlando Street where the Harrisons had lived for over ten years, but inside so very different – full of ornaments and pictures, warm with the smell of baking, and the grate piled high with glowing coals. In 1945, Dot put a big picture of Mr Attlee, the new Prime Minister, over the mantelpiece and kept a little candle burning before it, as if he were a saint.

When Annie and her family were there, there was so much furniture you could scarcely move, because stuff from the parlour had been moved out to make room for a double bed for mam and dad. Annie and her sister slept upstairs with Auntie Dot. Then the war ended and Uncle Bert came home and, somewhat unreasonably Annie thought, expected to sleep with his wife. She was indignant when another bed was acquired from a secondhand shop and put in the boxroom for her and Marie. This meant the settee from the parlour had to be placed precariously on its side, and they had to climb over an armchair to get in and out of bed – which was too small, anyway, even for two little girls.

Still, Annie loved the crowded house, swarming with people, though it was irritating to have to stand in a queue for the lavatory at the bottom of the yard, or compete for food with three growing, hungry boys. The boys were older than Annie, having been born before the war, and she thought Dot was sensible not to have more whilst Bert was away, because they were a handful. Not that Marie was much better. Despite being only three, she was as 'mischievous as a sackful of monkeys', as Dot put it.

'I don't know what I'd do without you, Annie,' Dot said frequently. 'You're the only one who knows how to behave proper, like. You'd never think you were only four.' Annie helped make the beds and dry the dishes. Her favourite job was dusting the ornaments on the sideboard: souvenirs from Blackpool and Rhyl and Morecambe, places where Dot and Bert had gone when they were courting.

'Poor little mite,' Dot said sometimes, ruffling Annie's mop of copper curls. 'What's to become of you, eh?'

Annie had no idea what she was on about. She didn't feel the least bit poor, but warm and secure in the shambolic house where, as far as she knew, the Harrisons would stay for ever. In September she would start school, the one the boys went to, and life would be even better. She loved Auntie Dot with all her heart, and Uncle Bert, once she forgave him for taking over the bed. A tall man with a halo of sandy hair, red cheeks and a bushy moustache, he reminded her of a teddy bear, and bought little presents for the children on pay day: sweets or magic painting books or crayons. Bert was an engine driver who worked shifts, and they had to be quiet when he was on nights and slept during the day.

But gradually, Auntie Dot, who laughed a lot and was always in a good mood, began to get bad-tempered. Perhaps it was because she was getting fat, thought

Annie, noting the way her auntie's belly was swelling, getting bigger and bigger by the day. She snapped at the boys and told Annie and Marie to get out of the bloody way, though her bark was worse than her bite. If anyone at the receiving end of her temper got upset, she was instantly and extravagantly remorseful. Once, when Marie began to cry, her auntie cried, too.

'I'm sorry, luv,' she sobbed, gathering Marie in her arms. 'It's just . . . oh, hell, I dunno, I suppose everything's getting on top of me.'

It was a blustery rainy day in April when Dot threw the cup. Annie and Marie were in their best frocks, having been to nine o'clock Mass with their aunt and uncle and the boys. The pegs in the hall were full of damp clothes, with a neat row of Wellingtons underneath. After Mass, Uncle Bert had gone to bed, with a stern warning to the boys to keep the noise down. Dot knotted a scarf turbanwise around her ginger hair, pulled a flowered pinny over her head and tied it around her nonexistent waist, making her belly look even bigger. She began to iron on the back room table. As each item was finished, she placed it in a pile, until there were two neat folded heaps of clothes and bedding.

'Can't put this lot away till Bert gets up or I can get in the parlour,' she muttered to herself. Every now and then, she changed the iron for the one left on a low gas ring to re-heat. As the fresh iron was brought in, she spat on it with gusto.

The boys, restless at being kept indoors by the rain, disappeared upstairs. After a while, they began to fight, and there was a series of muffled howls and bumps. Dot went into the hall and hissed. 'Tommy, Mike, Alan! Shurrup, or ye'll wake your dad.'

She smiled at the girls, who were squashed together in the other armchair from the parlour. 'Oh, don't you look a picture! The royal princesses don't hold a candle to you pair. What are you drawing? Do your Auntie Dot a nice picture for the kitchen, there's good girls.'

Their best drawings were pinned to the larder door, but now Annie abandoned hers to watch Dot at work. Her aunt's movements always fascinated her, they were so quick and efficient. She would have offered to help, but Dot didn't like anyone under her feet when she was ironing.

The ironing finished, Dot put both irons on the back step to cool and went into the kitchen to prepare dinner, deftly peeling a stack of potatoes and chopping up a cabbage. There was already a pan boiling on the stove, a corner of muslin sticking out under the lid. Annie licked her lips. Suet pudding! She hoped it was syrup, her favourite.

Dot lit the oven and placed a big iron casserole dish of steak and kidney on the middle shelf. To Annie's surprise, she remained stooping for several seconds, wincing. She grasped the draining board, panting, before lighting another ring on the stove and pouring almost a whole pint of milk into a pan. Then she took a big tin of custard out of the cupboard, mixed the remainder of the milk with two tablespoons of powder, poured the whole lot into the pan and began to stir vigorously, her face creased in a scowl. Making custard was a hazardous business: if you didn't remove the pan at just the right time, it burned.

Sitting watching, listening to the spoon scraping the side of the pan, the spit of water on the hot stove, the muffled voices of the boys upstairs, Annie, in the warm, comfortable chair pressed close to her sister, felt a sense of perfect happiness. In about an hour – and although an hour seemed an age away, it would pass eventually – Dot would ask her to set the table, then nine plates would be spread on every conceivable surface in the kitchen and the food would be served, with Dot moving bits of potato and spoonsful of steak and kidney from one plate to another, 'to be fair, like', as she put it. In the middle of this, Dot would say 'Tell your dad the dinner's ready, luv', and Annie would knock on the parlour door and her dad would emerge and collect two meals, one with only minute portions for mam, and take them back with him. Uncle Bert's dinner would be kept warm for later.

The boys began shouting and there was a crash, as if they'd knocked something over. Uncle Bert thumped on the floor and yelled, 'Keep the noise down!' just as there was a sharp rap on the front door.

Dot groaned. 'See who that is, Annie.'

Annie trotted to the door. Father Maloney stood outside. He gave Annie a brief nod, and, without waiting for an invitation, pushed past and walked down the hall, straight into the room full of ironing and thick with the smell of cooking dinner – boiling cabbage predominated.

'Why, Father!' Dot's pretty, good-natured face flushed as bright red as her hair with embarrassment. She pulled the turban off and dragged the pinny over her head, dislodging one of her pearl earrings. It fell on the lino-covered floor with a little clatter and, as she rushed forward to greet the priest, she stood on it, 'I wasn't expecting you today. Annie, Marie, get up and let Father have the armchair.'

She closed the kitchen door and called the boys. They came down and stood meekly against the wall, hands behind their backs, whilst Dot carried out a quick inspection, straightening their collars and smoothing down the tousled ginger heads they had inherited from their mam and dad. Father Maloney gave them a cursory glance. As soon as his back was turned, Mike pulled a face and Marie stifled a giggle.

'Who is it?' Uncle Bert shouted.

'It's Father Maloney, Dad,' Tommy shouted back. Uncle Bert said something incomprehensible and the bed creaked.

The priest didn't stay long. He asked the children if they'd been good, and they assured him they had in their most convincing voices. When he turned to Dot, Mike stuck out his tongue as far as it would go. Annie did her best to keep a straight face. Mike was the favourite of her cousins. His hair was redder than his brothers', he had twice as many freckles, and his blue-green eyes danced with merriment.

'And how are you, Dorothy?' Father Maloney asked gravely.

'I'm fine, Father,' Dot replied with a glassy smile and a killing look in the direction of Mike, whose tongue was performing contortions.

'You look tired, child.' He frowned at the stack of ironing. 'You should treat Sunday as a day of rest, someone in your condition.'

'It's a bit difficult, Father, y'see . . .'

But Father Maloney wasn't interested. He blessed them quickly and departed. Annie and Marie immediately reclaimed the armchair.

The front door had scarcely closed, when Uncle Bert appeared, fully dressed. He'd even managed his tie, though the knot was crooked.

'You're too late, Dad. He's gone,' said Mike.

'Bloody hell!' Uncle Bert swore, and stumped back upstairs. The bed creaked again. He must have thrown himself on it fully clothed.

Dot was scraping her earring off the floor when Alan said, 'What's that smell?'

'Jaysus, the custard!' She opened the kitchen door and a cloud of smoke billowed out. The top and front of the stove were covered with a brown, blistering mess.

7

'I like it burnt,' said Mike.

'I don't,' Tommy countered.

As if this were a signal for another fight, the boys fell upon each other and began to wrestle.

And that was when Dot threw the cup.

It shattered against the wall and the pieces fell onto the sideboard. 'I can't stand it!' she screamed. 'I can't stand it another sodding minute!' She stood in the kitchen door, her hands on her hips, looking madder than anyone had ever seen her look before.

Marie burst into tears, and the boys stopped wrestling and looked at their mother in alarm. Something terrible must have happened, something far worse than burnt custard.

'Is Mr Attlee dead, Mam?' Tommy asked nervously.

Dot glared. Upstairs, the bed creaked and Uncle Bert's weary footsteps could be heard descending. The parlour door opened and the tall gaunt frame of Annie's dad appeared. His hair, paler than Dot's, almost salmon coloured, was plastered close to his narrow head, and his face wore an expression of unrelieved gloom. He looked at everyone nervously, but didn't speak.

Uncle Bert came in and, to Annie's surprise, he sat down and clumsily dragged Dot onto his knee. 'What's the matter, luv?'

Dot buried her head in his shoulder and gave a deep, heartrending sigh. 'I can't stand it another minute. This morning was the last straw.'

'Here, youse lot, buy your mam a bar of Cadbury's milk chocolate and get something for yourselves and the girls while you're at it.' Bert handed Tommy half a crown. 'Take a ration book off the mantelpiece.'

Dot lifted her head. 'Put your coats on, it's still raining.'

Marie's sobs ceased at the prospect of the chocolate, and as soon as the boys had gone, Annie's dad crept into the room and sat down.

'Come on, luv, spit it out.' Bert stroked his wife's arm.

'It's just there's so much to do, Bert, looking after nine people; all the washing and ironing and the cooking. And when Father Maloney came, walked right in and there I was in the middle of the dinner and washing everywhere, I just wished I had me parlour back, that's all.'

There was something significant about this last remark which Annie didn't understand, because everyone fell silent.

It was Dot who spoke first. She looked at Annie's dad directly. 'I'm sorry, Ken, but it was only supposed to be temporary, and it's been over four years. Now, what with Bert back, and another baby on the way – well, the house just isn't big enough.'

There was another silence, and once again it was Dot who broke it. 'If only Rose could give a hand, that'd help a bit.'

Uncle Bert said awkwardly, 'Dot said the corporation came up with a house in Huyton, a nice modern one with three bedrooms.'

Annie's dad spoke at last, and the words came out in a breathless rush. 'It's too far away. Me work's on this side of town, Litherland and Waterloo. I couldn't ride me bike to and from Huyton every day, it must be fifteen or twenty mile.'

Dot took a deep breath. She was still sitting on Bert's knee, clinging to him as if it gave her the courage to speak out. 'Ken, you're me little brother, and I know you've been through a lot with Rose. If this was a bigger house, you could stay for ever, but . . .' She broke off and began to cry quietly. 'Oh, soddit! I hate saying this.'

9

'It's not right, y'know, Ken,' Uncle Bert said gently. 'Rose'll never get better as long as you and Dot wait on her hand and foot. If you had a place of your own, the responsibility might do her good.'

Annie's dad stared at his shoes. 'I'll see what I can do tomorrer. Bootle lost so many houses in the Blitz, there's not much going . . .'

'Good lad!' Bert said heartily as Annie's dad got up and left the room without another word.

Dot looked worried when the parlour door slammed shut more loudly than it need have. 'Now he's got the hump!'

'Never mind, luv. It had to be said.'

'I could kill that sodding Hitler for what he did to Rose.'

Annie, listening avidly, wondered what her auntie was on about.

'She weren't the only one, Dot,' said Uncle Bert. 'Other folks had as bad – and some had worse.'

Dot sighed. 'I know. Even so . . .' Her voice trailed away and they sat together companionably on the chair. 'I suppose I'd better see to the dinner before something else burns.'

'I'll give you a hand, luv.'

Dot giggled. 'You know what our Tommy said when I threw that cup? He asked if Mr Attlee had died. Jaysus, if anything had happened to ould Clement, I'd've thrown the whole bloody tea service.'

Three weeks later, the Harrisons went to live in Orlando Street, Seaforth, and life changed so completely that Annie felt as if they'd moved to the other side of the world.

2

Orlando Street seemed to stretch for miles and miles. More than one hundred polished red brick houses were on either side, built directly onto the pavement, identical, and as seamless as a river. The paintwork was severe: bottle green, maroon or brown doors and window frames, a few black. Once a year, Annie's dad repainted the outside woodwork the same bitter-chocolate colour.

When Annie was older, she would remark disdainfully: 'The world would end if someone painted a door blue or pink. *I'm* going to have the front door of *my* house bright yellow!'

In all the years she lived there, she always had to check the number to make sure it was the right house, and her heart sank when she turned the corner into Orlando Street. The awful day the Harrisons moved to Number thirty-eight remained for ever etched in her mind.

Uncle Bert turned up with a lorry and the beds were loaded in the back, along with their possessions, which Dot had carefully packed in cardboard boxes. Dad's bike was fetched from the back yard.

Dad looked bewildered and angry when he emerged with Mam. She wore her best coat made of funny, curly fur, and blinked at the daylight, as if she rarely saw it, her face all tight and pale.

'The girls'd better go in the back, they can sit on one of the beds,' Dad said curtly as he helped his wife into the cab.

Dot pursed her lips and yelled, 'One of you lads, come here.' When Mike appeared, she said, 'Go with them, luv. Poor little mites, they'll be scared out of their wits stuck in there all on their own.'

Mike evidently thought this a treat. His face lit up, and he leapt into the lorry and threw himself onto the bedsprings with a whoop.

When Uncle Bert picked up Marie, Dot burst into wild tears. 'There's no need to take the girls, Ken. Why not leave them with us?'

Annie, unsure what was going on, had a feeling this would be preferable, and grabbed her auntie's hand, but Dad shook his head.

'No,' he said in a thin, stubborn voice. 'It's about time Rose took some responsibility, like Bert said.'

'Jaysus!' Dot sobbed. 'He didn't mean the girls. Oh, if only I'd kept me big mouth shut!'

An hour later, Annie and her sister watched Uncle Bert drive away, Mike hanging out of the passenger window, waving. They waved back until the lorry turned the corner, then looked at each other nervously and went back into their new house.

Annie hated it as much as she hated the street. She hated the dark, faded wallpaper and the furniture left by the previous tenant, which Dad told Dot he'd got at a knock-down price.

The parlour was scary. There was something sinister about the tall cupboard with its leaded glass doors, the panes like a hundred eyes, glaring at her, unwelcoming and unfriendly, and the big black sideboard, full of whirls and curls, was something the devil himself might have.

She went upstairs and gasped in amazement. A bathroom! She climbed onto the lavatory with some difficulty, and stayed perched on the wooden seat for several minutes to get the feel of it, then pulled the chain. It was odd using a lavatory indoors, and rather exciting, though she'd prefer to be with Dot and Bert and the lavvy at the bottom of the yard.

She tiptoed into the rear bedroom which overlooked the backyard. 'Strewth!' she gasped, in exactly the same tone as Auntie Dot used. Like the parlour, the room was full of dark, gloomy furniture. A dressing table in front of the window shut out most of the light. Another single bed was already there, as well as their own, which meant they could have one each. Their clothes were in a box on the floor.

One by one, Annie gingerly opened the drawers in case anything interesting had been left behind. 'Strewth!' she said again, when the smell of mothballs made her sneeze. Apart from their lining of yellow newspapers, the drawers were empty, as was the wardrobe, except for three coathangers which she couldn't reach.

She unpacked their clothes and put most away, leaving the frocks for Dad to hang up. As she gravely carried out this task, she felt grown up and responsible, though she knew she was only delaying the time she dreaded: the time when she would have to go downstairs and face her mam.

Eventually, when she could put it off no longer, Annie crept down into the living room. Mam was in the armchair by the window, her head turned towards the wall.

Annie stared at her curiously. This pretty lady with the sad grey eyes and cascade of dark cloudy hair was supposed to be her mam, yet she seemed like a stranger. It was Auntie Dot who'd brought them up, taken them to the clinic and to Mass. It was into Dot's warm, rough arms they snuggled when they needed love, whilst their mam remained in the parlour, emerging occasionally on Sundays or at Christmas or if Dot had arranged a birthday tea, when she would sit, wan and pale and silent. Sometimes, at Dot's urging, the girls went in to

13

see her. Mam would be in bed or in a chair, staring vacantly out of the window. The girls never stayed long, because Mam never spoke, hardly looked at them, and a few times she hadn't even opened her eyes.

'It's not her body that's sick, it's her mind,' Dot had told them only a few days ago, and Annie imagined inside Mam's head being full of sores. 'It's that sodding Hitler what done it!' Dot, angry, slammed the iron down onto the collar of Bert's working shirt. 'Poor girl, such a pretty thing she was, well, still is, but the life's been squeezed out of her.'

'What did Hitler do to me mam?' Annie asked, imagining the monster personally squeezing the life out of her mother.

Dot sighed as she steered the iron around a row of buttons. 'Oh, I suppose you've got to know some time, and now's as good a time as any. It's just that you and Marie would have had an older brother if he hadn't been taken to heaven at eighteen months.' She made the sign of the cross. 'Johnny. Lovely little lad he was, dark, like your mam and Marie. He was born the first month of the war, just after our Alan.' She folded the shirt and reached for another. 'One night, after the siren went, your mam left him by himself for a minute, just a minute, mind, when the house was bombed and Johnny was killed. Poor Rose, she's never got over it.' Dot paused over a cuff. 'Mind you,' she said thoughtfully, 'she should be better by now, it's six years. Lots of terrible things happened to people during the war, but they pulled through.'

Standing by her mam, Annie felt overcome with misery. She didn't want to be in this dark, quiet house, away from Dot and Bert and her boisterous cousins. She badly wanted to be kissed and cuddled and told everything was going to be all right. Marie was in the kitchen, chattering away. Dad just grunted in reply. Mam didn't appear to have noticed Annie was there; her face was still turned away. Annie climbed onto her knee and lay there, waiting for an arm to curl around her neck. But her mother remained as still as a statue. After a while, Annie slid off and went upstairs to sit on the bed and wonder what was going to happen to them.

A few minutes later, Marie crept in, her impish little face downcast. 'Don't like it here,' she said tearfully. 'Want Auntie Dot.'

'Sit on me knee,' commanded Annie, 'and pretend I'm your auntie.'

So Marie climbed on her sister's knee, and they sat there, sniffing miserably, until Dad called to say tea was ready.

A month later, Dot appeared with a black pram containing a tiny baby with bright red hair and bright blue eyes. Her belly was back to its normal size, and she looked lean and pretty, in a white cardigan over a green skirt and blouse, and with a green ribbon around her carroty curls.

'This is Pete,' she said proudly. 'Your new cousin.'

She left the pram outside and carried the baby indoors. The girls were so pleased to see her they clung to her skirt, hugging her legs. They'd feared they might never see Dot again.

'Where did he come from?' Marie demanded.

'Can I hold him?' asked Annie.

'I found him under a gooseberry bush,' Dot twinkled. 'Sit down, Annie, and you can nurse him for a while. Careful, now. I'd have come before, but as you can see, I've been rather busy.' As soon as the baby was deposited in Annie's arms, Marie climbed onto her aunt's knee.

Dot turned to Mam, who was in her usual chair by the window. 'How are you, Rose? Have you settled in, like?' she asked brightly.

Annie looked up from examining the baby's face, his short ginger lashes, his petal pink ears, curious to see Mam's reaction. She scarcely moved from the chair all day except to make the tea, when she would waft in and out of the kitchen like a ghost to peel potatoes laboriously and mince meat in the curious rusty machine left by the previous tenant. Often, the potatoes hadn't boiled long enough and were hard inside, and Dad had to do them again. He brought the meat home in his saddlebag, and at weekends did the washing, hanging their frocks and petticoats and knickers on the line. When Mrs Flaherty, the widow next door, offered to help, 'Your poor wife being ill, like,' he churlishly refused.

Mam rarely spoke. Even if the girls asked a question, she mostly didn't answer, just looked at them in a vacant way, as if they were invisible and she wondered where the voice had come from.

'I think so,' Mam whispered in response to Dot's enquiry.

'And how are you coping with the girls, Rose? Don't forget, I'd be happy to have them if they're too much for you. We've missed them a lot. In fact, Alan cried every night for a week after they'd gone.'

Not to be outdone, Marie said quickly, 'We cry too, Auntie Dot. Me and Annie cry every single night.'

'Do you now!' Dot said in a tight voice. 'And what do you do with yourselves all day?'

Annie and Marie looked at each other.

'We draw.'

'And play with our dolls.'

'Have you been to the park yet? And there's sands not far away.'

'No, Auntie, we haven't been anywhere, 'cept to the shop for a loaf sometimes,' Annie said importantly. 'Our dad leaves the money.'

'I see!' Dot's voice was still tight. 'Shall we go to the sands now?'

'Yes, please!' they chorused.

'Get your coats, then. There's a chill in the air for June.'

Dot didn't say another word until they were outside. As they walked along Orlando Street with Pete tucked up in his pram and the girls skipping along each side clutching the handle, she asked casually, 'Are you eating proper? What do you have for breakfast?'

'Cornflakes,' replied Annie, 'and we have bread and jam for dinner.' She didn't add, because she felt Dot wouldn't approve, that it was she who got the cornflakes because Mam usually forgot, and by the time they were hungry again and there was no sign of food on the horizon, she would cut four thick slices of bread and smear them with margarine and jam. Twice she'd cut her finger as well as the bread, but the blood merged with the jam and was hardly noticeable.

'Bread and jam? Jaysus, that's no meal for two growing girls,' Dot said caustically. 'You got better than that in our house.'

'Bread and jam's me favourite,' Marie piped, so Dot said no more, though later, as she steered the pram across the busy main road, she said firmly, 'From now on, your Auntie Dot'll come as often as she can.' Then she muttered, half to herself, 'As for your mam, I'm not sure whether to feel sorry for her, or give her a good kick up the arse!'

Annie started school in September. On her first day, Dad went into work late and took her on the crossbar of his bike.

St Joan of Arc's was in Bootle. Her cousins were already there and could 'keep an eye on her', Dot promised. It was a long walk, but Annie was glad to return to the familiar bombscarred streets, where women sat on their doorsteps on sunny days, and children played hopscotch on the pavements or whizzed around the lampposts on home-made swings. No-one played out in Orlando Street. Most residents were old, and if a child dared so much as kick a ball, they were told to play elsewhere.

One of the best things about school was the dinners. Dinners were almost as nice as lessons. Because she wanted the nuns to like her, Annie paid close attention during class. She was one of the first to learn to read and do sums, but her favourite lesson was drawing. The nuns called it 'Art', and were impressed with her pictures of 'pretty ladies in nice dresses'. One, Sister Finbar, wrote a note to Annie's mam to say she must be 'encouraged with her artwork', but Mam merely held the unopened envelope on her knee till Dad came home and read it.

'Good,' he mumbled tiredly.

Annie's dad was an insurance collector. He went into the office each morning to 'bring the books up', and spent the rest of the day riding round on his bike collecting payments, a penny here, twopence there. He came home at seven, exhausted. This was because he had a gammy leg, Dot told them. He'd broken it when he was little and it hadn't set properly.

'That's why he didn't fight in the war like your Uncle Bert. Poor Ken, he should have a sitting-down job, not be riding round on that sodding bike eight hours a day,' Dot sighed. 'Who'd have thought our Ken would end up like this, eh? Your gran, God rest her soul,' she crossed herself, 'thought the sun shone out his arse. She hoped he'd go to university, him being a scholarship boy an' all, but he met your mam, and . . . Oh, well, it's no use crying over spilt milk, is it?'

Annie hadn't been at school long when Colette Reilly asked her to tea. She enjoyed being made a fuss of by Mrs Reilly.

'Our Colette's little friend!' she cooed. They sat down to jelly and cream and fairy cakes with cherries on top. Then Mrs Reilly cleared the table and they played Ludo and Snakes and Ladders and Snap.

'When can I come to yours?' Colette demanded as Annie was leaving.

'Don't be rude,' Mrs Reilly laughed. 'Wait till you're invited.'

'I'll have to ask me mam,' said Annie. She pondered over the matter for days. If she could go to Colette's, it seemed fair Colette should come to hers, but she couldn't imagine Mam making jelly or fairy cakes, and she felt uneasy asking someone to the dark, gloomy house which was exactly the same as the day they'd moved in. Although Uncle Bert had offered to decorate – 'A bit of distemper'd go over that wallpaper a treat, Ken, brighten the place up no end' – her dad had turned him down as churlishly as he'd done Mrs Flaherty when she'd offered to help with the washing. 'I like it the way it is,' he said stubbornly.

Eventually, Annie plucked up the courage to approach her mam. 'Colette wants to come to tea,' she said nervously.

Mam was in her dressing gown, the blue one with silk flowers round the neck and cuffs. The red one with the velvet collar had gone to the dry cleaner's on Saturday. Mam wore her dressing gowns a lot. She looked at Annie, her lovely grey eyes vacant, empty. 'No,' she said. 'No.'

That night when Annie was in bed, Dad came in.

'You must never ask children to this house,' he said in his faint, tired voice. 'Never.'

So Annie never did. In a way, she felt relieved. She didn't want anyone to know her mam couldn't make jelly and wore a dressing gown all day and didn't know how to play Snakes and Ladders.

If the nuns expected another star pupil when Marie Harrison started school, they were to be sadly disappointed. Marie was in trouble from the first day, when she stole another new girl's ball and threw it on the roof where it lodged in the gutter. Annie had been looking forward to her sister's company, but at going-home time, Marie was nowhere to be seen. She was off to play on a bomb site or down a crater or in North Park with a crowd of boys, and came home hours late with grazed shins and torn clothes, though Mam didn't seem to notice.

Not to be outdone, Annie began to wander the streets of Bootle and Seaforth, staring in shop windows or through the gates of the docks, where dockers unloaded cargoes from all over the world. Her imagination soared, visualising the boxes of fruit and exotic-smelling spices being packed in sunny foreign climes. As the nights grew dark, though, and the cruel Mersey winds whipped inland, her adventurous spirit wilted, and she wished she were at home in front of the fire with someone to talk to and something to eat. Since both girls started having school dinners, Mam didn't make a meal till Dad came home.

One day in November, when it was bitterly cold and raining hard, she went down the entry and in the back way, and was surprised to be met by Auntie Dot, looking extremely fierce. 'Where the hell have you been?' she demanded. 'It's gone five. And where's Marie?'

Dot was growing fat again, but this time Annie knew it was because she was having another baby. She jealously hoped it wouldn't be a girl. Dot mightn't love them so much if she had a daughter of her own.

Her aunt grabbed her arm, full of angry concern. 'Look at the state of you! You'll catch your death of cold. Get changed this minute and put your coat in the airing cupboard while I make a cup of tea.'

When Annie came down in a clean frock, she found Pete, now eighteen months, playing happily with wooden blocks. She glanced at her mam, and was surprised to see her cheeks were pink and she was twiddling with the belt of her dressing gown. Dot came in with a cup of steaming tea.

'Get those wet shoes off and put them on the hearth,' she barked. 'And I'd like an answer, madam. Where have you been till this hour, and where's your sister?'

'I went for a walk and Marie's gone to North Park.' Annie thought it wise not to mention the bomb sites and craters.

'Really!' said Dot caustically. 'It's not what I'd call walking weather, meself. As for the park . . .' She shook her head as if the situation was beyond her comprehension. Annie fidgeted uncomfortably.

'Do you know what day it is?' Dot demanded.

'Tuesday,' Annie replied, adding, 'the seventeenth of November.' She remembered thinking when Sister Clement wrote the date on the blackboard that it had a familiar ring.

'That's right, Marie's birthday! Nice way for a five-year-old to spend her birthday, in the park in the rain – isn't it, Rose?' She turned on the hunched woman in the corner. 'I come round with a cake and presents from us all, thinking there'd be a birthday tea, and what do I find? You've *forgotten*! Forgotten your own daughter's birthday! Not only that, there's no food in the offing of any description.'

This was said with such derision that Annie winced. For some reason she felt guilty. Her own birthday had fallen on a Sunday in October and they'd gone to Dot's for tea. Mam didn't answer, but began to shake her head from side to side. Dot, well into her stride, continued, 'Even worse, the girls aren't even in, and you're sitting here in your sodding dressing gown and don't give a shit, you selfish cow!'

Annie gasped. Her mam's head turned faster and faster and her eyes rolled upwards. She started to moan, and Dot leaned across and slapped her face, hard. 'Don't put on your little act with me, Rose,' she said in a low, grating, never-heard-before voice. 'You've had me fooled for years, but no longer. You're taking our Ken for a ride. If he's idiot enough to be taken in, that's his concern, but you're not getting away with it with these two girls. They're little treasures, the pair of them. I love them as if they were me own and you'll look after them proper or I'll have them taken off you. Do you hear?'

To Annie's surprise, Mam stopped moving her head and nodded. For a while, her mouth worked as if she were trying to speak, and perhaps she would have if Marie hadn't come bouncing in. Her shoes squelched and she was soaked to the skin and covered in mud, though she gave Dot a cocky smile. The smile vanished when Dot removed the shoes none too gently, and ordered her upstairs to change.

Then Dot turned to Mam, and in a gentler voice said, 'This can't go on, Rose. Two little girls wandering the streets, it's just not right. God knows what sort of trouble they could get into. In future, I'll get our Alan to stand by the gate and make sure they go home.'

Poor Alan, thought Annie, he'd have a fit. Dot

dropped to her knees, somewhat clumsily due to her big belly, and grasped Mam's hands. 'I know what our Ken was up to that night, luv, but it's time to forgive and forget, if only for the sake of your girls.'

At this, Mam's face grew tight and she turned away, just as Marie came running downstairs.

Dot sighed and got awkwardly to her feet. 'Where's the ration books? Keep an eye on Pete for me while I get some cold meat, a few tomaters and half a pound of biscuits from the corner shop. There'll be a birthday tea in this house today or my name's not Dot Gallagher.'

Dot stayed till Dad came home, and after the girls had gone to bed there came the sound of a big argument. Annie crept onto the stairs to listen.

'I've told you before, Ken,' her aunt said loudly. 'If you can't cope with the girls, Bert and me will have them.'

'They're my girls, Dot,' Dad said in the quiet, mutinous voice he often used with his sister. 'They're my girls, and I love them.'

Things improved, but only slightly. There was a meal waiting when they got in – beans on toast, or boiled eggs – and Mam was dressed properly. Their normally curt and reticent dad gave them each a front-door key, as well as a stern lecture on coming straight home, describing the bloodcurdling things that could happen if they didn't. A girl had been murdered during the war, he told them, strangled with a piece of string in a back entry a mile away. Marie, easily frightened, rushed home panic-stricken, clutching Annie's hand.

But Mam stayed enclosed in her own private, grief-stricken world, hushed and uncommunicative. She only showed signs of life in the minutes before her husband was due home, when her head would be cocked like a bird's, waiting for the sound of the latch to be lifted on the backyard door, the signal of his arrival. During the meal, she sat watching, noting his every move, her listless eyes lifting and falling as he ate.

The meal finished, Dad would turn his chair towards the meagre coke fire and read the newspaper, the *Daily Express*, his wife still watching with the same hungry, melting expression on her face. No-one spoke. After a while, Annie and her sister would go upstairs and play in the chilly bedroom, and later on they'd go to bed of their own accord, and Dad might put his head in to say goodnight if he remembered.

Except for the occasions when Dot and Bert came round, this was how every evening passed; there was never any variation.

As the years went by, Annie became protective of her mother. She lied when Dot asked questions. Although her aunt only had their best interests at heart, she'd hated seeing Mam slapped and bullied.

'Mam made a cake for tea the other day.'

'We play Snakes and Ladders nearly every night.'

Anyroad, Dot didn't come round much nowadays. As soon as she'd had the new baby, another boy called Bobby, she'd fallen pregnant again and Joe was born a year later. Now she had six boys, 'Three little 'uns and three big 'uns', as she cheerfully put it. 'By the time afternoon comes, all I want to do is put me feet up.' It meant it was Dad who took Annie to the shops to buy a white dress and a veil for her First Holy Communion. The same outfit did Marie the following year.

Auntie Dot insisted the girls visit on Sundays. They did for a while, until Annie, conscience-stricken, decided she should stay at home and help her dad. Despite the long hours he worked, he spent all weekend doing housework. At eight, Annie was doing the week's shopping and even wrote the list herself. 'Poor little mite,' Dot said sorrowfully. 'She's old before her time.' Annie learnt to iron, and, as she knelt on the chair in front of the table, she couldn't help but wonder what the hunched, helpless woman in the chair by the window was thinking. About Johnny, her brother? Did she know she had two daughters? Once, Dot said Mam should be in hospital, but that was silly, thought Annie. Where would they put the bandages?

On the Sundays her mother could be persuaded to go to Mass, Annie felt proud as they walked along Orlando Street, just like a normal family. Mam looked so pretty in her curly fur coat, her long hair tied back with a ribbon, though Annie couldn't help but notice curtains twitching in the windows of some houses as they passed; curious neighbours watching 'the funny woman from number thirty-eight' on her way to church – which was how she'd once heard her mam described whilst she waited, unnoticed, at the back of the corner shop.

It would be nice to have a mam who wasn't 'funny', Annie thought wistfully, and a cheerful dad like Uncle Bert. One day, she found a wedding photo in the drawer of the big black sideboard. She stared at it for quite a while, wondering who the handsome couple were; the bright-eyed, smiling girl in the lacy dress clutching the hand of a young man with dashing good looks. The pair stared at each other with a strange, intense expression, almost sly, as if they shared a tremendous secret. It wasn't until Annie recognised a younger Dot, and Uncle Bert before he'd grown his moustache, that she realised it was her parents' wedding.

She showed the photograph to Marie, who looked at it for a long time before her face crumpled up, as if she were about to cry. Then she turned on her heel and left the parlour without a word.

Annie put the photo back in the drawer and resolved never to look at it again.

3

When Annie was eleven, she sat the scholarship. The entire class were to take the exam, but she was one of the few expected to pass. Passing the scholarship meant attending a grammar school instead of an ordinary secondary modern.

Marie was contemptuous. 'Seafield Convent! You'll never catch me at an all-girls' school. When *I* sit the scholarship, I'll answer every question wrong for fear I pass.'

The exam was set for nine o'clock one Saturday morning early in June. Annie's dad, who rarely became animated, was concerned she wouldn't arrive on time.

'I'll wake you when I leave,' he said in his flat, tired voice.

'Don't worry, Dad,' Annie said cheerfully. 'It's like any other day, except it's Saturday. I'm never late for school, am I?'

When the morning came, she was woken by the pressure of his hand on her shoulder. 'It's seven o'clock,' he whispered. 'There's tea made. Mam's still asleep,' he added somewhat superfluously, as if Mam were likely to be of use if she were awake.

'Rightio.' Annie snuggled under the clothes. She heard him manoeuvre his bike into the back entry and the wheels creak as he rode away. Sunlight filtered through the thick brown curtains. She lay, dazzled by the long bright vertical strip where the curtains didn't meet. She didn't feel at all nervous. She liked exams and was looking forward to the scholarship. They'd been doing special homework for weeks.

But after a while, she began to feel uneasy. Something was wrong. The bed felt sticky and her nightie was glued to her legs at the back. Annie stayed there for a good five minutes trying to work out what it was, then, gingerly, she got up. She gasped in horror. The sheet was stained with blood! Terrified, she twisted her nightdress round, and found it even bloodier.

She was going to die!

There was a dull, tugging ache in the pit of her stomach, as if heavy weights were suspended there about to pull everything out. Annie shook with fright and uttered a thin, high-pitched wail. The sound disturbed Marie, who turned restlessly and pulled the eiderdown over her head.

'Marie!' Annie shook her sister awake. She had to talk to someone.

'Whassa matter?' Marie sat up, pushing her dark hair from her eyes.

'Look!' Annie pointed to the bed, then to her night-dress.

'Jaysus!' said Marie in a startled voice. 'It must be that thing.' Despite being younger, Marie was better versed in the ways of the world than her sister. Months ago, she'd described how babies were born.

'What thing?' Annie cried piteously.

'I can't remember what it's called, but it happens to everyone – women, that is.'

'Why didn't you tell me!'

Marie shrugged. 'I thought you already knew.'

Her sister's lack of concern calmed Annie somewhat, though she still felt frightened. So, she wasn't going to die, but would she bleed like this for the rest of her life? The thought was infinitely depressing.

'What shall I do?' It didn't cross her mind to approach her mam.

'Tell Dot,' Marie said promptly, which was what Annie had already decided as soon as the words were out of her mouth.

The questions in the scholarship paper didn't make sense. Annie read and re-read them, but all she could think of was the lump of old petticoat between her legs and the fact that blood might come rushing forth and drown the whole class. She forgot entirely how to do decimals, and couldn't remember what an adjective was.

The two and a half hours dragged by interminably. When the time was up, she left the paper on the desk, knowing she had failed miserably.

Tommy opened the door to Annie's knock. The eldest of Dot's boys, at seventeen he was as tall as Bert, though as thin as a rake like his mam. He wore a blue shirt under his best suit, and his ginger hair was cut Tony Curtis style. If he hadn't been her cousin and she hadn't felt so wretched, Annie would have thought him immensely attractive.

'I'm just off into town to the pictures,' he said vaguely as she entered the house. Music came from a wireless upstairs; Alma Cogan sang 'How much is that Doggie in the Window?' In the kitchen Dot was singing along at the top of her voice. There was no sign of Bert, and Annie had already noticed the younger boys playing in the street.

'Hallo, luv,' Dot smiled, but the smile faltered when she noticed Annie's tragic expression. 'What's the matter?'

'I've failed the scholarship!'

Dot's face fell, but only slightly. 'It's not the end of the world, luv, I don't believe in grammar schools, anyroad. Most kids pay to go and they're just a crowd of snobs. You'll be far better off in an ordinary secondary modern like the boys.'

'It's not only that,' said Annie tearfully, 'it's . . .'

Mike came banging down the stairs, pushed Annie to one side, and began to clean his teeth in the sink. Alan had taken up the singing where Dot left off, and he was trying to mimic Alma Cogan's gutsy tones in a way which, at any other time, would have made Annie smile.

'What, luv?' urged Dot, then seeing Annie's eyes flicker to her cousin, she said, 'Come on, let's go in the parlour.'

The parlour had long been returned to its former glory. The three-piece suite was in its proper place and the polished gatelegged table in the centre took up an inordinate amount of space considering it was only used on special occasions. In the corner, in pride of place, stood a new addition, a television, covered with a brocade cloth and a statue of Our Lady. A few days ago, at least twenty people had crowded into the room to watch the coronation of Queen Elizabeth and listen to Richard Dimbleby's commentary, almost drowned out at times by Dot's vigorous condemnation of royalty and all it stood for.

As she sat in the grey moquette armchair, Annie began to weep the tears she'd longed to weep all day. 'When I woke up this morning, the bed and me night-dress were covered in blood . . .'

'Oh, you poor love!' Dot dropped on her knees and stroked Annie's face with her chapped hand. 'And you weren't expecting it?'

Annie shook her head dolefully. 'That bloody Rose, I could strangle her!' Dot raged. 'I should have told you, shouldn't I? It's just that having boys, it didn't cross me mind.' She began to cry, her emotions seeming to swing wildly from sympathy for Annie, anger with Rose, and recriminations against herself. After a while, she wiped her face with her pinny. 'Tell you what, let's have a treat! A little drop of whisky each, eh? Do your tummy good and calm your nerves.'

She opened the sideboard, took out a half full bottle, and poured an inch of liquid into two glasses. 'I often have a tot meself,' she said, cheerful again. 'But only one, mind; more, and I'm not responsible for me actions. Bert'll kill me when he finds it half gone.'

Annie choked on the whisky at first, but it seemed to warm her insides and she began to relax.

One of the boys suddenly yelled, 'Mam, where's me blue shirt?'

'Jaysus!' gasped Dot. 'I'm sure that's what our Tommy went out wearing. It's in the wash!' she screamed.

'Oh, Mam!' the voice said mournfully.

Dot grinned. 'Do you feel better now, luv?'

Annie nodded. She felt pleasantly light headed.

'I'll fit you up with something before you go,' Dot promised, 'and tell you what to buy each month.'

'You mean it's not for ever? It stops sometimes?'

'It's just a few days once a month, that's all. You'll soon get used to it,' Dot said comfortably. 'Some women look forward to the curse.'

'The curse!' Annie smiled for the first time that day. 'You won't tell me dad, will you?'

'No, luv, but what about your mam? Are you going to tell her?'

Annie avoided Dot's eyes and shook her head.

Dot gave a disgusted, 'Humph! You've been having me on, haven't you, Annie? Rose playing Snakes and Ladders! You must think I was born yesterday. I never said anything, because Bert told me to mind me own business. He said as long as you and Marie seemed all right, I shouldn't interfere.' She absent-mindedly poured herself another glass of whisky.

Annie fidgeted with a loose thread of grey moquette on the arm of the chair. She noticed faint smudges of crayon in the rough loops of the material. It must be from the kitchen, where she and Marie used to draw.

'Will me mam ever get better?' she asked Dot directly. It was something she'd wanted to know for a long time.

As if it had provoked a chain of thought, instead of answering, Dot said, 'Oh, your dad! He was a real ladykiller in his day, just like our Tommy. He'd got more girls in tow than a sheikh with a harem.'

Annie resisted the urge to laugh. Dad, her stooped, weary father with his peaked face, the man who brought meat home in his saddlebag and spent the weekends doing housework – a ladykiller!

Dot noticed her incredulous expression. 'He was, Annie,' she said indignantly. 'He attracted women like a flypaper attracts flies. Out with a different girl every night he was, until he met your mam. Then, wham, bang! It was love at first sight.'

Annie recalled the wedding photograph in the sideboard drawer, the couple sharing a great secret.

'I'm glad I didn't fall in love like that!' Dot said primly. 'I love Bert with all me heart, but with our Ken and Rose, it was too hungry, too . . .' she searched for another word, 'too overwhelming,' she finished.

'Dot,' Annie said cautiously, knowing her aunt was slightly drunk and might reveal things that ordinarily she wouldn't, 'what was me dad up to the night Johnny was killed? You said something about it once . . .'

'I remember,' Dot said darkly. She leaned back in the chair and finished off the whisky. Suddenly, the wireless was switched off and Mike and Alan came stamping down the stairs like a pair of elephants.

'Tara, Mam,' they shouted. The front door slammed, then there was a clatter, and 'Tara, Annie', came through the letterbox.

Dot smiled and looked as if she might cry again. 'Aren't they lovely lads? I'm a lucky woman, what with Bert an' all.' She didn't speak for a while, and Annie thought she'd forgotten her question, until she leaned over and took her niece's hand. 'I suppose you've a right to know, luv. You're nearly grown up, specially with what happened today.' She took a deep breath. 'Your mam and dad had their own house off Chestnut Grove in those days. The night Johnny died, your dad was late; he should have been home long before the siren went. The shelter was only at the bottom of the street and Rose got all the things together you need for a baby. She took them to the shelter, meaning to come straight back for Johnny, and . . . well, you know the rest. She'd only set foot inside when the bomb fell. If your dad was there, they'd have taken Johnny with them.' Dot paused and eyed the whisky bottle, but made no move to touch it.

'And what was me dad up to?' whispered Annie.

Dot stared into her empty glass. 'He was an awful weak man, your dad. He couldn't resist a pretty face, even if Rose was the only woman he wanted. It came out he was with someone else, and no, Annie, I don't think your mam will ever get better, because she's too eaten up with jealousy and hatred, all mixed up with terrible love, and in my opinion, it's nowt to do with Johnny dying, but because your dad betrayed her.'

'I see,' said Annie, wondering if she did. Her aunt was still clutching her hand, and now her grip tightened, so hard that Annie winced.

'He's me little brother, and he did an awful thing, but no man has paid more thoroughly for his sins than our Ken.' Dot's voice began to rise and became grating, almost hysterical. 'Sometimes I wonder if it's all a sham with Rose, if she's putting it on, trying to squeeze every last drop of remorse out of him. But no-one could put on an act like that for so long, surely? No-one could be so twisted as to wreck so many lives, including their own, could they, Annie?'

Annie wished she'd never raised the subject. Dot frightened her. Her eyes glinted strangely and she looked almost unhinged. She tried to extricate her hand, but her aunt's grip was too strong.

'She was already expecting you when it happened,' Dot said hoarsely. 'We thought another baby'd do the trick, bring her back to her senses, but it made no difference. As for Marie, she was an accident.' She laughed bitterly and eyed the whisky bottle again.

Annie managed to drag her hand away. She returned the bottle to the sideboard and said brightly, 'Shall we have a cup of tea, Auntie Dot?'

Later, when they were having the tea, Dot recovered her good humour. 'I'm sorry, luv, for letting off steam just now. I should never have had that second glass of whisky.'

Annie was relieved her aunt was back to her amiable, good-natured self. She was glad she'd come, after all. She'd learnt a lot about Mam and Dad, though she doubted if it would help to understand them better.

When the letter arrived to say she'd failed the scholarship, Dad merely shrugged his shoulders wearily and didn't say a word.

Grenville Lucas Secondary Modern school had been built after the war. It was a light, airy two-storey building with modern desks and equipment. The walls were covered with drawings, the work of the pupils themselves, done in the art room overlooking the tree-lined playing fields.

Annie went into the top stream, though soon discovered she was no longer a star pupil. There were many boys and girls cleverer than she would ever be. After a while, being clever didn't matter. What mattered was making friends, being one of the 'in-crowd'. The worst thing that could happen was not being invited to join a clique, being an outsider.

To her surprise, she found herself quite popular, and eventually attached herself to Ruby Livesey, leader of a nameless sisterhood of about a dozen girls. Ruby was stout, with the gait of a heavyweight boxer and the reputation of being a bully. It seemed wise to be in her good books, though Annie was to regret this decision in the years to come.

Also, she was flattered to be asked. The other girls in Ruby's gang were all in their second year. When she asked why they'd chosen her, the reply was astonishing. 'Because you're so pretty.'

Pretty! That night, Annie studied herself in the misty, scarred wardrobe mirror. 'Do you think I'm good-looking?' she asked her sister.

Marie was lying on the bed reading *Silver Star*. 'You're okay,' she shrugged. 'Your face is quite a nice shape, though I couldn't stand having red hair meself.' She tossed her own brown tresses. 'What are the boys like at Grenville Lucas? Have you been asked out yet?'

'Of course not!' Annie hooted. 'I'm not quite twelve.'

'I've been going out with boys since I was five.'

'If me dad knew, he'd kill you.'

'He wouldn't give a shit!'

'Don't swear!' The reproof was automatic. Marie swore like a trooper.

'Dot swears,' countered Marie.

Annie couldn't be bothered arguing. She continued examining her face. It *was* a nice shape, sort of oval, rather pale and slightly freckled between the eyes. Her

34

hair was more copper than red, darker than the Gallaghers', and thicker, a mass of natural waves and curls.

'You've got nice eyes.' Marie put down her magazine and regarded Annie speculatively. 'Sometimes they're blue and sometimes they're grey, and your lashes are a lovely gold. I'd advise you not to use mascara when you're older.'

'Thanks!' Annie said sarcastically. 'Do you think we'll grow tall, like Dad and Auntie Dot?'

Marie frowned at the ceiling, as if her height were something she often put her mind to. She was remarkably adult, though in a different way from her sister. Whilst Annie ran the house as confidently as a woman, Marie did nothing to help at home, but *thought* like a woman. She read adult magazines and spent hours in front of the mirror combing her hair and posing like a film star. The effect of the lecture Dad had given all those years ago had long since worn off. Annie knew her sister went to North Park with boys after school. When she tried to reason with her, Marie laughed in her face. Last term she'd been caught smoking, and the nuns had written to Dad, though nothing had been said. He was increasingly tired nowadays, as if everything were too much for him.

'I reckon I'll be the same height as our mam,' Marie said after serious consideration. 'Dot always says I'm the spitting image of her. You'll probably end up tall. Fortunately, you've already got more curves than Dot, who's as skinny as a scarecrow, so I reckon you'll look okay.'

Annie went to bed that night feeling unusually happy. It was nice to discover at such a late age that you were pretty!

One good thing about Grenville Lucas was that,

although Annie was asked to some girls' houses, they didn't automatically expect to come to hers. It was taken for granted that not all parents welcomed their daughters' friends. After school, Ruby Livesey and the gang went to the shops in Waterloo, where they hung around Woolworth's and Boots. A few girls shoplifted. When this happened, Annie edged into another aisle so she wouldn't appear to be with them if they were caught.

Other days, they went to a café for a cup of tea, where they often met up with boys from Merchant Taylors, and Annie was amazed at the change which occurred in Ruby. Normally overbearing and bossy, she collapsed into simpering giggles and her gruff voice went up an octave. No-one else seemed to find this transformation in any way remarkable; indeed, they were too busy simpering themselves.

It was at this time Annie realised she needed money of her own. It was embarrassing when someone else had to pay for her tea, and she was never able to buy anything from Woolworth's. When the girls went to the pictures on Saturdays, she had to refuse.

'Ask your dad for some pocket money,' Dot urged when Annie explained her predicament. 'He can afford it.'

'Can he?' Annie felt bewildered, having assumed they were poor.

'Of course he can. One thing our Ken's always been is a good insurance salesman. His wages aren't up to much, but he earns as much again in commission.'

So Annie approached her dad for pocket money, and was surprised when he offered five shillings a week, much more than the other girls.

The incident was a revelation. Since they'd moved to Orlando Street, nothing new of any description had been bought for the house. Their food was basic, almost meagre. The only expensive item on the weekly shopping list was fresh fruit for Mam, which Annie had never seen her eat, but she must have done some time, because the fruit had always gone by Saturday when she went shopping again. Even at Christmas nothing extra was bought, because they always went to Dot's on Christmas Day.

Annie wasn't sure whether to be angry or pleased at the discovery they weren't poverty-stricken. Emboldened, she approached her dad for new clothes. In December, the gang were planning a day in town to go Christmas shopping, and she didn't fancy wearing her school uniform.

Her dad's expression was one of sheer bewilderment when she asked for a coat, as if it had never crossed his mind his daughters might want anything other than the barest essentials. Annie stared at his drawn, white face. She hadn't noticed before, but his features seemed to be collapsing in on themselves as the years took their toll, smudging and blurring, and she felt scared that the day might come when he'd have no face at all. His light blue eyes were sinking back into his narrow skull, and there were little silvery channels glistening underneath where the eyes had watered. They looked like eternal tears.

Annie felt a pang of guilt for having bothered him. She touched his sleeve. 'It doesn't matter, Dad, honest.'

He glanced down at her hand with a look of faint surprise, as if he were unused to human contact. She could feel the sharp bones in his wrist. 'It doesn't matter, Dad,' she said again.

To her astonishment, he smiled, and the change was so enormous it almost took her breath away. His thin, almost invisible mouth quivered upwards and his face took shape again. For a brief, magical moment, Annie glimpsed the ladykiller in him.

'I suppose you want to look nice for the boys,' he said

in a jokey voice which Annie had never heard before and would never hear again.

'That's right, Dad.' She didn't disillusion him, but it wasn't the boys she wanted to look nice for, but herself.

'Well, my girl must look as good as the others,' he said simply.

Straight after work the following Saturday, he took her to Stanley Road in Bootle, and bought her an emerald green winter coat, two jumpers and a skirt, and a pair of black patent leather shoes.

'Oh, Dad, it's lovely,' she breathed as she twirled in front of the mirror. The green was a perfect contrast to her bright copper curls.

But Dad was no longer interested. He nodded briefly and paid the assistant. They walked home without saying a word, and so fast that Annie could scarcely keep up.

4

Pupils who hadn't been at Grenville Lucas from year one, who appeared in class suddenly and without warning, were regarded with the deepest suspicion. The suspicion was even greater if they had a strange accent. It took Ian Robertson from Glasgow a whole term to make friends.

So when Sylvia Delgado arrived during Annie's third year, she was looked upon with loathing – but only by the girls. When Mr Parrish, the headmaster, ushered the new girl into class halfway through a Geography lesson in November, several boys risked a cheeky wolfwhistle.

Annie was in the process of colouring a map showing the wheat-growing areas of Canada. She looked up to see a tall, slender girl beaming at them with a heroic and slightly aggressive self-confidence, as if she expected everyone to like her on the spot.

The wolfwhistles weren't surprising. The girl was the first genuinely beautiful person Annie had ever seen, with fine, delicately-formed features and ivory, almost translucent skin. Her long blonde hair was dead straight, cut in a jagged fringe on her forehead. Even from the back of the room, it was possible to see the startling azure blue of her eyes, the thick dark lashes under equally dark, perfectly shaped brows.

'This is Sylvia Delgado,' Mr Parrish said brusquely. 'She's from Italy, and I hope you'll make her very welcome.'

Italy! There was an excited buzz. There'd never been a foreigner at school before. The girl nodded at the class and smiled again.

'It is so very nice to be here,' she said, in perfect English with just the faintest suggestion of an accent.

The headmaster exchanged a few words with the teacher, Mrs Wayne. After he'd gone, Mrs Wayne looked around for an empty seat. As usual, there were vacant desks near the front. She indicated to the girl where to sit and told the class sharply to settle down.

The agricultural map of Canada forgotten, Annie glanced covertly at the new girl, who was on the next row to her, several desks in front. Her long slim legs, clad in honeycoloured stockings and crossed elegantly at the ankles, protruded into the aisle, as if the desk were too small, and the heel of one black suede ballerina shoe was dangling from her toes. She wore a uniform of sorts: a gymslip made from fine serge material, more like a pinafore frock, with a scooped neck instead of square. The folds of the full flared skirt fell in a half circle beneath the seat. Annie felt convinced that the white blouse underneath this remarkably fashionable garment was pure silk from the way it shimmered when the girl bent her elbow and began to write.

She would love Sylvia Delgado to be her friend, Annie thought longingly, not just because she was beautiful and wore expensive clothes, but because there was something appealing about her demeanour. She felt sure that, if they got to know each other, they would have lots in common – though probably every other girl felt the same. New pupils weren't usually accepted for ages, but it was bound to be different with this girl. Everyone would be clamouring to be her friend.

But Annie couldn't possibly have been more wrong.

She had no idea where the new girl sat at dinner time, but when they emerged from the dining room, Annie saw her standing alone in the playground, looking rather deflated.

'Who's that?' demanded Ruby Livesey.

'Her name's Sylvia Delgado, she's Italian,' Annie said importantly. 'She only started this morning.'

'Italian!' Ruby expostulated rudely. 'Why's she blonde, then? I thought Italians were dark.'

'I've no idea.' Annie had wondered the same. 'Shall we talk to her?'

'Not bloody likely,' Ruby snorted. 'Being Italian's almost as bad as being German. We fought them bloody Eyeties during the war.'

Even Sally Baker, Ruby's trusted first lieutenant, felt bound to remark, 'But the war ended ten years ago, Ruby.'

'Yeah, but even so!' Ruby stared belligerently at the new girl. 'I've changed me mind. I *will* have a word with her, after all. Tell her what I think of bloody foreigners.'

'No!' cried Annie, but she was ignored. As the girls,

Ruby at their head, marched across the playground, Annie trailed miserably behind. She couldn't wait for the summer term when Ruby Livesey, who was already fifteen, would leave. She was sick of belonging to her gang, fed up going to the pictures and seeing only Ruby's choice of film, and hanging around in cafés talking to stupid boys. She would have broken off relations long ago, but lacked the courage, having witnessed what Ruby did to those who got on her wrong side. She didn't fancy being dragged into a back entry and beaten up on the way home from school.

Two boys were already chatting to the new girl when they arrived. 'Sod off!' Ruby barked. The boys looked at her in surprise. They laughed, but readily departed. She plonked herself squarely in front of the girl and sneered, 'So, you're a bloody Eyetie!'

The girl's lovely dark blue eyes grew puzzled. She threw back her head. 'I am Italian, yes,' she said with dignity.

'Me Uncle Bill was killed by your lot during the war.'

This was a lie. Uncle Bill's ship had been sunk by a German U-boat, but it was more than Annie's life was worth to point this out.

The girl replied with the same quiet dignity, 'I'm sorry about your uncle. But my father is a communist who hated Hitler and spent the war fighting the Germans in Yugoslavia.'

Annie gasped. Although Russia had been an ally of Britain during the war, for some reason she couldn't quite understand it was now her greatest enemy, ready to atom bomb the country any minute. Russia was made up entirely of communists. Fortunately, Ruby seemed ignorant of this fact and appeared momentarily confused. She swiftly recovered her composure, 'What the hell are you doing in our country, anyroad?' she demanded.

'My father has bought a hotel in Waterloo. My mother is English, she was born in Formby. We have decided to make England our home.' The girl tossed her long blonde hair defiantly and Annie admired her spirit. Although clearly shaken, her manner was proud, almost queenly.

'You got any brothers or sisters?' one of the girls asked curiously.

'No. I am a lone child.'

The gang tittered, and Ruby said threateningly, 'We don't like foreigners in this country, particularly Eyeties, so keep out of our way in future. Understand?'

Sylvia Delgado nodded stiffly. 'I understand.' Her dark eyes swept slowly over the group, as if she were memorising them. Annie dropped her own eyes and wished she could crawl under a stone.

To emphasise that her threat was real, Ruby gave the girl a vicious shove, grabbed her leather satchel and flung it across the concrete yard where it slithered to a halt in a cloud of dust.

As if taking their cue from Ruby, not one of the girls spoke to Sylvia Delgado, apart from Ruby's own frequent verbal, and sometimes physical, assaults. Wherever Sylvia was, she would be tracked down and given the sharp edge of Ruby's tongue, along with a blow if her tormentor happened to be in a particularly foul mood. Sylvia became the sole topic of conversation, and Annie was shocked by the sheer spite of the comments.

'Me dad said columnists are a load of shit. He reckons Sylvia's dad should be shot.'

'He's a communist, not a columnist,' Annie said hotly. 'When I told me Auntie Dot, she said he was a hero.' But no-one was willing to listen to a word in Sylvia Delgado's favour.

'Have you seen where she lives? It's that big hotel opposite the Odeon. S'not fair, a foreigner living in a dead posh place like that.'

'What gets me is she don't half fancy herself. She walks around as if she owns the place. You'd think she was Marilyn Monroe or something.'

'Not Marilyn Monroe, she's nice. I wouldn't mind being her meself. No, Grace Kelly. She always looks as if there's a bad smell under her nose, and she's living in a palace with that French prince, isn't she?'

'It's that cruddy gymslip that gets me,' complained Sally Baker. 'If any of us wore one like that, Mr Parrish'd have a fit.'

'We should rip it off her back and tear it to pieces,' Ruby said balefully. 'Tell her to get one the same as ours.'

The girls glanced at each other nervously. 'Perhaps that's going a bit far, Ruby.'

'Y'reckon!' Ruby sneered. 'Well, something's got to be done to take the bitch down a peg or two.'

'But she hasn't done anything,' Annie protested. She felt angry. Although Sylvia Delgado still walked with her head held high, she looked slightly desperate, as if she were gradually being worn down. Annie wished she were brave enough to ignore Ruby, because she liked Sylvia Delgado more than ever and longed to be her friend. She didn't care if she came from Italy or Timbuctoo.

Ruby turned on her and began to list all the terrible, imaginary things Sylvia had done to justify her treatment. Intimidated, Annie didn't say another word.

As the autumn term drew to a close, the subject of Sylvia Delgado was put aside temporarily as plans were made for Christmas. The gang were going to the pictures on Christmas Eve, but Ruby hadn't yet made up her mind what to see. On the Saturday after school finished, a shopping trip to Liverpool was planned. Several girls were having parties.

Annie had asked for more housekeeping and had been buying extra groceries for weeks: a tin of assorted biscuits, a plum pudding and a fruit cake she intended icing herself, several tins of fruit. She was determined the Harrisons would enjoy the occasion for once, and had even bought decorations and a little imitation tree.

The sisters put the decorations up one day after school. Throughout the entire operation, their mam sat in her usual chair, her head turned away, her long dark hair falling like a curtain over her incredibly girlish face. She seemed oblivious to everything, even when Marie climbed on the table and banged a nail directly above her head. The girls would have been astonished if she'd acted any differently.

'What do you think, Mam?' Annie nevertheless asked when the decorations were up and the room actually looked quite cheerful. She saw Mam's hands were clasped tensely on her lap, the knuckles white and strained. 'Perhaps she's frightened,' Annie thought with compunction.

Mam didn't answer, and Marie said contemptuously, 'It's no use asking her, is it? You'd only drop dead if she answered.'

'Shush!' Marie frequently made horrible, insensitive comments in Mam's hearing – at least, Annie assumed she could hear.

'Why should I?' Marie demanded. 'She's way out of it, drugged to high heaven.'

'What on earth are you talking about?'

Marie looked at her sister impatiently. 'Honestly, Annie, you're not half thick. You haven't a clue what's going on. Mam's got all sorts of tablets in the cupboard. She takes pills all day long.'

'You mean aspirin?' Aspirin were the only pills Annie knew of.

'I've no idea what they're called, but they're different shapes and colours. They deaden your brain so you don't have to think. I pinched one once when she went to the lavvy. It was a nice feeling, nothing seemed to matter, but I fell asleep in the pictures and it was *Singin' in the Rain.*' She pouted. 'I missed most of it.'

With that, Marie flounced upstairs to get ready for a date. She spent all her pocket money on clothes and cosmetics. In a while, she'd come down dressed to the nines, her face plastered with Max Factor pancake, burgundy lipstick, and far too much shadow and mascara on her lovely grey eyes, looking as glamorous and pretty as a film star, and more like eighteen than thirteen.

Annie knew it was a waste of time saying anything, and neither Mam nor Dad seemed to care. She sighed as she went to get the tea ready – Mam had given up the ghost ages ago when it came to preparing meals.

Grenville Lucas held their customary party on the day school broke up. Lessons finished at mid-day. After a turkey dinner, festivities would transfer to the gym. It was the only day in the year when the pupils could dispense with school uniform and wear their own clothes. Marie even got up early as she couldn't make up her mind what to put on.

Annie wore a new plaid skirt and her favourite jumper, pale blue cable knit with a polo neck. The two girls set off at half past eight full of excited anticipation, Annie little realising the day would turn out to be one of the most momentous of her life.

In class the girls were eyeing each other with interest, assessing the various fashions, when Sylvia Delgado came in wearing the most beautiful frock Annie had ever seen. Made of fine, soft jersey, it was turquoise, with a high buttoned neck and full bishop sleeves gathered into long, tight cuffs. A wide, tan leather belt accentuated her incredibly slender waist.

A girl behind gasped involuntarily, 'Doesn't she look lovely!'

Sylvia's long blonde hair was tucked behind a gold velvet Alice band decorated with tiny pearls. When she sat down, Annie saw she was wearing tan leather boots with *high heels*! Annie's skirt and jumper suddenly seemed very drab, and her feeling of envy was mixed with alarm. The outfit would drive Ruby Livesey *mad*!

'Who the hell does she think she is, coming to school tarted up like a bloody mannequin!' said Ruby for the fifth, possibly the sixth, time.

Christmas dinner was over and they were in the gym watching the dancing; Mr Parrish was playing his Frank Sinatra records. Sylvia Delgado had been up for every dance, but not a single boy had approached Ruby or her gang, though some girls danced with each other. Annie felt a stirring of interest in the opposite sex. She hated dancing with girls, particularly Ruby, who insisted on being the woman and it was like pushing a carthorse round. It was particularly irritating to see Marie floating past, always in the arms of a different boy.

'I hate her!' Ruby spat. 'If it wasn't for her, those boys'd be dancing with us.'

The logic of this escaped Annie, as there was only one Sylvia Delgado and eleven of them. As far as she was concerned, the party had turned out to be a wash-out. She couldn't wait for it to be half past three when she could throw away her paper hat and leave – not that she intended going home. They were going shopping; Ruby might well get on her nerves, but was infinitely preferable to her silent mam.

It was almost dark by the time they reached Waterloo, and freezing – the road led straight down to the River Mersey. Little icy spots of rain were blowing on the biting wind which gusted under their skirts and up their sleeves, penetrating the thickest clothes.

Despite the cold, they were happy. Every now and then, they would burst into song, 'White Christmas', or 'I saw Mommy kissing Santa Claus', though it ended in a giggle after a few bars when their jaws froze.

Annie had recovered her good humour. It was difficult not to when there were decorations everywhere, and coloured lights, and the shops were packed with happy people. There was a lovely atmosphere, and she felt heady with excitement.

Carols could be heard along the road, and they came to a churchyard, where five black-cloaked nuns were standing around a large crib with almost life-sized figures, singing 'Away in a Manger' at the top of their glorious soprano voices. A large crowd had stopped to sing with them.

Annie paused, entranced. The scene was like a Christmas card. The churchyard was surrounded by frost-tipped holly trees strung with sparkling lanterns, and the vivid colours were reflected over and over in the gleaming, thorny leaves. The white starched headdresses of the women were like giant butterflies, quivering slightly as if about to soar away. Above it all, icy drops of rain could be seen against the navy-blue sky, blowing this way and that like tiny, dancing stars. As Annie watched, a real star appeared, which seemed to be winking and blinking especially at her. The other girls were already some distance ahead. 'Let's sing some carols,' she called.

They stopped. 'It's bloody freezing,' Ruby complained.

'Just one,' pleaded Annie. 'After all, it's Christmas.'

'Oh, all right, just one.'

The nuns began 'Silent Night', and everyone joined in. Annie was singing away when Sally Baker nudged her. 'See who's over there!'

Sylvia Delgado was standing at the back of the crowd, staring wide-eyed, as if as entranced as Annie by it all. She wore a thick suede coat with a fur collar which looked incredibly smart.

Annie only half heard the message being passed along the line of girls. 'See who's over there!' She felt annoyed when her arm was grabbed and someone hissed, 'Come on, quick! Let's get out of here.'

'Why?' she asked. 'The carol hasn't finished.'

A man's voice shouted angrily. 'Look what someone's done to this poor girl!'

Ruby and the gang were nowhere to be seen. Puzzled, Annie left the church and saw them running down the road, laughing. They disappeared into Woolworth's and were still laughing when she caught up with them.

'What happened?' she demanded.

'Ruby pushed Sylvia Delgado right into the middle of a holly tree. You should have seen her face! One minute she was there, then, "whoosh", she'd completely disappeared!'

Annie said nothing. She thought of Sylvia innocently watching the lovely Christmas scene, little realising she was about to be attacked.

The girls were at the jewellery counter discussing what presents to buy each other. 'What would you like, Annie?' Sally Barker called.

'I wouldn't be seen dead with anything off youse lot,' Annie said coldly.

They stared at her in surprise. One or two had the grace to look ashamed, as if they knew the reason for the normally easy-going Annie Harrison's strange behaviour.

'Merry Christmas,' she said sarcastically. Turning on her heel, she marched out of Woolworth's to cries of, 'But Annie . . .'

The nuns were still in the churchyard, but there was no sign of Sylvia Delgado. Minutes later, Annie stood by the Odeon opposite the hotel where Sylvia lived. The traffic was heavy, and every now and then her view was blocked when a doubledecker bus or a lorry crawled by. The hotel was called the Grand, an appropriate name, she thought, because it was very grand indeed. Three storeys high, it was painted white and had little black wrought-iron balconies outside the windows of the first and second floors, and a red-and-black striped awning across the entire front at ground level. The doors were closed, and she wondered if it was more a posh sort of pub, rather than a hotel where people stayed.

She wasn't sure how long she stood there, hopping from one foot to the other, and swinging her arms to try and keep warm. Time was getting on, and if she didn't take her courage in both hands soon, she would be late with Dad's tea. She didn't want him coming home on such a bitter night to find there was no hot meal waiting.

Eventually, she took a deep breath and dodged through the traffic across the road. She peeped through the downstairs window of the hotel. Apart from a string of coloured lights across the bar, the big room was in darkness. She went around the side and found a small door, where she rang the bell and waited, her stomach knotted with nervousness.

After a while, the door was opened by a slim woman whom Annie recognised immediately as Sylvia's mother. Not quite so beautiful, eyes a slightly lighter blue, and several inches shorter than her daughter, but lovely all the same. Her blonde hair was cut urchin style, in feathery wisps around her face. She wore black slacks and a pink satin shirt blouse, and smiled kindly at the visitor.

'Is Sylvia in?' Annie gulped.

'I heard her come home a minute ago. Are you a friend from school?' The woman looked delighted. 'Come in, dear. Quickly, out of the cold.'

'Thank you.' Annie stepped into the neat lobby and the change from numbing cold to instant heat was almost suffocating. She noticed a metal radiator fixed to the wall, which explained why Sylvia's mother could walk round in a satin blouse in the middle of the winter!

'And who are you? You must call me Cecy, which is short for Cecilia. It's pronounced, "Si Si" – "yes" in Italian. I can't stand being called Mrs Delgado by my daughter's friends. It makes me feel very old.'

'I'm Annie. Annie Harrison.'

'Come along, Annie. I'll show you up to Sylvia's room.'

Annie felt uncomfortable when Mrs Delgado – Cecy – linked her arm companionably and they went upstairs together. Would the welcome be quite so warm if Sylvia's mother knew she hadn't exchanged a single word with her daughter since she'd started school?

When they reached the first-floor landing, Cecy shouted, 'Sylvia, darling, one of your friends is here.' She pointed up the second flight of stairs. 'First door on the right. I'll bring coffee in a minute.'

'Thank you, Mrs . . . I mean, Cecy.'

The knot in Annie's stomach tightened. What sort of reception would she get? It would be quite under-standable if Sylvia ordered her off the premises. As far as she was concerned, Annie was an acolyte of Ruby Livesey, someone who'd made her life a misery for weeks.

She was about to knock on the door when it opened, and Sylvia regarded her haughtily. There was an ugly red scratch on her creamy cheek. The two girls stared at each other.

'Hello,' Annie said awkwardly.

'Hello. I was wondering if you'd come. I've been watching you across the road for ages.' Sylvia gestured towards the window.

Annie took a deep breath. 'I came to say it wasn't me. I knew nothing about it till afterwards. Are you badly hurt?'

'Did they send you to find out?' Sylvia looked angry. 'I wouldn't have thought they cared.'

'No!' Annie said quickly. 'I came of me own accord. They don't know I'm here – not that it'd worry me if they did.'

'If you must know, there are tiny scratches all over my head. It's a good thing I went in backwards or I could have been blinded.' She shuddered. 'The scratch on my cheek happened when I was being pulled out. Cecy will have a fit. I've managed to avoid her so far.'

'I'm awful sorry,' Annie mumbled.

'Are you truly?' Sylvia looked at her keenly.

Annie nodded her head. 'I'm sorry about everything.'

Sylvia's lovely face broke into a smile. 'In that case, why don't you come in and sit down, Annie – it is Annie, isn't it?'

'That's right.' Annie entered the room and sat in an armchair. The suede coat Sylvia had been wearing lay over the arm.

'I think my coat's ruined,' Sylvia said sadly. 'Bruno bought it for me because he said England would be cold.'

Annie saw the coat was scored with little jagged marks. 'Bruno?'

'My father. It cost two hundred thousand lire.'

'Jaysus!'

Sylvia laughed. It was an attractive laugh, like every-thing else about her, deep and faintly musical. 'That's not as expensive as it sounds, about a hundred pounds in English money.'

'Jaysus!' Annie said again. Her coat had cost £8.9s.11d. 'If you use a wire brush, the marks won't show so much.'

'Perhaps,' Sylvia shrugged. 'It's my own fault. I was only showing off. I wore my most elegant dress and Cecy's boots as a way of thumbing my nose at those awful girls. Why should I look drab to please them?'

It was Annie's turn to laugh. She forgot that until very recently she'd been one of the awful girls herself, albeit unwillingly. 'You couldn't look drab if you tried!'

Sylvia tossed her head conceitedly and looked pleased. Her eyes met Annie's for a long moment, and in that moment, Annie knew the ice had been broken. There was no need for more explanations and apolo-gies. Sylvia had forgiven her and from now on they would be friends.

'Is this room all yours?' Annie had only just noticed the bed tucked underneath the white sloping ceiling. The room was large, almost twenty feet square, thickly carpeted from wall to wall in cream. Some-what incredibly, because Annie was unaware such a thing was possible, the fresh daisy-sprigged wallpaper was exactly the same pattern as the frilly curtains and the cover on the bed. There were a wardrobe and dressing table in pale creamy wood, a desk and two armchairs.

'It's what's called a bedsitting room,' explained Sylvia.

'It's dead gorgeous!' Annie breathed. 'It's like a film

star's.' Sylvia even had her own gramophone with a stack of records underneath. Amidst the paraphernalia on the dressing table, the silver-backed mirror and hairbrush, several bottles of perfume and pretty glass ornaments, stood a pearl crucifix with a gold figure of Jesus. Sylvia was Catholic. It meant they had something in common.

'What's that?' She pointed to a small wooden shield on the wall.

'Our family coat of arms,' Sylvia explained. 'Please don't tell anyone at school, but my father is a Count. He has another, much larger shield in the bar, and thinks it a great joke to tell everyone he's a Count, then tell them he's a communist. Bruno is very gregarious; he loves arguing, particularly about politics. That's why he bought the Grand, so he would have an audience for his views. He's not interested in money. We already have pans.'

'Pots,' said Annie. 'You have pots of money, not pans.'

There was silence for a while, then Sylvia said shyly, 'What are you doing on Saturday, Annie?'

'Nothing.' Annie had decided to have no more to do with Ruby Livesey. The decision would cause unpleasantness when she returned to school, but she didn't care. She and Sylvia would face it together.

'I haven't bought a single present yet. I wondered if you'd like to go shopping in Liverpool? We could have lunch and go to the cinema.'

'I'd love to!' cried Annie. 'Having lunch' sounded dead posh. If she did the washing on Friday, she'd have Saturday to do as she pleased.

Cecy came in with coffee and a plate of chocolate biscuits. She yelped in horror when she saw her daughter's scratched face, and immediately fetched disinfectant and cotton wool.

'I caught it on a tree,' Sylvia explained.

'You silly girl!' Cecy said fondly as she dabbed the wound.

Annie would have loved a room like Sylvia's, and a two-hundred-thousand lire coat, but what she would have loved most of all was a mam who cared if she came in hurt. 'Mam wouldn't notice if I came home carrying me head underneath me arm,' she thought drily.

5

At ten o'clock on Saturday morning, Annie waited on Seaforth station for the Liverpool train. Sylvia was catching the five past ten from Waterloo and they would meet in the front compartment. It was colder than ever. A pale lemony sun shone, crisp and bright, in a cloudless blue sky.

Annie thought of the rack in the kitchen which was crammed with clothes she'd washed the night before, the larder full of groceries, and the beef casserole slowly cooking in the oven. There was nothing for Dad to do when he came home from work. He could read the paper or watch sport on the recently acquired television which had been bought at Annie's insistence. Even Marie stayed in one night to watch a play.

She stared at the signal, willing it to fall and indicate the train was coming, and did a little dance because she had never felt so happy. Next week, it would be Christmas and today she was going into town with her friend! On the platform opposite, a porter watched with amusement.

'Someone's full of the joys of spring, even if it is December,' he shouted.

The silver lines began to hum, the signal fell, and a few minutes later the train drew in, and there was Sylvia, exactly where she'd said she'd be! She wore a red mohair coat and a white fur hat and looked every bit as happy as Annie.

Liverpool was glorious in its Christmas splendour. Carols poured out relentlessly from every shop and the pavements were crammed with people laden with parcels struggling to make their way along.

The first thing they did was buy a copy of the *Echo*. In the Kardomah over coffee, they excitedly scanned the list of films. They had to finish shopping in time for the afternoon performance.

'Which one do you fancy?' asked Sylvia.

'You say first.'

'I'd love to see *Three Coins in a Fountain*. It's set in Rome and I miss Italy awfully.'

'Then that's what we'll see.'

'Are you sure?'

'Positive,' Annie said firmly. 'I saw Rossano Brazzi in *Little Women* and I thought he was dead smashing.'

'Next time, you can have first choice. Now, as soon as we've finished our coffee, you must take me to George Henry Lee's. According to Cecy, it's the finest shop in Liverpool.'

On her few excursions into town, Annie had never ventured inside George Henry Lee's, deterred by the mind-boggling prices in the window. Once there, Sylvia began to spend at a rate that took Annie's breath away; a black suede handbag for Cecy, a silk scarf for Bruno, a fluffy white shawl for her grandmother.

'My grandparents are flying over for Christmas,' she explained. 'Now, what shall I get for Grandpapa?'

They went to the menswear department, where, after much deliberation, she chose a long-sleeved cashmere pullover. 'Aren't you going to buy any presents?' she asked Annie after a while.

'Not here,' Annie said, embarrassed. She'd managed

to save nearly five pounds by assiduously putting aside a shilling a week from her pocket-money for a whole year. 'I'll get mine in a less expensive shop.'

Sylvia was profusely apologetic. 'I'm so tactless! Shall we go somewhere else? You lead the way.'

They linked arms as they made their way towards the exit. At the jewellery counter, Sylvia paused. 'Are we going to exchange presents? Those bracelets are very elegant. I'd like to buy one for you.'

The bracelets were diamanté, huge dazzling stones in a chunky dark gold setting. They were very elegant indeed, but they were also £4.19s.6d!

'No, ta,' Annie said quickly. 'They're lovely, but your present must cost the same as mine. I couldn't afford that much.'

Sylvia nodded understandingly. 'What about these pretty little pendants? Nine and elevenpence. Is that too much? I haven't got the hang of English money yet.'

'That's half an English pound.' Annie stared at the pendants on a display card on the counter. There were ten different designs, tiny enamelled flowers no bigger than a sixpence on a fine gold-plated chain.

'This one would suit you perfectly, an orchid.' Sylvia pointed to the second pendant down, a red and blue and gold flower. 'You are like an orchid, Annie, you seem to change colour all the time. One minute your hair is red, then the light changes and it's gold. Your eyes are different, too; blue, then grey, then blue again.'

Annie felt as if she could cry. No-one had ever paid her such a lovely compliment before. 'I'd like it very much,' she whispered.

'In fifty years' time,' Sylvia said sagely, 'you will see this little orchid in your jewellery box, tarnished, faded and old, and will always be reminded of Sylvia Delgado and the day she bought it for you.'

'That's a very profound remark from such a young

lady!' the elderly assistant said, wrapping the orchid in tissue paper and tucking it inside a cardboard box.

'Thank you,' Sylvia said demurely.

Annie noticed one of the pendants was shaped like a rose. She'd never bought a present for her mam before, it seemed a waste of time. 'I'll have a pendant, too,' she said impulsively. A rose for a Rose!

Later, when they were having their lunch in Owen Owen's restaurant – special Christmas fayre, roast chicken and plum pudding – Annie said, 'Why didn't you go to a private school, seeing as you're so well off?'

Sylvia made a face. 'Because Bruno doesn't believe in private education. He considers it a basic right which should be the same for everyone, rich and poor alike. No-one should be allowed to pay for better teachers, better schools. He's the same with most things. When Cecy had me, he insisted she use the local hospital, where they left her in labour for days because they were so backward. Then she was stuck in a ward with peasant women who hated her. That's why I am a lone child. She had such a terrible time, she swore she'd never have more children.'

'Bruno'd get on with me Auntie Dot and Uncle Bert. They're in the Labour Party.' Bert was chairman of the local branch.

'I doubt it,' Sylvia said darkly. 'He hates socialists almost as much as he hates fascists. Don't ask me why, it's something to do with state ownership and banks and shares and capitalism.' She glanced at her minute gold watch. 'We have half an hour before the film starts. Just time enough for you to show me St George's Hall.'

Annie gaped. 'What on earth do you want to see that for?'

'Bruno said it's one of the most beautiful buildings in Europe.'

'Is it really?' Annie had never noticed anything remarkable about it. 'I haven't bought you a present yet!' She'd got dad a tie, earrings for Marie, a box of handkerchiefs for Dot and tobacco for Uncle Bert.

'I told you, I'd like those red gloves.'

Annie screwed up her nose. 'But they'll wear out.'

'What else do you expect gloves to do?'

'It means one day you'll throw them away. I'd like to get you something permanent, like my pendant.'

'Maybe we'll see something on the way to St George's Hall.'

But by the time the curtains closed on *Three Coins in a Fountain*, and Frank Sinatra crooned the last notes of the haunting theme song, Annie still hadn't bought Sylvia a present.

Sylvia was in tears. The picture had made her feel homesick. 'The music is so beautiful,' she sniffed. 'I could listen to it for ever.'

Annie had a brainwave. 'I'll buy you the record for Christmas! In fifty years' time, when I look in my jewellery box and think of you, you can play *Three Coins in a Fountain*, and think of me!'

It was an anti-climax after the glorious day to walk into the house in Orlando Street: like entering a tomb, Annie thought miserably. The television was on without the sound and Dad looked up, but didn't utter a word of greeting. Mam's face was turned away. Annie wondered if they spoke to each other when they were alone.

Marie was out, as usual. Annie could go out later if she wished. She'd been invited to a party, but as Ruby Livesey would almost certainly be there, she decided to stay in and watch television.

She went upstairs to unpack the presents. She still had Sylvia's record, and had been invited to the Grand on

Christmas Eve to get her pendant. She opened the box containing Mam's rose and touched the little petals with her finger. Downstairs, her father's footsteps sounded in the hall and the door slammed. He must be going to the corner shop.

Annie was never quite sure afterwards what prompted her to do what she did. In fact she could remember nothing between Dad slamming the door and finding herself standing in front of her mother, gazing down and marvelling at her girlish face. How incredibly pretty she was! She hadn't aged a bit, not like Dad. In fact, she looked much younger than Cecy, who, according to Sylvia, spent a small fortune on creams to keep the wrinkles at bay. Annie noticed the almost childish curve of her chin, the way her long dusky lashes rested on her smooth cheeks. It was such a shame, she thought sadly, such a waste.

'Mam,' she said loudly. 'I've got you a present.'

Mam didn't stir. It was as if Annie had never spoken.

'I've got you a present, Mam,' she said again, even louder, but still there was no reaction. She leant down and twisted the frozen face towards her. 'I've got you a present. It cost nine and elevenpence and you've got to take it off me,' she shouted.

Annie fell to her knees until the face was level with her own. It was of tremendous importance that she make her mother hear. 'Look, Mam, it's a pendant, a rose.' She took the pendant out of its box and dangled it by the chain. 'A rose for a Rose. I bought it specially because it's so pretty. Please, Mam, please take my present.'

Mam opened her eyes and looked directly at her daughter, and Annie stared deep into the pools of grey, seeing little shreds of silver and gold that she'd never known were there. Mam gave an almost audible gasp, as if she'd never seen Annie before.

'Let me put it on for you, Mam.' Annie's hands trembled as she reached behind and fastened the clasp. Mam's hands went up to her throat and she began to finger the little pink rose.

'There!' Annie said with satisfaction. 'It looks dead nice.'

'Thank you,' Mam whispered.

Annie felt the urge to weep. She stayed at her mother's feet and laid her head on her lap. Slowly, surreptitiously, she slid her arms around the slim legs until she was hugging them tightly.

They stayed that way for a long time. Then Annie felt her body tingle as there was a soft, almost imperceptible movement, and Mam was gently stroking her head.

'Oh, Mam!' she whispered.

There came the sound of Dad's key in the door, and the hand was abruptly removed. When Annie looked up, her mother's head was turned away and her eyes were closed.

She scrambled to her feet, heart thudding, and was in the kitchen by the time Dad came in. What did it mean? Had it been a charade all these years, a sham, as Dot suspected? Why did Mam stop when she'd heard the key?

Annie let the clothes rack down and began to feel the washing, removing the items that were dry, spreading the still damp clothes out so they'd be ready for ironing by tomorrow. Her hands were shaking as she pulled the rack up and wound the rope around the hook in the wall.

Could it be that Mam really was so full of a mixture of hate and love that she'd deliberately shut herself off from the world just to punish Dad? Or maybe it was herself she was punishing for leaving Johnny alone. Either way it wasn't fair, Annie thought bitterly.

60

In the end, she decided she'd probably imagined the whole thing. Mam hadn't been stroking her head, not really. It had merely been an involuntary action and she didn't know what she was doing.

Any other explanation didn't bear thinking about.

On Christmas Eve, Annie set off with Sylvia's record tucked under her arm and permission from Dad to stay out late – not that Marie, who came home at all hours, ever asked. After the Grand had closed they were all going to Midnight Mass, even Bruno, who, said Sylvia, had promised not to sneer. He'd offered to bring Annie home by car. Annie had been looking forward to the evening ever since Sylvia had suggested it.

'If you've nothing else to do on Christmas Eve, why don't you come and have supper? We could play records and talk.'

Supper! Annie hadn't realised you could ask someone to supper, and they were going to have *a glass of wine* with the meal!

Although it was only half seven, through the window she could see the Grand was already packed with customers. Every table was occupied and there were crowds massed around the bar. The noise was deafening.

She went round the side and rang the bell, and had to ring a second time before Sylvia answered. To Annie's surprise, she wore a plain black dress and a white apron. The scratch on her cheek had faded to pink.

'Oh, Annie!' she cried dramatically. 'How I wish you were on the telephone and I could have prevented you from coming!'

Annie's heart sank. 'What's wrong?' she asked, hoping her awful disappointment didn't show on her face.

'Two of the waitresses haven't turned up.' She dragged Annie into the lobby. 'We are all at sevens and eights at the moment.'

'Sixes and sevens.' Annie made an attempt at a smile.

'There's a dinner for thirty in the Regency Room and a party in the Snug. I'm so sorry, Annie, I was really looking forward to tonight, but I can't desert Cecy when she only has one helper.'

'I'll help,' offered Annie, praying the offer would be accepted. She would do anything rather than return to Orlando Street.

'Sylvia!' Cecy shouted impatiently. 'The soup's waiting.'

'Coming!' Sylvia shouted back. She turned to Annie, looking sceptical. 'Another pair of hands would be more than welcome, but it's not a very exciting way to spend Christmas Eve.'

'I don't mind a bit what I do.'

Sylvia still looked sceptical. 'Are you sure?'

Annie nodded with all the enthusiasm she could muster. 'Positive!'

'In that case, hang your coat up and come into the kitchen.'

'*Sylvia!*' Cecy screamed.

The kitchen was a long room at the back which ran the entire width of the hotel. Several pans, lids rattling, steamed on the eight-ringed stove. Wearing a white overall, a red and perspiring Cecy was carving a massive turkey. A middle-aged woman dressed like Sylvia was just leaving with a tray laden somewhat precariously with bowls of soup.

'Annie's come to help,' said Sylvia.

'Take those sandwiches to the Snug,' Cecy snapped.

'I'll show you.' Sylvia picked up a tray of soup. As they went upstairs, she said, 'My grandparents are asleep in all this chaos. Their plane was held up, the train was late and they're exhausted. That's the Snug.' She nodded towards a door on the left.

Annie knocked. There was a buzz of voices inside,

but no-one answered, so she cautiously opened the door and went in. The room was thick with smoke. A dozen people in armchairs seemed to be engaged in a furious argument with everyone else. A dozen hands reached for the sandwiches and she found herself holding a magically empty plate.

A voice called, 'I say, miss, we'd like another round of drinks.' The man turned to the others. 'What are you having?'

'I'll have a beer.'

'Me, too.'

'Whisky and ginger for me.'

The orders came thick and fast and Annie did her best to memorise them; four beers, three ciders, a whisky and ginger, two gin and tonics, a Pimms No 1, an orange cordial.

Repeating the order under her breath, she raced back to the kitchen. 'Four beers, three ciders . . .' She searched wildly for paper and pencil and wrote it all down with a sigh of relief.

'Whew!' She mopped her brow. 'The people in the Snug want these,' she said, handing the list to Cecy.

'Take it to the master in the bar,' Cecy said cuttingly. 'Say it's for his bloody Marxist friends. Once you've done that, there's sausage rolls to take up. I daren't give them all the food at once, else they'd eat the lot and still ask for more.'

After trying several cupboards and a lavatory, Annie found the door to the bar. It was like walking into a wall of noise. She gave the order to a tall, incredibly handsome man with smooth jet-black hair and the face of a Greek god, whom she assumed was Bruno.

'It's for the people in the Snug,' she yelled.

'Who are you and why aren't you in uniform?' His dancing brown eyes belied the apparent curtness of the question.

63

'I'm Annie, Sylvia's friend,' Annie explained. 'I've got to rush, I've something else to do.'

She had 'something else to do' for the next three hours. It wasn't how she'd expected to spend Christmas Eve, but she enjoyed herself immensely. She made more sandwiches when the bloody Marxists declared themselves on the verge of starvation, and helped wash and dry the dishes when they appeared out of the Regency Room in great numbers, thirty of everything.

It was almost half ten by the time Cecy sank into a chair, crying. 'Why did I let Bruno buy this place? I've never worked so hard in my life.' Her eyes lighted on Annie. 'What are you doing here?'

'Who do you think looked after the bloody Marxists?' Sylvia laughed.

'Was that you, Annie, dear? I was too busy to notice.'

'Is it all right if I go now, Mrs Delgado?' The other waitress had removed her shoes and was wearily massaging her feet.

'Of course, Mrs Parsons. Would you like a lift home?' Cecy was gradually becoming her normal charming self.

'No, ta. It's only round the corner.'

'Now, what do I owe you? The master insists I pay double for anti-social hours, so five pounds should do nicely. Is there much in tips?'

'There's a pile of silver from the Regency Room.' Sylvia pointed to the plate of coins on the table. 'You take it, Mrs Parsons.'

'Oh, I couldn't, miss. You did half the work.' The waitress eyed the money longingly.

At Sylvia's insistence, Mrs Parsons emptied the coins into her bag. 'Happy Christmas!' she cried happily as she left.

'The bloody Marxists didn't leave a penny,' Sylvia

64

snorted. 'I bet they'd say the workers should be better paid and not rely on tips.'

'They're just too mean to put their hands in their pockets.' Cecy looked disgusted. 'Annie! I seem to recall a red-haired young person dashing in and out all night and washing loads of dishes. I insist on paying for your hard work. You weren't here as long as Mrs Parsons, but you didn't get a single tip.' She handed Annie a five pound note.

'But I didn't expect to be paid,' Annie said faintly.

'It would have cost twice that if the other waitresses had turned up.' Cecy adamantly refused to take the money back.

'Ta very much,' gulped Annie. *Five pounds!*

Bruno appeared at the door. 'How did things go, darling?'

'Don't darling me,' Cecy snapped. 'We've been worked off our feet whilst you've been in your element behind the bar.'

Bruno laughed and blew a kiss. Despite Cecy's cross words, she smiled and blew one back. Annie sighed, because it seemed terribly romantic. They obviously loved each other very much.

'I suppose I'd better wake the old folks ready for Mass,' Cecy said wearily, 'but how anybody can sleep in this din is beyond me. As for you pair, help yourselves to food. There's wine opened in the fridge.'

Sylvia piled sausage rolls and mince pies onto a plate. 'Come on, Annie. I'm dying to hear my record.'

Halfway upstairs, she paused. 'You can see everything going on from here. It's how Bruno keeps an eye on the bar when he's not there.'

Annie hadn't noticed the little oblong window in the wall before. The girls sat on the stairs and peered through. The bar was more crowded than ever and people were still coming in. A few customers were singing drunkenly and there was the sound of breaking glass.

'Normally, we'd be closed by now,' Sylvia explained, 'but there's an extension because it's Christmas Eve. It's not usually so crowded, either. Scarcely any of these are regulars and one or two are getting out of hand. Bruno will throw them out if they continue. He's very particular who he allows in his pub.' She pointed. 'See that lot over there! They look awfully common and are very much the worse for wear.'

Annie followed her gaze. Half a dozen men and two young women were at a table in the centre of the room. As she watched, one man knocked a glass onto the floor with his elbow, but was too engrossed in the woman next to him to notice. The woman said something and the man grinned and kissed her full on the lips.

Oh, Jaysus! Annie felt her blood run cold. The young woman was Marie! She wore a tight-fitting black jumper, emphasising her budding breasts. Annie gasped as the man on her other side angrily pushed the first away, and it looked as if there could actually be a fight. Marie appeared quite unconcerned. She seemed to be enjoying herself, and threw back her head, laughing uproariously, as the second man dragged her into his arms. The first got up and made his unsteady way towards the Gents.

'Is something the matter?' Sylvia asked.

Annie nodded numbly. 'The girl in the black jumper is me sister!'

Sylvia frowned. 'But you said your sister is at Grenville Lucas and she's younger than you!'

'That's her. That's our Marie. She's only thirteen.'

'But she looks years older,' Sylvia gasped. 'Shall I tell Bruno? He'll throw them out immediately. He's strict about that sort of thing.'

'I'd sooner you didn't.' Annie felt unable to watch another minute. What on earth was she going to do about Marie?

'Come on, Annie,' Sylvia said gently. 'I'll play my new record and you can tell me all about it.'

It was half one when Annie let herself in and she felt almost cheerful again. She'd told Sylvia everything, from living with Dot and moving to Orlando Street, to Mam stroking her head – or *possibly* stroking her head – the other day. It was a relief to share her worries with someone else.

She crept upstairs and felt in the dark for her night-dress so as not to disturb her sister, but as her eyes got used to the darkness, she realised Marie's bed was empty and her heart sank. Where was she?

Despite being so tired after all her hard work, she couldn't sleep. She tossed and turned, thinking about her sister. They weren't 'boys' she'd been with, but grown men. Did they know she was thirteen?

Eventually she began to doze, but was jerked awake by a sharp noise. She sat up, trying to work out what the noise had been when it came again. Stones were being thrown at the window. Marie!

Annie got out of bed. Her sister was in the yard about to throw another stone. She flew downstairs and let her in. 'Where the hell have you been?' she demanded.

'Out and about,' Marie said airily. 'Ta, sis. I forgot me key and I didn't want to wake the old fool up.'

'He's not old, and he's not a fool,' Annie hissed when they were in the bedroom. 'He's a poor helpless man trying to do his best for us.'

'Really!' Marie said sarcastically. She threw her clothes on the floor and pulled on her nightdress. 'Goodnight, Annie. Merry Christmas,' she said in the same sarcastic voice as she got into bed.

'I saw you in the Grand tonight,' Annie said accusingly.

Marie hiccupped. 'Did you now! And what were you doing in the Grand, Miss Goody Two-Shoes!'

'Me friend lives there. I was helping in the kitchen.'

'Honest!' Marie sat up. 'You're friendly with that Italian girl? What's she like?'

'I'm the one asking the questions,' Annie snapped. 'What were you doing with those horrible old men? They looked at least twenty-five.'

Marie snorted. 'Mind your own business!'

'No, I won't. I felt ashamed, seeing them paw me sister in public. Things aren't so bad at home that you have to do horrible things like that. You could have stayed in and watched television.'

'You didn't!'

'I was working,' Annie said virtuously.

'And what do you mean, things aren't so bad at home?' Marie guffawed incredulously. 'Are you blind or something? It's Christmas Eve, and if we hadn't put those decorations up, there'd be no sign of it here. There never has been, not even when we were little; no presents by our beds, nothing.' She leaned forward and said fiercely, 'As soon as I'm old enough, I'll be out this house like a shot, and I'm never coming back.'

Annie sighed. There seemed little she could say because Marie was right. She was drifting off to sleep again, when a small voice tinged with desperation and misery said, 'I've got to have someone to love me, Annie. That's what I was doing tonight, looking for someone to love me.'

'I love you, Marie,' Annie said quickly. They weren't as close as she would have liked, they were two such very different people, but she loved her sister dearly.

'It's *them*!' Marie began to cry. 'They make me feel invisible, as if I don't exist. It's all right for you, you do things. You make yourself useful so they know you're there, but if I disappeared tomorrow, neither of them would notice.'

Annie got out of bed and climbed in with her sister. 'Never mind, luv,' she said soothingly. 'Never mind.' She tried to think of some comforting words to cheer her sister, but there didn't seem to be any. 'Never mind,' she said again.

Minutes later, the two girls were fast asleep in each other's arms.

On the day they returned to school, Annie and Sylvia met outside so they could face the inevitable storm together. They linked arms, marched through the gates and waited for the fireworks, but there was no sign of Ruby Livesey and no-one else took the slightest bit of notice.

Feeling let down, they wandered around the playground, arm in arm. After a while, Sally Baker came up. 'Hello, Annie. Why didn't you come to my party?' She didn't wait for a reply, but went on, 'Hey, you'll never guess, Ruby's left. She's got a job in Jacob's Biscuit Factory. I'm dead glad, I never liked her.'

They were joined by another girl from Ruby's old gang. 'Our Brian went to the Grand on New Year's Eve. You never said your dad was a Count, Sylvia. Isn't it smashing news about Ruby? Who'd like a peppermint cream? I got a whole box in my Christmas stocking.'

6

Tommy Gallagher married Dawn O'Connell in the summer of 1956, soon after he had done his National Service. Dawn was a skinny, darkly dramatic girl who wore an enviable amount of eyeshadow and too much lipstick. As she had no sisters, she asked Annie and Marie to be her bridesmaids.

'Now, about the dresses,' Dot said, full of importance. 'Dawn fancies blue, which should suit both your colourings.'

'Blue's fine,' Annie said blissfully. She would have agreed to black, she was so thrilled.

'Don't worry about the money,' Dot assured them. 'I'll have a word with our Ken. I think I'm the only one who can get through to him. Bert says it's because I've got the most penetrating voice in the world.'

The dresses were bought at a discount from Owen Owen's, where Dawn worked in Ladies' Underwear. Pale blue slipper satin, they had a low neck, a gathered skirt and a dark blue sash. 'You can get them altered afterwards,' said Dot. 'They'll do to go dancing in when you're older.'

'You lucky thing!' Sylvia said enviously when she heard. 'I'd love to be a bridesmaid.'

'You can be mine,' Annie offered, though she couldn't visualise getting married.

'And you can be mine! Though that means one of us will be a matron of honour. I wonder who'll get married first?'

'You will,' Annie said with conviction.

Sylvia had been invited to the wedding, and spent an entire evening modelling her vast wardrobe in front of Annie. 'Which dress do you like best? Perhaps I should buy something new. Oh, dear!' Sylvia said distractedly. 'I don't know what to wear!'

Annie laughed. 'You've got too many clothes, that's the problem. The peachy coloured frock really suits you.'

'Does it? You don't think it's too old – or possibly too young?'

'It's just right,' Annie assured her. 'You're dead

conceited, Sylvia. You don't half fancy yourself.' Their friendship had reached the stage where they could be critical of each other without causing offence. Sylvia stuck out her tongue, but otherwise ignored the comment.

Annie had never heard Mam and Dad argue before – well, not exactly argue, Mam wasn't saying a word, but Dad was going on and on in the voice that had turned husky of late and sounded like an old man's.

'But you've got to, you've got to,' he insisted. After a while, he came into the kitchen and said wearily to Annie. 'I'd like you to buy your mam a dress for Tommy's wedding. How much d'you think it'll be?'

So that was it! 'Okay, Dad,' Annie said, in the forced cheerful tone she used with her father. 'She'll need shoes and a hat as well – about fifteen pounds, I reckon. I'll go after school tomorrow. Don't worry, I'll get something nice.'

Dad sighed. 'You're a good girl, Annie.'

With Sylvia in tow, the following day Annie went to Waterloo in search of a dress. 'Pink,' she said firmly. 'It's got to be rose pink.'

She'd almost given up hope by the time they entered the final shop ten minutes before closing time. The assistant looked up impatiently when they came in and began to go through the rows of dresses.

'This one's perfect!' Annie had reached the last few frocks on the final rack when she took one out. 'And it's her size.'

The dress was deep pink grosgrain with a square neck and little puffed sleeves. The bodice was fitted and the panels widened into a full, almost circular skirt.

'It's pretty,' Sylvia said admiringly. 'I'm sure she'll love it.'

The assistant perked up and became co-operative

71

when she realised she was about to make a sale without the garment being tried on. She helped Annie choose a hat from the small millinery selection.

'This could have been made to go with the dress.' She picked up a pink feather band with a tiny veil. 'It's exactly the same colour.'

Annie tried it on. 'What do you think?' she asked Sylvia.

'It looks ghastly with red hair, but the style is very flattering.'

'In that case, I'll take it,' Annie said thankfully.

'Shall we put some lipstick on her?'

'Leave her alone, Marie. She looks fine. She's lovely as she is,' Annie glared at her sister.

Marie had adopted a proprietorial air with their mother on the morning of the wedding, spending ages combing her hair into a variety of different styles until she settled on a big fat bun at the nape of her slender neck. Mam stood in the middle of the room, a lost, confused figure, whilst Marie prowled around, adjusting the sleeves of the dress, straightening the little rose pendant.

'A bit of lipstick'll finish her off.'

'She's not a doll,' Annie snapped. 'Anyroad, why the interest in what Mam looks like all of a sudden? You've never cared before.'

'I never realised she was so gorgeous. Just imagine, sis, if the girls at school knew we had a Mam who looks more like our big sister!'

'Hmm,' Annie sighed.

'You should have got her a pair of lace gloves.'

'I didn't think.' She was pleased the dress fitted so well, the material clinging to Mam's lean hips, the short sleeves revealing milky-white arms. The hat looked perfect on her dark hair.

'I wouldn't mind those shoes afterwards. I mean, she'll never wear them again.' Marie stared enviously at the black suede shoes with little narrow heels. 'They're too small for you.'

'You're like a bloody vulture. Would you like her nylons, too?'

'I wouldn't mind. Or that bag.'

'That's Cecy's, Sylvia bought it her for Christmas. I'd run out of money by the time I remembered a hand-bag.'

'Where's Dad?' Marie demanded.

'Outside, waiting for the taxi.'

'Doesn't he think the driver's capable of finding the house himself? Keep still, Mam. I think I'll comb her hair loose, after all.'

The taxi would drop Mam and Dad off at Dot's, then take the girls to Dawn's house where they would change into their bridesmaids' frocks.

'I wonder if she realises what's going on?' Marie combed their mother's hair loose and began to curl the ends under her finger.

'I hope not. She'll think she's turned into a tailor's dummy.'

'Did you see Dad's face when he saw her dressed?' Marie giggled. 'It went all gooey and stupid, as if he was about to cry.'

Annie didn't answer. She had also noticed Dad's incredulous expression, as if he were seeing his wife for the first time and had fallen in love all over again. Annie had looked away, feeling as if she were intruding on something intensely private. Unlike Marie, she didn't find it the least bit funny.

Annie stared at her reflection in Dawn's wardrobe mirror. 'Gosh, I look *strange*.' She was growing taller, as Marie had predicted, and filling out. She'd been wearing a brassiere for more than a year and took a thirty-four, though suspected she'd soon need a bigger size. Her hips were quite broad, but shapely, she told herself, because her waist was narrow, the narrowness accentuated by the wide sash of the dress. She placed the coronet of blue flowers on her hair.

'Do you want this straight?' she asked Dawn, who looked radiant in her white satin wedding gown, 'or tipped towards the back?'

Dawn pursed her lips as Annie placed the coronet in various positions on her red curls. 'Straight, I think, almost on your forehead. It looks sort of regal.'

Marie sidled up. 'Are you sure you've got the right frock? This one feels really tight.'

'Mine's bigger. If that feels tight, it wouldn't go near me.'

'I'd better not eat anything, else I'll bust the zip.' Marie mopped her brow. 'I wish it wasn't so hot. I'm sweating like a cob already.'

'Tara, Tommy, lad,' Dot screamed. 'Have a nice honeymoon. Don't do anything I wouldn't do!'

As the newly-married couple's car turned into the traffic, Dot and the bride's mother burst into tears and fell into each other's arms.

Everyone began to drift back into the big room above the pub where the reception was being held. The musical duo, pianist and drummer, started to play 'Jealousy', and seconds later Bert swept a still tearful Dot across the floor. In no time the wooden floor shook as more couples began to tango. The children played tick, darting in and out of the dancers, and the room rapidly turned into a steambath with the heat.

'Oh, Bert,' Dot sobbed when the dance had finished. 'One of these days, I'll have no boys left. The house'll be empty.'

'Never mind, luv, you'll still have me,' Bert said comfortingly.

At this, Dot began to cry even more. Bert grinned. 'She always gets maudlin when she's been at the whisky. Fetch us some of that fruit punch, Annie, luv. Least if she's got a glass in her hand she mightn't notice it's non-alcoholic.'

Annie helped herself to another glass at the same time. The punch was an invention of Alan's, who was at catering college training to be a chef. He came up and regarded the nearly empty bowl with satisfaction. 'Another lot gone! I'd better make some more.'

'It's delicious,' Annie said. 'I could drink gallons in this heat.'

'I bet our Mike'll be gone within the year,' Dot sniffed when Annie returned. 'He's dead serious about that Pamela girl.'

'He was until today,' said Bert. 'Pamela's been given her cards. Ever since our Mike laid eyes on Annie's friend, he's gone as soppy as a puppy. Look at them dancing together!'

Mike was staring at Sylvia fixedly, an expression of total adoration on his face. A girl of about seventeen glared at them from the side of the room. Sylvia caught Annie's eye and winked.

'Have you noticed our Ken?' Dot was saying. 'He looks like a skull and crossbones. I'll have a word later, make him get a tonic off the doctor. Give them some punch, Annie. Our Alan's brought a fresh lot.'

'Isn't she lovely?' Dad said brokenly when Annie appeared. 'Isn't my Rose a picture?'

'Jaysus, Dad, have you been drinking?' He looked slightly idiotic, his head poised in a peculiarly stiff, lopsided way as if he were scared it might fall off. Tears were trickling down his hollow cheeks.

'Only that punch. Your mam really likes it.'

'Everybody's crying,' Annie complained. 'Dot, Dawn's mam, now you!'

The evening wore on. Night brought no respite from the sticky, suffocating heat. The men forced open the old sash windows, to such an extent they would probably never close again, but there was still no breath of wind to relieve the perspiring guests, and Dawn's grandma fainted in the middle of the Hokey Cokey.

Annie was dancing with the best man, Colin Donnelly, when Sylvia tugged her shoulder. 'Come quickly. Your cousin is in a state!'

'Which cousin?' Annie asked irritably as she reluctantly detached herself from Colin's arms. She'd actually found herself flirting for the first time in her life.

'Mike. He wants to kill himself because I won't marry him,' Sylvia burst out laughing. 'I don't think he means it, but what are we to do?'

'I'll see to him,' Colin said manfully. 'Where is he?'

Mike, usually so cheerful and full of beans, was in the kitchen, beating the wall with his fist and sobbing hopelessly. 'I love her, Annie,' he cried when they arrived, 'but she won't marry me.'

'Is he drunk?'

Sylvia shook her head. 'He's only had the punch, like me.'

'Come on, old chap, pull yourself together.' Colin slapped Mike on the back. 'Act like a man!' He glanced covertly at the girls to see if they were impressed. Annie and Sylvia burst out laughing.

Colin looked hurt. 'What's so funny?'

'I've no idea,' Sylvia giggled. She and Annie ran back into the main room and watched the revellers, trying not to laugh. Mike joined them after a while. He sat beside Sylvia and watched her soulfully. Every now and then he gave a pathetic sniff and the girls tried not to laugh even more. The discarded Pamela had gone home in tears hours ago.

Colin returned and gave Annie and Sylvia a cold look before asking Marie to dance.

The lights darkened for the 'Anniversary Waltz', and Annie was amazed when her mam and dad danced past. Mam's eyes were closed, but she was smiling, her head cocked on one side, and holding the hem of her skirt in her right hand so that it fell like a fan. Dad was watching her, his mouth half open and a glazed, inane look on his face.

To Annie's horror, she felt an overwhelming urge to giggle! What on earth was wrong with her? She clapped a hand over her mouth and tried her best to keep a straight face. She became aware that, beside her, Sylvia was sobbing quietly. 'What's the matter with you?' she snapped.

'Your mother and father! She is so incredibly beautiful. It's so sad, Annie.' Mike slid his arm around her shoulders and she collapsed against him. Mike began to cry, too.

'Bloody hell!' Annie said disgustedly. She went into the kitchen, where she found Alan pouring a bottle of vodka into a bowl of punch. 'You bugger!' she cried. 'No wonder everyone's crying, they're drunk!'

Alan looked unperturbed. 'Seemed like a good joke. Those who don't drink are more pissed than those who do! I got the vodka off this mate at college, a whole crateful. It fell off the back of a lorry.'

'All of Bootle'll have a head in the morning, including me!' No wonder she'd flirted with Colin and laughed at poor Mam and Dad.

Marie came bursting into the kitchen, red-faced and perspiring. 'Eh, Annie, our dad's just had a nervous breakdown,' she panted.

'But he was dancing with me mam a few minutes

77

ago!' Annie said dazedly. She wondered if the world had gone insane.

'I know, but he suddenly slid down on the floor and began crying his eyes out. Dot and Bert are seeing to him in one of the bedrooms.'

'I'd better go and look after Mam.'

'There's no need. She's doing the rumba with the best man, though she's got a face on her like a zombie.'

'Jaysus, Mary and Joseph! This is a madhouse, not a wedding. It's all your fault!' Annie turned accusingly on Alan. 'None of this would have happened if you hadn't spiked the bloody punch.'

'No-one was forced to drink it!' Alan departed with another bowl.

Marie turned her back to Annie. 'Undo the zip will you, sis, I can hardly breathe.' She wriggled uncomfortably as Annie struggled with the zip. 'I can't understand it. This dress fitted perfectly a few weeks ago. Even me breasts feel bigger, all swollen.'

'Oh, Marie!' A terrible suspicion swept over Annie. 'You're not, you're not . . .' She couldn't bring herself to finish.

'Pregnant?' Marie said calmly. Then her pretty face wrinkled in horror. 'Jaysus, Annie, that explains it!'

The sisters stared at each other without speaking for several seconds, then they both burst into tears.

'What are we to do?' asked Annie. It was the day after the wedding, Sunday; they were in the bedroom discussing Marie's predicament.

'I've no idea,' Marie said sullenly.

'How far gone are you?'

'I've no idea,' Marie said again. 'I've never been regular like you. That's why it didn't cross me mind.'

'Didn't you take – what are they called, precautions?' Annie was still in a daze of shock. Marie had been going out with boys since she was little, but even after seeing her with those awful men in the Grand last Christmas, she'd never imagined her doing that *thing* with them.

'Don't talk so stupid.' Marie's grey eyes blazed. 'If I'd taken precautions, I wouldn't be up the bloody stick, would I? Anyroad, where the hell was I supposed to get precautions from?'

'It's no good getting stroppy with me,' Annie said in a hurt voice. 'I only want to help.'

'I'm sorry,' Marie muttered.

If only it weren't such a horrible day! It was still hot, but the sky was black and heavy, as if there was going to be a storm. The light was on, but the dim bulb behind the dark yellow shade made the room look even more miserable and depressing.

As if Marie had read her thoughts, she said, 'I hate this room, I hate this house and I hate this street. I went into another girl's bedroom once, and it was full of pictures of film stars: Frank Sinatra and Gene Kelly and Montgomery Clift. This place stinks.'

Annie, sitting crosslegged on the bed, began to fiddle with the eiderdown, feeling at a loss. Marie's attitude was so belligerent, as if the whole thing were Annie's fault. Perhaps she should have done more to protect her sister, she thought guiltily.

Thunder rumbled in the distance, and seconds later the room was lit by a brilliant flash of lightning, followed by another and another.

'We've got to sort this out today, Marie,' Annie said firmly. 'I take it you don't intend to have the baby?' A child would be the last thing Marie wanted. She was little more than a child herself.

She was surprised when Marie's hard expression softened. 'I wish I could,' she said longingly. 'I'd love a baby of me own, someone to love and love me back. There's no way I'd be like *them*!' She gestured at the door as if their mam and dad were outside. 'But I'm only thirteen, I couldn't stand living in one of them homes for unmarried mothers.' Her voice became harsh. 'I suppose I'll just have to get rid of it, though apart from having hot baths and drinking loads of gin, which doesn't usually work, I haven't a clue how to go about it.'

An abortion! Annie hated the very word. It actually sounded cruel, and so very final. 'Neither have I,' she said. 'We could ask Dot?'

Marie shook her head. 'Once Dot's had a good yell and called me all the names under the sun, she'll be all right, but she won't help get rid of it. Some woman from down the street had an abortion and Dot hasn't spoken to her since. She'd offer to bring the baby up, that's all.'

'Perhaps that would be the best solution,' Annie said hopefully.

'No!' Marie said vehemently. 'I couldn't bear to see me own child being brought up by another woman.' Rain splattered against the window and within seconds became a downpour. The panes rattled in their frames.

Annie began to play with the eiderdown again, pleating and unpleating the shiny cotton between her fingers. Marie was so grown up at times, and seemed to have feelings and emotions she found alien. There was far more to her sister than the flighty, hard-hearted impression she usually gave. It made Annie feel rather inadequate, as if she herself were incapable of feeling strongly about anything.

'Abortion is against the law,' she said. 'You have to have it done in a back street or something.' Ruby Livesey had known a girl who'd known a girl who'd had one and she'd bled for days and ended up in hospital where the nurses treated her like dirt. 'Have you any money?'

'I've still got last week's pocket money, five bob.'

'I've three pounds saved for Christmas. I wonder what it costs?'

Marie shrugged. 'Search me!'

'I bet that's not enough. What about the father, would he help?'

'No, he wouldn't,' Marie snapped.

'Are you going to tell him?'

'No!'

'I think you should.'

'I think I shouldn't.'

'Why not?' Annie persisted.

'Because,' Marie breathed on her nails and polished them on the sleeve of her dress, 'it could be more than one person.'

'Oh, Marie!' Annie felt herself grow very hot. She stared at her sister, scandalised.

Marie said furiously. 'Don't look at me like that! Sometimes, Annie, you're so holier-than-thou it makes me sick.'

'You're taking it out on me again,' Annie said through gritted teeth. More than one person! She could easily be sick herself. She was about to say how utterly disgusted she was, but noticed Marie's jaw was trembling as if she were about to cry. All the nonchalance, the couldn't-care-less attitude was put on. Marie was hurting badly inside.

Annie got off the bed and reached inside the wardrobe for her best coat. She'd ask around at school as tactfully as she could to see if anyone knew about abortions – and how much they cost.

'Where are you going?' Marie demanded.

'To the Grand for tea. Afterwards, me and Sylvia are going to the pictures in Walton Vale.'

'Leaving me all by meself! Thanks, Annie. You're all heart.'

'I promised.' Earlier, she'd thought of ringing Sylvia from the phone box at the end of the street and cancelling the arrangement, but had changed her mind. It would be embarrassing, but she'd ask Sylvia for a loan. She'd bring the subject up on the way home.

They'd been to see *The Last Time I Saw Paris*, and were strolling arm in arm along the little stretch of sand where Dot had taken the girls when they'd first moved to Orlando Street. No-one brought their children to play on the sands these days. It was stained with oil and littered with debris from the sea, and with human debris; rusty cans and sodden mattresses, old clothes and scraps of paper. After the thunderstorms that afternoon, the air was refreshingly cool.

'Isn't Elizabeth Taylor too beautiful for words?' Sylvia breathed. 'As for Van Johnson!' She put her hand to her forehead and pretended to swoon. 'I think I'm in love.'

'Mmm,' muttered Annie.

'What's the matter, Annie? You've been awfully quiet all night. Didn't you enjoy the picture?'

'It was dead lovely,' Annie had scarcely taken it in.

'There's something wrong, I can tell.'

Annie took a deep breath. 'I want to borrow some money,' she said in a rush. 'I'll pay back every penny, I promise. I hate asking, but it's an emergency and I've no-one else to turn to.' She was glad it was dark so Sylvia couldn't see her shamed expression. She kicked violently at a tin can, suddenly angry that it was her who'd been put in the awkward position of having to get her sister out of the mess.

'You can have all the money you want,' Sylvia said instantly. 'How much: five pounds, ten, a hundred?'

'Oh, Sylvia!' Annie felt close to tears.

Sylvia squeezed Annie's hand. 'Don't be upset.

What's it for? Don't tell me if you'd sooner not,' she added hastily.

'It's for Marie,' Annie sniffed. 'She's pregnant. I don't know how much, because I've no idea what an abortion costs.'

'*Pregnant!*' Sylvia stopped dead and her mouth fell open. 'Pregnant!' she said again.

'Isn't it terrible? It makes me go all funny, *thinking* about it.'

'I wonder where she did it?' Sylvia shuddered.

'I didn't ask.' Annie had visions of her sister under shadowy trees or in dark back alleys with men who had no faces.

'Where will she get the abortion done?'

'I don't know that, either.'

'Come on.' Sylvia veered them towards Crosby Road. 'Let's go back to the Grand and we'll discuss it over a cup of coffee.'

Annie paced nervously up and down the pale cream carpet. The coffee had long been drunk, and it was half an hour since Sylvia had gone downstairs promising, 'I won't be long.'

Cecy might regard Annie as a bad influence when she knew what her sister had done, and refuse to let Sylvia see her again. She'd think there was bad blood in the family and Annie could do the same thing.

The longplaying record finished, but she couldn't be bothered to turn it over. Anyroad, the music, the jazzy score of *Guys and Dolls*, had begun to get on her nerves.

Suddenly, Sylvia burst into the room. 'It's all settled,' she said breathlessly. 'Marie's booked into a nursing home in Southport this coming Saturday. She'll have to stay overnight.'

Annie sat down, overcome with relief. 'I can't thank

83

Cecy enough,' she began, but Sylvia interrupted with a horrified, 'Don't mention a word of this to Cecy! She'd never approve. It's all Bruno's doing, with the help of the bloody Marxists.'

'I'll pay him back as soon as I can,' Annie vowed.

Sylvia shook her head. 'Bruno's only too pleased to help. It makes him feel good, doing something for the proletariat.'

Bruno Delgado picked Annie and Marie up from the corner of Orlando Street on Saturday morning. Sylvia was in the front of the big black Mercedes car.

Marie was subdued throughout the journey to Southport, overawed by the handsome, garrulous Bruno, who lectured them on politics the whole way. The law should be changed, he declared, so women could have an abortion legally. 'A woman's right to choose,' he called it.

'Your Parliament makes me sick,' he exploded at one point. 'All those middle-aged, middle-class men pontificating on what should happen to a woman's body. What the hell do they know about it? It's even worse in Italy, where the church makes all the rules.'

They were nearly there when he enquired, 'What excuse did you give at home to explain Marie's night away?'

'We didn't need an excuse,' Annie said carelessly. 'They won't notice she's gone.' She could have bitten off her tongue when she saw in the rear mirror Bruno's dark eyebrows draw together in astonishment. Marie stiffened at her side. 'I feel invisible,' she'd said once. In a moment of awareness, Annie knew why she'd let the men make use of her body. They'd made her feel wanted, though for all the wrong reasons. She pressed her sister's hand. 'It'll be over soon,' she whispered.

Sylvia's attitude didn't help. She completely ignored Marie, not once even glancing in her direction. Annie had known she disapproved since Christmas Eve, but she didn't realise the dislike was so intense.

'She's led a charmed life,' Annie thought wryly. 'She doesn't know the half of it.' Marie had only been trying to survive as best she could.

Bruno and Sylvia remained in the car when the sisters went into the nursing home, a gracious detached ivy-covered house in a wide tree-lined avenue. 'They're expecting you,' Bruno said. 'It's all arranged.'

A woman in a white starched overall came towards them, her face expressionless. 'Miss Harrison?' She looked from one to the other. Annie pushed Marie forward. 'Come with me, please.'

Marie turned, and Annie felt a fierce stab of pity at the sight of her stricken face. 'Do you want me to stay?' she said.

The woman in the overall said coldly, 'That's not allowed. You can pick her up at the same time tomorrow.'

Annie put her arms around her sister. As their cheeks touched, she said softly, 'Don't worry, Marie. We'll come through. One of these days, everything will be all right, you'll see.'

7

'I'm glad the summer holiday's nearly over,' Annie said with a sigh. 'School seems a nice change when you've been off six whole weeks.'

'I suppose it does.' Sylvia echoed Annie's sigh. They were bored, having done everything there seemed to be to do; gone to Southport and New Brighton numerous times, seen so many pictures that the plots had become muddled in their minds, and they were sick to death of Liverpool city centre. School offered variety to what had become tedium.

They were sitting on the sands, having removed rubbish to make a clear space, watching a small cargo boat sail towards a rippling green and purple sunset.

'Have you made up your mind what to do when you leave?' Sylvia enquired. 'You'll be fifteen in October.'

Annie frowned. 'Dot thinks I should stay at school till next July. After that . . .' she paused, picked up a handful of sand and let it fall through her fingers. 'The thing is,' she burst out, 'I can't imagine things ever being different. I've got to look after me mam and dad.'

'You can't look after them for ever, or you'll end up with no life of your own,' Sylvia said warningly.

'Dot said that. She suggested I go to Machin & Harpers – that's a commercial college,' she explained in response to Sylvia's puzzled look.

Sylvia nodded her smooth blonde head. 'Good idea, but it doesn't solve the problem of your parents. What happens when you fall in love?'

'In love?' Annie burst out laughing.

'All women fall in love,' Sylvia said wisely, 'even if all men don't. I can't wait. Bruno gets angry with me. He wants me to go to another school and get some qualifications, then go to university, when all I want to do is fall in love and get married.'

'You never told me that before!' Annie said in astonishment. Sylvia seemed too much in love with herself, her clothes, her hair, her figure. 'I thought you didn't like boys much. When we went on that double date, we decided afterwards it was more fun being with each other.'

They'd gone out in a foursome, their first dance and first date. The boys had them in stitches when they met

86

on the New Brighton ferry, pretending to be Dean Martin and Jerry Lewis, but on the date, the spark had gone and everyone was stiff and formal. Annie and Sylvia kept going to the Ladies for a laugh.

'We won't always feel that way. One day we'll each meet a man who'll be far more important to us than anyone else in the world.'

Annie felt slightly hurt. 'Will we?'

'Yes, though we'll still meet. We can take our children for walks together and ask each other to dinner.'

But no matter how hard Annie tried, she couldn't visualise Sylvia's version of the future. It was impossible to imagine living anywhere other than Orlando Street, and leading a life different from the one she led now. She would merely go to work each day, instead of school.

'How's Marie?' Sylvia asked politely.

It was almost two months since Marie had had her 'termination', as the nursing home called it. 'Quiet. She stays in watching television.'

'She'll bounce back up again. She'll feel better at school.'

'As long as she doesn't bounce back up as high as she was before,' Annie said darkly.

There was a new teacher at Grenville Lucas when they returned. Mr Andrews didn't look much more than a schoolboy himself. The girls fell hopelessly in love, despite the fact he wore glasses and wasn't exactly good-looking. There was just something carefree and exhilar-ating about Mr Andrews that appealed to everyone, girls and boys alike. He had an enthusiasm for life that the other teachers lacked. Nor did he dress as they did, but wore corduroy trousers and a polo-necked sweater under his shabby tweed jacket.

'Good morning, class!' He'd burst into the room,

eyes shining and rubbing his hands as if he were genuinely pleased to see them.

'Good morning, Mr Andrews,' they'd chorus – they'd been ordered not to call him 'sir'. English lessons were turning out to be fun. Shakespeare wasn't rubbish any more, and *The Mill on the Floss* and *A Tale of Two Cities* suddenly seemed quite interesting.

'If only we could study something written by a twentieth-century writer,' Mr Andrews grumbled one day, 'but the bloody education authorities won't let us.'

The class gasped. A teacher, swearing!

Mr Andrews decided a drama group was needed. 'Who'd like to join?' he cried. 'It's both educational and enjoyable at the same time.'

The entire class raised their hands. Annie and Sylvia were always on the look-out for something interesting to do.

'Perhaps I should have mentioned, but the drama group will meet *after* school.' Mr Andrews' eyes twinkled mischievously.

Half the hands went down. He laughed. 'Thought you were in for a skive, did you? Well, you've got another think coming. All you budding Thespians meet me in the gym at four o'clock. What is it, Derek?'

'What's a budding Thespian, sir? It sounds rude.'

'I told you not to call me sir. A budding Thespian, Derek, is someone who wants to be an actor, which you quite obviously don't.'

Mr Andrews thought the new group should cut their teeth on something simple like a pantomime. After a majority vote for *Cinderella*, he said he'd write the script himself.

'Why turn down a part?' Sylvia linked Annie's arm on the way home.

'I couldn't bear to go on stage with everybody looking at me!' Annie shuddered. 'He made me wardrobe mistress, though the men's costumes will be hired. Wardrobe mistress! Doesn't it sound grand? I'll borrow Dot's electric sewing machine. It can go in the parlour, no-one uses it. I'm dead excited! You'll make a marvellous principal boy, Syl.'

'I hope Bruno hasn't got some prejudice against them. He has some weird ideas sometimes. Shall we go for a coffee?'

'We're awfully late and there isn't time,' Annie said regretfully, 'I've got to make the tea.'

'If only I could help! I've become quite good at cooking since we moved to the Grand. I can peel potatoes like a whirlwind.'

Annie felt uncomfortable. 'You don't mind not coming, do you, Syl? I mean, I'm forever in the Grand, yet you've never set foot in our house. It's just that me dad's dead funny about letting people in.'

'Of course I don't mind,' said Sylvia.

'Anyroad, if you came once, you'd never want to come again. Me mam never opens her mouth. It's like a grave compared to yours.'

Sylvia looked sympathetic. 'It must get you down.'

Annie said nothing for a while. 'It's funny, but it doesn't get me down a bit,' she said eventually. 'I scarcely think about it.' She looked worriedly at her friend. 'Dot's always on about how ill me dad looks. It sounds awful, but I don't notice. I just make the tea and can't wait to meet you so we can go to the pictures or the youth club.'

They stopped in front of a small haberdashery shop. The window was piled high with packets of cellophane-covered wool, and half a dozen cheap cotton frocks hung crookedly from the partition at the back.

'Who on earth wears such ghastly rubbish?' Sylvia said scathingly.

'Women who can't afford anything else, I suppose.'

'Oh, God!' Sylvia clapped a hand to her forehead. 'What a terrible snob I am! Why do you bother with me, Annie?'

Annie laughed. 'Because I like you!'

Sylvia looked forlorn. 'I must tell Father MacBride what a snob I've been at my next confession.'

'Is snobbery a sin?'

'I'll confess it just in case.' Sylvia took confession very seriously. 'What do you tell at confession, Annie? I can't imagine you doing anything wrong.'

'I've never committed a mortal sin,' Annie said earnestly. 'Least I don't think so. I'm not sure how the church would regard helping Marie with the abortion – not that I confessed that. The priest can see you through the grille, that's if he hasn't already recognised your voice. I tell lies occasionally, but only white ones, and I'm a bit vain, though not nearly as vain as you. I just mumble I've had a few bad thoughts and get five Hail Marys and five Our Fathers as a penance.'

'But you don't really have bad thoughts, do you?'

They turned into Orlando Street. The long, red brick walls seemed to stretch for ever and ever. There wasn't a soul about. Annie shivered. Sometimes she wondered if her life might reflect the street: empty, dull, with every year exactly the same, like the houses.

She stopped, and Sylvia looked at her questioningly. 'What's wrong?'

'You asked if I had bad thoughts. I don't, but what worries me is that I don't have any thoughts at all,' she said tragically.

'Don't be silly,' Sylvia said warmly. 'We discuss all sorts of things and you always have an opinion.'

'It's hard to explain . . .' Annie paused as she struggled for words. 'I suppose I mean *deep* thoughts. The reason Marie went off the rails is because everything's so horrible at home. Why haven't I done something equally bad? Why am I always so calm and normal? Nothing seems to affect me. I never cry or make a scene or even lose my temper. It's as if I haven't any feelings underneath the surface.'

'Oh, Annie!'

'Most of the time I'm happy, least I think I am, but it doesn't seem right to be happy with things the way they are. Sometimes, I wonder if I'm completely dead inside because I'm always so bloody cheerful.'

'It's your defence mechanism,' Sylvia said knowledgeably.

'What's that?'

'You don't allow yourself to feel things, otherwise you'd go mad, but deep down at heart it's affecting you all the same.'

Annie managed to smile. 'Where did you get that from?'

'Bruno, who else! You should talk to him some time, Annie. He admires you tremendously.'

'Does he?' Annie gaped in astonishment.

'He calls you a "little brick". Compared to you I am no more than a useless flibbertigibbet. Oh, look, we've walked right past your house.'

'I usually do,' Annie said bitterly.

'You've done a wonderful job with Cinderella's ball-gown, Annie,' Mr Andrews said, impressed. 'Where did the material come from?'

'Me and Sylvia . . .' Annie corrected herself; after all he was the English teacher. 'I mean, Sylvia and I went to a jumble sale in Southport. We bought heaps of stuff for just pennies. I made the gown out of an old frock and a curtain.'

The jumble sale had been Cecy's idea. The church hall had been like an Aladdin's cave, full of clothes, many as good as new. Even Cecy had been delighted to find an old-fashioned Persian lamb coat, which she was going to have remodelled.

Annie had removed the skirt from the blue-and-pink striped taffeta frock, and made another, full length, from one of the blue curtains, faded at the edges. She'd sewn little blue and pink rosettes around the hem, and turned the other curtain into a hooded cloak for Cinderella's entrance to the ball. There was enough material left over for a muff.

Mr Andrews shook his head admiringly. 'You have quite a talent for this sort of thing.'

'I used to love drawing dresses when I was little,' she said shyly.

'The Ugly Sisters' costumes are just as remarkable.'

'They're not quite finished. I brought them to see if they fitted.'

Mr Andrews looked at her keenly. 'What do you intend to do when you leave school?'

'I'm going to Machin & Harpers Commercial College next September.' Dot had had a serious talk with Dad, and it was all agreed.

He wrinkled his rather stubby little nose. 'That seems a waste. You should go to Art College, take a dress designing course. What does your mother think about these outfits? They're quite outstanding.'

'She liked them,' Annie lied. Only Marie had been interested enough to enquire why Annie was spending so much time in the parlour.

'I should hope so! Perhaps one of your parents could pop in and have a word with me some time,' Mr Andrews suggested. 'A talent like yours shouldn't be squandered at Machin & Harpers.'

'I'll ask them,' promised Annie. Two lies within as many minutes! At least she'd have something real to confess next time she went.

That night, she thought about Mr Andrews' words.

She'd loved making the dresses. It was like painting a picture or writing a story, because she kept having fresh ideas what to do next, where to put a bow, how to shape a neckline, finish off a sleeve. As the material sped through the machine, she felt a thrill of excitement, because she couldn't wait to see what the finished garment would look like. When it was hanging on the picture rail in the parlour, she looked at it for ages, scarcely able to believe the beautiful gown had recently been odds and ends thrown out for jumble. Not only that, it was all her own work, a product of her industry and imagination.

But it would be too much effort explaining this to her dad, she thought tiredly. Bruno would be different. He'd move heaven and earth to ensure Sylvia went to Art College, but Annie's father would never understand. Anyroad, the course might take years, and Machin & Harpers only took nine months.

Annie woke up a few weeks later with butterflies in her stomach. Today was the dress rehearsal, and she was worried the costumes might clash on stage, or Cinderella would trip down the plywood steps into the ballroom and it would be her fault for making the dress too long.

She met Sylvia in their usual place on the way to school. 'I've forgotten my costume,' she announced crossly when she arrived. 'It's Cecy's fault. She insisted on ironing it and left it in the kitchen.'

'Honestly, Syl. You'd forget your head if it wasn't screwed on!'

'Only if someone left it in the kitchen instead of in my bedroom as they'd promised.'

'You should have ironed it yourself,' Annie sniffed. 'Cecy waits on you hand and foot. If me mam ironed something for me I'd drop dead.'

'Thanks for the lecture, Annie.' Sylvia grinned. 'Anyway, it means I'll have to rush home at dinner time.'

'I'll come with you.'

It was a glorious December day. The sun shone with almost startling intensity out of a luminous, clear blue sky.

Sylvia took deep breaths as they walked swiftly to the Grand. 'Isn't it exhilarating! Bruno says Liverpool air makes him feel quite drunk.'

'Sunny days in winter are much nicer than summer ones.' Annie pointed. 'Look at those people queueing outside the Odeon. Fancy going to the pictures on a lovely day like this!'

'What's on? *The King and I*. We must go one night. Apparently, Yul Brynner is completely bald.'

Cecy shrieked when they appeared. 'What are you doing here?' She made something to eat and offered to take them back in the car.

'No, thanks,' Sylvia said with a martyred air. 'We'll walk, but we'd better hurry.'

The queue outside the Odeon had begun to move. People were paying to go in at the glass cubicle in the foyer. A dark-haired woman with a bright scarf around her neck bought a ticket and disappeared into the darkness. Annie froze.

'Come on!' Sylvia dragged her arm impatiently.

Annie didn't move. She turned to her friend and opened her mouth to speak, but nothing would come.

Sylvia left her hand on Annie's arm. 'What's the matter?'

The power of speech had returned. 'I could have sworn that woman was me mam!' Her head swirled with the shock.

Sylvia gasped. 'Are you sure?'

'Yes. No. Not really.' Annie grimaced. 'I only saw her for a second, but it looked just like her.'

'What was she wearing?'

'All I noticed was her scarf. It had a swirly pattern, like that new blouse of Cecy's.'

'Paisley?'

'That's right, Paisley.'

'Why not go home and see if she's there? Who cares if we're late?'

'But say she isn't?' Annie stared at her friend in horror.

Sylvia rolled her eyes dramatically. 'Gosh, Annie, I don't know.'

'I don't know, either.' Perhaps some things were best left undiscovered, she thought dazedly, otherwise the entire world would be turned upside down. 'Oh, come on,' she said with an attempt at indifference. 'If we run, we might get back to school in time.'

'If that's what you want.'

'It's what I want,' Annie said firmly, though she couldn't get the incident out of her mind all afternoon. Perhaps she should have gone home – and if Mam hadn't been there . . . ?

Although Annie racked her brains and puzzled over the matter at the expense of the History and French lessons, she couldn't for the life of her visualise what would have happened then.

The dress rehearsal was a complete disaster. Everyone forgot their lines, the prompt couldn't be heard without shouting, and Cinderella fell headlong down the steps on top of Dandini and burst into tears.

Mr Andrews remained serene throughout. 'A lousy dress rehearsal is a sign of a good show,' he assured the petrified cast. 'Thank goodness you didn't do well. I would have been really worried.'

Annie arrived home, pleased to find Dot in the back kitchen where she'd already started on the tea. 'Have you been here long?' she asked.

'Since about four o'clock, luv. Why?'

'I just wondered.'

'It's no use coming before you two get here, is it? I'd only end up talking to meself.' Dot jerked her head angrily in the direction of the living room, where Annie's mother was in exactly the same position she'd been in when the girls left for school that morning.

'Oh, Dot!' Annie laid her cheek on her aunt's bony shoulder. If only she could tell Dot what she'd seen, or thought she'd seen, but it would only cause ructions. She smiled, imagining Dot pinning Mam down on the floor the way wrestlers did on television, and twisting her arm until she conceded she'd been to see *The King and I*.

'What's the matter, luv?' Dot laid down the sausages she was unwrapping and took Annie in her arms.

'Nothing.'

'Feel like a cuddle, eh?' Dot said tenderly. 'Pity you're not little any more, or you could sit on me knee the way you used to.'

Annie was now as tall as Dot, perhaps slightly taller. 'I wish we could have stayed with you and Uncle Bert in Bootle,' she sighed.

'So do I, luv! Oh, so do I!' Dot patted her niece's back. 'It was all Father Whotsit's fault, walking in when I was in the middle of the dinner. If only I hadn't burnt the custard and got in such a temper!'

'You threw a cup at the wall, remember?'

'I remember. It was out me next-to-best tea service, too. I said things I didn't mean to say, and it got your dad all stubborn.'

'Still, the house wasn't big enough – and you've had three more boys since.' Annie moved out of her auntie's arms to put the kettle on.

'We could have asked the landlord for a bigger house. In fact, that's what Bert and me intended,' Dot said surprisingly. 'I was going to approach our Ken as tactfully as I could and suggest he found somewhere for him and Rose and we'd keep you and Marie. I think he might have agreed.' Her mouth curled in an expression of disgust. ' 'Stead, I go and lose me flaming rag, don't I?' she finished bitterly.

Such a little thing, a few unguarded words, and the whole course of their lives had changed, Annie thought.

'Never mind!' Dot patted her arm. 'Deep down at heart, our Ken thinks the world of his lovely girls. Christ knows what you'd have turned out like if you'd stayed with Bert and me.' She cut a sliver of lard for the frying pan and lit the gas underneath. 'I'll leave these sausages for you to finish, Annie. I'd better be off. And oh, there's a Blackledge's cream sandwich in the larder.'

'Ta, Auntie Dot.'

Marie came in, saw the sausages sizzling in the pan, and said, 'Dad hardly ever eats his tea lately. He puts it in the dustbin.'

Annie glanced at her in surprise. 'I hadn't noticed!'

'You're never here, are you?' Marie said, with a hint of accusation in her voice. 'You just plonk his dinner down, then you're out the door like a shot.'

'Has he seen the doctor yet?' Dot demanded.

'I don't know,' Annie said guiltily.

Dot flushed angrily. 'It's not your job to mind your dad, Annie.' Her voice rose so it could have been heard out in the street, let alone the living room it was intended to reach. 'But we know whose job it is. Our Ken could die on his feet, but some people couldn't give a damn.'

'I'm going to the lavatory,' Annie said abruptly. It was too much; what with Dad ill, Marie moping around looking dead miserable, and Mam, or someone who looked very much like Mam, going to the pictures.

'Tara, Annie!' Dot shrieked after a while. 'I've left the spuds and sausages on a low light.'

When Annie emerged, she found Marie sitting on her bed, looking sulky. 'Did Dot tell you?' she said.

'Tell me what?'

'We can't go to their house for Christmas dinner this year, they're going to their Tommy's. What are we going to do all day, Annie?'

Annie's heart sank. The highlight of the festive season had always been the cheerful, chaotic meal at Dot's. Once Sylvia knew, she would be invited to the Grand, but she couldn't desert Marie on Christmas Day.

'What can we do,' she said patiently, 'except make our own Christmas dinner? We've got decorations – in fact, it's time we put them up.'

'That sounds fun!' Marie said scornfully. 'Like the most miserable Sunday you can think of with knobs on. I'd sooner stay in bed.'

'What do you expect?' Annie demanded. 'I can't pluck another auntie out of the air for us to have Christmas dinner with. Anyroad, unless you go to Midnight Mass, you've got to get up for church.'

'Sod church,' Marie pouted.

'Marie!'

Marie squirmed uncomfortably. 'I've felt really peculiar in church since . . . you know! I keep expecting the priest to point at me during his sermon and denounce me as a murderer.'

'Don't be silly,' Annie chided gently.

'I'm not being silly. Me baby would have been born in January if I hadn't had him murdered. It was a boy, they told me.'

'You must stop brooding.' Annie felt very inadequate. 'Why don't you go out with some of the girls from school?' she said cautiously, half expecting to have her head bitten off. It was.

'Because they're stupid!' Marie snapped. 'They watch *Muffin the Mule* on television, and some still play with dolls.'

'I'd better get the tea,' Annie paused in the doorway. 'By the way, have you ever seen our mam with a Paisley scarf?'

'No,' Marie said abruptly. She seemed too preoccupied to ask why Annie had asked such a funny question, and Annie was left wondering if she'd ever have the courage to look for the scarf herself.

According to Dot and Bert, the pantomime went down a treat. 'It was better than the ones you see at the Empire,' Dot claimed. She gave a sarcastic laugh. 'I see your mam and dad didn't come.'

'I didn't ask them,' said Annie.

'Our poor Mike nearly fainted when Sylvia walked on stage,' Bert said, smiling broadly. 'He only came to see her in tights. Now he's in love all over again. Not that I blame him. She's a real Bobby Dazzler, that Sylvia. If I wasn't already married to the best-looking woman in the world I could fancy her meself.' Dot dug him sharply in the ribs with her elbow, but at the same time looked girlishly pleased.

Mike had Sylvia, in white spangled tights and red frock coat, pinned against the wall, where he was talking to her earnestly. Later, she said to Annie. 'Your Mike wants to take me out. What should I do?'

'He's dead nice, but he'll never be able to keep you in the manner to which you're accustomed. He's only an apprentice toolmaker.'

'He asked me to the pictures, not for a lifelong commitment. I know, I'll suggest he brings a friend so we can make a foursome!'

'No!' cried Annie, but Sylvia departed, grinning, just as Mr Andrews came up holding a cardboard folder, looking strangely sheepish. To the chagrin of the girls, he'd brought his fiancée, a pretty girl with China-blue eyes and long straight hair who looked like Alice in Wonderland, and seemed entirely unaware she'd ruined several Christmases.

'This is a play I wrote at university,' he mumbled. 'I thought we'd do it next term. I wonder if you'd mind reading it over the holiday? I'd like to know what you think.'

Annie took the folder, flattered that he was interested in her opinion. '*Goldilocks!*' She looked at him, puzzled. 'Another pantomime?'

'It's a play.' He shuffled his feet awkwardly. 'Goldilocks is the nickname of the main character.'

'Do you want me to be wardrobe mistress again?'

'No, I want you to play Goldilocks.'

'Me!' Annie looked at him askance.

'You'd be perfect, Annie.' Suddenly, he was the old Mr Andrews again. His eyes sparkled with an enthusiasm which was catching. 'You've got the right air of authority – and the red hair! I didn't know it at the time, but the part could have been written specially for you!'

Goldilocks was an orphan. Having lost both parents in a car crash, she arrives at an orphanage where she sets about altering the strict, oppressive regime. By the end, it is the orphans who are in charge, ordering the staff around with the same unfeeling cruelty used on them.

'What's that you're reading?' Marie enquired. She was brushing her hair in front of the dressing-table mirror.

Annie threw the folder onto the bed. 'A play. Mr Andrews wrote it.'

'Honest! What's it like?'

'Dead good.' It was incredible that a play could be so sad and so funny at the same time.

'Can I read it?'

'If you like. Mr Andrews wants me to play the main part.'

'Are you going to?'

'I'm not sure.' She felt admiration for Goldilocks, who despite all her adversities, was able to take control of her own life. Unlike me, she thought wryly, who just bumps along from day to day.

'We're going to see *The Ten Commandments* at the Forum on Saturday,' Sylvia announced gaily the next day. 'Mike's bringing his best friend, Cyril Quigley, for you.'

'Cyril! There's no way I'm going out with anyone called Cyril,' Annie said in a horrified voice.

'He's called Cy for short. That's not so bad, is it? In fact, it sounds a bit American.'

Annie looked grudging. 'I suppose so.'

Cy Quigley – Annie refused even to *think* of him as Cyril – had short, very black curly hair, and dark eyes which seemed to be laughing all the time. To her intense relief, she quite liked him. It was difficult not to. He had her in stitches in the cinema, making fun of Moses, particularly when he received the Ten Commandments from God.

'Not another one!' he groaned when number six was reached.

The people nearby kept demanding they be quiet, and even Sylvia got annoyed. 'Don't be sacrilegious,' she hissed.

'Fancy doing this again next Saturday, Annie?' Cy asked when they were in Lyons having coffee and he was rolling a cigarette. He'd already smoked twice as many ciggies as there were commandments.

'I don't mind,' Annie said casually. Inwardly, she was thrilled.

He held her hand on the way to Exchange Station. Annie stiffened when they arrived, hoping he wouldn't kiss her. She wasn't ready for her first kiss just yet. To her relief, he shook hands politely.

'See you next week, then.'

'Have a nice Christmas,' Annie said.

He grinned. 'Same to you.'

Annie watched him cross the road. He stopped and bent his head, cupping his hands around a cigarette as he lit it. She sighed happily.

'Where's Mike?' she asked in surprise when she turned to find Sylvia alone and looking rather glum. They walked onto the platform where the Southport train was waiting, doors open.

'Gone!' Sylvia said abruptly. 'Let's get in the last compartment so as to avoid him.'

The girls sat facing each other. The doors closed and the train started. 'I know he's your cousin, Annie,' Sylvia continued in a complaining voice, 'but he bores me silly. He asked me out again, but I refused. I think he's taken umbrage.'

'But I'm seeing Cy next week!' Annie said in consternation.

'I know, I heard,' Sylvia said stiffly.

'I thought we'd be going in a foursome again.'

'You'll just have to go in a twosome, won't you!'

Annie felt terrible. 'We always go out together on Saturdays.'

'Well, next Saturday I'll just have to stay in alone.' Sylvia turned to look out of the window, her face cold.

'Why didn't you say you didn't want to see Mike again?' Annie said reasonably. 'I wouldn't have made another date with Cy.'

'Why didn't you discuss it with me beforehand?'

'In the middle of Lyons! Don't be silly, Sylvia. It would look as if I was asking for your permission or something.'

Sylvia tossed her head and didn't answer. 'Anyroad,' Annie went on, 'the whole thing was your idea. I didn't want any part of it, did I?'

Neither girl spoke for several stations. The train reached Marsh Lane and Annie saw her cousin get off further down the platform. He looked as miserable as she felt as he went through the exit without a backward glance.

She'd never had a row with Sylvia before, and felt all shaky inside, particularly as she couldn't quite understand what she'd done that was so wrong. 'It was you who said we'd both meet a man one day who'd be more important to us than each other,' she said accusingly.

'I meant when we were really old, eighteen or nineteen,' Sylvia said accusingly back.

'I'm getting off in a minute, we're nearly at Seaforth.'

'So?'

'So, I'll see you tomorrow afternoon, shall I?'

Sylvia shrugged carelessly. 'If you like.'

The train drew into the station, the doors opened. 'Tara, Sylvia.'

'Goodbye, Annie.'

Annie's legs nearly gave way when she stepped onto the platform. Her friendship with Sylvia had come to an end, she thought tragically. There was no way she'd go to the Grand tomorrow, although it had come to feel like home and she was dead fond of Cecy and Bruno.

The guard had blown his whistle and the doors were whirring as if they were about to close, when a figure launched itself out of the train and half fell beside her.

'Oh, Annie!' Sylvia cried. 'What a truly horrible person I am! I'm jealous, that's all. You had such a lovely time with Cyril . . .'

'*Cy!*'

'Cy, and I was so miserable with Mike. Will you ever forgive me?'

'I thought we weren't going to be friends any more,' Annie said in a small voice.

'Just as if!' Sylvia linked Annie's arm affectionately.

'I'll ask Mike for Cy's address and cancel the date,' Annie offered.

But Sylvia pooh-poohed the offer vehemently. 'I wouldn't dream of such a thing. I hope you have a lovely time on Saturday. Just spare a thought for me occasionally, listening to records in my lonely room . . .'

8

'Well, Annie, what did you think?' Mr Andrews' eyes blinked nervously, as if he would be devastated if she hadn't liked his play. It was the first day back at school, and Annie had stayed after the English lesson.

She coughed importantly. 'I think it's very good. Me sister read it and she really liked it, too.' Marie had been so impressed, both with the play and the pantomime, that she couldn't wait to join the drama group when she reached her final year. She'd decided she would like to be a proper actress when she grew up.

Mr Andrews looked relieved. 'What about playing Goldilocks?'

'I dunno.' Annie wriggled uncomfortably.

'I'll be vastly disappointed if you don't give it a try. In fact, I might give up without you. You're the only one I can see in the part.'

He was so nice she didn't like to let him down. 'I mightn't be any good. I've never acted before.'

'All of us are acting all the time,' he said enigmatically.

'I'll give it a try, then.'

'Good girl!' he said delightedly. 'In that case, keep this copy and start learning your lines. I'll cast the rest of the parts on Monday.'

Perhaps she'd known deep down she would play Goldilocks, because, with Marie's help, Annie already knew the lines off by heart.

'I hardly ever see you,' Sylvia complained on the way home from school. 'You go out with Cyril – I mean Cy – every week, and tonight you're staying in again. We always go to the youth club on Wednesdays.'

'I've only been out with Cy three times, and I changed it to Friday last week, didn't I, so I could see you on Saturday.'

Sylvia said petulantly. 'You've been really funny all week, just because he kissed you.'

'It was only a peck on the cheek.' She felt a little thrill every time she thought about it.

'I think it's getting serious.'

'Don't be silly!'

'Promise you won't go to that club, The Cavern, with him. It's our own special place. I'd be upset if you shared it with Cyril.'

'Cy! I promise. I don't think it's his cup of tea.' The girls had gone to the new club last week, the night it opened. The queue snaked right round the block and they'd been almost the last to be allowed in. Down a narrow street of old warehouses in the centre of Liverpool, the rough basement with its bare brick walls and foot-tapping music had made them feel very cosmopolitan and sophisticated. Ever since, they'd sung 'When

The Saints Go Marching In' as they went through the gates to school.

'Anyway,' said Sylvia, returning to the matter in hand, 'why can't you go to the club tonight?'

Annie sighed, 'I don't like leaving our Marie. She's dead upset over losing the baby.'

'It's taken her long enough to find out.'

'She's been upset all along. I didn't know how bad until recently.'

Sylvia snorted derisively. 'If I remember rightly, she didn't lose the baby. It was taken from her at great expense.'

'Oh, Sylvia! What a horrible thing to say!'

'It's not your job to act as a social worker to your sister, Annie,' Sylvia said with an irritating air of self-righteousness.

'Then whose job is it?' Annie asked simply. She was determined not to get annoyed, because she knew what would happen. Any minute, Sylvia would collapse like a pricked balloon and declare herself to be the most horrible person in the world.

'It's your mother's job, or your father's. What about Auntie Dot?'

'Don't be stupid! Me mam and dad live in a world of their own and Dot knows nothing about it. I'm the only one Marie's got to talk to.'

Sylvia stopped dead. 'Oh, Annie! What a dreadful person I am!' She stared at Annie soulfully. 'How do you put up with me?'

'I dunno, I must be daft.' Annie jerked her head. 'Come on, stop posing, else there won't be time for a coffee.'

'Posing?' Sylvia caught her up. 'Was I posing?'

'You pose all the time. You'd think you were Vivien Leigh.'

'Do I actually look like Vivien Leigh?' Sylvia tossed back her long blonde hair with a slender hand.

'Not in the least,' Annie said bluntly. 'You just pose and look dramatic, the way she did in *Gone With the Wind*.'

Sylvia looked puzzled. 'Was that a compliment?'

'It was a statement, that's all.'

When they were in the café, Sylvia said, 'Why don't you ask Marie to come with us to the youth club?'

'I did once, but she refused. She knows you don't like her.'

Sylvia looked hurt. 'I've never said I didn't like her.'

'You didn't have to, Syl. It's obvious. Still, it was generous of you to offer, under the circumstances,' Annie said kindly.

'I've got an idea!' Sylvia's lovely blue eyes brightened. 'Cecy's terribly short-handed. Two women left after Christmas. Would Marie like a job? She'd be so busy, she wouldn't have time to be upset.'

'A job? What sort of job?' Marie demanded.

'Working in the kitchen in the Grand. It's good fun. I did it once and I really enjoyed meself.'

Her sister looked dubious. 'I'm no good at that sort of thing.'

'How do you know?' Annie enquired. 'You've never tried. The pay's good, five shillings an hour, plus tips.'

'Why don't you do it, then?' Marie asked suspiciously.

'Because I don't like taking money off me best friend's mother.'

'Five bob an hour!' Marie pursed her lips thoughtfully. 'How many nights a week?'

'You'd have to sort that out with Cecy. As many as you want, I expect, though they don't do meals on Sunday and Monday.'

'Gosh! I could earn pounds. I could buy meself stacks of clothes.' Marie looked animated for the first time in months. Annie reminded herself her sister was only fourteen. She might have lost a baby, but she was still childish enough to be excited at the idea of buying clothes.

'You'd have to work really hard,' she said sternly.

Marie looked virtuous. 'I don't mind hard work.'

'You could have fooled me!'

'I really fancy one of those taffeta petticoats that make your skirt stick out,' Marie said longingly.

'We'll go to the Grand tonight and you can discuss it with Cecy.' Annie felt hopeful that the problem of Marie might be solved. 'By the way, she knows nothing about that business with the nursing home, so don't mention it whatever you do.'

Annie felt certain that everyone on the train was looking at her. It was as bad as – worse than – having nothing on. She caught the eye of an old woman, who quickly turned her head away.

'I feel dead stupid,' she whispered to Sylvia.

'For goodness' sake, Annie,' her friend snorted impatiently. 'You'd think you were the first woman in the world to wear slacks.'

'My bottom's *huge*!'

'No-one can see your bottom whilst you're sitting on it.'

'I wish I hadn't let you talk me into buying them.' It had seemed a good idea in Bon Marché. Lots of the girls in The Cavern wore slacks.

'Don't start putting the blame on me!' Sylvia said indignantly. She grinned. 'You'll soon get used to them.'

Annie wriggled. She felt as if she were being slowly cut in half. 'I suppose so,' she sighed.

'Where did you go last night with Cy?' Sylvia asked casually.

'For a Chinese meal. It was horrible, like eating

roots.' Annie glanced slyly at her friend. 'I'm not seeing him again.'

Sylvia tried not to look glad. 'I hope it's nothing to do with me!'

'It's because he kissed me!'

'But he kissed you before and you said you liked it!'

'This time he kissed me on the lips and his breath *stinks*! Honestly, Syl, it was like being kissed by a sewer! Phew!' Annie waved her hand in front of her face. Between kisses, he'd whispered how much he loved her and how beautiful she was, but all she could think of was how to escape from the rotten smell coming from his mouth. In the end, she'd pulled away and run into the station, where she'd jumped on a train before there was time to make arrangements for another date.

Sylvia burst out laughing. 'It's all those cigarettes!'

'I know. He'll just have to find a girl who smokes as much as he does. Anyroad, I couldn't have gone out with him next Friday, could I? We're going to the theatre with Mr Andrews.'

After discovering that not a single member of the drama group had seen a real play in a real theatre, and, worse, they'd never heard of the Liverpool Playhouse, Mr Andrews decided it was time they paid a visit.

'It'll be my treat,' he said, 'though that's not as generous as it sounds. It's only a bob each at the back. That's where I used to sit in my hard-up student days.'

The play was *School for Wives*, a period piece which told the story of a disreputable old man in search of a young wife. Sylvia spent all week deciding what to wear and turned up in a long black coat and a Greta Garbo hat. She complained bitterly she was getting creased as more and more people squeezed into the next-to-back row until they were squashed to-gether like sardines.

'What do you think so far?' Mr Andrews asked in the first interval.

'It's the dead gear, sir – I mean, Mr Andrews.'

'That old man's a marvellous actor,' one of the boys said.

Mr Andrews' eyes twinkled. 'That "old man" is called Richard Briers and he's only twenty-one! When he becomes famous, which he surely will, you can tell people you first saw him at the Liverpool Playhouse.'

'I wish I hadn't come,' Annie said miserably. 'It makes me realise how awful my Goldilocks is.'

'Don't be silly,' Sylvia chided. 'I think you're very good. I've been telling you so for weeks.'

'She's still a bit stiff,' Mr Andrews said easily. 'She needs to relax a bit, that's all.'

'Are Mam and Dad going to see *Goldilocks*?' Marie asked.

'I haven't mentioned it,' Annie replied. Her sister was helping to prepare the Sunday dinner. Since working at the Grand, she gave the occasional hand at home. 'I didn't ask them to the pantomime, did I?'

'That was different. This time you're the star. They went to Tommy's wedding, and they'll go to the christening when Dawn has her baby, so they should go and see their daughter in a play!' Dot and Bert would be grandparents at Easter. 'Cutting it fine,' Dot said darkly. 'Nine months to the day. I'll kill our Tommy if it's early. The whole street'll talk.'

'I suppose I could ask them,' Annie mused.

Later, on her way to see Sylvia, she thought, 'I've never made demands. In fact, it's *me* who's looked after *them*, rather than the other way round. When Mr Andrews asked what they'd thought of the pantomime, I had to lie again, say Mam was ill. It would look dead funny if they didn't turn up for *Goldilocks*.' People would wonder what sort of mam and dad she had.

She'd definitely ask them. 'It's time they did something for me.'

'That was brilliant, Annie,' Mr Andrews enthused when the dress rehearsal finished. 'Absolutely brilliant.'

'I got quite carried away,' Annie said modestly. It was Wednesday and the play was only two days off. Today, she'd actually managed to get *inside* Goldilocks, and feel her bitterness and frustration at the hand that fate had dealt her.

'That's as it should be.' Mr Andrews came onto the stage. 'Gather round, cast, I've some news.' They sat on the floor at his feet. 'We've nearly sold out of tickets for the main performance, and Mr Parrish wants us to do an extra one on Friday afternoon just for the school.'

Everyone groaned affectedly and pretended it would be a bore.

Mr Andrews wasn't fooled. 'I knew you'd be pleased. There's a reporter coming from the *Crosby Herald*, so you'll have your names in the paper next week. Now, who's brought money for tickets? You'd better be quick, there's only a few left.'

Annie supposed she'd better buy tickets for Mam and Dad before it was too late. She kept putting off asking them, but perhaps if she produced the tickets and waved them in their faces, it would be harder for them to refuse. The more she'd thought about it, the more important it seemed that they should come. It proved something, though she wasn't sure what. As soon as Dad finished his tea tonight, she'd bring it up.

Marie was about to leave for work when Annie got home. 'There's a big dinner tonight, Crosby Conservative Association. Bruno nearly hit the roof when he found out. Cecy said he was nothing but a bloody Marxist. They had an awful row.'

'They often row, but it doesn't mean anything,' Annie said.

'I know. They're terribly in love. It's dead romantic.' Marie sighed happily. 'It's smashing there, sis.' She kissed Annie's cheek. 'Ta!'

'Get away with you!' Annie flushed with pleasure. She couldn't remember her sister making a spontaneous show of affection before.

Marie left, and Annie began to prepare her father's tea. Since hearing he was throwing his dinner away, she'd been making appetising little treats. She smeared butter on a piece of plaice and slid it under the grill, peeled two small potatoes and opened a tin of peas.

She made herself a jam butty and ate it in the kitchen, staring through the window at the wall separating the house from Mrs Flaherty's. She felt restless and on edge, aware of the blue tickets in the breast pocket of her gymslip. She moved to the door where she could see her mam. The television was on without the sound. Once, when Mam was in the lavatory, Annie had looked in the cupboard, and there, as Marie had said, were several bottles of tablets with funny names she'd never heard of.

'God, it's *horrific*!' she thought. 'It's like a nightmare – Mr Andrews could write a play about it.'

The clock on the mantelpiece struck seven, and she saw her mother's body tense. Her head cocked slightly as if she were listening for something. She was waiting for the sound of the latch on the backyard door, the signal that her husband was home.

As soon as her father had cleared his plate, Annie fetched the tea. 'Would you like a pudding? I've got a Battenburg, your favourite.' He'd never said it was his favourite, but whenever she bought one it rapidly disappeared.

'No, ta,' he grunted. He turned his chair towards the fire, opened the *Daily Express* and began to read.

The clock struck half past seven. If she didn't leave soon, she'd be late meeting Sylvia – she realised she'd forgotten to change out of her uniform. She stood irresolutely in the middle of the room, wondering whether to go upstairs and change, but the tickets seemed to be burning a hole in her pocket. 'I'll ask now,' she decided. If she didn't, she wouldn't stop thinking about it all night.

She sat down, took a deep breath, and said in a voice that shook for some reason. 'I've got tickets for the school play. They're only ninepence each. I've got the main part. I'm the star. Please come, *please*!'

There was no answer and in the ensuing silence Annie felt as if her words were still there, hanging in the air full of urgent desperation. But Mam had heard, she could tell. Her mother's body shrank. She hunched her shoulders and folded her arms and stared down at her knees, which were clenched together like teeth. Dad looked up from his paper, but instead of looking at Annie, he looked at the television, at the characters talking soundlessly to each other. Then he shook his head, not at Annie, but at the screen, though she knew it was meant for her. There was a finality about the gesture. She knew straight away there was no point in trying to change his mind.

So that was it. They weren't coming.

Jaysus! With a feeling of reckless rage she'd never experienced before, Annie took the tickets from her pocket and threw them on the fire. She watched them curl, turn brown, catch alight, and as they were consumed by the blue, flickering flames, she felt a similar flame begin to kindle in her heart. She loathed them! She loathed them both, particularly her mother. You never knew, Dad might have come if it hadn't been for her.

The floodgates broke. 'Why didn't you leave us with Auntie Dot?' she cried in a voice raw with hate and anger. 'You're not fit to be parents, either of you.'

Her father was still staring at the screen. He didn't even glance in Annie's direction during her outburst. If he turns the sound up, I'll hit him, she vowed.

'*Why don't you listen to me?*' Suddenly she was screaming. 'I'm your daughter. I'm Annie. Don't you know I'm here?'

She had to get through to them! She had to say something that would touch a nerve, instigate a response. 'Marie had an abortion last year. Marie's your other daughter, in case you've forgotten. She had an abortion because she'd been looking for someone to love her, and when I started my periods I thought I was going to die! That's why I failed the scholarship.'

Annie remembered the mothers waiting outside school to collect their children when it was raining, the sportsdays and speechdays which she hadn't bothered to mention because she knew they wouldn't come, the pantomime. But what she'd missed more than anything was a knee to sit on and arms to embrace her when she'd needed them. She wanted to explain the aching misery of her childhood to her parents in words they would understand, but perhaps she wasn't clever enough or literate enough, because she couldn't think of a way of phrasing how much she'd missed their love. Instead, she got to her feet and began to walk back and forth, waving her arms furiously, and all that came pouring out was a stream of bitterness and despair that she'd never known, never dreamt, she'd been storing up for years, perhaps her entire life.

'I hate you. I hate you both!' she screamed finally.

Still silence. Oh, if only they would speak! If only they would answer back. Why didn't they at least make excuses, defend themselves?

Mam's eyes were closed, screwed tight, as if she were shutting everything out. Annie turned on her. 'I saw you going into the Odeon, Mam,' she said brutally. 'There's nothing wrong with you, is there? All this is a sham.' She gestured around the room. 'You're just getting back at me dad because he was out with another woman the night Johnny was killed. You've ruined his life, and you've ruined my and our Marie's lives, because you're so eaten up with sheer bloody spite!' She bent down and began to shake her mother by the shoulders. 'Are you listening to me, Mam?' she demanded shrilly.

'Don't,' said Dad. 'Don't.'

Annie glared at him, ready to continue with her invective, but the words choked in her throat. Jaysus, his face! Why hadn't she noticed how grey it had become, the skin like rubber, pitted and eaten away, his eyes almost invisible in dark, shrunken sockets? In a moment of blinding clarity, she realised he was very ill, that he was dying. She could actually smell the sickness, the sweet, rotten odour of decay that came from somewhere deep inside him.

Annie turned on her heel wordlessly and left the room. She snatched her gabardine mack off the rack in the hall, left the house and walked quickly to the youth club. A vicious wind had sprung up; she shoved her hands in her pockets because she'd forgotten her gloves.

'Where on earth have you been?' Sylvia demanded crossly when Annie came into the church hall where the youth club was held. 'We've lost our place on the table tennis rota.'

But Annie didn't care. 'Let's go for a walk,' she said abruptly.

'A walk?' Sylvia looked startled. 'Gosh, Annie, are

you all right? You haven't changed and you're as white as a sheet.'

'Come on!' Annie marched towards the door.

'I'm coming!'

Annie was halfway down the street by the time Sylvia caught up with her, still struggling into her suede coat.

'Where are we going?'

'Nowhere. Anywhere.'

'Something awful's happened, hasn't it?'

Annie nodded. 'I can't tell you, not yet,' she replied in a flat, emotionless voice. 'I just want to walk.'

'All right, Annie, that's what we'll do.'

Sylvia linked Annie's arm and the two girls walked silently for a long time. After a while, the monotonous clatter of their shoes on the pavement began to get on Annie's nerves. The sound seemed to echo, magnified, in the near-empty streets.

'Talk to me,' she demanded.

'What about?'

'I don't know.'

Sylvia began to speak, hesitantly at first. She told Annie about Italy, about the little village in the south surrounded by misty lavender hills where she was born. They'd lived in a big house, 'Almost as big as a castle, Annie, with little turrets on each corner and acres and acres of vineyard at the back.' During the war, Cecy had been worried she'd be arrested because she was English, but no-one in the village informed on her and she'd been left alone. Bruno had gone away to fight with the Communists in Yugoslavia soon after Sylvia was born and she hadn't seen him till she was four. 'When the war ended and he came back, I was thrilled to discover this tall, magnificent man was my father. I wouldn't let him out of my sight. He had to take me with him everywhere. Then he decided he wasn't prepared to tolerate the Mafia any longer. They virtually ruled the village and demanded a huge share of the profits from our wine business.' And Sylvia had started school. 'All we did was say prayers, I learnt scarcely anything.' So they'd moved to Turin. 'Such an elegant city, Turin, Annie. It's where Bruno and Cecy met. He has a cousin there, and Cecy was on holiday with one of her aunts. I went to a proper school, but soon Cecy became homesick. She yearned for Liverpool. Now, you'll never guess, Bruno is quite gloriously happy, and Cecy occasionally feels homesick for Italy!'

Sylvia's voice trailed away. Annie saw they'd reached a crossroads and there was a pub on the opposite corner. 'Have you got any money?'

'Of course. How much do you want?'

'I'd like a drink, a whisky.' A whisky had helped once before, the day she'd failed the scholarship. Perhaps a drink would help calm her pounding heart and the turmoil in her stomach.

'You're still in uniform!' Sylvia bit her lip. 'Turn your collar up to hide your tie. Stay away from the bar so the landlord won't see you.'

The pub was packed. Annie found two stools and carried them to a corner. Sylvia was ages getting served at the crowded bar. She arrived looking flustered. 'I got you a double.'

'Ta.'

Two men approached. 'Mind if we join you, girls?'

'Yes,' Sylvia said crisply. 'Go away!'

'Toffee-nosed pair of bitches!' one man muttered audibly.

The whisky had the opposite effect from what Annie hoped for. It made her feel worse, as if a kettle was boiling inside her stomach, emitting clouds of steam, and her heart was pounding even louder.

'I think I'm going to be sick,' she said plaintively.

'Come on, you need some fresh air.'

Back outside, Sylvia said, 'Shall we go to the Grand? You can rest in my room and Cecy will make a nice cup of tea.'

The idea was tempting, but Annie shook her head. 'I should go home,' she said tiredly. Go home and apologise for saying such terrible things.

'What time is it?' she asked when they reached Orlando Street.

'Nearly ten o'clock. We've walked for miles, Annie. I'm surprised we found our way back.'

Annie had left her key in her satchel. She knocked on the door of number thirty-eight. 'Thanks, Sylvia,' she muttered.

'What for?'

'For putting up with me tonight.' Sylvia hadn't complained, not once. 'I'll never forget it.'

Sylvia laughed shyly. 'That's what friends are for. Whatever happens, I'll always be there for you, Annie.'

Sylvia had disappeared by the time Annie knocked a second time. She stepped back and looked up at the window of her parents' room; the curtains were open and the room was in darkness, which meant they were still up. Perhaps Dad was so angry he'd decided not to let her in. Annie rather hoped this was the case. She'd welcome anger, understand it. It was the mute, uncomplaining acceptance of her tirade that had driven her to say more and more wicked things.

She knocked a third time, then peered through the letterbox. Total blackness! Marie wasn't due home for half an hour, when Bruno or Cecy usually brought her in the car.

Perhaps the back door was open; it wasn't usually locked until they went to bed. Annie walked to the end of the street and turned down the narrow passage leading to the back entry which ran between the two rows of houses. The path was unlit. Dad had warned them never to use the entry in the dark, reminding them of the girl who'd been murdered in such an entry less than a mile away. Remembering, Annie started to run. She stumbled against a dustbin and nearly screamed when she saw two luminous eyes staring at her from on top of a wall. It was a cat, who spat and snarled as she passed. At last, she reached thirty-eight and almost fell into the yard. Her fingers shook as she fumbled with the latch on the back door. She sighed with relief when the door was safely closed behind her.

There was a light in the kitchen, but not the living room, which was odd. Annie squinted through the net curtains, but no-one was there. They must be out, but it was unheard of for her parents to go out unexpectedly. Perhaps one had been taken ill! If so, it was entirely her fault.

She tried the kitchen door, convinced it would be locked, and was surprised to find it open, and even more surprised when it jammed after a few inches. There was something preventing it from opening further. Annie pushed hard with her shoulder and the door gave way.

The smell hit her immediately. Gas, so powerful, that she instinctively put her hands to her face to prevent herself from retching. Then she screamed.

Mam was lying on the floor, her head on a pillow, rosary beads threaded through her still, white fingers. Dad's head was in the oven, his body half draped over his wife's. One of his hands lay protectively on her breast. His poor legs were twisted crookedly because Annie had pushed at them trying to get in.

Annie screamed again and couldn't stop screaming. She screamed so loudly she didn't hear windows opening and irritable voices demanding to know what the hell was going on, nor footsteps in the entry and the latch lifting on the back door. She was unaware that the back yard was suddenly full of people. It wasn't until she was roughly yanked aside that she came to.

'Jesus Christ!' a man's voice said hoarsely. 'Get the kid out of here. Someone call an ambulance, quick!'

'Come on, luv. Come indoors with me.' Mrs Flaherty from next door took hold of Annie's arm and tried to lead her away.

She stared at the old woman, eyes wild with terror. 'I killed them! I murdered me mam and dad.'

Shrugging off the restraining arm, she fought her way out of the yard. Her ankles struck the pedal of Dad's bike, which was propped against the wall. It slid to the ground with a crash.

There were more people in the entry outside. 'What's going on?' someone asked.

'It's the Harrisons. They've done themselves in.' The speaker's voice throbbed with excitement. 'Gas, I think it was.'

Annie emerged from the entry into Orlando Street. People were pouring out of the pub on the corner. Above the sound of the shouting and the laughter, she could hear a voice calling, 'Empty your glasses, *please*!' There was something strangely familiar about the desperate cry. 'Please come, *please*!'

She stood outside the pub for a long time, being jostled by the crowd and in everyone's way. Several men, unsteady on their feet, began to cross the road and she followed them blindly, then began to run again.

After a while, Annie stopped running. Her breath was raw within her pounding chest, and her legs felt as if they were about to give way. She'd come to the stretch of sand where Dot used to bring them in the summer when they were little, and where she and Sylvia came on warm evenings to talk.

Now, at half past ten on a bitter March night, she felt herself drawn towards the dark isolation offered by the litter-strewn beach . . .

Upper Parliament Street

Sylvia stuck her head round the office door. 'Lunch time!' she sang.

'Already?' replied Annie without looking up. Her eyes were glued to the paper in her typewriter. 'Are you sure?'

'You must be the only typist in Liverpool who doesn't watch the clock all day long,' Sylvia said as she came into the tiny room. She wore a knitted shawl with a long fringe over an ankle-length black jersey dress, boots, and a red scarf tied around her head like a gypsy. Gold hoops dangled from her ears. The outfit looked casual, as if it had been thrown on without a thought, yet she'd probably spent ages deciding what to wear that day for Art College.

'I'll just finish this letter,' Annie murmured. Sylvia stood behind and watched, impressed, as her friend's fingers flew over the keys.

'There!' Annie typed 'Yours faithfully', left five clear spaces, then 'J. Rupert', and withdrew the sheet with a flourish. 'I'll do the rest this afternoon.'

'I should think so!' Sylvia lounged against a filing cabinet and said with a twinkle, 'Where's your boss?'

'Now as he's seen you, likely to come in any minute, I reckon.'

The words were scarcely out of her mouth when, through the glazed wall separating her cubbyhole from Jeremy Rupert's luxurious office, they saw a bulky figure rise from the desk. Sylvia was as visible to him as he was to them. The girls grinned at each other.

Annie's door opened and a man entered. His roly-poly figure and noticeably short arms and legs must have presented a challenge to his tailor. Chubby red cheeks and round spectacles gave him a Billy Bunter look. He had tiny feet and walked in a curiously dainty manner for someone of his bulk. 'Can I have a copy of this please, Annie.' His eyes widened in surprise which both girls knew was entirely faked. 'Oh, hello, Sylvia, I didn't know you were here.'

'Hello, Jeremy.'

Annie could never get used to Sylvia addressing her boss as 'Jeremy'. 'I don't work for him, so if he calls me by my first name, I shall call him by his,' Sylvia argued.

'You look a sight for sore eyes, I must say,' Jeremy Rupert's mouth almost watered as he looked Sylvia up and down.

'Thank you,' Sylvia said prettily. 'I'm about to whisk your secretary off to lunch. She's already five minutes late.'

'Then she must take an extra five minutes for her lunch hour,' Annie's boss said expansively. 'No, another ten. In fact, Annie, I don't expect to see you back until two fifteen.'

As his own lunch hour was quite likely to stretch to three or even later, there was no likelihood of him seeing Annie at two fifteen. Nevertheless, she unhooked her coat from behind the door, and said demurely, 'Thank you, Mr Rupert.'

'Well, we're off,' smiled Sylvia. 'Nice seeing you, Jeremy.'

Jeremy Rupert opened the door with exaggerated courtesy. As the girls went through, he put a heavy arm around Sylvia's waist to usher her out. Sylvia paused deliberately, and with an expression of distaste, took his cuff between her thumb and forefinger and let the arm drop. No words were spoken, but the man smiled as if it were a great joke.

'Is he always like that?' Sylvia asked when they were outside.

'Like what?'

'Like a bloody octopus. He can't keep his hands to himself.'

'I do have a job fighting him off sometimes,' Annie conceded. She'd only worked for Jeremy Rupert for two months. At first, she thought the way he slipped his arm around her waist or shoulders was merely a paternal gesture on his part – he had two daughters slightly older than herself – but lately she'd noticed his hand brush her breasts. She hadn't said anything because she couldn't think of a way to put him off without risking her job. She acted as if the incidents hadn't occurred.

'You should slap his face,' Sylvia said indignantly.

'And get the sack?' Annie hooted.

'If Bruno knew, he'd give the creep a good punch on the nose.'

'In that case, I'd get the sack and Bruno would end up in jail.'

'Bruno wouldn't mind. He'd think it a cause worth fighting for.'

'But I would,' Annie argued. 'It's a good job. I get eight pounds ten a week, which is at least a pound more than in another solicitor's. Not only that, I really enjoy the work since I was promoted.'

Stickley & Plumm, solicitors, were situated in North John Street, in the business centre of Liverpool, where they occupied three floors above an exclusive gentlemen's outfitters and a travel agent. An old-established, highly reputable firm, Mr Stickley and Mr Plumm were old bones, and of the four partners, Jeremy Rupert was the most junior. There were nine other solicitors, ranging from very young to very old.

Annie had started in the typing pool two and a half years ago. She was sixteen and had just left Machin & Harpers with the next to highest speeds in her class; 120 words per minute shorthand, 60 typing.

Just as she had been a good pupil, Annie was an equally good worker. She was neat, both in her dress and in her work, conscientious and punctual. Only Annie herself was surprised when, despite her youth, she was offered the job of Jeremy Rupert's secretary when the current occupant retired. The other secretaries were more than twice her age.

Not only did it mean an increase in wages, but Mr Rupert was head of the Litigation Department, where the work was vastly more interesting than conveyancing or probate, involving simple but fascinating disputes from litigants squabbling over the situation of boundary walls and fences, to violent criminal activities including the occasional murder.

Annie loved the work. Lately, though, Mr Rupert's roving hands had become a problem.

Sylvia linked her arm. 'Let's have lunch in the New Court.'

'But it'll be nearly all men,' Annie protested.

Sylvia flung the corner of her shawl over her shoulder with a flourish. 'Why do you think I want to go?'

'You know what you are?' said Annie as they strolled along. The streets were packed with office workers. It was a crisp, sunny December day and the small shops were tastefully decorated for Christmas. 'You're a prickteaser. You enjoy flaunting yourself in front of men.'

Sylvia raised her fine eyebrows. 'That's a rather vulgar expression coming from the prim and proper Miss Annie Harrison!'

'That's how Mike described his new girlfriend. Mind you, Dot still gave him a clip round the ear, even though he's twenty-three.'

'Mike! Is he still so depressingly boring?'

'Mike isn't the least bit boring.' Annie sprang to the defence of her cousin. 'Anyroad, he considers you incredibly conceited.'

'That's because I've got plenty to be conceited about.' Sylvia glanced at her reflection in a shop window as if to confirm the truth of this remark: not that there was any need for confirmation, the admiring looks from passers-by, particularly the men, were enough to convince any girl she was outstanding.

The looks weren't just for Sylvia. The two girls were in stark contrast to each other: Sylvia in her flamboyant outfit, her straight creamy hair spread fanlike over her woollen shawl, and Annie, quietly dressed in a sensible coat, the frill of her white blouse spurting from under the collar, yet, in her own way, equally flamboyant with her russet curls, cheeks pinker than usual from the cold, and gold-lashed blue-grey eyes. Both were tall, though Sylvia was as slender as a model and two sizes smaller than her more voluptuous companion.

The men in the New Court were suitably impressed when the girls went in. Sylvia swept haughtily up to the bar and ordered shandy and cheese sandwiches, apparently oblivious to the stir they had created. She winked at Annie. 'If you ignore them, it drives them wild.'

'Do you like my shawl?' she asked when they were seated.

'It's very nice,' Annie said dutifully.

'Cecy had it made. She'll order one for you, if you like.'

'I don't want to hurt her feelings, but tell her no ta. I can't see meself in a shawl.'

'She misses you terribly, Annie,' Sylvia said, serious for once.

'I miss her, too – and Bruno.'

'You didn't have to leave. You can come back any time you want.'

'I know, Syl,' Annie said patiently. They had the same discussion at least once a week. 'But it was time me and Marie lived together.'

'But Marie will be moving to London once she finishes her drama course. You can't live in that horrible little flat all on your own!'

'It's not little and it's not horrible. I really like it there.'

'Better than the Grand?' Sylvia looked hurt.

'Of course not!'

The girls finished their meal and left the pub. Outside, they made arrangements to meet when Annie finished work at Saturday lunchtime. 'We'll go shopping, catch a movie, and finish off at the Cavern,' Sylvia announced.

Annie couldn't help but smile at the 'catch a movie'. Her friend had become very Americanised since she started College. She referred to men as 'guys' and said 'kinda' instead of 'kind of'.

Sylvia kissed her cheek and said, 'See ya, Annie', and waltzed off into the crowd. Annie submitted to the kiss, embarrassed. It was something else Sylvia had started to do. They must be a pretentious lot at Art College.

As she climbed the stairs to her office on the second floor, she passed Reception, where Miss Hunt, secretary to Mr Granger, the senior partner, was on the telephone. She put the receiver down and glanced pointedly at her watch.

Annie stuck her head inside. 'Mr Rupert said I could have an extra fifteen minutes. I was late leaving.'

Miss Hunt was the longest-serving female employee

in the firm. A tall, painfully thin woman with a penchant for pastel twinsets and tight perms, she was the butt of cruel office jokes of which Annie hoped she was ignorant, or her permanent anguished frown might have grown deeper. Miss Hunt had spent most of her adult life attending to Arnold Grayson's every whim. She shopped for him, to the extent, it was rumoured, of buying his underwear. On his behalf, she sent birthday presents to his wife and children, arranged his holidays, paid his bills. More than once, she had been seen kneeling on the floor tying Arnold Grayson's shoelaces.

Outside his office, Miss Hunt was a different person. She was nominally in charge of female employees, who often felt the lash of her acerbic tongue if they were late or their work didn't come up to scratch, and woe betide them if they spent too much time gossiping in the Ladies.

Her narrow yellow face twisted into what might possibly be a smile when Annie spoke. 'I thought it wasn't like you to be late, Miss Harrison. Was that your friend who came for you earlier?'

'Yes, Sylvia. It's all right for her to come in, isn't it?'

'Of course. She looks rather Bohemian,' Miss Hunt said wistfully, as if she wouldn't have minded being a bit Bohemian herself.

'She's at Art College,' said Annie, as if that explained everything. She was never sure if Sylvia was a Bohemian, an Existentialist or a Beatnik. 'We only lunch on Thursdays, when she has a free period.'

Back at her desk, Annie flicked through her shorthand notebook and found only two more letters, both short. She typed them quickly, put them in the blotting folder on Mr Rupert's desk ready for him to sign along with those done that morning, and swept the leather top clear of cigarette ash. She then caught up with the filing. It wasn't yet half two and she had nothing else to do. In practice, she was supposed to collect work from the typing pool to fill in time before her boss appeared, but Annie wasn't in the mood to be a model secretary that afternoon.

She sank her chin onto her hands, laid palm downwards on the typewriter. She'd hated leaving the Grand and upsetting Cecy, but there'd been Marie to consider. Marie was living next door to Auntie Dot with an increasingly ailing old lady, and Annie was left with the old, familiar sensation of guilt, of feeling responsible for her sister.

The telephone rang in Mr Rupert's office. Annie picked up her extension, which usually made her feel very important, and made an appointment for a client to see him the following week.

Downstairs, someone called, 'Rose, Ro-ose. Mr Bunyon and his client would like a cup of tea straight away.'

'I've only got one bloody pair of hands. I'll be as quick as I can,' a hoarse voice replied. Rose, the tealady, could be heard angrily banging dishes in the kitchen. Almost eighty, Rose was a breath of fresh air in the dull and stultifying atmosphere that prevailed in the offices of Stickley & Plumm. She never hesitated to speak her mind. If anyone didn't like it, all they had to do was sack her, she said challengingly.

Annie returned to her reverie. *Rose!*

'*How are you getting on with the girls, Rose? Don't forget, I'd be happy to have them if they're too much for you.*'

'*Don't put on your little act with me, Rose.*'

'*It's time to forgive and forget, Rose.*'

Dot's voice. Then another, throbbing with excitement. '*It's the Harrisons, they've done themselves in. Gas, I think it was.*'

Although she was sitting down, Annie's legs felt

weak, as if she'd been running too fast and too far. Perspiration trickled down her armpits, despite the deodorant she'd rubbed on that morning, as she began to relive that terrible night. She'd relived it a thousand times already. Lately the memory returned less and less, but it took the smallest thing, like someone calling 'Rose', for it all to come flooding back.

She left the sands and ran towards the Grand, trying to keep a look-out for Bruno, but the cars that whizzed by all looked the same. Suppose he just dropped Marie off at the end of Orlando Street!

Bruno was about to leave when Annie came stumbling up. She threw herself onto the bonnet, and the Mercedes stopped with a screech of brakes. 'For goodness' sake, Annie!' came Bruno's irritable voice. 'Are you trying to commit suicide?'

She tried to explain, but the words refused to come. There seemed no words in the dictionary to describe what she'd just seen. 'Me mam, me dad' she croaked, but that was all. She stood, ice-cold and trembling. Even when Bruno shook her by the shoulders, she still couldn't speak.

Then Cecy and Sylvia came and took her inside. Bruno said crisply, 'Stay here, Marie.' He got into the car and drove away.

Cecy made a cup of tea and Annie drank it gratefully. 'Perhaps a drop of whisky?' Cecy suggested, but Sylvia said in a scared voice, 'She had whisky earlier and it made her sick.'

Marie looked terrified. 'What's happened, sis?'

Annie opened her arms and her sister fell into them. Words came at last. 'They're dead, Marie. Our mam and dad are dead.'

Cecy gasped. 'God rest their souls.' She crossed herself.

'The thing is,' Annie sobbed, 'it's all my fault. I killed them. They wouldn't come to see the play and I said the most terrible things.'

'You can't kill people with words, Annie,' Cecy said, puzzled.

'*I* did!'

'I don't understand, dear.'

But no matter how Annie tried, she couldn't even begin to describe the horrific sight she'd so recently witnessed.

After a while, Bruno returned with a weeping Auntie Dot. A neighbour had known she was a relative and the police arrived with the tragic news. Bruno found her and Bert in Orlando Street. Bert stayed behind to deal with all the questions that had to be answered.

'Oh, my poor little lambs!' Dot embraced Annie and Marie in her scrawny arms. 'Trust our Ken! Even at the very end, Rose is the only one he gives a toss for. Didn't care, did he, that one of you girls was bound to find them? Poor Annie!' She stroked Annie's curls. 'What a thing to happen, eh? I could strangle the bugger with me bare hands,' she added.

Bruno had been talking quietly to his wife and daughter, and Cecy began to cry. Sylvia stared at Annie unbelievingly.

'But Dot, none of it would have happened if it wasn't for me,' Annie cried hoarsely. 'It was my fault. I drove them to it. Oh, if only I'd kept me big mouth shut, they'd still be alive.'

'What are you talking about, luv?'

'I'm the wickedest person in the world.' Annie felt as if her head would burst. How was she going to live with this for the rest of her life? 'The things I said!'

'Hold on a minute.' Bruno grabbed Annie's arm. 'Your father killed your mother, then himself. It was nothing to do with you.'

'It was, it was,' Annie wept.

'He left a note,' Bruno said harshly. 'He was dying of cancer. There were only a few weeks left. He took your mother with him.'

Annie shook her head. 'That was just an excuse. He didn't want me to think I was responsible.'

'No, luv,' Dot broke in. 'The note was typed. Your dad must have done it in the office before he came home. Nothing you said would have made any difference. He had it all planned.'

It was long past midnight by the time Bruno took Dot home. Marie went with them. Cecy had offered to keep both girls, but Marie preferred to be with her aunt. 'She can sleep with me. Bert won't mind dossing down in the parlour for a night or two,' said Dot.

Annie went to bed in the spare room feeling light-headed with relief, but when she woke next morning she could smell gas and, every time she closed her eyes, she saw the bodies of Mam and Dad lying in the kitchen. I pushed his legs all crooked, she remembered.

When Cecy came in, she found Annie almost hysterical with guilt and grief. 'They were still terrible things to say when he felt so ill, when he was dying,' she said in a cracked voice.

Cecy stroked her forehead. 'He probably wasn't listening, dear. He almost certainly didn't take in a word you said.'

'But what if he did? And another thing, if I'd looked after them better, he wouldn't have felt the need to take Mam with him.'

'Annie, dear, you're only fifteen,' Cecy said softly. 'You've had far too much responsibility in your young life. Soon, you can put this all behind you and start having a nice time, like other young girls do.'

'I was already having a nice time. I neglected them. I

should have stayed in more often. I should have stayed in all the time.' Annie began to cry. 'I'd never have gone out if I'd known me dad was dying.'

'Of course you wouldn't,' Cecy said gently. 'You know, your forehead's awfully hot. I think I'll call the doctor.'

The doctor came and prescribed tablets. For the next few days, Annie swam in and out of nightmarish sleep and periods awake when everything in the room seemed to be moving silently. The furniture would loom up as if it were about to fall on top of her, then recede just in time. The pictures on the wall detached themselves and floated around like leaves in a breeze. Dot came, and Marie. Sylvia and Cecy seemed to be there all the time. Heads were unnaturally large, voices slow and deep like a broken record on a gramophone.

'I'm a terrible nuisance,' Annie would say in moments of lucidity.

One morning, she woke up feeling better. She sat up. The furniture stayed in place and the pictures remained on the walls. Annie looked around with interest. She hadn't noticed what an elegant room this was, with its silver and grey wallpaper and dove-grey satin curtains that hung in smooth folds over the narrow windows. The eiderdown and coverlet were the same material, and even the furniture was a pale bleached grey. By contrast, the carpet was deep rippled pink.

Cecy came in. Her head was a normal size and she gave a delighted smile when she saw Annie sitting up. 'Ah, I think this is the old Annie. You're looking well, dear. The colour's already back in your cheeks.'

She rushed away to make a cup of tea. A few minutes later, Sylvia appeared in a white quilted dressing gown, her blonde hair mussed. She gave a sigh of relief. 'Jaysus, Annie, you had us worried.'

'You caught that from me Auntie Dot.'

Sylvia sat crosslegged on the plump eiderdown. 'Caught what?'

'The "Jaysus". She always says it.'

'"Jaysus" is such a lovely word!'

They grinned at each other. Sylvia reached for Annie's hand. 'Oh, it's good to see you your old self again.'

Annie sighed. 'I doubt if I'll ever be me old self, Syl.' She had memories, terrible memories, that she'd never had before.

Sylvia looked grave. 'In the long run, what happened was probably for the best. Your father was going to die, and Dot thinks your mother wouldn't have wanted to live without him.'

'How did he do it?' She wasn't too sure if she wanted to know.

'The police said he put sleeping tablets in her tea.'

'Then he carried her into the kitchen and lay down beside her . . . Jaysus!' Annie bit her lip and tried not to cry, just as Cecy swept into the room with a tray of tea things. She took one look at Annie's distraught face and said sharply to Sylvia, 'Is this your doing?'

'I was only telling her about the sleeping tablets.'

'It was me that asked,' Annie put in.

'Oh, well, I suppose you had to know some time.'

'What day is it?' Annie asked suddenly.

'Monday,' Sylvia replied.

'The play, *Goldilocks*. It should have gone on last Friday!' She'd let Mr Andrews down.

'Don't worry,' Sylvia assured her. '*Goldilocks* went ahead as planned. Mr Andrews managed to get a red wig, and according to all reports, Marie played Goldilocks to perfection.'

'Marie? *Our* Marie?'

'Who else? She knew the part as well as you did.'

Annie felt relieved. It was time her sister got some recognition.

'Now, get dressed the pair of you,' Cecy said impatiently. 'I'll make breakfast, and if Annie feels well enough, we'll all go into town. I feel in the mood to spend lots of money today.'

There was no question of the girls going back to Orlando Street. In fact, they never went back at all. Dot and Bert cleared the house of its contents, and brought Annie's few possessions to the Grand. To everyone's astonishment, it was discovered the house had been purchased, not rented, and the small mortgage had almost been paid off.

'He was always a secretive bugger, our Ken,' Dot said, shaking her head. They were in the Grand, in the vast private lounge which was big enough to hold two suites. Cecy and Bruno were working, and Sylvia was upstairs supposedly doing her homework, but probably playing with the hulahoop she'd just bought. 'What do you want to do with the money, Annie? Bert said the house is worth eight or nine hundred pounds. I suggest you and Marie put it in the bank and when you're a bit older, you can buy a little house between you.'

It was a month later. The Harrison girls were back at school. The news of their parents' deaths had been in the newspaper and everybody was treating them with a mixture of kid gloves and ghoulish curiosity.

Annie had remained with the Delgados, who had assured her that she could stay in the silver and grey room permanently, whilst Marie had moved into the house next door to Dot's which was occupied by an old lady, though she had all her meals with the Gallaghers, and still came to work in the Grand several nights a week. Marie appeared entirely unaffected by recent events. She actually seemed slightly more cheerful, as if she'd been freed from a great burden.

The girls had been shielded from the inquest – even the police understood that Annie had suffered enough – and weren't told about the funeral until it was over. Annie didn't ask, but she'd once read that suicides couldn't be buried in consecrated ground. She tried to stop herself from even formulating the thought that Dad wasn't just a suicide, but a murderer – unless, and she wasn't sure if this was worse, Mam had actually *wanted* to go with him!

'I think the money should go in the bank,' she said to Dot. 'I'll want the fees for Machin & Harpers – oh, and me and Marie will need pocket-money.' She had no intention of sponging off Cecy and Bruno. She would help in the kitchen in return for her keep.

'Are you happy here, Annie?' Dot sniffed. 'That Cecy's all right, but she's a bit toffee-nosed if you ask me.'

'Cecy's anything but toffee-nosed,' Annie assured her. 'And Bruno is the nicest person in the world.' She had quite a crush on Bruno.

Dot winked. 'Oh, that Bruno. He's dead gorgeous, he is.'

'Auntie Dot!'

'Well, I'm not so old that I don't recognise a handsome-looking feller when I see one. Bruno's so good-looking I could bloody eat him.'

'I'll tell Cecy you've got designs on her husband,' Annie threatened. 'Not that she'd care. They're mad about each other.'

'There's no need to tell Cecy anything, luv,' Dot said comfortably. 'I'm happy with my Bert. He's no oil painting, but he's the only man I've ever wanted. Anyroad, you're wrong about those two. There's something funny about that marriage. It's not all it's cracked up to be.'

Annie had no intention of getting embroiled in an

argument about the Delgados' marriage. She said cautiously, 'Dot?'

'Yes, luv?'

'When you sorted through me mam's things, did you happen to come across a Paisley scarf?'

Dot went over to the window. It was April, still daylight at eight o'clock. 'It must be nice to live right opposite the pictures – and on top of a pub,' she said. 'You've got all the entertainment you need close at hand.' Then she shook her head. 'A Paisley scarf, luv? No, I never found anything like that.'

'Are you sure?'

Dot turned and looked straight at Annie. 'Sure I'm sure. Most of your mam's things were only worth throwing away, except for that dress she had for our Tommy's wedding, and your Marie snapped that up. I would have remembered seeing a Paisley scarf.'

Annie was relieved to leave school in July. She felt she was cutting herself off from her childhood. The long summer holiday was spent as it had been the year before, in Southport and New Brighton, at the pictures. Now the Cavern had been added to their list of activities, and they regularly went dancing; to Reeces, the Rialto, the Locarno. Annie turned her blue bridesmaid's frock into a dance dress.

It wasn't until she was in bed that she thought about Mam and Dad. Some nights, she woke up in the darkness to the smell of escaping gas, but the smell always disappeared when she sat up.

Bruno insisted his daughter transfer to Seafield Convent where she could take O and A levels in readiness for university, whilst, shortly before her sixteenth birthday, Annie began a shorthand and typing course at Machin & Harpers Commercial College.

'It's such a shame,' Mr Andrews complained when

told. He wrinkled his stubby little nose. 'You should take a course in fashion or design.'

'But it would be years and years before I could get a job,' said Annie. 'I need to support meself as quickly as possible.'

'Your sister doesn't think like that. Marie wants to take a drama course when she leaves next year.'

Annie smiled. 'Perhaps she's got more guts than me.'

'That's not true, Annie. You're too sensible for your own good.'

Machin & Harpers found employment for their students when they finished the nine-month course. Within a week of leaving, Annie started work in the typing pool at Stickley & Plumm.

Shortly afterwards, Sylvia got the results of her O levels. She'd failed the lot except Art, in which she achieved a B grade.

'Well, I suppose we should be thankful for small mercies,' Bruno said glumly. 'I didn't know you were good at Art.'

'Neither did I.' Sylvia had no desire to go to university and didn't care a jot. 'I've never done oil painting before. I quite enjoyed slapping the colours on. I felt sort of reckless. According to Sister Mary, my pictures had a message, though I don't understand what it was.'

'Well, you needn't think you're leaving Seafield,' Bruno snapped. 'You're going back for A levels.'

'Okay, Bruno.'

As Sylvia later explained to Annie. 'I don't mind it there. The nuns like me because I'm half Italian. They seem to think I've some connection to the Pope. And if I don't go to school, Bruno might make me get a job.' She shuddered. 'Having seen you leave at eight every morning and not get home till six, *and* work Saturday mornings, I'd sooner go to Seafield Convent any day. It's only a few minutes down the road.'

'You're dead lazy, Syl.'

Sylvia yawned. 'I know.'

Time passed pleasantly. She and Sylvia went dancing several times a week, and always to the Cavern on Saturdays to hear the Merseysippi Jazz Band. Sometimes they went on a Wednesday, Skiffle Night, when Lonnie Donnegan or the Gin Mill Skiffle band played.

Marie developed a passion for the theatre and dragged her sister to the Playhouse and the Royal Court, where they saw Margaret Lockwood, Jean Kent, Jack Hawkins and Alec Guinness. Marie insisted on waiting for almost an hour outside the stage door for Sam Wanamaker's autograph, only to discover he'd left by a different door. One night, they followed Michael Redgrave and Googie Withers along Lime Street as they made their way to the Adelphi.

'Just think,' Marie crowed as they trailed several feet behind. 'One day, there might be fans following *me* back to my hotel!'

'Only if they're idiots,' Annie snapped. 'Frankly, sis, I feel dead stupid. They might think we're private detectives.'

Marie left school and enrolled part-time at the Sheila Elliott Clarke Drama School in Bold Street. With a tenacity Annie never dreamed her sister possessed, she increased her hours at the Grand, and took a Saturday morning job as a waitress. She had no intention of spending her share of the money from Orlando Street on another house; apart from which, the sum was considerably depleted, what with school fees and other expenses. Anyroad, house prices were soaring. Someone Marie knew had actually paid an unbelievable three thousand pounds for a semi-detached in Childwall.

'As soon as I've saved enough money, I'm off to London,' Marie declared. 'It's the only place if you want to become an actress.'

It all sounded terribly exciting. Annie felt very dull, particularly when, much to Sylvia's astonishment, her friend got an A level in Art, and managed to obtain a place at Art College.

It even seemed a tiny bit unfair. Annie would have loved to have taken a course in dress design as Mr Andrews had urged, but it had always seemed out of the question. Now Sylvia was about to take 'Art in Advertising', yet she wasn't the least bit interested. It was merely a way of passing a few years in an enjoyable way without going to work.

What future was there for her at Stickley & Plumm? If she stayed long enough, Miss Hunt would retire and she might become Mr Grayson's secretary, and it would be *her* turn to tie his shoelaces!

She supposed one day she might get married, but so far had rarely met someone she would go out with twice, let alone marry. Apart from Cyril Sewerbreath, most males seemed incredibly childish. They had spots, dirty fingernails, and giggled all the time. It would be nice to go out with someone of at least twenty-five. 'Perhaps I'll have to wait till I'm twenty-five meself.'

Mrs Lloyd, the old lady Marie lived with, was becoming more feeble by the day. Dot gave a hand when she could, but Marie had to get the woman out of bed each morning, and lately had felt obliged to help her dress.

'The other day, I found the chamber pot and it was full to overflowing,' Marie said when she turned up for work. 'I emptied it, but it didn't half pong. I nearly puked. I'll ring her son later. The thing is, he seems to think she's my responsibility, but I'm just the lodger.

I'm quite fond of Mrs Lloyd, but it's horrible, sis. It reminds me of home.'

She didn't want to move elsewhere. 'I'm fed up being a lodger, and I don't earn enough for me own flat. Still, never mind, eh! In another nine months I'll be off to London. In the meantime, I'm terrified one morning I'll find poor Mrs Lloyd dead in her bed.'

It was then Annie decided it was time she left the Grand. She would be eighteen soon, and couldn't live with Cecy and Bruno for ever.

'But Marie's old enough to find herself a bedsit, surely,' Sylvia said crossly when Annie broke the news.

'You're older and you haven't,' Annie pointed out.

'And it wouldn't do her any harm to look after a sick old lady for a while,' Sylvia's voice was tart.

'She's looked after a sick old lady for more than a while, apart from which, you wouldn't look after a sick old lady for five minutes. Mrs Lloyd would be long dead if she'd had you for a lodger.'

Sylvia grinned. 'I'd probably have killed her – which reminds me, it'll kill Cecy when she hears you're going to leave.'

Cecy was devastated. 'But Annie, there's no need for you to go,' she cried. 'I hoped you'd stay till you got married. Bruno and I think of you as our daughter.'

'But Marie . . .'

'There's room for Marie! It would be lovely having you both.'

Cecy didn't know this was out of the question. Marie and Sylvia scarcely spoke. Although Annie felt wretched at the thought of leaving the people who had supported her through the worst time of her life, in her heart, she knew it wasn't solely to do with Marie. It was time she became independent. To her relief, she found Bruno on her side.

'You must allow Annie to make her own decisions,

darling,' he told Cecy. 'Just as you must allow Sylvia to make hers – if she ever gets round to making one,' he added darkly.

Bruno helped Annie find the flat. It was on the top floor of a gracious four-storey house in Upper Parliament Street, a short bus ride from Stickley & Plumm – within walking distance, if she felt energetic. Thin partitions had been erected to form a small bedroom and kitchen on one side of what had once been a large attic, and a second bedroom and bathroom on the other, leaving the middle section as the lounge. The bath was full of rust stains and the kitchen had no ventilation, but the view from the pretty arched window was magnificent, encompassing the entire centre of Liverpool with the protestant cathedral protruding upwards like a candle and the River Mersey twinkling in the distance. Everywhere was very shabby and urgently in need of decoration, but it was cheap and Annie fell in love with it at first sight.

'Upper Parliament Street!' screeched Dot when she heard. 'Jaysus, girl, it's dead scruffy there. It's where the prostitutes hang out.'

'As long as no-one takes me for a prostitute . . .' She'd found the area very interesting. People of all shades and colours lived there.

Dot said scathingly. 'Upper Parliament Street was once the poshest part of Liverpool. All the shipping and cotton merchants lived there, but it's been going downhill for years.'

'I like it,' Annie said stubbornly. 'And the rent's not much. I'll be able to afford it when Marie goes to London.'

'I should bloody hope so,' Dot grumbled. 'I'm amazed they've got the cheek to *ask* rent, in an area like that.'

*

The sisters were excited as they settled into their new home. They covered the walls with posters to hide the dirty marks and did their best to polish the scratches out of the furniture. Annie made new curtains for the lounge.

Cecy and Dot came, breathless after climbing four flights of stairs, to make sure they'd settled in. They grudgingly agreed the place looked quite homely, but Dot swore she'd been propositioned on the way.

'This geezer asked how much I charged. I told him, "More than you're ever likely to earn in your bleedin' lifetime, mate".'

'What did he say?' asked Marie, fascinated.

'He said, "You look worth every penny, Missus".'

Annie didn't believe a word of it.

The door flew open and Rose hobbled in with a cup of tea. 'Here you are, darling. A nice hot cuppa to warm the cockles of your heart.'

Annie looked at the old woman vacantly. Rose snapped her fingers, 'Wake up, Annie. It's tea time.'

'Oh! Thanks, Rose.'

'You were miles away, darling. Your boss is on the way up.'

'Is he?' She began to shuffle papers around in order to look busy.

Jeremy Rupert appeared in the doorway. 'I've some letters I'd like to get rid of before my four o'clock appointment arrives, Annie. You can bring the tea with you.'

Groaning inwardly, Annie picked up her things and took them into his office. She was longing for her tea, but it would inevitably go cold while he reeled off the letters without pausing. She was about to sit beside the desk, when Mr Rupert pushed past and pinched her bottom.

Annie gritted her teeth and said nothing.

2

The Cavern was packed to capacity. Cigarette smoke mingled with the condensation on the walls, so they appeared to be shrouded in steam. On the small stage, a band was playing traditional jazz with pulsating exuberance. The rows of wooden chairs in front were packed with an equally exuberant audience, who tapped their feet and clapped their hands to the music and from time to time burst into spontaneous applause.

There were as many people standing as sitting. Almost all were in their teens or early twenties, and scarcely any were even mildly intoxicated. Alcohol was not on sale at the Cavern, though a few youngsters secretly brought their own, adding gin, rum or other spirits to their soft drinks when no-one was looking.

The atmosphere was friendly. Merely to be there meant that normal reservations had been dispensed with. Everybody talked to each other as if they all belonged to the same family, rather than just a club.

Annie and Sylvia were with a group of students from the Art College. Nearly all wore black, even the boys. Sylvia was dressed in tight black slacks and an over-long black sweater that came almost to her knees. With her black-rimmed eyes, lashes stiff with mascara and pale lipstick, she looked like a ghost. Annie didn't feel out of place in her red-and-blue striped slacks and white sweater. She'd tied her hair back with a white chiffon scarf and draped the ends over her shoulder.

She loved the Cavern. It was the only place in Liverpool where she felt unconventional. It was the sort of club you would find in London, perhaps even Paris!

One of the boys asked her to dance, and they went into the dark, arched section given over to dancing.

They jigged to and fro, not touching – Annie never knew what to do with her hands. The noise was too great to talk, unless you yelled at the top of your voice.

After a few minutes, she and the boy smiled at each other and returned to the group. An older man had arrived who looked the longed-for twenty-five. Sylvia hung onto his arm and stared at him provocatively. Annie managed to discern his name was Ted and he was a lecturer at the college. He was attractive, with untidy brown hair and an engaging grin, and as shabbily dressed as the students.

As the night wore on, Annie felt she would melt in the heat. She made her way to the rather disgusting Ladies to powder her nose, in case it was shining like a beacon. It didn't look too bad when she examined it in the mirror attached crookedly to the wall. Even so, she gave it, and the freckles between her eyes, a dab of pancake, and freshened up her lashes with spit. The door flew open and Sylvia came whirling in.

'I saw you sneak off, Annie,' she shrilled excitedly. 'Oh, isn't Ted Deakin delicious? I'm sure he fancies me.'

'He's okay. He's a bit old.'

'You hypocrite, Annie Harrison! You're always on about preferring older men.'

Annie made a horrible face. 'For me, not you.'

'Anyway, we're going to Bold Street for a coffee. Are you coming?'

'And be a gooseberry! Not likely.'

'There's a crowd of us going, silly. Come on, Annie,' Sylvia said coaxingly. 'Live a little.'

Annie glanced at her watch. 'I'd better go home.' It was almost midnight, and she wanted to go to Holy Communion in the morning, which meant coffee was out as it would break her fast. Marie was staying at the Grand, not that Annie minded being alone. Although meals weren't usually served on Sundays, it was Cecy's uncle's Golden Wedding and she was providing lunch for forty. It wasn't worth Marie's while to come home and go back in the morning.

She collected her coat, said goodbye to Sylvia, who was sulking, and took her time walking home. As she neared the house where the flat was, she blinked in astonishment when a taxi skidded to a halt outside and Sylvia and Ted Deakin climbed out. Sylvia was flushed and no longer sulking. She gave Annie her most charming smile.

'Ted's missed the last train. Could he sleep on your sofa tonight?'

'Well . . .' Annie wasn't sure if she wanted to spend the night alone with a strange man.

'I thought I'd sleep in Marie's room, if you don't mind,' Sylvia went on coaxingly. 'She's staying at the Grand, isn't she?'

It would be churlish to refuse. Annie took them upstairs. In the flat, she spread the spare blankets on the worn tapestry sofa. 'I'm afraid there's only a cushion for a pillow.'

Ted grinned. 'It looks very comfortable. I'm sure I'll sleep well.'

She doubted it. He was about two foot longer than the sofa, which had several protruding springs. She went to bed herself and fell asleep as soon as her head touched the pillow. When she awoke, she was greeted by the sound of church bells. She sat up, stretched her arms, then leapt out of bed to go to the lavatory.

To her surprise, the blankets on the sofa hadn't been touched. To her even further surprise, she could hear voices coming from the other bedroom. Ted and Sylvia were in the room together.

Annie turned cold. *Sylvia had slept with Ted Deakin!*
She rushed into the kitchen, made a pot of tea, put everything on a tray, and carried it to her room. She

returned to bed, fuming. It seemed an age, and she'd already drunk four cups, before the door to Marie's room opened. There was a pause, then the front door banged. Sylvia had actually *slept* with a man. It made Annie feel dead funny. She was annoyed that her heart was beating so rapidly, as if something truly dreadful had happened.

There was a tap on her door. 'What?' she growled.

The door opened and Sylvia stuck her head round. 'Morning!' she cried. She was wearing Marie's flowered dressing gown, and looked bright-eyed and incredibly beautiful.

'Bitch!' Annie snorted.

Sylvia looked startled. 'What?'

'You're a bitch.'

'Now, look here, Annie . . .'

'No,' interrupted Annie. 'You look here. How dare you make a fool of me by pretending Ted had missed his train?'

'But he had missed his train.'

'Then how dare you make a fool of me by pretending he wanted to sleep on the sofa?'

Sylvia looked ever so slightly uncomfortable. 'We couldn't very well say what we really wanted, could we?'

'Why not? I'm no prude.'

'Huh! Are you sure about that? Anyway, I wasn't completely sure if he *did* want to sleep with me. Until he came into the bedroom, I thought he could well have intended to sleep on the sofa.'

'You make yourself very cheap, Sylvia,' Annie said haughtily.

'You're just jealous, that's all. I'm going to make myself a cup of tea.' She slammed the door.

'You'll have a job,' Annie shouted. 'I've got the teapot here.'

The door flew open. Sylvia strode in and picked up the tray. Her face was expressionless.

'Was it the first time?' asked Annie.

'Yes,' Sylvia said briefly. On the way out, she tripped over Annie's slippers and nearly fell headlong.

Annie got up for the second time that morning. 'What was it like?' she asked from the kitchen door.

'Okay.'

'Okay! Is that all? I thought it was supposed to be glorious, y'know, mind-boggling and world-shattering and all that sort of thing.'

'I read in a book once, women don't always like it straight away. The more you do it, the more likely you are to have an organism.'

'An orgasm, not an organism. An organism is a structure.'

'How on earth did you know that?'

'You're not the only one to read books,' sniffed Annie. 'Would you like bacon and eggs for breakfast?' She took it for granted Sylvia wasn't going to Holy Communion after spending the night with Ted Deakin, and it was entirely Sylvia's fault that she herself had unwittingly drunk a whole pot of tea, which meant Holy Communion was out for her as well.

'Only if you do the egg both sides,' Sylvia said as if she was granting a great favour.

Annie saluted. 'Yes, ma'am.'

Sylvia slammed into the bedroom. She emerged shortly in her black trousers and long sweater, just in time for breakfast. They ate in silence. Both seemed to find the view from the arched window of tremendous interest.

When they'd finished, Annie began to clear the table. 'Do you feel different?' she enquired.

Sylvia thought hard. 'Not terribly.'

'I'd feel incredibly different. Just the thought of a

man seeing me with nothing on makes me go all funny.'
Annie disappeared into her room to get dressed. 'Did it hurt?' she shouted.

'A little bit,' came the reply.

'A girl at school did it with a sailor. She said it hurt a lot.'

'Well, it only hurt a little bit with me,' Sylvia said crossly. 'I wish you'd stop going on about it, Annie.'

'It's just that I can't get over the fact that one of us has slept with a man.' Annie paused whilst fastening a suspender. 'I feel we should have done it at the same time – not that I feel the urge, mind.'

'Perhaps if you'd come into the bedroom, Ted might have managed the operation slightly better. He quite liked you, Annie.'

'What do you mean?' Annie hopped to the door with a stocking half on, and just managed to dodge out of the way as Sylvia came hurtling into the room and threw herself onto the bed. She burst into tears.

'He couldn't manage it. He said he was important or something.'

'Impotent. Do you mean to tell me you're still a virgin, after all?' She felt slightly let down.

'I'm not sure.' Sylvia's voice was muffled in the pillow. 'He did it with his finger. He called it finger pie.'

'Jaysus!' muttered Annie, shuddering and giggling at the same time.

'He tried to put a French letter on, but it just fell off.'

Annie turned away to hide her face as she finished fastening her suspenders. She felt her cheeks grow red as she tried to stifle the hilarity she felt at the idea of a French letter dropping off a tiny penis. She slapped her hand over her mouth, so hard it hurt. Her shoulders heaved. Eventually, the laughter bubbling up from her stomach refused to be contained another second, and she collapsed in a heap on the floor, shrieking hysterically.

'Annie!' Sylvia twisted round until she was leaning over the edge of the bed, watching her friend's contortions. Her long hair hung down like curtains. 'It's not the least bit amusing,' she said in a hurt voice. 'In fact, it's tragic. I had a terrible night. He kept wanting to try again and again. We had to watch it, like waiting for bread to rise.'

Which only sent Annie into shrieks of laughter all over again.

'You're terribly cruel, Annie Harrison.' Even as Sylvia spoke, her lips began to twitch. 'I suppose it *does* have its funny side.'

With an effort, Annie managed to bring her hilarity under control. 'What made you do it, Syl?'

'I'm not sure.' Sylvia rested her face in her hands. 'Lots of girls at college have been with guys. I thought it was time I did. Ted Deakin seemed perfect to start with. He's old, he's experienced. Trouble is, he's too experienced. He's never been able to do it since his wife divorced him. He thought *I'd* get him started again. Trust me to pick someone who's past it,' she added moodily.

Ted being divorced only added further piquancy to the night's events. It was as if Sylvia had stepped into the adult world.

'Poor Ted,' Annie said soberly. He'd seemed quite nice. She recalled his rather engaging grin. 'Are you going to try again?'

Sylvia grimaced. 'Not bloody likely! Last night did my ego no good at all. Mind you, I'm glad I'm a woman. We don't have to put on an act. If we're not in the mood, we can just lie back and think of England.'

After lunch on Christmas Eve, Stickley & Plumm held

their customary office party. It was a formal affair, with everyone gathering in Mr Grayson's office for a glass of sherry and one of Miss Hunt's mince pies. The conversation was forced, the atmosphere drier than the sherry. Everyone breathed a sigh of relief when, at half past three, Mr Grayson said jovially, 'Happy Christmas to one and all,' which meant it was time to leave. They could go home or do last-minute Christmas shopping.

Annie scurried upstairs. She was buttoning her coat when the rotund figure of Mr Rupert appeared in the doorway. 'Going, Annie?' he said with mock incredulity. 'I haven't wished you Merry Christmas.'

'You wished it me downstairs,' she stammered.

'That was just a handshake.' Before she knew what was happening, he had pressed his plump face against hers and was kissing her wetly on the lips. 'Merry Christmas, Annie.' He tried to kiss her again, but she managed to duck underneath his arm. As she ran downstairs, she rubbed her mouth on her sleeve. She felt dirty. If he didn't keep his hands to himself, she'd leave, even if it did mean getting less money elsewhere.

'But why should *you* leave?' Marie said angrily. 'He's the one who should leave. Why don't you tell this crabby Miss Hunt what's going on?'

'I'll see what happens after Christmas.'

'Where are you going tonight?' Marie was getting ready for the Grand. She put her white apron in a bag, along with a pair of flat shoes. Her face was beautifully made up. She still wore plenty of make-up, but drama school had shown her how to use it with skill.

'There's a crowd of us going to the Cavern.'

'Think of me whilst you're enjoying yourselves. There's a big dinner tonight as well as a party in the Snug.' Marie smiled happily. 'We seem to have swopped places. It used to be me out on the town

every night, and you were left to look after our parents.'
Elocution lessons had ironed out Marie's Liverpool
accent, and she no longer said mam and dad.

'I'm ever so proud of you, Marie,' Annie said quietly.
Her sister was so busy working that she'd never been to
the Cavern.

'I'm proud of you, sis.' Marie looked through the
window at the dark streets, a far-away expression on
her face. 'Remember the day Bruno took us to the
nursing home in Southport? As you were leaving, you
said, "Don't worry, Marie. We'll come through. One of
these days, everything will be all right, you'll see." They
were your exact words. I kept thinking about them after
they'd taken the baby from me. At the time, I didn't
believe them, but they've come true. We're okay, aren't
we, sis?'

'Apart from the loathsome Jeremy Rupert, we're
fine.'

It was bedlam at the Gallaghers' on New Year's Day.
There were far too many decorations, for one thing, and
they kept falling down. The parlour was out of bounds,
being occupied by Alan and his fiancée, Norma.
Tommy's girls, Marilyn and Debbie, had been left
with Grandma whilst their mam and dad went to the
pictures. The girls were playing with their dolls on the
floor. Upstairs, Mike was listening to Elvis Presley's
'Blue Suede Shoes' on his new record player, whilst the
three younger lads mooched about picking at food and
generally making a nuisance of themselves. Uncle Bert
had wisely taken himself to the pub.

Annie watched Pete help himself to Christmas cake.
It seemed only yesterday that his mam had brought him
round to Orlando Street, shortly after the Harrisons
moved in. She remembered him sitting on her knee, a
few weeks old, whilst she examined his tiny fingers and

little pink ears. Now Pete was fourteen and his voice was already beginning to break. She was taken aback by how quickly time flew, and said as much to Auntie Dot.

'I know, luv,' Dot agreed, 'and the older you get, the quicker it flies. I'll be fifty this year, not that I feel it, but it seems like only yesterday I was twenty-one.'

She didn't look fifty, either. Although her ginger hair was streaked with silver, the skin on the sharp bones of her face was shiny and unlined. A few years ago she'd started wearing glasses and her latest pair had fancy blue and silver frames which Annie thought grotesque.

Uncle Bert walked in that very minute, accompanied by a man Annie had never seen before who was introduced as Lauri Menin.

'Lauri with no "e" at the end,' said Bert. 'He's a comrade from the Labour Party. This is me niece, Annie Harrison.'

'She's a secretary at one of those big posh solicitors in town,' bragged Dot.

'How do you do.' Annie shook hands amidst the chaos. Lauri Menin's grip was firm and hard. He was a tall man, well built, with broad shoulders and twinkling brown eyes. She rather liked his moustache, which suited him perfectly, being just the right size: not small enough to look like Hitler, not big enough to look ridiculous. After taking this much in, she never gave him another thought. He was really ancient, at least forty, and probably already had a wife and several children.

Bert said, wincing at the noise, 'I'll take Lauri into the parlour, luv. We want to talk politics for a while.'

'Unless you want to talk with our Alan and Norma canoodling on the sofa, I wouldn't if I were you,' Dot said tartly.

'Is there anywhere in this house I can get some privacy?' Bert demanded exasperatedly.

Tommy and a very pregnant Dawn arrived to take their daughters home, and the house quietened down a little. Annie helped Dot make a pile of brawn sarnies, and Mike took his upstairs to eat with Elvis Presley. Alan and Norma were allowed theirs in the parlour on the strict condition it was vacated as soon as they'd finished. 'Your dad's got political matters to discuss,' Dot said importantly.

'Did you say you worked for a solicitor?' Lauri Menin asked Annie.

'Well, Dot did. It's Stickley & Plumm in North John Street.'

'I'm thinking of buying a house. Do they do conveyancing?'

'Oh, yes. The conveyancing department is the biggest.'

His brown eyes twinkled. 'I've never done this sort of thing before, and I'm rather nervous. Are they a reputable company?'

'One of the most reputable in Liverpool – and one of the oldest.'

Not much escaped Dot's sharp ears. 'We'd never let our Annie work in a place that wasn't completely above board,' she said firmly, as though she'd personally inspected the office and interviewed the staff.

Annie gave him the telephone number, and enquired where the house was he was thinking of buying. She wasn't sure whether to call him Lauri or Mr Menin.

'It's not built yet,' he replied. 'It's on a small estate of just fourteen houses in Waterloo, very ordinary, but there will be a view of the Mersey from the upstairs window. I was born within sight of a river, so it will remind me of my childhood in Finland.'

'Finland!' exclaimed Annie. She'd never dreamt he was a foreigner. His English was perfect.

'He came over to fight in the war when he was only

nineteen,' explained Dot. 'And he couldn't bring himself to go back after the Finns ended up on the side of the Germans.'

Bert was beginning to get impatient. The younger lads had disappeared, Alan and Norma had gone out, and the parlour was vacant. He wanted to get down to politics. 'C'mon, Lauri. See you later, Annie.'

'No you won't, Uncle Bert. As soon as I've helped Auntie Dot with the dishes, I'll be off.' She'd only come to wish everyone a Happy New Year. 'Sylvia and I are going to the pictures tonight to see *Marjorie Morningstar* with Gene Kelly.'

'Hang on a minute,' Dot waved her arms. 'We can't let our Annie go without making a toast.' She produced a bottle of sherry and quickly poured some into four glasses and handed them round. 'To 1960,' she cried merrily.

'To the sixties,' Lauri Menin murmured. 'Let's hope they bring happiness and good fortune to us all.'

The sixties! All the way back to the flat, Annie wondered what the sixties would bring for her.

In February, without telling a soul, Annie decided to look for another job. Jeremy Rupert's attentions were beginning to wear her down.

She searched the Vacancies in the Liverpool *Echo*, but the secretarial jobs invariably called for someone aged 'twenty-one plus', and the wages for ordinary shorthand typists were so low, she'd have to give up the flat. Of course, she could always return to the Grand – Cecy would welcome her with open arms – but that seemed a retrograde step to take.

If only she'd been more careful with the money from Orlando Street! Her share had nearly all gone. Apart from the fees for Machin & Harpers and three months advance rent, she had recklessly bought a refrigerator, because food in the unventilated kitchen went bad within a day. The rest of the money had disappeared in dribs and drabs, whilst Marie had carefully held onto hers, adding to it over the years.

In the end, she decided her only option was to put up with Jeremy Rupert a while longer until a suitable job came up, though it seemed degrading. 'I'm letting him maul me 'cos I won't give up the money,' Annie thought to herself. 'In a way, I'm a bit like one of them prostitutes Auntie Dot's always on about.'

On a grey, drizzly Good Friday morning, Marie Harrison left Liverpool for London. She had over six hundred pounds in her bank account. A room was waiting for her in a house with four other budding actresses.

After Mass, Annie went with her sister to Lime Street Station. Marie found a seat, then leaned out of the window.

'Look after yourself, Marie,' Annie pleaded. She had never felt so sad and was doing her utmost not to cry. It was a different feeling altogether from when Mam and Dad had died. The sight of Marie's happy, hopeful face tugged at her heart-strings. She prayed her sister wouldn't be hurt, wouldn't be lonely, that she'd quickly be successful.

'You look after yourself too, sis. Give that Jeremy creature a kick in the groin next time he tries something.'

'I will, don't worry.' Annie tried to laugh. The train began to move and she ran along the platform holding onto her sister's hand. 'Tara, Marie. Tara.'

'Goodbye, Annie. I'll write soon, I promise.'

Annie watched the dark-haired figure waving from the window and waved frantically back until the train curled round a bend and Marie could no longer be seen.

The centre of Liverpool was deserted on Good Friday. She hurried through the empty, wet streets, trying to hold back the tears. It wasn't until she arrived home that she felt able to let them flow. She cried for ages. Her sister was the only flesh and blood she had left. She remembered cuddling Marie the day they moved to Orlando Street, recalled her anguished face when they'd discussed what to do about the baby, and how upset she'd been when it had been taken away. Even now, all these years later, it still seemed unbearably sad; a thirteen-year-old girl longing for a baby, longing for someone to love.

Later, when the tears had finally stopped, she had a long soak in the brown-streaked bath, using the last of the pine bubble bath she'd got for Christmas. It seemed a more cheerful thing to do than make the Stations of the Cross, which she usually did on Good Fridays. She felt better when she emerged with crinkly skin and a face pack hardened to concrete.

It was nearly five o'clock. At half seven she was meeting Sylvia off the train at Exchange Station. They'd not made up their minds what to do, but in case they decided to go dancing, Annie used her best deodorant, put on a set of fresh underwear, her new green dress with the pleated skirt that she'd been saving for a special occasion, and her black ballerina shoes with buckles on the toes. She put her hair up for a change. The style looked rather flattering as little curls escaped from the enamelled slide onto her neck.

The whole operation made her feel even better. After all, it was unreasonable to be unhappy when her sister was embarking on a great adventure. As soon as Marie had settled in, Annie was going to stay for the weekend. She decided to make a list of which clothes to take. As she wrote, a weak sun appeared and the lounge was flooded with pale yellow light. By the time the list was finished, Annie was her old self again, and began to look forward to the evening ahead. She and Sylvia always ended up having a good time and a good laugh.

A pleasant smell seeped up through the floorboards from the flat below. The horrible man with the big buck teeth who lived there was making curry for his tea. The smell made her feel hungry and she realised she'd been too upset to have dinner. She'd just slid two slices of bread under the grill and put half a tin of beans in a pan to heat, when she heard light footsteps running up the stairs.

For a moment, her heart leapt at the thought it might be Marie who'd caught the same train back, having decided to stay in Liverpool after all. There wasn't time to decide whether this was good or bad before there was a knock on the door and Sylvia shouted, 'It's me.'

'You're miles early.' Annie felt annoyed when she saw Sylvia was wearing her black slacks and jumper, which meant a dance was out of the question. 'Here's me, dressed up like a dog's dinner.'

Sylvia walked into the room and sat down without a word.

'What's wrong?' Annie frowned.

'The most awful thing has happened,' Sylvia replied in a small voice. 'I've brought a bombshell.' It was rare for Sylvia to sound so subdued. 'Cecy and Bruno have had the most terrible row. They followed each other round the Grand all afternoon, shouting and screaming.'

'Is that all!' Annie said, relieved. Cecy and Bruno rowed all the time, though she had to concede their fights were usually over quickly. She'd never known one last for more than half an hour, after which they usually made up with extravagant hugs and kisses.

'You don't understand, Annie.' Sylvia's blue eyes were frightened. 'Bruno's been having an affair and

Cecy's just found out. The woman's called Eve, a waitress who worked for us a short while last year.'

'An affair!' Annie was horrified. 'I don't believe it. Not Bruno!' Bruno Delgado epitomised everything true and honest in the world. He was perfect. She couldn't visualise him doing any wrong.

'The thing is, it isn't the first. He's had affairs before. He told Cecy all about them, confessed them one by one.'

Annie gaped. 'Did they know you were listening?'

Sylvia nodded bleakly. 'Every now and then one of them would say, "Keep your voice down, Sylvia will hear", and they'd be quiet for a while, then they'd get so mad, they'd start shouting all over again, sometimes in Italian, sometimes in English, as if they didn't care whether I heard or not.'

'Oh, Syl! Do you hate him?'

'I don't know. He said the oddest things. He said, "Everyone's entitled to a healthy sex life. I'm a normal man with normal needs. If you weren't so bloody religious, the situation wouldn't have arisen." '

Annie tried to make sense of this, but couldn't. 'What did he mean?'

'There's something burning,' Sylvia said.

Annie looked perplexed. 'I don't understand. What's religion and a healthy sex life got to do with burning?'

'I meant I can smell something burning.' Sylvia jumped to her feet. 'There's smoke coming from the kitchen.'

'Me beans on toast!'

The toast was cinders and the pan was ruined. The man with the buck teeth came stamping up to make sure Annie hadn't set the house on fire. He went away, disgusted, when she explained what had happened.

Sylvia opened the windows to let the smell out and Annie gave the cooker a superficial clean. She made a cup of tea to calm their nerves.

'That's a nice dress,' Sylvia said when they were sitting down again. 'Green's your best colour.'

'I got it from C & A. I thought we might have gone to a dance tonight. I prefer making me own frocks, but I can't manage pleats.'

'Your hair looks nice, too. It suits you up.'

Annie patted her curls. 'I was trying to cheer meself up. I felt dead miserable because our Marie had gone.'

'I forgot about Marie.' Sylvia made a face. 'She telephoned earlier. Cecy said to tell you she'd arrived safely.'

'There must be a phone in her new flat.'

A long silence followed. Sylvia stared into her cup. Annie didn't raise the subject of Cecy and Bruno until she was ready to talk again.

'They actually spoke about divorce, Annie,' Sylvia said suddenly. 'Least Bruno did. Cecy said she'd never divorce him. Never.'

'Oh, no!' Nothing was permanent. Nothing could be relied on to stay the same. Marie had gone, and now another part of her life was falling apart. She still didn't understand what had happened. Bruno had had an affair – affairs – but why, when he had always seemed so completely in love with Cecy? She said as much to her friend.

'He still loves her,' Sylvia explained carefully, 'he said so, but from what I could gather – and this is truly incredible, Annie – they haven't made love since I was born. Bruno yelled, "Do you think I'm made of stone? Eighteen years, Cecy, eighteen years." You see, Cecy had an awful time with me and she was too frightened to have another baby. I think I told you that once.'

'But you can use things.'

'Apparently she won't. The Catholic Church forbids it.'

'Me Auntie Dot's every bit as religious as Cecy,'

Annie said, 'but she says that's a load of rubbish. It's all right for the Pope to lay down the law, but he hasn't got to look after the unwanted babies. Anyroad, there's something called the rhythm system . . .'

'It's not reliable. Even I know that.'

Annie sighed. 'Jaysus, Syl. It must have come as a terrible shock.'

To her surprise, Sylvia said thoughtfully, 'It did and it didn't. Over the years, I've had this funny feeling there was something wrong. Bruno used to look at Cecy with a strange expression on his face that I couldn't understand.' She smiled unexpectedly. 'I'm sick of talking about it. Let's go for a meal and the pictures. There's a new Alfred Hitchcock picture on at the Odeon, and I love all his films. *Rear Window* and *Vertigo* are two of my all-time favourites. It'll take our minds off things for a few hours.'

They went to a Chinese restaurant and had curried prawns and rice, not just because it was Good Friday and they couldn't eat meat, but because Annie had been longing for curry since the smell had drifted through the floorboards, though as she said to Sylvia over the tea that tasted like dishwater, 'I'll have to cut down on this sort of thing now that our Marie's not there to help with the rent.'

The new Hitchcock film was called *Psycho*. It was utterly terrifying, nothing like *Rear Window* or *Vertigo*. Annie kept her eyes shut most of the time, particularly during the last ten minutes.

'What happened?' she asked when the curtains thankfully closed and the stunned audience stood to leave. Instead of the usual buzz, everyone was strangely quiet.

'I've no idea. I didn't look,' Sylvia replied in a shaky voice. 'Thank God we haven't got a shower!'

A woman behind put her hand on Annie's arm and

she yelped in terror. 'What happened at the end?' she asked. 'I was scared to watch.'

'So was I,' said Annie.

Outside, Lime Street appeared dimly lit and had a gloomy, sinister air. Every man who passed looked like a potential murderer.

'Oh, Lord,' Annie groaned. 'I left all the windows open. Someone might have climbed in.'

'No-one's likely to climb in a fourth-floor window.'

Annie shivered. 'I'll be on me own tonight and that chap downstairs gives me the creeps. Have you noticed his eyes? The lids are heavy and they move dead slow, like a lizard.'

'Would you like me to stay?' offered Sylvia.

'*Please*, Syl. I'm petrified at the thought of going back by meself. I wish we'd never seen that picture. It took me mind off things all right. I'm scared bloody stiff!'

They looked for a telephone box so Sylvia could call the Grand. When she emerged, she gave Annie a sardonic smile. 'Cecy thinks I'm staying away because of the row.'

'Did you tell her the real reason?'

'No,' Sylvia said in a hard voice. 'She can think what she likes. If things get any worse, I shall leave home.'

'You've changed your tune. You were upset before.'

'I'm still upset, but it's no good crying over spilt milk, is it?'

The table was propped against the door, the bedroom doors were open and the beds had been moved so they could see each other across the lounge and communicate in case of emergency. Every light was switched on.

They sat up in bed and chatted about clothes, as if nothing out of the ordinary had happened. Annie was seriously considering making herself a plain black costume.

Sylvia looked surprised. 'I thought you were going to be hard up?'

'Once I've made the costume, I won't buy another thing,' Annie said virtuously, 'though I'd love a pair of those stiletto-heeled shoes.'

'They snap easily. I've had mine mended twice and Cecy complains about dents in the carpet. And don't get those winklepickers. A girl at college bought a pair. We thought she had deformed toes.'

After a while, Sylvia said she was tired and ready for sleep. Her blonde hair disappeared beneath the bed-clothes. 'Goodnight, Annie.'

''Night, Syl. Things'll probably seem better in the morning.'

There was an answering grunt. Annie's head was buzzing and she had rarely felt so wide awake. She lay down reluctantly and tossed and turned for ages. The traffic outside gradually faded to the occasional car and she began to drift off, but woke up seconds later with a painful jump. Eventually, she fell asleep and dreamt a buck-toothed man with an enormous knife was butchering Marie in the bathroom, and the brown stains on the bath had turned brilliant red. Marie was screaming, but to Annie's horror, she found herself glued to the bed, paralysed, unable to do anything but listen to her sister's agonised cries. She woke up again, heart pounding, bathed in perspiration, conscious of the pungent smell of escaping gas, but afterwards realised the smell was no more real than the dream.

It was a terrible Easter weekend. They went dancing on Saturday, but their gloomy faces must have put off any would-be partners. Not a soul asked either to dance. They left in the interval, more miserable than when they'd arrived. Sylvia telephoned an anxious Cecy to say she was spending another night with Annie.

The following morning they went to Mass, then caught the train to Southport, and had scarcely been there five minutes when the heavens opened and the rain poured down. As they sheltered in a doorway, Sylvia began to giggle. 'This has been the worst Easter of my life.'

'It's not over yet. We've got Monday to get through.'

'There'll probably be an earthquake.'

They laughed and the tension broke. They searched for a café and stumbled inside, drenched to the skin. Sylvia ordered a pot of tea, buttered scones and strawberry jam for four.

'I've led a charmed life up to now,' she said at one point. 'Bruno and Cecy have been magical parents. They always seemed superior to other people's. I'll just have to get used to the fact they're human like everybody else.'

It was still raining an hour later and there seemed little else to do but to return home. Sylvia thought it was about time she put in an appearance at the Grand, if only to change out of her wet clothes. They confessed they were sick of the sight of each other and wouldn't meet until the following weekend. Annie stayed on the train only as far as Marsh Lane Station. She was dying to see Auntie Dot.

Her shoulders immediately felt lighter when she went into the Gallaghers' noisy house. The rain lifted, the sun came out, and after dinner, she and Dot went for a walk to escape the din. She told her auntie about the Delgados.

'It's often the way when couples are all lovey-dovey,' Dot said soberly. 'It's only done to disguise the faults, from themselves as well as everyone else. I always suspected things weren't all they were cracked up to be between those two.' She nudged her niece sharply with her elbow. 'If it weren't for Bert, I wouldn't mind helping Bruno out!'

'Auntie Dot! You're terrible, you are.'

'I'm only joking, luv, but you must admit he's a bit of all right.'

Annie was about to climb the final flight of stairs to the flat when she nearly jumped out of her skin. On the shadowy landing, someone was sitting on a suitcase outside her door.

'Hello, Annie,' Sylvia beamed. 'Relations have completely broken down at home. They were using me to convey messages to each other. I'd like to move in, if you don't mind. I promise to be incredibly cheerful, do my share of housework and pay half the rent. We'll have a wonderful time. They say every cloud has a silver lining. I suppose this is it!'

3

She had lost her temper only once in her life, and Annie Harrison had vowed never to do so again. Occasionally, people would remark how calm she was, particularly for someone with red hair. But it was dangerous to lose your temper, dangerous to lose control and say terrible things you didn't really mean which you would regret until the day you died.

Despite her vow, the day came when Annie could easily have murdered Jeremy Rupert. Instead, she merely slapped his face.

By keeping a sharp eye on his movements, she managed to keep out of his way most of the time, but when summer arrived and along with it summer frocks and bare legs, he became more and more difficult to repel. His round eyes would devour her as she sat by his desk. Once again, she began to scan the paper for another job.

The days he was in court were best. He came into the office early, rattled off dozens of letters, and she was left to type them in peace.

He was due in court at eleven o'clock the day she slapped his face. She had already packed his briefcase with the files concerning the case he was defending, together with a lined pad and two freshly sharpened pencils, whilst he went for a quick confab with Mr Grayson. She fastened the case and put his wig in its white drawstring bag on top.

A few minutes later, he came in with Bill Potter, the junior solicitor who was accompanying him to court. He lit a cigarette and flung the lighter on the desk.

'Hallo there, Annie,' Bill smiled.

Annie smiled back. Bill was only twenty-three and quite attractive in a weedy sort of way, but unfortunately engaged to be married.

Mr Rupert picked up the briefcase. 'Everything here?' he puffed.

'Everything,' confirmed Annie.

'What about the Clivedon file, Jeremy?' Bill Potter said. 'Old Grayson thought it might prove useful.'

Jeremy Rupert clicked his fingers impatiently at his secretary. 'The Clivedon file, Annie. Quickly, there's a good girl.'

The Clivedon file was in the end cabinet, third drawer down. Annie disturbed the file behind as she hastily pulled it out. Mr Rupert shoved the folder in his briefcase and the two men left.

Before closing the drawer, Annie bent down to straighten the files. Suddenly, Jeremy Rupert was back in the office. He snatched the lighter off the desk and held it aloft. 'Nearly forgot this.'

Annie muttered something meaningless and returned to the filing. She never felt his hand reach beneath her flared skirt until it was directly between her legs, squeezing.

'Hmm, nice,' he murmured.

She felt herself grow dizzy with hot, uncontrollable rage. She span round and slapped his face with such force that his head turned ninety degrees and his glasses flew off. '*How dare you!*' she gritted.

He went pale and retrieved the glasses, which were miraculously all in one piece. There was a bright scarlet patch on his right cheek. 'But . . . but, Annie,' he stammered. 'You've never said anything before.'

Annie didn't reply, but slammed into her own office without another word. She was shaking because she'd completely lost control. Had she been holding something heavy, she could have killed him.

For the remainder of the week, he appeared slightly shamefaced, but over the weekend must have decided he'd done nothing wrong. On Monday, he began a reign of terror. He found fault with her work where no fault existed, insisted he'd said one thing during dictation, when her notes proved he'd said another. They argued fiercely over the situation of commas and semicolons, and Annie found herself with no alternative but to type letters a second time, usually long ones, when there was nothing wrong with the first. He insinuated she was incompetent, that she was slow, unintelligent. He claimed one of his clients had said she was rude on the telephone.

'Who was it?' Annie demanded. 'I'll ring up and apologise.'

'I've already apologised,' Mr Rupert snapped.

'Liar!' Annie muttered underneath her breath.

In the lunch hour, she remained at her desk and applied for every single secretarial vacancy in the *Echo*.

She knew she was finished at Stickley & Plumm. Her lip curled when she thought about her boss. He was utterly despicable, using his little bit of power to harass a helpless young girl – she forgot, for the moment, that she'd nearly knocked his head off. He'd probably like to sack her, but was scared she'd make a fuss and he'd get into trouble. Instead, he was trying to drive her into leaving of her own accord, but Annie's blood was up. She was damned if she would leave before she found another job.

'What's up with you?' Sylvia asked one night when they were clearing the table after tea.

'What do you mean, what's up with me?' Annie snapped.

Sylvia pretended to back away in fright. 'I mean exactly that. You don't speak normally, you explode. Is everything all right at work?'

'Everything's wonderful at work. Jeremy Rupert is the perfect boss.'

'Are you being sarcastic?'

'Yes,' Annie said briefly, but refused to say what was wrong. 'I'm in the middle of a feud. I'll tell you about it when it's over.'

The crunch came one Thursday, nearly three weeks after she'd slapped Mr Rupert's face.

He dictated a long Writ that morning. The Litigant was called Graham Carr. 'How do you spell that?' Annie enquired.

'C-A-R-R.'

The document was complicated and full of legal jargon, it had to be done on very thick paper with two carbon copies, which meant the typing was slow, hard work. It was three pages long when finished, and had taken two hours, but there wasn't a single error. Mr Rupert had gone to lunch, so she put it on his desk, and quickly typed half a dozen letters applying for jobs advertised the night before. She'd already been rejected by five of the firms she had applied to; she was either over-qualified, under-qualified, or too young.

Jeremy Rupert returned at three. A few minutes later, he waddled into her office and threw the Writ on the desk. 'You've spelt the name wrong. It's Kerr, K-E-R-R. Same as Deborah,' he added with a sneer.

'But you spelt it the other way,' cried Annie. She produced her notebook and turned to the page. 'See!'

'You misheard. It's Kerr with a K. You'll have to type it again. I'd like the correct version by five o'clock, if you don't mind.'

He'd done it deliberately! Every shred of anger fled and she felt close to tears. She reached in her stationery drawer for a sheet of special paper, two flimsies, two carbons.

'C'mon, girl, c'mon.' Mr Rupert was watching her slow movements. Annie jutted out her jaw. She'd sooner die than let him see her cry. It was a ludicrous thing to think of, but she desperately wished she had a mam or dad to go home to, someone who would stroke her head and say her boss was the most evil man in the entire world and she wasn't to work for him another minute. She was fed up being on her own. Sylvia wasn't the same as a proper adult.

'I need to go to the cloakroom,' she said abruptly.

'Don't forget, I want that Writ by five o'clock,' Mr Rupert called after her. She could have sworn she heard him chuckle.

She would never get the Writ done in time. Her hands were already shaking and her fingers would turn to thumbs with nervousness. She sat on the lavatory for a good ten minutes and made up her mind what had to be done. She would hand in her notice and hope one of the jobs she'd applied for would turn up soon, though it went against the grain to be forced out by a bully.

After splashing her face, she went to see Miss Hunt and told her she was leaving.

'Leaving, Miss Harrison! But why?' Miss Hunt's long jaw dropped.

'I think I would be happier in another job.' Annie had no idea why she should feel uncomfortable, as if she were letting Miss Hunt down. It was she who had recommended Annie for promotion.

'Happier? But I thought you were happy in your present job. We have had glowing reports about your work from Mr Rupert. Even Mr Grayson has expressed his pleasure more than once at the way you have progressed.'

'I love the work, it's just . . .' Annie paused, wondering how she could explain to this prim and proper woman what her boss had done.

'It's just that what, Miss Harrison?' Miss Hunt's permanent frown deepened in annoyance.

'Me and Mr Rupert don't get on all that well.'

The frown turned to one of surprise. 'Have you been crying? Your eyes are all red.' She no longer seemed annoyed.

Annie felt her eyes fill up again. She nodded.

'Sit down, Miss Harrison, and tell me all about it.' The older woman pulled up a chair. 'Mr Grayson has a client, so we won't be disturbed.'

'It's awfully embarrassing.'

'Despite appearances to the contrary, I am not easily embarrassed.'

Annie explained about the Writ. 'He definitely spelt it Carr. I can show you my notebook. I'll never get it done by five o'clock.'

'In that case,' Miss Hunt said briskly. 'We'll get the typing pool to do it. The girls can type a page each. Now, why on earth should Mr Rupert do such a mean thing?'

Annie took a long breath. 'I slapped his face. He's been . . . well, too free with his hands. I couldn't stand it any longer. He . . . he did something awful, and I couldn't help myself, I hit him really hard.'

Miss Hunt's face emptied of expression. 'And how long has Mr Rupert been behaving like this?'

Annie shrugged. 'Since I started working for him. Oh, I know you're going to say I should have mentioned it before, I should have stopped him, but I was scared of getting the sack.'

'I see,' said Miss Hunt. She pursed her yellow lips.

In the next room Mr Grayson could be heard showing his client out, a woman with a loud, pleasant laugh. Annie felt envious; she was so miserable, she was convinced she would never laugh again.

Mr Grayson returned to his office and pressed the buzzer for his secretary. 'Come with me, Miss Harrison. I'd like you to repeat what you just told me to Mr Grayson.'

Annie gasped. 'But I couldn't *possibly* . . .'

'I'm afraid you must. Come along.'

Mr Grayson looked mildly surprised when they both appeared. 'Miss Harrison has something to tell you,' Miss Hunt announced.

Throughout her halting and muddled explanation, Mr Grayson stared grimly at his blotter and didn't look at her once. 'Thank you, Miss Harrison,' he said pleasantly when she'd finished.

Miss Hunt showed her to the door. 'Don't forget the Writ,' she said.

The Writ delivered, Annie returned to her office. A few minutes later Jeremy Rupert's internal telephone rang, and she heard him say, 'Yes, sir, right away.' He immediately went downstairs.

The only person he called 'Sir' was Mr Grayson. Annie tried to get on with her work, but kept making mistake after mistake, and the waste-paper basket became increasingly full of crumpled letterheads.

It was a good hour before her boss returned. Through the thick glass, she saw him sit at his desk and put his head in his hands.

Not long afterwards, a girl from the pool brought the Writ. Annie thanked her. 'I would never have got it done in time.' She read the document through. There were two spelling errors which hadn't been on the original, but she didn't care. She combed her hair in the mirror behind the door and briefly practised looking as if she didn't have a care in the world before taking the Writ into Mr Rupert's office.

He hadn't moved from the desk. His face was ghastly white and he was gazing into space, entirely unaware she had come in. She stared at him nervously. She hadn't planned on it going this far. If only she'd put a stop to things months ago!

She told Sylvia the whole story when she got home. As she expected, Sylvia howled with laughter. 'He's gross, Annie, gross in more ways than one. I hope he's got the boot, he deserves it.'

'I didn't want him to lose his job.'

'But you were quite willing to give up yours! When we get to the Grand, I think I shall ask Bruno to give you a little pep talk.'

'I'd sooner you didn't mention it. I feel dead ashamed.' She'd saved her own job, but at the cost of Mr Rupert's. It was an uneasy feeling.

The situation at the Grand had become bearable. Cecy and Bruno no longer rowed; instead they were scrupulously polite to each other. Bruno was openly consorting with Eve, the former waitress, and there was nothing his wife could do about it. Cecy looked worse each time they saw her. Although only forty-two, she could easily have been taken for fifty. Her blonde hair was thinning, her face was haggard and her blue eyes were glazed with sadness – whereas Bruno seemed younger. Annie found herself glancing at him surreptitiously from time to time. She'd always had a crush on him, but now, although it was shameful to admit, since she'd learnt about the affairs he was even more attractive. She felt a little shiver when she thought about him making love to Eve, a plump and comely woman with a jaunty walk, as dark-haired as he was.

Shortly after the girls arrived, Cecy announced she intended buying herself a little bungalow.

'You mean move out?' Sylvia said in astonishment. 'But what will Bruno do without you?'

'Bruno already does quite well without me.'

'You know what I mean, Cecy. I meant the food, that sort of thing.'

Cecy turned away with a sour twist of her lips. Eve had worked in the Grand. She could easily take over Cecy's role in the kitchen.

Mr Rupert had recovered slightly by next morning. His manner was bland, as was his voice. He asked Annie to come in with her notebook, but stumbled badly over the dictation, as if his mind was unable to grasp the intricacies of the work involved.

'That will do for now,' he said after a short while.

Annie remained in her chair, wondering if she should say something, perhaps express some regret. She was searching for the appropriate words when Mr Rupert said again, 'That will do, Miss Harrison.'

Pauline Bunting from Accounts came round with the wages at the usual time, directly after lunch. Annie's brown envelope was unusually thick.

'Hey! It feels like I've got a bonus!' she chortled.

Pauline gave her a strange look. She didn't stay for a

chat as she often did, but mumbled she was in a hurry and quickly left.

The envelope contained twice the usual number of notes. Bemused, Annie searched for her wage slip. It was still in the envelope, along with a folded letter. She felt a flicker of alarm, followed by a sensation of dread. She knew exactly what the letter would say. Signed by Mr Grayson, it was short and to the point; he would be obliged if she would leave the offices of Stickley & Plumm when they closed for business that afternoon. A week's wages were enclosed in lieu of notice.

She'd been sacked!

Angry tears pricked her eyes, and she was simmering at the cruel injustice of it all when Miss Hunt came in. Her initials were beside those of Mr Grayson on the letter, AFG/DH, so she must have typed it.

'I'm sorry, Miss Harrison,' she said stiffly, her long, thin body poised clumsily, like that of a gauche young girl.

'Why on earth should I be dismissed when I've done nothing wrong?' Annie cried. She felt like throwing her typewriter through the window. Either that or bursting into tears.

'I'm afraid it's the way of the world, dear. Us little people are no more than pawns on a chessboard. When the powerful want us out of the way, we just get shoved aside.'

Annie blinked at this rather emotive response. 'If you hadn't made me tell Mr Grayson, this wouldn't have happened.'

Miss Hunt's yellow face grew bleak. She nodded. 'I know. The fact is, Miss Chase is emigrating to Australia at the end of the month and I felt sure Mr Grayson would allow you to take over as secretary to Mr Atkins. Unfortunately, he feels it would be better all round for the firm if you weren't here. Of course,' she went on caustically, 'the firm is all that matters where Arnold Grayson is concerned.'

Annie laughed contemptuously. She nodded towards Mr Rupert's empty room. 'What's happening to him?'

'Mr Rupert has been given a severe dressing-down. It would be difficult to get rid of a partner. Nevertheless, his behaviour falls far short of what is considered acceptable.'

'In other words, he's got off scot free!'

'He has been warned it must never happen again.'

'Did you say anything to Mr Grayson when he dictated the letter?' Annie asked curiously.

Miss Hunt averted her eyes. 'It would have been a waste of time.'

'I'd like to leave right now. I'm up to date with me work.' She couldn't stand the thought of seeing Jeremy Rupert again.

The older woman frowned briefly, then her face cleared. 'Perhaps that would be wise.' She went to the door. 'Good luck, Miss Harrison. I hope your next job turns out more happily than this one.'

She was about to go, when Annie called, 'Miss Hunt?'

'Yes, Miss Harrison?'

'How do you stand it?'

'I don't know,' Miss Hunt said as she closed the door.

Annie gathered together the belongings accumulated over the years; spare make-up, emergency sanitary towel, paper hankies, aspirins, soap and towel, toothbrush, and all the other odds and ends she had acquired. She had nothing to put them in, so helped herself to a stout envelope with plackets in the sides – the first thing she had ever stolen.

Throughout, her cheeks burned and her hands shook with anger. She glanced around the tiny office to make sure she'd got everything. It was important to get away quickly. Pauline Bunting might have passed on the news of her dismissal and the office would be agog. She didn't want to discuss why she'd been sacked with anyone, no matter how sympathetic they might be.

Feeling like an outcast, she slipped quietly downstairs with the envelope clutched to her chest, and was about to open the front door leading to North John Street when the enormity of what had happened sank in. For over three years, she had been coming in and out of this door regularly, without once being late. She had always given conscientiously of her best, yet where had it got her?

Annie sat on the bottom stair and sniffed hard several times. It had got her nowhere. She was brooding over the unfairness of it all when the door opened and the stairs flooded with sunlight. Annie cursed inwardly for not making herself scarce. If it was Jeremy Rupert . . . ! But the man who entered was a stranger, jacketless, with crumpled navy cotton trousers and a long-sleeved check shirt.

However, he turned out to be a stranger who knew her. 'Hello,' he said pleasantly. 'This is a coincidence. It's Annie, isn't it, Annie Harrison? I was going to come and see you today.'

Annie stared at him for several seconds. There was something familiar about his affable features and bright brown eyes, but it was the moustache that finally did it; a moustache that was not too big and not too small, but just the right size for his face, though she had to search for his name.

'Mr Menin,' she said eventually. 'We met at Auntie Dot's on New Year's Day.' He was buying a house in Waterloo and she'd recommended Stickley & Plumm. She had forgotten all about the incident.

'Lauri, please!' he protested. 'Mr Menin makes me

feel very old. I have an appointment at three to sign the final contract for my house.'

'It's taken a long time!' she remarked.

'The building work has just finished. It'll be ready to move into soon.' He was still holding the door. 'Are you coming in or going out?'

'Going out,' Annie said brightly. She went past him into the street. 'Goodbye, Mr . . . Lauri.'

To her astonishment, he let the door go and began to walk along the pavement beside her.

'What about your appointment?' she stammered.

'That can wait,' he said gently. 'There are more important things at the moment, such as why does Miss Annie Harrison's face show so many different emotions? Her eyes say one thing, her lips another and her forehead is full of worried lines. None of the emotions are happy ones, and her voice tells the same story. What's wrong, Annie?'

'Oh!' She had rarely felt so moved. It was incredible that this virtual stranger was able to see through her so easily. She'd thought she'd put on a brave face when they just met. She stared up at him. Her head came to just above his shoulder and she didn't think she'd ever seen such a kind, concerned expression on a face before. His brown eyes smiled into hers. She noticed his eyebrows were like little thatches and his luxuriant brown hair curled onto his broad neck. Why hadn't she noticed how nice he was on New Year's Day?

'May I invite you for a coffee? Or would you prefer to tell me to get lost and mind my own business?' he twinkled.

'I'd love a coffee.'

The first place they came to was a long, narrow self-service snack bar which was virtually empty after the mid-day rush.

Lauri Menin brought two coffees over to the plastic table. 'The truth is,' Annie blurted as soon as he sat down, 'I've got the sack.'

'I thought as much. At least, I thought you were leaving.'

'How on earth could you possibly guess?'

He nodded towards the envelope. 'The contents told me the whole story. People don't usually walk round with stuff like that. Changing jobs is a bit like changing house, on a smaller scale.'

Annie felt glad the sanitary towel was hidden. To her astonishment, in a rush of scarcely stoppable words, she found herself explaining the reason she'd lost her job, yet she didn't feel a bit embarrassed. Lauri Menin listened to the whole sorry tale right up to the point where he'd found her on the stairs. He didn't interrupt once. When she finished, he said seriously. 'This Jeremy Rupert sounds a most disagreeable creature, but also rather tragic. How terrible to have to get your kicks out of forcing your attentions on a young girl. You must feel very sorry for him.'

Pity was the last thing Annie felt. 'I never looked at it that way.'

Lauri continued, 'Mr Grayson – who my appointment was with – is even more to be pitied. The man is totally unprincipled.'

'Why were you coming to see me?' she asked shyly.

He folded his broad arms on the table. 'To thank you,' he said. He had a soothing, slightly husky voice with only a trace of Liverpool accent. She couldn't imagine him sounding angry. 'For all their faults, Messrs Stickley & Plumm handled the purchase of my house efficiently.'

She murmured something about it being a highly reputable firm, and he said that under the circumstances, that was open to question and it was time to change the subject from Stickley & Plumm. 'What do you know about interior decoration?' he asked.

'Absolutely nothing!' Annie replied.

'According to your Uncle Bert, you're very artistic. The thing is, I'm in a quandary over what colours to have my house painted. The decorators are waiting on my instructions. If I don't let them know soon, they'll paint everywhere white, including the front door.'

'You must have the front door bright yellow,' Annie said quickly. She knew he was only being kind and trying to take her mind off things. 'Our front door used to be a horrible dark brown. I swore if I had a house of me own I'd have the front door yellow.'

Lauri Menin grinned. He had large, slightly crooked white teeth. 'Then yellow it shall be. It's lucky I spoke to you. I could well have chosen horrible dark brown. What about the lounge? My favourite colour is red, but I have a feeling that might not look so good.'

Annie cringed. 'Red would look dead awful. Pastel colours would be best, pale pink or lemon, with matching wallpaper on the breastwork. According to the women at work, that's the latest fashion.'

'No wallpaper, I'm afraid, until the building has settled. Pink or lemon sounds fine. I like the sound of it.'

'What about your wife? Isn't she allowed a say in the colours?'

He drained his cup, 'I haven't got a wife.'

'You don't look like a bachelor.' According to Sylvia, bachelors were either men of the world or mothers' boys. Lauri Menin appeared to be neither.

'I'm a widower,' he said lightly.

Annie clapped her hand to her mouth. 'Gosh, I'm awful sorry. I mean, I'm sorry about taking you for a bachelor and sorry about your wife.'

Lauri looked amused by her confusion. 'There's nothing to be sorry about. The bachelor thing I don't mind, and Meg died more than half a lifetime ago. Our time together was short but sweet. We were only twenty. She was killed in the Blitz.' He returned to the subject of his house. 'I would like a young person's opinion on furniture. Having lived in rooms for more than twenty years, I possess nothing of my own except clothes and books. I need to furnish the place from top to bottom.'

Annie thought he was the most splendid person she'd ever met. How fortunate she'd sat on the stairs those extra few minutes, or they wouldn't have run into each other! He seemed genuinely interested in her views. She suggested he describe the new house and she would offer advice, though warned that up to now the only household item she'd bought was a refrigerator.

'I'll do better than describe it. My car is parked just round the corner. As you appear free for the rest of the day, if you fancy a trip to Waterloo, I'll show it you.'

The tiny estate was shaped like a light bulb. There were fourteen identical creamy brick semi-detached houses. Two pairs, which already had people living in them, lined the narrow opening. Infant climbing plants had begun their long journey up the front walls. There was a half-built rockery in one garden, freshly dug flower beds and borders in the others, a tiny hedge. A bright new road sign said, 'Heather Close', with 'Cul-de-Sac' underneath in smaller letters.

'Heather is the name of the main contractor's daughter,' Lauri said.

Once past the opening, the houses flared out into an oval, with two pairs on either side, some of which were already inhabited, and one pair directly ahead completing the oval. Annie thought the top pair were in the best position. It was where the king and queen would live, with their subjects spread out either side and on guard at the entrance. She was pleased when Lauri drove his Ford Anglia car into the drive of one of the furthest houses, the left one, number seven.

'Oh, it's *lovely*!' she breathed when he unlocked the door and they went inside. The hallway was light and bright and airy, with bare pink plaster walls and glass panelled doors.

'This is nice.' She stroked a glossy wooden cupola-shaped knob on the bannisters.

'It's the only house to have that particular feature,' Lauri said.

'Why is that?'

'I was employed on the site as a carpenter. I took the opportunity to make a few additions to my own property.' They went into the lounge, which had a small curved bay at the front and French windows leading to the back garden. The long red-brick fireplace with little niches each side for ornaments and a rough slate hearth was a work of art. Lauri said it was something else unique to this house.

'It's super – and I love French windows!' Annie could scarcely contain herself. 'They're the sort of thing you see in films. I've never come across them in real life before. Can we go outside?'

'Of course, but I'm afraid it's a sea of mud and clay out there.'

The large newly-fenced back garden was almost triangular, like a slice of cake with the house at the narrow end. Wild new grass and a million dandelions had thrust through the upturned clods of earth, but what caused Annie to gasp with pleasure was the tree almost in the centre; a big willow tree with lacy branches trailing the ground.

The estate had been built in the grounds of an old house, Lauri told her. 'Unfortunately, the beautiful gardens were destroyed by the builders. Only a few trees escaped.' He went on to say he'd always wanted a garden. 'I keep my landlady's tidy, but it's very small.'

Everywhere was very quiet except for the subdued chirrup of invisible birds and the drone of a bee which had landed on a nearby dandelion. It dawned on Annie what a lovely day it was. She'd been too preoccupied to notice until now. The entire garden was flooded with dazzling June sunshine and the yellow dandelions shone and flickered like candles. Annie blurred her eyes and saw a smooth green lawn bordered by flowering shrubs, a vegetable patch, a garden shed, and small children dodging in and out of the delicate tendrils of the willow tree. She sighed.

'What's the matter?' asked Lauri Menin.

'Nothing. I was just thinking how beautiful it will be one day.'

They went back inside. Annie oohed and aahed over the little breakfast room and the kitchen, which had a double stainless steel sink, white units and a black and white tiled floor. She was equally impressed with upstairs, particularly the bathroom with its pale green suite. The main bedroom was at the back. Through the window, Lauri pointed out the River Mersey shining glassily in the distance.

She remembered him saying the river would remind him of his childhood in Finland, and asked if he missed his old country.

'Only that.' He nodded towards the view, and said he'd lived on the edge of a river and the beginning of a forest. 'It was enchanting, but after my mother died, I was very unhappy. My older brothers married and went away, my father was a taciturn man who rarely spoke. When war broke out in 'thirty-nine, I was glad of an excuse to leave.' He'd never felt any urge to return. 'I think of myself as a Liverpudlian.'

'It's the nicest house I've ever been in,' Annie declared once she'd seen everything there was to see. The Grand was – well, too grand in a way, and compared to Orlando Street, Heather Close was a palace.

Lauri smiled appreciatively at her breathless admiration and duly noted her suggestions of colour for the walls. 'Would it be too much trouble for you to come with me when I buy the furniture?' he asked.

Annie vowed it would be a pleasure. The next best thing to spending money was spending someone else's.

He murmured it was about time he took her home and she was startled to find it was nearly six o'clock. Sylvia, knowing how critically things hung at Stickley & Plumm, would be concerned.

When the Anglia drew up in Upper Parliament Street, she shyly invited him inside. 'For a coffee and to meet me friend, Sylvia.'

She was disappointed when he refused. 'Sorry, but I have a meeting at half past seven – in fact, I'm seeing your Uncle Bert.'

Of course, he belonged to the Labour Party. She gave him her phone number – Sylvia had declared she couldn't live without a telephone and had one installed shortly after she moved in.

His brown eyes twinkled down at her when he shook hands. 'Goodbye, Annie. Thank you for your help. I'll be in touch soon.'

'Tara, Lauri.'

'Annie! Where on earth have you been? I've been worried sick about you.' Sylvia stood with her hands on her hips like a fishwife.

'I met this lovely chap, Syl,' Annie said dreamily. 'His name's Lauri Menin. We went to see his new house in Waterloo.'

'What happened at Stickley & Plumm? I kept

imagining Jeremy Rupert had got the push and attacked you with a knife, like that chap in *Psycho*.'

'It wasn't Mr Rupert who got the push, it was me. All he got was a thorough dressing-down or something.'

'Why aren't you upset?' Sylvia demanded.

'Because I feel sorry for him. It's tragic, getting your kicks out of forcing your attentions on a young girl. As for Mr Grayson, the man is totally unprincipled.'

'What the hell are you talking about?'

'I'm not sure. Is the kettle on?' Annie threw herself onto the sofa.

'There's tea made. Who's this Lauri chap?'

'Lauri Menin. We got on like a house on fire and I really liked him. The trouble is,' Annie said wistfully, 'he's ancient, nearly forty.'

'Jaysus, that's *old* old. Bruno's not much more than that. By the way, there's a pile of letters for you on the table.'

There were more rejection letters, and two inviting her to attend an interview. One was from the English Electric in Longmoor Lane, where Mike Gallagher worked as a toolmaker. It was a long bus ride to the outskirts of Liverpool, but according to Mike, working there was a laugh a minute. The company had tennis and badminton courts, a dramatic society, and all sorts of other leisure activities.

First thing on Monday morning, Annie telephoned and arranged an interview. She discovered the wages were twenty-five shillings a week more than at Stickley & Plumm, easily covering her bus fare. The following week she started work as secretary to the Sales Manager of the Switchgear Department.

The English Electric was as different from Stickley & Plumm as chalk from cheese. Annie's boss, Frank Burroughs, insisted she call him by his first name. He was a harassed man in his thirties with five children and a demanding wife who telephoned several times a day to tick him off for something he'd done or hadn't done, or to complain about the children. An engineer, Frank hated paperwork, and left his secretary to do everything that didn't involve technical detail. His first action was to show her how to forge his signature.

Annie immediately joined the tennis club. Members were free to invite their friends, so Sylvia bought a tennis frock which had no sleeves, no back and scarcely any skirt, and with Annie in her more demure white shorts they flaunted themselves on the courts all summer. They never went without male partners, though were hopeless at tennis.

When winter came, they played badminton. Sylvia had a mad, month-long fling with the star player, the English Electric dentist. A *proper* affair! She went to his house in Childwall two or three times a week and didn't return until the early hours. Annie lay in bed listening for her return, wishing she could bring herself to be more free with her favours. Kissing was as far as she'd gone, and she hated having a tongue thrust in her mouth. It seemed grossly unhygienic.

Sylvia broke off with the dentist when he wanted to photograph her with nothing on. Meanwhile, Annie had met a young man from the Fusegear Department who'd been in the same class at Grenville Lucas. She went out with him several times, but after they'd dredged up every single memory of their schooldays, there seemed to be nothing else to talk about.

She had lots of other dates, but rarely felt inclined to go out with the same boy twice. She preferred being with a crowd at parties or the Cavern, where the music and the musicians had suddenly changed. The groups had funny names, like Rory Storm & The Hurricanes and Cass & The Cassanovas. They played something called 'rock and roll' instead of jazz. Sylvia went out with a drummer called Thud.

Once every few months, Annie went down to London to see Marie. After taking part in numerous off-beat plays in suburban pubs and run-down theatres, Marie had managed to get an Equity card, which meant she could call herself a professional actress. Stardom was waiting just around the corner. In the meantime, her savings having run out, she'd taken up waitressing to keep the wolf from the door.

Cecy moved to a bungalow in Blundellsands. Bruno was devastated, but didn't ask her to stay. He loved Cecy, but the relationship was doomed. His affair with Eve came to an end and he remained in the big hotel, alone.

'It doesn't seem right, us having such a good time when so many people are dead miserable,' Annie commented.

'It's the best reason in the world,' Sylvia snorted. 'Considering the way our parents ended up, I think we should put everything we can into enjoying ourselves. After all, we're nineteen. We're getting on.'

Lauri Menin's house was gradually becoming a home. The walls were pretty pastel colours, the curtains up, carpets had been fitted throughout. He seemed content to do things slowly, and every now and then would ring Annie from the red telephone at the bottom of the stairs to ask for her advice. 'What do I need for the breakfast room?'

'A table and chairs, of course, and a dresser if there's space.'

'Will you help me choose?'

Annie would meet him in town the following Saturday and they would tour the furniture shops until they found something she considered just right. He seemed happy to leave the selection entirely to her.

'You must be made of money,' she said one day just before Christmas, when they were in George Henry Lee's and he'd just paid cash for the final major item, a burgundy moquette three-piece that would tone in perfectly with the pink walls and beige carpet in the lounge.

He shrugged his muscular shoulders. 'I've had nothing else to do with my money but save it all these years. I don't drink, apart from the occasional beer, I don't smoke. I have no expensive vices.'

Annie laughed. 'Do you have any inexpensive ones?'

'I bite my nails in times of stress,' he admitted.

She loved spending time with him, and wished she got on half as well with the boys she met. She would store up things to tell him because he was always interested in what she'd been up to. It was irritating that Sylvia judged him boring, which was the worst sin of all in her book.

'He's anything but boring,' Annie maintained hotly when the judgement was delivered. 'He's the most interesting man I've ever met. I could talk to him for ever.'

Two days after another hectic Christmas, Sylvia and Annie went to Litherland Town Hall to see a group called The Beatles, four scruffy young men in desperate need of a haircut and decent clothes. They talked and smoked the whole time they played their instruments – one held his guitar in a most peculiar way, like a machine gun. But their music was raw, uninhibited, wild.

Perhaps it happened that night, no-one was quite sure, but from then on, the entire city of Liverpool began to reverberate to the urgent, pounding beat of rock and roll. The sound gradually spread around the world, but Liverpool was the place to be, particularly if you were young, unattached and had money to spend.

Annie and Sylvia joined the new clubs that had sprung up and travelled far and wide to the most unlikely venues: town halls, church halls, ballrooms, to hear Gerry & The Pacemakers, The Vegas Five, The Merseybeats . . . The Beatles began to play regularly at the Cavern, where Mike Gallagher could often be seen, always with a different girl. Dressed in black, with long red hair and a turned-up collar, Mike looked very much a part of the club scene. He studiously ignored Sylvia and she studiously ignored him back.

In August, the girls went on holiday to Butlin's in Pwllheli. They had a glorious time, but on the Wednesday Annie met Colin Shields from Manchester, a tall, thin young man, desperately shy, with a prominent Adam's apple which wobbled when he spoke. He regarded Annie with sheepish, adoring eyes which she found hard to resist. She willingly gave him her address, and a few days after they'd arrived home, she received a beautiful letter, as lyrical as a poem. The minute he'd set eyes on her, he'd fallen in love, he wrote. She was like a lovely exotic flower. He raved on about her perfect lips, her limpid eyes and peachlike skin. Please, *please* could he see her again? Manchester was no distance away. He could come on Saturday. If she refused, he didn't think he could go on living.

Annie didn't show the letter to Sylvia. She wasn't sure whether to be touched or amused. She wrote back and told him she'd meet him at Central Station.

Over the next few months, she enjoyed having such a nice young man hopelessly in love with her, hanging on to her every word and fetching chocolates and flowers all the way from Manchester. But Annie didn't want to take advantage. She genuinely tried to love Colin Shields back, particularly when he proposed and suggested they get engaged at Easter.

'What should I do?' she asked Lauri Menin. His house was furnished, though it looked bare without a single ornament or picture. He said he was too busy getting the garden into shape to think about such things; laying a lawn, planting shrubs, laying coloured slabs outside the French windows to make something called a patio. He'd even built a garden shed with a verandah. Every few weeks he asked Annie out to dinner, which Sylvia said was utterly sick considering his great age.

'You should follow your heart,' said Lauri.

'But I don't know where my heart wants to go,' Annie cried.

'What does your friend have to say?'

'Sylvia thinks I should turn him down, but only because she wants to get married before I do.'

Lauri gave his benign smile. 'That seems rather selfish.'

'Sylvia's as selfish as they come.' Annie sighed. 'The thing is, Colin and me get on, though not as well as I do with you. And he's got a good job in an insurance company – he's what Auntie Dot would call "a good catch". His mam and dad are nice, too. He took me to meet them the other week. They made ever such a fuss of me.'

'I'm not surprised. You're a catch, Annie Harrison. Whoever gets a nice old-fashioned girl like you will be a very lucky man.'

Annie blushed. It was the first time he'd made such a

personal remark, though she couldn't understand the bit about being old-fashioned. She considered herself extremely modern and with it. 'I'm not in love,' she confessed, 'but is everyone in love when they first get married? Perhaps love comes after you've lived together a while.'

'What if it doesn't?' He raised the thick clumpy eyebrows that she always wanted to comb and regarded her kindly. 'I don't want to influence you,' he went on, 'but you asked what you should do. In my opinion, no-one should require advice on getting married.'

'I just thought if you said, "go ahead", or "definitely not", it might help me make up my mind.'

'Go ahead then, Annie.' His voice was rather brusque, and she wondered if she was getting on his nerves.

She thought for a long time. 'See!' she said eventually, 'I knew it would help. As soon as you said, "go ahead", I knew I couldn't possibly. I'll turn him down.'

There was the strangest expression on Lauri's face which she must have misunderstood. She could have sworn he looked relieved.

She told Colin gently that she could never marry him, but that one day he would meet a girl who would make a far better wife than she would, a wife who genuinely loved him.

Nineteen sixty-two dawned, by which time it seemed as if every young man in Liverpool belonged to a rock group. The Cavern gave up jazz altogether and every night was rock and roll. Mike Gallagher took up the guitar and drove his family insane.

Jerry Lee Lewis came to the Tower Ballroom in New Brighton, followed by Little Richard, with The Beatles on the supporting bill. Annie and Sylvia were there, of course. They went everywhere. At night, they fell into bed, exhausted. Annie was glad she was no longer at Stickley & Plumm because her work was suffering. She was tired and made endless mistakes, but as she signed most letters herself, Frank Burroughs didn't notice.

She knew one day it would end. It was bound to. She couldn't go on enjoying herself in this crazy way for ever. In June, Sylvia would finish college and begin her career in advertising. She was thinking about moving to London, which meant Annie would once again be left in the flat by herself. But when June came, Sylvia decided to stay put. 'Who in their right mind would leave Liverpool when it's the epicentre of the universe? I'll have a few months off, I don't need the money.'

The city was changing in other ways: new buildings were going up, bomb sites at last being cleared, the city centre looked different. There was a new *avant garde* theatre. Sculptors and poets blazed a cultural trail from Liverpool to the world outside. The narrow streets of homely little houses off Scotland Road, where everyone knew their neighbours, were ruthlessly razed to the ground and the people dumped in soulless new estates like Kirkby where they didn't know a soul, and the architects and town planners, despite their degrees and vast salaries, hadn't thought to provide shops and pubs beforehand.

Liverpool was changing all right: sometimes for the better, sometimes for the worse.

Annie would be twenty-one in October. She was lucky, her birthday fell on a Saturday. Cecy offered to provide a party at the Grand. She and Bruno were now on quite amicable terms, and she often turned up to help organise big functions.

'It's your twenty-first the month after,' Annie remarked to Sylvia. 'I'd have thought she'd have enough to do with one party.'

'I told her I don't want any fuss. I can't stand the thought of the pair of them drooling over me. I'd prefer to go to dinner with you.'

The dining room in the Grand held forty guests, fifty at a pinch. 'They can use the Snug if they want some quiet,' Cecy said excitedly when she went through the arrangements. It was pathetic, thought Annie; it wasn't even as if she were her daughter. However, the excitement was catching; she was looking forward to her party.

It was easy to find fifty guests. Annie made a list. The first person she put down was Lauri Menin. The Gallaghers made up fourteen, what with all the wives and children and Mike's current girlfriend, and there were loads of people she could ask from the English Electric and the Cavern. There was also Marie, though her sister had never been back to Liverpool, and Annie doubted if she'd come just for a party. She gave the list to Cecy, who was having proper invitations printed.

There was endless discussion on what to wear. Sylvia bought a daring white tube thing, more like a stocking than a frock, which showed off every single curve, but Annie could find nothing she liked. She ended up buying several yards of ivory taffeta, polka-dotted with black, and made herself a ballerina length, off-the-shoulder dress with a wide velvet sash which tied in a long trailing bow at the back.

When the day came, the woman from the ground floor flat came up with the cards which had just come through the letterbox. Sylvia was still in bed. 'You must be popular, Annie,' the woman said. 'There's dozens!'

There was a lovely one from Marie which had pressed flowers in the shape of a key – and a message; 'Sorry I won't be there, sis, but I've got an audition which is too good to miss. If I get the part, my name will be in lights by Christmas.'

Colin Shields hadn't forgotten it was her birthday; he couldn't forget her, he wrote, and never would. The 'never' was underlined. Nearly everyone in Switchgear had sent cards, even those who hadn't been invited to the party. There were cards from Dot and Bert, her cousins, Cecy, Bruno, and people she hadn't seen for years. One was particularly huge. To Annie's astonishment, it was signed by everyone at Stickley & Plumm. She searched for Mr Grayson and Jeremy Rupert's signatures and was annoyed to find them there. Hypocrites!

She'd opened the lot when a white envelope was slid under the door. The man with the buck teeth in the flat below wished her the happiest of birthdays.

Sylvia emerged, yawning, 'Happy birthday, Annie,' she grunted. She handed over yet another card, along with a box containing a pair of onyx and ivory pearl earrings and a necklace to match.

'They'll go perfectly with me dress,' Annie breathed.

'Which is precisely why I bought them, idiot.'

Annie indicated the cards covering the table. 'I never realised I had so many friends. Even the man downstairs sent one.'

Sylvia didn't appear the least impressed. 'That's because you're so nice,' she said in a bored voice. 'Everybody likes you. You never get on people's nerves or rub them up the wrong way. Me, now! On my birthday, I'll get half a dozen cards and certainly not one from the horrid man downstairs because I completely ignore him. That's one of the reasons I didn't want a party. I haven't got stacks of friends like you.'

'Don't talk silly,' Annie began, but Sylvia interrupted. 'Don't argue. I'm arrogant and conceited and, on the whole, I don't like people, unlike you who likes everybody.'

She disappeared to get dressed, leaving Annie, for

some reason she couldn't quite define, offended. She wasn't sure if she wanted to be the sort of person who never rubbed people up the wrong way or got on their nerves. It made her feel like . . . like an anonymous jelly, something that couldn't possibly be taken offence at.

Hurt, she went into the bedroom where Sylvia was rubbing body lotion on her thighs, announced she was offended and explained the reason why.

'An anonymous jelly!' Sylvia hooted. 'Seriously, Annie, you've got a sharp tongue on you. You can be sarcastic and funny, but no-one would believe me if I told them what the real Annie Harrison was like.'

'You mean I'm playing a part all the time?'

'No, you're too anxious for people to like you. It probably stems from looking after your parents; you were walking on eggshells, trying to please everybody.'

To Annie's irritation, the phone went before the rather interesting discussion could be taken further. It was Dot, who'd just had a telephone installed, ringing to wish her niece a happy birthday. After that, the phone didn't stop all day.

Bruno said his lungs would never be the same after blowing up fifty balloons of all shapes and sizes – the long sausage ones were the worst. They were pinned in bunches to the walls of the oak-panelled Regency room. The tables had been removed and the chairs pushed back.

It was a wonderful party. To Annie's delight, Cecy had booked a group, Vince & The Volcanoes, who weren't quite as good as The Beatles, but nearly, though Dot said caustically she'd never really appreciated how well her Mike could play until she heard Vince erupting.

Annie felt loved and very precious as she was showered with gifts and kisses. She was always the first to be asked on the floor – everybody wanted to dance with the birthday girl.

Except Lauri Menin.

Where was he, Annie wondered, when they stopped for refreshments and there was still no sign. She hadn't heard from him in weeks, and she was looking forward to dancing with him more than anyone, though Bruno came a close second. Cecy had lost track of who'd replied to the invitations; some people had telephoned, others had written, and she had no idea if Lauri Menin was coming.

Everyone had gone down to the kitchen to collect the food that Cecy had been all week preparing. Annie went up to Sylvia's room to give her freckles a coat of pancake. Impulsively, she searched through the records until she found *Three Coins in a Fountain*, and put it on the gramophone. She sat in front of the dressing table and listened to Frank Sinatra's haunting, mellow voice whilst she powdered her nose. It was nearly six years since the record was bought – she still had the little orchid pendant, but it was too tarnished to wear.

How different things were now from then! Mam and Dad were dead, Marie was in London, too busy to come to her party. She recalled the Christmas Eve when she'd served the Bloody Marxists in the Snug, and Bruno and Cecy seemed so much in love. Now she was twenty-one, a proper grown-up, able to vote in the next election, with . . .

Annie stopped powdering her nose and stared at her reflection.

With what?

With a decent job, a shabby flat, but that was all. There was nothing exciting ahead of her, no dazzling career in advertising or on the stage like Sylvia and

Marie. She had never met a single man she'd like to marry, except for . . .

Annie saw a pretty, red-headed young woman in a polka-dotted dress put a startled hand to her startled face.

Except for . . .

There was a knock on the door. 'Come in,' she shouted.

Lauri Menin entered the room. 'Dot told me you were here. I'm sorry I'm late. We had a rush job and didn't finish till seven.'

She'd never seen him in a formal suit before. Even when he took her to dinner, he wore a sports jacket. The suit was dark grey, with a blue shirt underneath and a light grey tie. His wavy hair was flattened with Brylcreem, his eyebrows were neatly combed. He looked so solid and reassuring. She knew she would be safe with Lauri, that she would trust him with her life.

She stared at him wide-eyed and unspeaking. It seemed a miracle that he should appear just when she'd been thinking about him so intensely.

'I've brought you a present.' He handed her a small box clumsily wrapped in brown paper.

Her voice returned. 'What is it?'

'Open it and see.'

The box contained a Yale key. She'd received dozens of keys that day. This was the first real one. She held it up and looked at it curiously. 'What's it for?'

'Number seven Heather Close.'

'I don't understand.' She understood completely and wanted to cry.

He knelt beside her. 'Annie, it's been murder, but I vowed I'd wait till you were twenty-one before I asked you to marry me. I hope I'm not making a fool of myself, but I love you, Annie. I want you to be my wife more than I've ever wanted anything.'

'Lauri!' She twisted round and fell into his arms. 'I love you, too. I've loved you ever since you found me sitting on the stairs at Stickley & Plumm.' She hadn't realised until just before he'd entered the room.

His brown eyes had lost their twinkle. Instead, they glistened darkly and she felt as if she was staring into his very soul. 'Then I'm not making a fool of myself, it's "yes"!'

'Oh, yes, Lauri. Oh yes, it's "yes"!'

Annie had a blazing row with Auntie Dot when she turned up at the flat next morning. Sylvia took one look at Dot's face and quickly made herself scarce. 'I'm off to Mass,' she declared, though they'd already been to the nine o'clock one.

It would have been too much to announce she was going to marry Lauri in front of everyone last night. She would have only burst into tears and made a show of herself. She merely whispered the news to Dot and Bert as they were leaving. Dot looked stunned and muttered something incomprehensible; Bert kissed her warmly, slapped Lauri on the shoulder, and shook his hand several times.

Dot had obviously been brooding overnight. 'The thing is, luv,' she began cautiously, 'he's twice your age.'

'Not for ever,' Annie said calmly. 'After a while, he'll just be twenty years older.' She'd have thought Dot would be thrilled at the idea of her settling down with a responsible man who had his own house.

'It's not as if he's like Bruno, full of life and with an eye for the girls. Lauri's already dead set in his ways.'

'Perhaps I should marry Bruno, then,' Annie said sarcastically. 'He'd be having affairs behind me back within a couple of months.'

'But you've hardly had any proper boyfriends, luv,'

Dot persisted. 'You haven't "played the field", as we used to say.'

'That's because I didn't want to, Auntie Dot. I don't care if Lauri's dead set in his ways. I love him. He makes me feel all safe and comfortable.'

Which was the worst thing she could have said. Dot immediately lost her famous temper. 'Safe and comfortable!' she screeched. 'That's no way to begin a marriage. *Un*safe and *un*comfortable more like. Marriage is an adventure. It's not till your kids have grown up and you're growing old together that it's time to feel safe and comfortable.'

'I'd have thought you'd want me to be happy,' Annie said stiffly.

'Not with a man old enough to be your bleedin' father,' yelled Dot. 'That's it!' A look of dawning awareness came over her gaunt face, and she struck the arm of the sofa with her fist. 'That's it, isn't it? Our Ken was never much of a dad, was he? You're looking for a father figure, and Lauri Menin fits the bill perfectly.'

'You've read too many newspaper articles, Auntie Dot.' Annie did her best to keep her own temper. 'You'd think you were Dr Freud.'

Dot turned her anger on the absent Lauri, 'He had no right to ask an impressionable young girl to marry him. I'll bloody well tear him off a strip next time I see him.'

'If you do, I'll never speak to you again!'

'Oh, luv!' Dot's face twisted in anguish. 'I want you to be happy.'

'I *am* happy, happy with Lauri. And he waited over two years before asking me to marry him. Why do you think he let me pick everything for his house? It was because he always hoped one day I'd live there, that the things would be mine, yet all the while he just sat back and let me enjoy meself. Oh, Auntie Dot,' Annie sat beside her aunt and took her hand, 'I'm no longer an impressionable young girl. I'm a woman and I want to settle down with Lauri. Please be happy for me. You're the only person in the world whose opinion I care about.'

Dot looked mollified. 'I suppose you're old enough to know your own mind,' she sighed. 'But what about religion, luv? Lauri's an atheist.'

'Yes, but he's happy for our children to be brought up Catholic.' Annie blushed when she thought about what happened before you had children.

'What's Sylvia got to say about it?'

'She thinks I'm nuts. According to her, Lauri's smug and boring.'

'The nerve of the girl! He's a lovely chap. I've always liked him.'

Annie gaped at the sudden swing in Dot's position. Dot saw the look and grinned. 'I'm just an ould meddler, aren't I?' She gave Annie a warm hug and said tearfully, 'I hope you'll be very happy with Lauri. You have my blessing, girl.'

Heather Close

I

The lawn looked thick and smooth, shimmering like emerald velvet in the summer sunshine, although close up the grass was thin. The turfs took time to reach the earth beneath and flourish. Lauri cut the lawn at least once a week with the electric mower. He said the more it was cut, the quicker the grass would grow.

There was scarcely a breath of breeze, just enough to make the branches of the willow tree give off a whispery rustle. The leaves changed colour; light-dark, dark-light, when they moved.

From her deckchair on the patio, Annie could hear Gary Cunningham next door bawling his head off. He either had a dirty nappy, was hungry, or just plain fed up. Gary was three months old and a difficult baby. Valerie, his mother, found it hard to cope.

The Cunninghams had moved into number eight at the same time as Lauri had moved into number seven. Gary, their first child, had been born in April. Valerie Cunningham, an intense, wiry woman with dark fiery eyes behind heavy horn-rimmed glasses and short crisp hair, was in her mid-twenties. Her husband, Kevin, who worked in a bank, was just the opposite, with a round soft face, pale lips and pale eyes. His rimless spectacles seemed so much a part of him that Annie couldn't imagine him without them.

They fought a lot, the Cunninghams. It was rare that an evening passed when the Menins weren't forced to listen to a row. They yelled at each other, sometimes for hours, whilst Gary cried in the background.

On the other side, Mr and Mrs Travers were talking in subdued voices as they worked in their showpiece garden, full of glorious flowers, rustic seats and arches. The Travers were an unfriendly couple, who'd lived all their lives in India. Perhaps they thought they'd come down in the world, coming to live in Heather Close, with a building worker on one side and a comprehensive schoolteacher on the other.

Annie had been thrilled to find Chris Andrews, the teacher she'd liked so much, living by the Travers'. Chris was just as pleased to discover his favourite pupil, or so he said, had become a near neighbour. He had married Lottie, the Alice-in-Wonderland fiancée who had come to the pantomime. They had no children, and no matter how hard she tried, Annie found it difficult to take to Lottie. Despite her wide-apart blue eyes and butter-wouldn't-melt-in-the-mouth expression, there was something sly about her.

Gary gave an unearthly scream and Valerie screamed back, 'Give us a minute, you little bugger.' Annie might go round soon and give a hand; change his nappy or make a bottle. It would be good practice.

Her own baby rolled gently in her stomach. He or she never kicked, just made little gentle movements. Annie imagined a tiny figure shifting position, stretching and yawning inside her womb.

She loved being pregnant, loved the feel of her swelling body under her hands. She hadn't had a moment of sickness. According to the clinic, everything was going perfectly, as if she'd been born to be a mother.

The baby was due in September. Two weeks ago, she'd left the English Electric, and been presented with a Moses basket, which made her feel guilty: it was only six months since the wedding, when she'd been bought a set of saucepans.

Annie stretched comfortably. It was lovely being at home with nothing to do except make baby clothes and read and watch Wimbledon on television. She'd already had stacks of visitors. Bruno had bought Sylvia a car for her twenty-first and she'd got a job in something called 'public relations', which meant she was sent out on assignments and always managed a detour to Waterloo. Cecy was so thrilled you'd think Annie was bearing her first grandchild, and of course Dot came bearing stern advice nearly every day.

The patio, a suntrap, was becoming too hot. Annie struggled out of the deckchair and went through the French windows into the cool house.

There were pictures in the lounge, reproductions of Impressionist paintings; Monet, Degas, Pissarro, Van Gogh.

'Why didn't you buy them before?' Annie asked Lauri. He'd had bare walls for more than two years.

'I wasn't sure if you'd like them. I wanted your approval.'

'They're beautiful!' Sunsets, rippling trees, Parisian streets, water lilies.

Brilliant sunshine flooded through the open windows and made the pictures look as if they were alight. The pink walls glowed softly, the dark red suite looked brighter than usual. Annie sighed with pleasure. It looked equally lovely when it was dark, the curtains drawn and the cream-shaded lamps on each side of the fireplace switched on. She would sit with Lauri on the settee, discussing names for the baby, what pattern wallpaper to put in the room which would be a nursery, or watching *Steptoe & Son* on television. Occasionally, Annie would compare their blissful situation with the Cunninghams', and Lauri would say something like,

'They've got to learn to adjust to each other, else life will be one big fight.' There'd been no need for Annie and Lauri to adjust; they hadn't exchanged a cross word since the day they'd met.

Oh, she was so *lucky*!

There was a framed photo of their wedding on the mantelpiece. To most people's disappointment, Annie had decided she didn't want a big posh do, about twenty guests at the most: the Gallaghers, the Delgados, Marie, one or two friends from work.

'Is that your idea or Lauri's?' Dot snapped.

'Mine,' lied Annie. Cecy had offered to pay for the reception and Uncle Bert for the cars, but Lauri felt as if he would be accepting charity. The bride was supposed to pay for the wedding, but Annie hadn't got a penny saved. It seemed silly for Lauri to spend hundreds of pounds when there were still things to buy for the house: neither of the spare bedrooms were furnished, and he wanted a garage built on the side. Anyroad, Lauri said he would prefer a quiet affair. It made such sense that Annie gave up the idea of the wedding dress which she'd designed years ago – very regal, slightly Edwardian, with a tiny bustle – and made herself a simple calf-length frock in fine, off-white jersey, with a high neck and bishop sleeves. Cecy loaned her a white hat covered with frothy white roses.

Sylvia was the only bridesmaid, and considerably put out when told to wear something plain. She thought she was being awkward when she bought a scarlet costume, but it turned out just right for a December wedding.

Annie traced Lauri's features on the photo with her finger. He was smiling, the contented smile of someone entirely happy with his lot. He was always happy, Lauri. His only dour words were for the politicians on television. Otherwise, he exuded good humour all day long. It was impossible not to be happy when Lauri was around.

A loud crash sounded through the separating wall, followed by a scream. Gary was still crying. Annie hurried next door.

Valerie was in the kitchen, almost in tears, a baby's bottle in her hand. The room, identical to Annie's own kitchen in reverse, was in chaos. Every surface was covered with dishes, clean and dirty – Valerie never bothered to put them away. The fronts of the white units were streaked with coffee and tea. On the floor were two buckets full of dirty nappies soaking, and a basket of clean ones waiting to be hung out. Also on the floor, the reason for the crash, an upturned drawer and a scattered assortment of cutlery in urgent need of polishing.

'The whole bloody drawer came out when I pulled,' Valerie groaned.

'Never mind,' Annie bent down, scooped the cutlery into the drawer and shoved it back in. 'What's the matter with Gary?'

'Bloody little sod wants his dinner, that's what, and I can't find the brush to clean his bottle.' Valerie had been a nervous wreck since Gary was born; her milk had dried up so she couldn't breastfeed.

'I think I saw the bottle brush in the drawer.' Annie took the bottle out of Valerie's hand, cleaned it thoroughly, stuck a funnel in the neck, discovered the milk powder amidst the mess and measured out three spoonsful. 'Is there any boiled water?'

'In the kettle, I'm not sure if it's too hot or too cold.'

The water felt just right. Annie poured some over the back of her hand the way it said to do in her baby book. Then she filled the bottle up to eight ounces, found a teat soaking in a bowl on the window sill, and gave the bottle a good shake. 'Would you like me to give it him?'

'You'd better. My hands are trembling.'

The carrycot was in the lounge, which was as untidy as the kitchen. Gary's little screwed-up face was bright red with rage. Annie picked him up and shoved the bottle in his mouth just as he was preparing for another mighty yell.

'Whew!' Instead of tidying up whilst she had a few minute's peace, Valerie threw herself onto the black velvet settee and lit a cigarette. She wore jeans and pumps and one of Kevin's old shirts, covered in stains. Her short dark hair was uncombed and her face bare of make-up. 'Look at me!' she groaned. 'I'm a sight. You'd never think this time last year I was a career woman who wore tailored suits and wouldn't have been seen dead without lipstick. Don't have children, Annie. They ruin your life.' Valerie had been manageress of a travel agency.

'It's a bit late to tell me that,' Annie said drily.

'Of course, I forgot. In a few months, your lovely house will be just like mine.'

Never! There was no way she would have a kitchen like Valerie's. Not only that, she would feed her baby regularly, *breast*feed, and take it for long walks if it cried – Gary always calmed down in his pram, but Valerie was too disorganised to take him.

Gary finished his milk, so Annie laid him on her shoulder and began to rub his back.

'You should have let him suck it longer,' Valerie complained. 'At least it keeps him quiet.'

'But he'll only get more wind, sucking at an empty bottle.' Which was something else she'd read in the baby book.

'Aren't you already the perfect mother!'

There was a sarcastic edge to Valerie's remark that Annie resented. After all, she'd only come to help. She didn't have to be in this rather smelly house trying to raise a burp from an equally smelly baby. Hurt, she stared silently at the brick fireplace, almost identical to the one Lauri had built. The Cunninghams had taken the standard tile one out and had this installed as soon as they'd seen next door's.

'Sorry, Annie,' Valerie said stiffly. 'My nerves are at breaking point. I had a terrible row with my mother on the phone this morning, and last night Kevin and I had an even worse one.'

'I know, we heard.' It was something to do with Kevin wanting a clean shirt every day, which Valerie felt was unreasonable considering all the washing she had to do for their son.

'He seems to expect *his* life to go on exactly as it did before; his dinner on the table, shirts ironed and the house looking like something out of a magazine. He even had the nerve to suggest I weed the garden in my spare time. Spare time, I ask you!'

Annie and Lauri had listened to the subsequent row. Lauri smiled. 'If I'd known the Cunninghams were going to live next door, I would have asked for extra thick walls.'

Lauri was nothing like Kevin. He brought her a cup of tea in bed each morning, helped with the housework at weekends, and had no inhibitions about washing dishes just because he was a man. He laughed the time she burned the rice pudding, and didn't give two hoots when she made a terrible mess of her first omelette and they ended up with scrambled egg.

Gary burped and began to bawl. 'I'll change his nappy, if I can find a clean one, and take him for a walk,' Valerie said tiredly.

Annie offered to change the nappy whilst Valerie had another cigarette. It was difficult to get the terrycloth square around Gary's flailing legs and even harder to fasten the pin without piercing his tummy.

'One of these days I'll stab the little bugger, so help me,' his weary mother remarked.

Ten minutes later, she went marching off pushing the big expensive pram, her baby dressed only in his nappy and vest because she couldn't find clean clothes. Everywhere was still in a mess and there was no sign of a meal being prepared for Kevin.

Annie presumed there would be another row that night.

Sara Menin, weighing eight pounds, arrived without a single hitch on the last day of September.

'Isn't she beautiful!' Annie whispered the first night home. Sara was fast asleep in her cot beside their bed. She had pale fair hair with a touch of red and a tiny, almost grown-up face.

'Like her mother.' Lauri kissed Annie on the cheek. He stared at Sara as if he couldn't believe he was a father. 'It's like a dream come true,' he murmured softly. 'My wife, my child – my family.'

'Why didn't you get married again years ago?' Annie asked curiously, at the same time thinking how terrible it would have been if he had.

'What a strange question!' He looked amused. 'Because I was waiting for Annie Harrison to come along.' He kissed her other cheek.

'But you decided to buy a house.'

'I was fed up with lodgings, that's why. You appeared quite fortuitously right after I had made the decision.'

Sylvia always found the baby most peculiar. 'She's so *helpless*. Horses can walk the minute they're born. You've got to do everything for her.'

'Well, Cecy had to do everything for you. You didn't come leaping from her womb and go for a run.' Annie transferred two-month-old Sara to her other breast.

'I never thought the day would come when I'd see you breastfeed, Annie. Does it hurt when she sucks?'

'No. Actually, it's rather nice.'

'Ugh!' Sylvia shuddered. The Bohemian look had gone since she entered public relations, and she wore a short green shift dress with a thick gold chain slung around her slim hips. She looked incredibly elegant with her long blonde hair tied in a knot on top of her head and dangling jade earrings. Her white mini was parked on the drive outside. 'I'm only joking. I half envy you, having Sara. She's lovely.'

'Only half envy me?' Annie raised her eyebrows.

'Well, you're missing everything, aren't you? Liverpool's the most famous city on the planet. The atmosphere in the clubs is terrific. You should hear the way girls scream at the Beatles nowadays.'

'Do you scream?'

'Jaysus, no, I'm too old. But,' she added wistfully, 'sometimes I wish we were still teenagers. I wouldn't mind a good scream.'

It seemed very juvenile to Annie. She listened to the old groups on the radio, but they seemed to belong to a world she'd left behind.

'Hey, you'll never guess who I saw the other day in the New Court,' Sylvia said. 'Jeremy Rupert.'

'I hope you spat in his eye for me.'

'I was contemplating doing that very thing, except he was with this gorgeous guy. I said "Hello" in the hope he'd introduce me, which he did. The gorgeous guy's a solicitor called Eric Church.' Sylvia smacked her lips. 'He's a Catholic and I'm going out with him on Saturday.'

Annie felt she'd been rather traitorous. 'I hope that doesn't mean Jeremy Rupert's likely to come to the wedding if you end up marrying this gorgeous Eric,' she grumbled.

After Sylvia had gone, Annie put Sara in her Moses basket and went to fetch the washing in; the gusty November wind had blown everything dry. Valerie was bringing in her own washing at the same time. After the initial turmoil, Gary had turned out to be a lovely baby. His nature had become quite sunny and he rarely cried. The Cunninghams were trying for another baby and Valerie was already a week late with her period.

They waved to each other and Valerie looked inclined to stop for a chat, but Annie explained she had to get Lauri's dinner ready.

'I thought he was working in Manchester at the moment?'

'He is, but it doesn't take long to get home. I'm about to make a cottage pie.'

Lauri Menin belonged to a co-operative with four other carpenters, skilled tradesmen like himself. Sometimes, all five might work together on the one site if a large estate was being built, or else they took on jobs which required just one or two men, jobs that could last for as little as a single day. Fred Quillen, the oldest and longest-standing member of the co-op, handled the bookings with scrupulous fairness, and the Quillens' address and telephone number was on the sign over the yard in Bootle where the materials and vans were kept. The men were often fully booked for months ahead. At the end of the month, their earnings were pooled so each man earned the same as the others, barring overtime which went to the individual himself.

At the moment, Lauri was the only one to be employed on the building of a luxury house on the outskirts of Manchester. It was dark by the time he arrived home. 'And how's our daughter been today?' he asked, after he'd kissed his wife affectionately.

'Fine. She couldn't possibly be finer.'

'The food smells nice, my love, I'm starving.'

Annie bustled round, making fresh tea before sitting down to the cottage pie. When they'd finished, Lauri went into the lounge whilst she washed the dishes. She removed her apron and went to join him. He was on the settee reading the paper and looked up, smiling briefly when she came in. Next door, the Cunninghams were having their nightly row, but in number seven everything was quiet. Sara slept peacefully upstairs. Lauri didn't approve of having the television on unless there was something they specifically wanted to watch.

Out of the blue, Annie had the strangest vision. Instead of Lauri, she saw her dad sitting in front of the fireplace of the silent house in Orlando Street. For a moment, she felt quite dizzy. What on earth had triggered off such an awful memory? Then Lauri patted the settee and said, 'Come on, love', and the vision went, but later she found herself thinking about Sylvia and the Cavern, the groups they'd travelled the length and breadth of Liverpool to see, the dances, the tennis club.

'Do you think we could go out one night?' she asked. Dot had already offered to babysit.

'Of course, my love. Where to, the pictures?'

'The pictures would be fine.' She'd look in the *Echo* to see what was on. 'And you know I couldn't think of anything to have for me birthday? Well, if we can afford it, I'd like a record player.'

'Then a record player it will be,' said Lauri.

There were three very good reasons for throwing a party: it was their second wedding anniversary, it was Christmas, and Labour had recently won a General Election. Dot's new heart-throb, Harold Wilson, was Prime Minister.

Sylvia said to ask twice the number of guests they could accommodate because half were bound not to come. The trouble was, everyone had come and there was scarcely room to stand. If it had been summer, they could have opened the French windows and let everyone spill out into the garden, but it was December and snowing outside and guests had spilled out into the hallway and the breakfast room instead. There were several people sitting on the stairs.

Still, everyone seemed to be enjoying themselves. Valerie and Chris Andrews were dancing to 'Good Golly, Miss Molly'. Lauri, the perfect genial host, beamed at everyone in sight.

'This is the gear, sis.' Marie came into the kitchen and helped herself to a sausage roll.

Annie was frantically cutting sandwiches. She hadn't done nearly enough food. 'I thought you didn't say things like "the gear" any more.'

'Scouse has become really fashionable in London. People are always asking me to say something in a Liverpool accent. When I tell them my sister was at the Cavern the night it opened, they're really impressed.'

Marie had arrived that morning and would stay for the next few months. She had a small part in the pantomime at the Empire. Pantomime wasn't what Marie had in mind when she'd gone to London in search of stardom, but, as she said with a shrug, it was better than nothing. She'd brought an actor friend who was staying just for Christmas, Clive Hoskins, a sunburnt Adonis with perfect features and a halo of golden curls. Annie couldn't very well object when they took it for granted they would occupy the twin beds in the spare room. Her sister's morals were her own affair. When Annie asked if it was serious, Marie merely said, 'Clive is a dear friend. I'm very fond of him.'

Marie grimaced. 'What possessed you to wear that dress, sis? It looks frumpy, particularly with those flat shoes. And why don't you do something with your hair? It's been like that since you were little.'

'Oh, do I look awful?' Annie put a distraught hand to her head. 'I intended putting me hair up, but people started arriving before I'd got me make-up on. I made the frock for me twenty-first. I thought it looked dead smart.'

'That length went out of fashion years ago.' Marie looked very smart indeed, in a black form-fitting tailored dress with a daring deep V neckline revealing an inch of black scalloped lace. The skirt finished just above her knees. Her dark hair was cut severely, the same length all round, level with her eyebrows and the tops of her ears. Dot remarked it looked like a plant pot.

'I'll ask Lauri if I can buy material for some new frocks.'

'Don't *ask*, sis. *Tell* him you need more clothes.'

Sylvia came floating into the kitchen, in a dazzling pink dress styled like a toga, which left one gleaming shoulder bare. The hem was edged with silver braid, and she wore spiky-heeled silver sandals. Marie immediately made an excuse to leave, and Annie wondered if they could still remember why they disliked each other.

'More wine,' Sylvia sang. 'White for me and red for Eric, and for goodness' sake, Annie, get out of the kitchen and enjoy yourself. We're all having far too good a time to want food. You look harassed.'

'Oh, Marie said I looked frumpy, now I look harassed. I'm not exactly the perfect hostess.'

'No-one expects you to be perfect.' She took hold of Annie's arm. 'Come on.'

'Will you finish the sandwiches?'

'No I bloody won't. Hang the sandwiches and have a glass of wine.'

'It'll only make me sick. Everything makes me sick at the moment.' She was not quite three months pregnant, but having this baby was already very different from the first time. She felt wretched every morning and almost everything she ate upset her stomach. If she'd known she would feel this bad, she wouldn't have suggested the party, but the invitations had gone out weeks ago.

Sylvia dragged her into the lounge, where Eric Church was leaning against the wall, smoking. Annie had taken an immediate dislike to Eric. Perhaps it was only natural not to like the man who was to marry your best friend; after all, Sylvia had been scathing about Lauri. So far, Annie had kept her thoughts to herself.

He reminded her of a Regency buck, and wasn't so much handsome as attractive, with a thin aquiline face and sleeked-back fair hair. Tall and rather dashing, she imagined him in a frock coat with a lacy cravat and a whip twitching in his long white hand.

The pair had been virtually living together in Upper Parliament Street since they met fifteen months ago, and were getting married at Easter, though how Sylvia had the nerve to wear white for virtue, Annie found hard to understand.

'Hi, Annie.' Eric looked bored. He took the glass off Sylvia and she draped herself over him and nuzzled his neck. Annie felt embarrassed. The pair could scarcely keep their hands off each other, even in public. Eric looked slightly less bored and licked his loved one's ear.

After a short conversation during which they had eyes for no-one but one another, Annie made her excuses, and was immediately captured by one of Lauri's colleagues from the co-op.

'Lauri told us about the baby, Annie,' Fred Quillen said in the high-pitched voice that always sounded odd coming from someone with the build of a heavyweight wrestler. 'Congratulations. When's it due?'

'The middle of July. Sara will be twenty-two months by then.'

'So, they'll be nicely spaced apart.'

'I would have liked them closer, but Lauri wanted to wait a while.'

It was difficult to hear above the din of the music and the buzz of animated conversation. Annie noticed Lauri, a wine bottle in each hand, had forgotten he was supposed to be refilling glasses, and was deep in discussion with Dot and Bert and the couple from the Labour Party whose names she couldn't remember. She excused herself for a second time, saying she'd like to take a peek at Sara in case she'd been awoken by the noise. She'd already taken several peeks, but an earthquake wouldn't have disturbed Sara once she was asleep.

'Smashing party, Annie.' Chris Andrews said as she pushed past. He was talking to her sister and Clive Hoskins and she briefly remembered his play, *Goldilocks*, had sparked off Marie's desire to be an actress.

Valerie came out of the bathroom as Annie went upstairs. She looked very glamorous in a sleek blue satin dress with a halter neck, her hair newly set that afternoon. Annie felt very drab, particularly as Valerie now had two small children, and she only had one. Kelly Cunningham had been born in June, and was now six months old.

'False alarm,' Valerie said.

'Sorry?'

'I told you I was a week late, didn't I? Well, I could have sworn I'd just started, but it was a false alarm. Looks like you and me will be going to the clinic together. By the way, have you seen Kevin?'

'No, but there could be a dozen Kevins down there and I wouldn't have noticed. I'm off to have a bit of peace and quiet with Sara.'

'Feeling rough, are you?' Valerie said sympathetically. 'I was like that with Gary. It makes you wonder why women keep on having babies, doesn't it?' With that, she ran downstairs.

Sara was in her own little room at the front of the house. The wallpaper was creamy yellow patterned with white lace. She was lying on her side, so still that Annie quickly checked she was still breathing, something she must have done a million times before. She stroked the pale curls which had just a touch of ginger. Sara didn't stir, despite the fact the floor throbbed in time to the music.

Annie felt her heart quicken. Did all mothers have this sense of overwhelming love, mixed with anxiety and all sorts of other emotions, when they looked at their small children? She wondered if it would stop when they grew older. Did Dot still feel the same about her lads? Tommy and Alan had families and mortgages and were anxious for their jobs. Mike had given up his perfectly good job at the English Electric to start a pop group which had failed, and now worked for an engineering firm that was little short of a sweatshop; the younger lads were only just starting out in the big wide world.

With a sigh, Annie went to the window and lifted the curtain to see if it was still snowing. It was, and the close looked like a Christmas card with its covering of white. Brightly decorated trees glittered in most windows. Some houses, including their own, had coach lamps outside.

She was about to drop the curtain, when two people came out of the Andrews' house and began to run towards her own. As they got closer, Annie felt herself grow cold. Kevin Cunningham and Lottie Andrews! Laughing, they hurried down the side path and went in the back way.

Perhaps there was an entirely innocent explanation. Annie hoped they could think of one if someone noticed the footprints going from one house to the other in the otherwise smooth snow. She let the curtain fall, took a final glance at Sara and opened the door to return to the party.

Sylvia and Eric were at the top of the stairs. They didn't notice Annie about to emerge from the bedroom. She took a step back and half closed the door, although she knew she shouldn't watch, but there was something odd about their posture, something still and wary, like animals about to pounce. They didn't touch, just stared at each other. There was a look on Sylvia's face Annie had never seen before. Her lovely eyes were half closed, her lips curved in a quivering smile. Then Eric clasped her face in his long white hands and kissed her, not an ordinary kiss, but savage. His jowls moved, his mouth was wide open, as if he was trying to devour her in front of Annie's startled eyes.

His hands moved down her body, rested fleetingly on her breasts, ever so slowly, almost teasingly. Sylvia said, 'Oh, *God*!' in a strange hoarse voice, and Eric opened the bathroom door and they went inside. The bolt clicked into place.

Annie remained transfixed, holding the half-open door. She had never looked at Lauri like that! Lauri didn't open his mouth when he kissed her – she would be horrified if he did. Making love with Lauri couldn't be nicer. He was gentle, always respectful. Even on the first night, he made sure it didn't hurt. She always felt content and satisfied, lying in his arms when it was over.

Sylvia and Eric had looked *disgusting*. For some reason, Annie felt extraordinarily disturbed.

She went downstairs, to find Kevin and Valerie dancing cheek to cheek. Lottie was in the kitchen making a sandwich. 'I hope you don't mind, Annie. I always feel hungry after . . .'

'After what?'

Lottie looked at her with wide, innocent blue eyes. 'After a few glasses of wine.' She giggled, as if at a private joke, but Annie understood only too well what she'd been about to say. After sex!

'That chap's a card, isn't he?'

'Which chap?' queried Annie. She hated this party and desperately wished it were over. Would anyone notice, she wondered, if she crawled underneath the coats on the bed and went to sleep?

'That Clive chap with your sister. I mean, it's obvious. I've never met a queer before. I thought it was against the law.'

Annie didn't answer. Lottie departed with a sandwich in each hand.

Marie was sleeping with a homosexual.

And if that wasn't enough, Sylvia and Eric were behaving like animals and Kevin Cunningham and Lottie Andrews were having an affair.

It was too much!

'I think that went very well, don't you?' said Lauri. 'Everybody seemed to have a good time.'

Annie nodded numbly. It was nearly three o'clock, the last guests had left, and Marie and Clive had gone to bed. She began to collect the dirty glasses, but Lauri took them off her. 'You look exhausted, love. I'll clear up in the morning. Go on up and I'll bring you some cocoa.'

She was sitting up in bed when he brought the drink. He put the mug on the bedside table and took both of her hands in his. He could read her like a book, and always knew when there was something wrong.

'What's the matter with my little girl?' he asked tenderly.

'I feel all peculiar, I don't know why,' she confessed.

'I expect it's the baby. Do you feel queasy?'

'A bit. But it's not just that . . .'

He ruffled her hair. 'What is it then?'

She told him what had happened over the evening, the things she'd seen and heard. Lauri smiled. 'And why should they make you feel peculiar?'

'I've no idea,' Annie sniffed.

'Do you think you're missing something?'

Oh, he was so astute. He'd guessed before she had herself. She bit her lip and said nothing.

'Does that mean you'd like an affair with Kevin Cunningham?'

'Of course not!' Annie was shocked.

Lauri wiggled his eyebrows. 'Do you want to sleep with a homosexual?'

She giggled. 'No.'

'Shall I bare my teeth and look at you like an animal then? What shall it be, an elephant maybe, or a squirrel?'

'Oh, Lauri!' She flung her arms around his neck. 'I'm a terrible person.'

'No you're not, my dearest Annie. It must be very boring stuck at home all day with Sara. Why don't you and Sylvia go to the Cavern one night? Or to the pictures?'

'As if I'd leave you all on your own!'

Lauri shrugged. 'But I leave you when I go to the Labour Party. I was out every night for weeks before the General Election.'

'Perhaps I could go to the Labour Party with you some time? Dot would always look after Sara. I'd feel a bit peculiar at the Cavern. I'm sure they don't get very many pregnant women there.'

218

To her surprise, because Lauri usually agreed to almost everything she asked, he shook his head. 'You'd find the meetings very dull, and anyway, you've never shown the least interest in politics.'

She thought she might if she went to a meeting and heard what people had to say, but didn't bother arguing. She felt much better. It was enough to know she could go out if she wanted. Maybe she and Valerie could go to the pictures. It was no good asking Sylvia because she went everywhere with Eric.

'I suppose the best marriages are slightly dull,' Lauri was saying. 'And I dread Valerie finding out that Kevin is up to no good with Lottie Andrews – we'll have to get sandbags for the walls.'

2

According to Dot, who joined the crowds outside St Edmund's church to watch, there had never been a more glorious, a more radiant bride than Sylvia Delgado. She didn't like to hurt anyone's feelings, but it was the God's honest truth.

In her dress of paper-thin taffeta with several petti-coats underneath, long fitted sleeves and a shawl collar thickly trimmed with lace, Sylvia looked almost unreal, out of this world, too beautiful to touch. Her filmy veil was waist length and a coronet of pearls encircled her gleaming blonde hair. Eric looked dazed as she came floating up the aisle towards him on Bruno's arm.

No expense had been spared for the wedding of the Delgados' only child. The men wore top hats and grey morning suits and the women's outfits came from the most exclusive shops. The hired cars were long and sleek, the flowers in the church had been flown from the Channel Islands, the organist was a professional hired for the occasion. Bruno didn't give a damn, but Cecy wanted to impress the family her daughter was marrying into.

There had been a Church & Son, Solicitors, in Liverpool for over a hundred years. The firm had been established by Eric's great-great-grandfather, and was more highly regarded than Stickley & Plumm, if such a thing were possible. Specialising in litigation, the name of Peter Church, Eric's father, was frequently mentioned in the national media when he defended infamous criminals in long, attention-grabbing trials. Eric was his only son and reputed to be as brilliant as his father. The family lived in a palatial house in Southport, where they employed a cook and a gardener. Peter Church drove a Rolls Royce.

They were an impressive couple, the Churches, Peter, with his prominent beak nose and piercing eyes, had the arrogant look of a man who wouldn't suffer fools gladly. His wife Mildred, in her oyster brocade suit and over-feathered hat, looked a pillar of the community, as indeed she was.

Cecy felt it was essential to prove, by spending as much as possible, that the Churches had met their financial match by marrying into the Delgados – Sylvia was the daughter of a Count, and she had the family coat of arms printed in silver on the invitations. She'd gone to London to buy her lilac chiffon dress and matching hat from Harrods.

The only thing to spoil what should have been a perfect wedding was the matron of honour. At least, so Annie thought.

'But, Syl,' she reasoned. 'The trouble Cecy's going to, the expense. It seems dead stupid to muck things up with a matron of honour who's six months pregnant.'

'I don't care if you're ten months pregnant,' Sylvia

said flatly. 'You shall be my matron of honour, and that's that.'

'I won't half feel silly. I'll look a sight.'

'I don't care about that, either. We promised each other, we took a vow, that when we got married one of us would be bridesmaid and the other matron of honour.'

Annie couldn't remember taking a vow, but perhaps she had.

'If you refuse, I'll never forgive you!' Sylvia stared menacingly at her friend. 'I suppose I could delay it for six months until you've got your slim, svelte figure back?'

'Syl! You know darn well I've never been slim or svelte. As for delaying it, you're joking, because Cecy would die of shock. Oh, all right, I'll do it, but I'll look like a bloody house!'

In fact, she didn't look too bad. The blue lace frock with its long jacket discreetly disguised the bump in her stomach. She loaned Sylvia a handkerchief for something borrowed, and she wore a daring garter for something blue. The something old was the pearl coronet which had been Cecy's when she married Bruno all those years ago.

It seemed an odd thing to wear, mused Annie, standing behind her friend as she was betrothed to Eric Church, because Cecy and Bruno's marriage had turned out to be a disaster. Her musings were forgotten when the baby gave her stomach a series of vicious kicks. She turned and caught Lauri's eye. He was sitting at the end of a pew with Sara, in her new white broderie anglaise frock, on his knee. He smiled and Annie felt a shiver of sheer happiness run through her.

Then Sylvia lifted her veil. Annie caught her breath because she was so beautiful. Her eyes had never looked so huge and the irises were the dusky blue of an evening sky. They shone with unshed tears as Eric kissed her on the lips. Annie distinctly recalled the day Sylvia Delgado had come into the classroom at Grenville Lucas. She'd known straight away that they were going to become friends. They'd had some wonderful times together, but now both were married women.

An era had ended. A new one had begun.

Daniel Menin decided to arrive late, very late. Nine uncomfortable months elapsed, but still he showed no sign of being born. Annie was huge, absolutely massive, as she lumbered round. It was impossible to turn over in bed; she had to get out and in again. She virtually lived in the clinic. The baby's head wasn't in the right place.

'It's too busy kicking to know it should turn upside down,' she moaned. 'If it doesn't come soon, I'll have to have it induced.'

It was in the butcher's one sunny afternoon in late July that the baby gave the first hint of his arrival, a painful hint. She never went far these days in case this very thing happened. The shop was only a few minutes away from Heather Close. She screamed and bent double when a searing pain scorched through her stomach. There'd been no previous warning, nothing to indicate that today was to be the day.

The butcher looked scared. 'Jaysus, luv! What's wrong?'

A woman in the shop said cuttingly, 'The girl's about to have a baby. Don't stand there like a pill garlic, man, ring for an ambulance. Come on, luv,' she said kindly. 'Hang on to me. If you have another pain, squeeze as hard as you like.' The woman began to tell Annie in bloodthirsty detail about her own deliveries. 'With the first, I was torn to shreds. Twelve stitches I needed. Twelve! The second saw me two days in labour and in agony the whole time. The third, you wouldn't believe what happened with the third . . .'

Fortunately, Annie never found out what happened with the third. She was seized by an even worse pain, just as the butcher returned with a glass of water and announced an ambulance was on its way.

'But me little girl,' Annie gasped. 'I left her with a neighbour . . .'

The bloodthirsty woman said, 'Where d'you live, luv, and I'll go round and tell her.'

'Seven Heather Close, and if you could ask me neighbour to contact me husband? She knows where he's working.'

'All right, luv. Don't worry, everything's going to be all right,' which Annie thought an odd remark considering all she'd said before.

The ambulance arrived and with it more pains, terrible contractions that made her feel she was being ripped in two. The next eight hours were a nightmare, a tortured daze of piercing contractions and anguished screams. Lauri arrived, his face grave.

'Is there something wrong with the baby?' Annie yelled.

'Of course there's nothing wrong with the baby,' a nurse said. 'He's just an awkward little bugger, that's all.'

It was midnight when Daniel kicked and fought his way out of his mother's womb. Those last few minutes brought agony so fierce that Annie felt convinced she was going to die.

'You've got a lovely little boy, Mrs Menin.' There was a slap and Daniel Menin sent up a great howl. 'He's a whopper, too. Not far off nine pounds, I reckon. What are you going to call him?'

Annie, totally exhausted, could think of a dozen names to call her new son, none of them favourable. 'Daniel,' she said.

'He's a fine little chap,' Lauri said when he was allowed to see her. His eyes looked all puffy, as if he'd been crying. He stroked her damp brow. 'That was a terrible experience, my love. I felt every contraction with you.'

'Lauri?'

'Yes, my dear Annie?'

'Promise we'll never have another baby.' She couldn't go through that again.

'I promise. Frankly, I couldn't stand it, either. Two children are quite enough, and now we have a boy and a girl, the ideal family.'

There were two deckchairs on the Menins' patio. In one, Valerie Cunningham was suckling month-old Zachary. Valerie had given birth to four children in just over three years, a fact she never ceased to boast about. Eleven-month-old Tracy was crawling purpose-fully across the Menins' lawn, a dummy in her mouth.

'Just look at the birthday boy,' Valerie chuckled.

Annie watched as Daniel tried to drag a doll away from two-year-old Kelly. The chuckle was a warning to tell him to stop.

'Daniel,' she called. 'Leave Kelly's doll alone.'

Daniel ignored her. A wilful scowl appeared on his handsome little face. He tugged even harder, the doll's head came off and Kelly burst into tears.

Annie went over to where the children were playing. She knelt by her son, took him by his sturdy waist and said firmly, 'Look, you got loads of presents this morning. Why don't you play with them?'

'No,' said Daniel. He stared at his mother mutinously. It was the only word he knew. Lauri said it was typical; other children's first word was 'Mummy' or 'Daddy'. Daniel's was 'no'.

'What about that lovely big ball Auntie Dot sent?'

'No.'

'Or the telephone off your Uncle Mike?'

'No.'

She released him, and he immediately went for the broken doll. Annie grabbed it off him. Fortunately, the head clicked back on. She gave it to Kelly and Daniel tried to get it back, so she picked him up and carried him to the deckchair. He settled on her lap and watched Valerie feeding Zachary with genuine interest in his intelligent brown eyes.

Dark-haired, dark-eyed Daniel had been a handful since the day he was born. Unlike his sister, he scarcely slept and demanded constant attention. Annie was driven frantic, trying to keep the house nice, prepare Lauri's meals, and keep her small son occupied. He was far more advanced than Sara had been, sitting up unsupported at five months, walking at ten. Lauri had to build a gate at the bottom of the stairs after the day Annie couldn't find Daniel anywhere and he was discovered upstairs, trying to climb into the lavatory. Fortunately, Sara was no trouble and very self-contained. At the moment, she was playing house all by herself in the willow tree. Annie glimpsed her golden daughter crouched inside the leafy shade making an imaginary meal for a row of furry animals and dolls, a serious expression on her gentle little face.

Gary, Valerie's eldest, was playing with Daniel's new blue and white ball. He charged after it, without noticing his small sister crawling across the grass, and tripped and fell headlong. Tracy, more frightened than hurt, dropped her dummy and started to wail.

'*Gary!*' Valerie screamed. 'Come here.'

The child came across, dragging his feet. Valerie delivered a stinging slap to his bare leg. 'Look where you're going in future,' she snapped. Gary's bottom lip quivered, but he didn't cry.

'I think it was an accident,' Annie said mildly. Gary was a nice little boy and she hated to see him punished unfairly.

'Accident or not, he should look where he's going.'

Valerie never hesitated to lash out at her children, but Annie had sworn never to lay a hand on hers. She wanted, more than anything in the world, for them to be happy, for them not to know a single moment of the misery she had suffered in her own childhood.

She wished Auntie Dot and Sylvia would come soon so they could have their tea and Valerie and her brood could go home. It had seemed only proper to invite them, because the Menins were always invited to tea at the Cunninghams when there was a birthday.

Valerie began to complain in a loud voice about Kevin. 'He's off to London next week, the lucky bastard. Some sort of conference.' She laughed unpleasantly. 'If I didn't know him better, I'd swear he was having an affair, he gets home later and later. He hasn't got the guts, though. He knows I'd kill him if he went with another woman.'

Chris Andrews had mentioned the other day that Lottie was staying with a friend in Brighton next week. Annie was wondering if there was a connection, when Auntie Dot and Sylvia came round the side of the house.

Dot beamed. 'Where's my Danny Boy? Come on, you lovely little lad, and give your ould auntie a nice big kiss.'

Daniel slid off his mother's knee and trotted into her arms. There was something about Dot, with her rough voice and exaggerated manner, that attracted children like moths to a flame. The little Cunninghams gathered round. Gary often asked for his Auntie Dot.

Annie noticed her daughter hanging back, as if unwilling to join the throng. Sylvia, Sara's Godmother, had also noticed. She sat on the grass and pulled the little girl onto her knee and gave her a present, a blue leather shoulder bag. 'I didn't want her to feel left out,' she said. 'Daniel always seems to be the centre of attention.'

'It only seems like that. Lauri idolises Sara. Daniel isn't the centre of attention when Daddy's here.'

Sylvia looked casually elegant in jeans and a loose shell-pink blouse. She'd given up work when she got married and spent her leisurely days caring for her beautiful bungalow in Birkdale. She was learning to play bridge and spent a lot of time helping her mother-in-law with coffee mornings to raise money for charity. Almost every night, she and Eric went to a dinner party, usually with the same crowd of up-and-coming solicitors, accountants and businessmen. Once a week, they held a dinner of their own. Annie and Lauri had been invited, but declined. 'I wouldn't know which knife to hold,' Annie confessed. 'Anyroad, Syl, I'd feel out of place with those sort of people, and Lauri said if there's one profession he can't stand above all others, it's accountants.'

The birthday tea was served in the breakfast room. Instead of blowing out the single candle, Daniel made a grab for it and burnt his fingers. He didn't scream, but regarded the burnt fingers curiously, then looked to his mother for an explanation. Dot declared he was a marvel, a miracle of a child.

The Cunninghams left. 'I suppose I'd better tidy up a bit before Kevin comes home,' Valerie said sullenly.

'She's a mardy girl,' Dot remarked after Valerie had gone. 'She doesn't know which side her bread is buttered. Four lovely kids, yet she's always moaning. Mind you, I've never taken to women who leave their pegs on the line.'

Dot took the children into the garden and Annie cleared the table. Sylvia ran water into the sink. 'I'll wash, you dry.' This had been the pattern when they lived in Upper Parliament Street. Sylvia loathed drying dishes. She claimed it sent her into a trance.

'You'll get your lovely blouse all wet,' Annie warned.

Sylvia rolled up her sleeves before plunging her hands into the soapy water.

'What have you done to your arm?' Annie exclaimed. There was an ugly purple bruise on her left forearm, stretching from wrist to elbow.

'Oh!' Sylvia laughed and made a half-hearted attempt to pull the sleeve down. 'Oh, it looks much worse than it is. I fell upstairs! It doesn't hurt at all.' As soon as she'd finished, she rolled down her sleeves and buttoned the cuffs.

Annie put the kettle on so they could have a cup of tea in peace. 'I can't tell you how welcome silence is. Daniel's on the go all day.'

'But he's a super little boy, Annie.'

'Don't get me wrong,' Annie said quickly. 'I'm not complaining. Both my children are adorable and I'm entirely happy with my lot.' She looked sideways at her friend. 'Aren't you?' She wasn't quite sure why she asked the question that way, as if there was some doubt about it. Perhaps it was the bruise that made her feel uneasy.

'Eric and I are blissfully happy,' Sylvia gushed. 'Though we'd love a baby – the in-laws are for ever dropping hints. Eric is their only son, and there must always be a Church & Son in Liverpool.' She winked. 'Eric and I go at it hammer and tongs, but I don't seem able to conceive.'

'There's plenty of time. You've only been married fifteen months.'

'Yes, but I'll be twenty-five soon, we both will, and I want to be a young mother for my children when they grow up.'

Then Dot came in with Daniel wanting his potty, and the peace was shattered until he decided to go to sleep that night at half past ten.

Annie told Lauri about Sylvia's inability to conceive. 'Not like me. I must be very fertile.' It made her feel very feminine and fruitful.

'No, Annie,' Lauri said firmly. He knew straight away what she was leading up to, the same discussion they'd been having for months.

'Please, Lauri,' she implored. 'I'd love another baby. In fact, I'd like two. Four children is the perfect number, two boys and two girls.' She'd already chosen the names; Sophie and Joshua.

But Lauri's face had the stubborn expression that always came when she raised the subject. 'After Daniel, you made me promise that we'd never have another baby. How on earth can you have forgotten that time? It was sheer torture, love. I couldn't go through it again.'

'I haven't forgotten,' Annie said eagerly, 'but, looking back, I realise it was worth it. We ended up with Daniel, didn't we? I wouldn't care if it was twice that bad for another Daniel or Sara. It's what women do to have babies. Dot had an awful time with Alan, and Valerie did with Tracy, and the woman in the butcher's . . .'

Lauri broke in. 'I know all about Dot and Valerie and the woman in the butcher's, but it's *you* I'm married to, not them. I couldn't stand it, Annie. I'd be on tenter-hooks – and what about the expense?'

'The expense?' Annie said, puzzled. 'We've already got a cot and a pram and all the things we need.'

'There'd be another mouth to feed – two, if you had your way.'

'I thought we had plenty of money.' They rarely talked about money. Lauri gave her housekeeping every Friday, and never protested if she asked for more if there was an extra expense that week.

'All my savings went on the house because I wanted it to be perfect. We're not short, but we're not flush either. Interest rates have gone up which means mortgages have gone up with them. Now, if you don't mind, Annie, I'd sooner not discuss it any further.' He rattled the newspaper and started to read.

After a long silence, Annie said, 'What would happen if I forgot to take my pill?' She'd threatened this before and the reply was always more or less the same.

Behind the paper, Lauri said, 'I would consider you very deceitful.'

There was another silence, then Lauri lowered the paper. His eyes were twinkling. 'Are you sure this isn't a bit of one-upmanship on your part, Annie? The Cunninghams had a fireplace put in like the Menins. The Menins must have four children like the Cunninghams.'

She conceded he was probably right. She was jealous of Valerie.

'Come here,' Lauri lifted his arm and she cuddled beside him. 'Why risk our happiness by treading into the unknown? We already have two beautiful children. Be content, Annie. Be content.'

She was nearly asleep when she remembered the purple mark on Sylvia's arm. She'd done it falling upstairs! She also remembered that the Churches lived in a bungalow which had no stairs. She imagined Eric, a Regency buck with a cane twitching in his hand, and knew, as surely as she'd ever known anything, that incredible though it might seem, it was he who was responsible for the bruise on her friend's arm!

Sara looked tiny and lost in her yellow overalls and pink

T-shirt, with her favourite Teddy clutched to her chest. She looked at Annie trustingly. 'It's all right, sweetheart,' Annie whispered and gave her a little push, though she felt like a torturer. More than anything, she wanted to snatch her daughter up and take her home.

Then a helper swooped on them. 'Hello, Sara.' The woman took Sara's hand. 'What a good little girl you are! I think you're the only new one who's not crying.' She turned to Annie. 'She'll be fine, Mrs Menin. Say bye bye to Mummy, Sara. I'm sure you're going to just love playgroup.'

There was a lump in Annie's throat when she got home. She played with Daniel for a while, but what she really needed was someone to talk to, someone who would understand how she felt. Valerie would be no good. Valerie would think her an idiot getting upset over Sara. She was always looking for ways to get her children off her hands and would consider Annie lucky to have got rid of Sara for three mornings a week.

Perhaps Sylvia would come round? She hadn't seen her since Daniel's birthday, nearly three months ago. Though they spoke on the telephone frequently, it always seemed to be she who called. Lauri laughed like a drain when she said she thought Eric was responsible for the bruise. 'She could have fallen up someone else's stairs, my love. Really, Annie, your imagination knows no bounds.'

But Annie *knew*, she just knew! Sylvia hadn't been round because she was black and blue all over and had to stay indoors.

She dialled Sylvia's number, and it rang out for a long time. She was just about to replace the receiver when it was picked up. Sylvia answered, her voice muffled.

'Are you all right?' Annie enquired. 'You sound dead funny. Oh, I do hope it's morning sickness.'

'It's not, I'm afraid. I'm just a bit off-colour, otherwise I'm fine.' Eric was also fine. Everything was fine. 'How are Lauri and the children?' she asked.

'Fine,' giggled Annie. 'I'd be fine, too, except I feel dead miserable. Sara started playgroup this morning.'

'I expect she'll love it there,' Sylvia said dully.

'Do you feel too off-colour to come and cheer me up?'

'Sorry, Annie, but I think I'll go back to bed.'

'I'd come and see you, except I've got to pick Sara up at twelve.' Anyroad, the few occasions she'd gone to Birkdale by train, Daniel had shown an unhealthy interest in the Churches' valuable ornaments.

'I'm not really in the mood for visitors.'

Why not? Annie was immediately suspicious. 'You sound peculiar!'

'So do you!' Sylvia rang off with a curt 'goodbye'.

Annie immediately took her son next door, where Valerie was vacuuming the lounge. Tracy and Kelly were on the settee, pretending to be terrified. 'D'you mind looking after Daniel for a couple of hours? Sylvia's not well and I'd like to go and see her.' Daniel wasn't clinging like Sara and Annie didn't feel uncomfortable asking, because Valerie often requested the same favour. 'I'll be back in time to collect Sara.'

'Of course, it's Sara's first morning at playgroup, isn't it? I suppose you're feeling rather sad,' Valerie said surprisingly. 'Don't rush back for Sara. I'll pick her up with Gary. You'll have a job getting to and from Birkdale in time.' She said to give Sylvia her love and hoped she'd soon be better.

Annie took a last glance at Daniel. He had already thrown himself on the settee and was trying to get a doll off Kelly.

The Churches' bungalow was in a quiet tree-lined road

close to Birkdale golf course. It had a white pebble-dashed exterior and a distinctly Spanish look, with an arched porch and smaller arches each side leading to the rear. The Venetian blinds on the big front windows were closed so the sun wouldn't fade the expensive carpets. Sylvia's new car, another mini, this time red, was visible behind the half-raised garage door.

Annie rang the bell, which sounded like Big Ben. No-one answered, so she went through the left arch and tried the side door, which was open. She went inside and called, 'Sylvia? It's me, Annie.'

The kitchen was spacious, nearly three times as big as her own, with marble-topped units and every conceivable modern device. There were a few dishes on the stainless steel draining board waiting to be washed.

Annie went into the hall, which was vast and thickly carpeted in eau-di-nil. There were genuine oil paintings on the walls, but none were as attractive as the Impressionist prints in her own lounge.

'Sylvia,' she called again. Faced with an array of doors, eight altogether, she couldn't remember which led to the main bedroom. She opened one and found a study, opened another and a broom fell out. She jumped back, startled. 'Sylvia!' she yelled.

Music was coming from somewhere, the Beatles' 'We Can Work It Out'. Annie tried another door and peered inside. Sylvia, in a Victorian nightdress, all frills and lace and pleats, was leaning against a heap of pillows reading a magazine and on the point of popping a chocolate into her mouth. She looked up and said casually, 'Hi.' She appeared fit, healthy and entirely at ease.

'Why didn't you answer when I shouted?' Annie said indignantly.

'Because I knew the indefatigable Annie Harrison – sorry, Menin – was bound to track me down.'

Annie blinked, taken aback. Sylvia sounded cold, almost rude. 'I was worried about you,' she stammered. 'I thought I'd come and make sure you were all right.'

'I said I was a bit off-colour, that's all. Thank God I'm not ill, else you'd have hired a helicopter and landed on the lawn.'

'I'd have thought you'd be pleased someone cared enough to come all this way.'

Sylvia said haughtily. 'There's already several people who care, thanks; Cecy, Mrs Church and, of course, my husband.' She pointed to the chocolates. 'The bumpy one is ginger cream, your favourite.'

'No, ta. But I wouldn't mind a cup of tea.'

'You'll have to make it yourself – *I'm* a bit off-colour.'

Annie's hands shook as she got together the tea things. Had she made a terrible mistake? No, not terrible, a *welcome* mistake, but if that was so, why was Sylvia so aggressive, as if she knew Annie had guessed and was resentful. Why was she wearing such a concealing nightdress? Was it to hide all her scars and bruises? Perhaps the best thing would be to have it out with Sylvia, face to face, and see what happened.

She took the tray into the bedroom. 'I want you to do something for me,' she said slowly.

'Anything, Mrs Menin. Name it and it shall be done.'

'I want you to take your nightdress off.'

Sylvia's jaw dropped in astonishment. 'Whoa, Annie! You're showing tendencies I never suspected. Are you going to rape me? The press will love it. You can get Peter Church to defend you. It's his sort of case.'

'Oh, don't be stupid, Sylvia,' Annie said, blushing furiously. 'I want to see if there's any bruises, that's all.'

'Bruises! And why should I have bruises, dear friend?'

Annie didn't answer. Sylvia undid the buttons down the front of her nightgown and pulled it off. She slid the whole thing down to her hips. Annie blushed again.

234

Although they'd lived together for years, she'd never seen Sylvia naked before. She was surprised at how small her breasts were. Sylvia turned round to show her back. The nobbles of her spine were like large white pearls. There wasn't a mark anywhere.

'Are you satisfied? I think you could say my skin is flawless. At least, that's what Eric says, "Sylvia, darling, your skin is flawless."' Annie recoiled at the anger in her eyes. 'I saw the look on your face on Daniel's birthday when you saw my arm. I hurt it in the Grand, by the way, but you immediately thought Eric had done it. I sensed it again in your voice this morning and as soon as I heard you shout I knew why you'd come. What a terribly, terribly wicked thought to have! Incredibly wicked. You've got too much ghoulish imagination. I feel sorry for you, having such wicked thoughts about entirely innocent people. Eric is the dearest husband in the world. We're desperately in love and he would never lay a finger on me.' She was so angry she was almost in tears.

Annie poured the tea and put Sylvia's on the bedside table. 'I only had your best interests at heart,' she said inadequately.

'I'd sooner you didn't in future.'

They drank the tea in silence, Sylvia still smouldering.

'I suppose I'd better go,' said Annie.

'It wouldn't be a bad idea. I'm harbouring the notion of throwing this cup at you once I've finished the tea. I might have thrown the lot, except it would have stained the carpet.'

Annie took the tray into the kitchen and returned to the bedroom. She had one last try. 'Are you sure everything's all right, Syl?'

'Everything is brilliant, Annie. I concede my social life is tedious compared to what it used to be, all the charity functions and dinner parties bore me shitless. I can't help recalling the fun we used to have at dances and the Cavern . . .'

'The Cavern's closed.'

'I know,' Sylvia said sharply, 'and The Beatles went to Buckingham Palace to collect their MBEs. The Mersey Sound is no more. Everything comes to an end eventually, including friendships.'

'I'll be off then.' Annie shuffled her feet uncomfortably. 'If you ever need . . . I mean, if there's ever any trouble, well, we've put Daniel in the spare bedroom, but there's an extra bed in Sara's room.'

'Why, thank you, Annie.' Sylvia's voice was gracious and edged with steel. 'And don't forget either, that there's always room for you and the children when Lauri threatens to bore you all to death.'

Annie gasped. 'That was a *horrible* thing to say!'

'Not quite as horrible as suggesting Eric is a wife-beater.'

'Tara, Sylvia.' Annie turned on her heel.

'Goodbye, Annie.'

Annie had opened the door, when Sylvia shouted, 'Don't call me, I'll call you.'

She waited on the path outside for a good ten minutes, half expecting Sylvia to come hurtling out, crying, 'Come back, Annie. Come back. You were right all the time.'

But she waited in vain. Her legs shook as she walked to the station. It was bad enough that a friendship of more than half a lifetime was over, but the thing was, she didn't believe a word Sylvia had said.

A few weeks later, Sylvia sent a card and a pretty dress on her god-daughter's birthday. Annie thought hard before replying. She wasn't sure if the dress was a peace offering and Sylvia wanted to make up. In the end, she wrote a polite letter of thanks, adding, 'If you're ever passing, do drop in. Sara often asks for Auntie Sylvia.' But Sylvia hadn't dropped in by Christmas, when more presents for the children arrived and an expensive card, signed just, 'Eric and Sylvia.'

The same thing happened next Christmas. The following year, Daniel started playgroup, and later Sara started school. Annie felt her heart contract at the sight of her daughter in her gymslip and too-big blazer.

Lauri, the most understanding husband in the world, took a rare day off on Sara's first day. He knew Annie would be upset, alone in the house for the first time in five years. 'Let's do something exciting,' he suggested. 'We have three hours before it's time to collect Daniel.'

'Such as?' Annie couldn't think of anything exciting you could do for three hours on a Tuesday morning.

Lauri put his hands on his hips and glanced thoughtfully around the room. 'I've been thinking, I'm fed up with pink walls. Let's buy some wallpaper! I fancy a geometric design, something ultra-fashionable that will drive the Cunninghams wild.'

'What a good idea,' said Annie. At that particular moment, nothing seemed less exciting than picking wallpaper.

Lauri went to get the car ready, and she glanced at the telephone. What she'd *really* like was a good laugh with Sylvia. It was two years to the day, to the minute, since she'd called and Sylvia said she felt a bit off-colour. She'd never told anyone, not even Lauri, how much she missed her friend.

Impulsively, she picked up the phone and dialled the Churches' number. She could still remember it by heart. No-one had answered by the time Lauri came back. She put the receiver down, feeling guilty for some reason.

'Who are you calling?' he asked.

'It rang,' she lied, 'but when I picked it up there was no-one there.' She supposed that was partially true.

They got in the car. Lauri was putting on weight. She was feeding him too well, he claimed when he couldn't fasten his trousers. 'I must adjust this seat one of these days.' He had trouble sliding behind the wheel. Annie leaned over and kissed him. 'What's that for?' he smiled.

'Because I love you,' she said. 'I love you with all my heart.'

Choosing wallpaper for the lounge was definitely not exciting, but the message, the reason, the meaning behind it, was. Loving someone, and that person loving you back, was the most exciting thing in the world.

3

Mike Gallagher got married on New Year's Day, 1969, but his poor mam was driven to despair beforehand. Dot wasn't sure which was worst: a register office ceremony which meant the union wouldn't be recognised in the eyes of God; the fact the bride, Glenda, was a widow, five years older than the groom, with two teenaged children; or the outfits the couple had planned.

'He's getting married in *cowboy* boots, Annie!' Dot fanned herself frantically with a newspaper. 'Cowboy boots and a leather jacket covered in fringes. I said, "At least you could get your hair cut, luv. You look like Diana Dors", but he told me, his own mother, to get stuffed.'

Mike had a glorious head of ginger hair which fell on his shoulders in lovely little ringlets and waves. Annie thought it very attractive, particularly with his gold earrings. Most young men had long hair, but Mike's was particularly outstanding. 'Lots of the girls at the English Electric had a crush on your Mike,' she said.

Dot patted her own hair self-consciously. It was more silver than ginger nowadays. 'Folks always said our Mike took after me. Mind you, I'm not sorry he's settling down. After all, he's nearly thirty-two. An unmarried man with earrings and hair like that might set tongues wagging, but not to that Glenda woman with two grown kids.'

'I quite like her.' Glenda had been a widow for ten years. She was small and plain, but had a lovely warm smile that made her look quite beautiful and you quickly realised why Mike had fallen in love. Her children, Kathy and Paul, were a credit to her.

'What are they going to live on, I'd like to know – fresh air?' Dot demanded aggressively, as if Annie could provide the answer. 'The kids are still at school, Glenda earns peanuts in that factory, and our Mike's job wasn't up to much, but at least there was a wage coming in.'

For the second time, Mike had thrown in his job to tread into the unknown. Along with a member of his failed pop group, Ray Walters, he had started Michael Ray Engineering & Electrical Services, with the intention of repairing vintage cars from a rundown shed on Kirkby Trading Estate. 'Never,' Dot said, in a flutter, 'did I envisage having a son with headed notepaper.'

She was in a worse flutter now. 'You should see Glenda's wedding dress. It's one of those mini things that hardly covers her arse. Oh,' she groaned tragically, 'I hope none of the neighbours come to that heathen register office. They'll think they're watching a circus, not a bloody wedding.'

'Actually, Auntie Dot, I'm making myself a mini dress for the wedding.'

'Where does it end?' Dot asked suspiciously.

Annie touched halfway down her thigh. 'There.'

'I hope it covers your suspenders.'

'Oh, Dot, I'll be wearing tights, won't I?' Tights were probably the greatest invention known to man – to woman. It was great to be able to do away with suspender belts and not have big red indentations on your legs when you got undressed.

'You'll never catch me in a pair of them tights,' Dot said, tight-lipped. 'I think they're disgusting.'

Lauri thought the red mini dress looked very nice when it was finished and Annie twirled around for his approval. The children were in bed and it was okay to use the sewing machine. Daniel watched, fascinated, as the needle flashed up and down, and it wasn't safe to use it when he was around.

'I'm not showing too much leg, am I?' she asked anxiously.

He regarded her thoughtfully. 'I reckon that's just enough. One inch higher and it would look indecent, an inch lower would be dowdy.'

'Are you making fun of me?'

'As if I would! I know hemlines are a very serious matter.'

'You don't think me legs are too fat?' She was fishing for compliments and he knew it. He grinned. 'You've got perfect legs, Annie.'

'You don't mind other men looking at them?'

'As long as they just look, why should I mind?'

Annie smiled with satisfaction. It was just the right answer. She looked in the mirror and said. 'I wouldn't mind having me hair cut very short.' She still wore it in the same style as she'd done all her life, which wasn't really a style at all.

Lauri murmured, 'You know I prefer it long.'

'It's *my* hair!' she pouted.

He looked at her, amused. 'No-one's arguing over the ownership of your hair, love. It's just that you asked my opinion on your frock, so I thought you'd like it on your hair.'

She threw herself onto his knee. 'Am I getting on your nerves?' Perhaps it was the frock, but at the moment, she felt more like a teenager than a woman of twenty-seven with two children.

He stroked her cheek. 'I like it when you act like a little girl.'

Annie fingered his moustache. 'Why don't you let it grow, Zapata style?' He'd already refused to grow his hair, saying he would look ridiculous at his age.

'I like my moustache the way it is.'

'Why is it I leave my hair long for you, but you won't grow your moustache for me?' She pretended to look hurt.

'For the same reason we have flowered wallpaper instead of geometric which I preferred. The wallpaper wasn't important, my moustache is. If it's important that you have your hair short, Annie, then get it cut.'

Lauri always talked the most astonishing common sense, which was probably one of the reasons they didn't have rows like the Cunninghams. In fact, they never rowed at all.

She decided to leave her hair alone.

Annie came hurrying home, having deposited Sara at school and Daniel at playgroup. Daniel was pleading to go five days a week instead of three. Perhaps next term . . .

She worked out her programme for the morning. The beds were already made, the breakfast dishes washed. Friday was the day she cleaned the fridge and vacuumed upstairs. After that, she'd make some gingerbread men and prepare a boiled fruitcake. One of the neighbours might pop in for coffee. She hoped it wouldn't be someone who'd stay long, as she wanted to get on with Sara's dressing gown. Sara was shooting up; that blazer was unlikely to last till she was seven.

It was March and appropriately windy. Old dried leaves whipped against her legs and skipped across the Close to become entangled in the tall hedge which bordered the Travers' front garden. The old couple were gradually being buried within a cultivated jungle of towering trees and shrubs. Later on, Mr Travers would emerge, remove the leaves and glare accusingly down the Close. Last autumn, he had swept up every single one of his leaves for his compost heap and resented those from less conscientious gardeners encroaching on his property.

Inside, the house was beautifully warm, since they'd had central heating installed. Annie checked the boiler in the kitchen for no other reason than she liked seeing the pilot light flickering behind the glass door. Daniel was convinced a fairy lived inside who lit the flame each morning to cook her breakfast, and put it out when she went to bed.

The fridge cleaned, Annie wiped the draining board with a sigh of satisfaction, and was about to take the vacuum cleaner upstairs when the doorbell rang.

She tut-tutted to herself and straightened her pinny before opening the door. Sylvia, startling in a short white fluffy coat over a brief black frock and thigh-length patent leather boots, stood posing on the doorstep like a model in a magazine. She wore sunglasses and a big black floppy hat with a white feather. 'Hi, Annie,' she sang, as if it were only yesterday they'd last met, not two and a half years ago.

'Come in,' Annie stammered.

Sylvia sailed into the lounge and parked herself on the settee. Annie stood awkwardly in the doorway. 'Would you like a coffee?'

'Please. No milk, no sugar,' she added, as if Annie didn't know.

When Annie returned with two mugs of coffee, Sylvia had removed her hat and sunglasses and was staring around the room with interest. 'I see you've got new wallpaper,' she remarked.

The wallpaper was misty pearly beige with a pattern of shadowy poppies. Annie still couldn't get over how different the room looked after plain pink walls for so many years. 'Lauri wanted something more regular, like squares or triangles, but I preferred flowers.'

'I bet that was a serious topic of conversation in the Menin household for at least a month.'

Annie plonked the mugs on the coffee table with such force that the liquid spurted out onto the varnished surface. 'Is that why you've come after all this time,' she snapped, 'to make nasty comments?'

Sylvia looked unabashed. 'I just came to see how you were.'

'I was fine until you arrived.'

'How are Lauri and the children?' Sylvia took an embroidered hankie out of her pocket and wiped the coffee up.

'Very well, ta.' Annie had been considering telling Sylvia to get lost, but felt slightly mollified by the gesture of concern for her coffee table. 'Sara loves school, and Daniel's settled in playgroup. They've both had mumps and German measles, but got over it all right. Lauri's put on a bit of weight, but otherwise he's fine. How's Eric?'

'Eric!' Sylvia's blue eyes shone brilliantly. 'Eric's doing ever so well. He has cases on his own nowadays. People say that he'll turn out to be even more successful than his father.'

'Good,' said Annie. 'And yourself?'

Sylvia tossed her blonde head proudly. 'Tip-top.

243

Never felt better, but I can see it's a waste of time asking how *you* are, Annie. You look very much the contented *hausfrau* with your pinny and new wallpaper.'

'I think you'd better go,' said Annie.

'But I haven't finished my coffee!' Sylvia raised her perfect eyebrows and pretended to look outraged.

'Well, finish it, then go.'

'If you insist.' Sylvia sighed and began to sip the coffee slowly.

Annie ignored her own coffee. Her head was in a whirl. What had happened? Sylvia had been her greatest and closest friend. They had sworn to let nothing come between them. Perhaps it was she who'd pushed in the wedge by suggesting Eric . . . How would she have reacted if Sylvia had accused Lauri of doing something far worse than being merely boring?

She opened her mouth to speak, to say she was sorry for what she'd said about Eric, and dammit, Sylvia, we're friends. We promised to be friends for ever. I've missed you more than I can say over the last few years. There's no-one I can talk to the way I talked to you. You're the only person I can tell *really* intimate things, like I'd love to go to bed with Warren Beatty. Remember when we used to disappear into the Ladies for a laugh because we were the only ones who found a situation funny when everyone else thought it deadly serious?

Sylvia swallowed the coffee and reached for her hat and sunglasses. 'Thanks for the refreshments, Mrs Menin.'

The moment was lost. They went into the hallway. Sylvia put her hand on the latch and gave Annie a dazzling smile. 'It's cheerio, then, or "tara" as you would say.'

Annie nodded. 'Tara.'

But she couldn't let Sylvia walk out of her life,

because this time she knew it would be final. She took a step forward, 'Syl!'

Sylvia didn't hear. She turned the latch, then suddenly her body seemed to crumple and she leant her forehead against the door and twisted her lovely face towards her friend. 'Jaysus, Annie,' she whispered, 'I'm so bloody miserable, I could easily *die*.'

Eric hated her because she hadn't given him a child. He wouldn't mind if it was a girl, because girls can become lawyers and everybody knew it was the father who influenced the sex of their children. By now, the whole family hated her because she'd let them down. And the more they hated her, the more ridiculously she behaved because it was the only way she knew to fight back, otherwise she would become cowed.

'I wear the most ludicrous outfits, Annie. Mrs Church winced when I turned up to Mass last Sunday in this hat. I get pissed and tell dirty jokes in a very loud voice at dinner parties and generally make a show of myself.' Sylvia gave a terse laugh. 'Actually, shocking people can be fun, but it only makes Eric hate me even more.'

'Oh, Syl!' Annie said sadly.

They had returned to the lounge and were sitting on the settee. Annie was holding her friend's hand. Sylvia hadn't cried, but her eyes were unnaturally bright, and there were tense lines around her jaw. Her grip on Annie's hand was so tight it hurt.

'Have you seen a doctor about why you can't conceive?'

'I've seen a specialist, no less, but he could find nothing wrong. He said I should relax, stop thinking about it all the time.' She gripped Annie's hand even harder. 'As if I could! Every time I start a period I feel physically sick.'

'It might be Eric's fault,' Annie suggested.

Sylvia pretended to look astonished. 'I hope you're not insinuating that a Church is not totally perfect!'

'Sorry, I didn't realise it was a crime.'

'Well, it is,' Sylvia said matter-of-factly. 'I once suggested that Eric see a doctor same as me. He was pouring tea out at the time and decided to pour it on my legs – it was the morning you came to see me. You didn't ask to see my legs, did you?' Sylvia released her hand. She got up and began to walk to and fro in front of the fireplace. 'You were right, Annie. Eric was responsible for the bruise on my arm. He doesn't hit me often and I give back as good as I get, but oh, God, if you knew how much I loathed you for guessing.' She glanced at Annie curiously. 'You never liked him, did you?'

'I thought he looked cruel.'

'The thing is, Annie, the terrible thing is, I love him.' She went over to the French windows and stared out. The fence between the Menins' and the Cunninghams' creaked in the wind and the willow tree shivered delicately. 'You'll never believe this, but Eric loves me back. He hates me and he loves me. Making love is heaven, but that's all that's left, making love. Everything else is shit.'

Annie found it all beyond her comprehension. 'If Lauri laid a finger on me, I'd walk out and never come back.'

'Perhaps you don't love him enough.'

'I think it's just a different sort of love.' She had no intention of getting cross. 'I understand why you were so angry when I came storming over to Birkdale. With me and Lauri getting on so famously, it must have made you feel lousy . . .'

'Oh, for Chrissakes, Annie!' Sylvia said savagely. 'I'd sooner be married to Eric any day than Lauri. I wouldn't marry Lauri Menin for a million pounds.'

Annie felt as if a fist had curled up in her stomach. 'That's stupid!' she said weakly. Rising from the settee, she went to the window at the front of the room. She noticed a gold mini parked outside.

'Jaysus, these boots are killing me.' Sylvia undid the long zips and kicked the boots off. 'Is there anything to drink?'

'There's sherry in the kitchen from Christmas.'

'That'll do. A large one, treble or quadruple or bigger.'

Annie poured herself half a tumbler of sherry at the same time. She was anxious for Sylvia to continue, even though she wouldn't like what she had to say. 'That's stupid,' she repeated, returning to the lounge.

Sylvia had settled crosslegged on the hearth. 'Oh, Annie, as if I'd resent you being happy just because I wasn't! What a trite person you must think I am! I love you, in the way I'd love a sister.' She swallowed half the sherry in one go. 'No, what got up my nose was you feeling sorry for me, and at the same time thinking you and Lauri were blissfully happy, when you're not. Well, Lauri may be, but not you.'

'You're talking nonsense,' Annie said doggedly. 'We couldn't possibly get on better. We never fight. He lets me do anything I want.'

'*Lets* you!' Sylvia raised her eyebrows. 'Marriage is a partnership. One half doesn't give the other permission to do things.'

Annie frowned irritably. 'I didn't mean it to sound like that.'

'Why haven't you got four children, Annie? Four's what you planned.'

'Well, Lauri thought . . .'

Sylvia interrupted. 'And if I remember rightly, you wanted another baby straight after Sara, not to wait nearly two years.'

'Lauri . . .' Annie began, but Sylvia seemed determined not to let her finish a sentence.

247

'Remember when we used to plan our grand weddings?' she said reflectively. 'When I married Eric I wore the dress I'd always wanted, but I can't recall you wanting that ghastly thing you wore in front of about half a dozen guests. As for my red suit, I gave it away.'

'Grand weddings don't come cheap,' Annie said weakly.

'Cecy offered to do the reception. Uncle Bert wanted to help.'

'Lauri didn't want charity,' Annie muttered.

'It wouldn't have been charity. Cecy thinks of you as a daughter, but Lauri wanted a small wedding to his child-bride and Lauri got his way, just as he gets his way on all the really important things.'

Without realising, Annie had drunk all her sherry. She stumbled to the settee, feeling light headed. 'Why are we discussing my marriage, when it's yours that's failed?' she enquired.

Sylvia leaned forward, her face screwed up with the effort of trying to explain. 'Because you're suffocating, Annie. It's time you snapped out of this eager-to-please, obedient-little-wife shit and became the sparkling, witty, intelligent Annie I used to know. I find it incredible you and Lauri have never had a fight. You must never talk about anything remotely controversial if you don't row from time to time.'

'Lauri . . .' Annie paused. 'I suppose it's me own fault. I give in too easily.' She resented the admission there could be something wrong.

'It's about time your husband knew he was married to someone with firm opinions and a temper.'

'I'm not sure what you mean,' Annie said faintly.

'I'm not sure myself. All I know is, since you married Lauri you've become a zombie.'

Annie giggled. 'I think you're exaggerating, Syl.'

'Is there any more sherry?'

'It's in the cupboard next to the fridge.'

Sylvia came back with the bottle and refilled their glasses.

'Why did you come?' asked Annie.

'Because Eric was particularly vile this morning and I desperately wanted to talk to someone.' She returned to her place on the rug. 'There was only one person. I've missed you awfully these last few years.'

'I've missed you.'

Sylvia smiled. 'But I wasn't prepared to have you dripping sympathy all over me. I thought it was time you knew the truth about yourself.'

'That's kind of you, I must say,' Annie said caustically. 'Your own marriage is up the creek, so you're trying to convince me mine is too!'

'It's not that. I was fed up watching you kowtow to Lauri all the time. You'd think he was your father, not your husband.'

Annie's head was swimming too much to get annoyed. She lay down on the settee and mumbled, 'Oh, bugger off, Syl.'

'Jaysus, Annie,' Sylvia sighed pleasurably. 'I'm pissed out of my mind.' She put down her glass and fell back full length on the rug.

'Where do we go from here?' Annie said carefully.

'From here? Once I'm sober, I'm going to Liverpool to buy a frock I saw in a boutique for tonight's dinner party, a truly cute little purple number made entirely of fringes. It's the sort they used to do some dance in during the 1920s. I can't remember what it's called, the dance, I mean.'

'The Charleston.'

'That's right.'

'Mike Gallagher got married on New Year's Day in a leather jacket covered with fringes.'

Sylvia raised her head, dismayed. 'Mike's married?'

'Auntie Dot nearly did her nut, but I thought he looked fab.'

'Wow! I never told you this, Annie, but when we saw Mike in the Cavern, I thought he looked fantastic with that gorgeous hair, like Henry the Fifth. I was sorry I dumped him all those years ago.'

Annie hiccupped. 'Well, it's too late now, you've lost him.'

'Shit!' Sylvia beat the rug with her fist in mock chagrin. 'I thought, if I ever left Eric, I could have Mike.'

'Are you likely to leave him?' Annie tried to look deadly serious.

'It's inevitable. One of these days, the sex will wear off and we'll hate each other completely. Of course we can't get divorced, his family would never stand for it.' She put her hands behind her neck, stared at the ceiling, and said reflectively, 'I might become a nun.'

'In your purple frock with fringes?' Annie laughed.

'I'll start a new order; the Little Sisters of Rock and Roll. We'll chant Beatles' songs and worship at the shrine of Paul McCartney.'

'Not John Lennon?'

'No. He was at Art College before me, but nobody liked him.' Sylvia suddenly sat up and cried, 'Oh, Annie! Why are we both so miserable?'

'Believe it or not, Syl,' Annie said slowly, 'I don't feel the least bit miserable, despite you saying I should be.'

'That's because your brain has turned to cotton wool.'

'Then perhaps everyone should have cotton wool for brains and the world would be a happier place.'

The back door opened and Valerie Cunningham called, 'Annie, are you there?' She came into the room with Daniel. 'You didn't turn up at playgroup, so I thought I'd better bring him home.'

She'd actually forgotten to collect her son! Annie made a brave attempt to sit up, but fell back with a groan. 'Jaysus, me head!'

'Hello, Sylvia,' Valerie said brightly. 'It's ages since I've seen you.' She made them both black coffee. 'This is a turn-up for the books,' she remarked. 'I never thought I'd find Annie Menin as drunk as a lord at this time of the day.'

Annie still had a hangover when Lauri came home. He was amused and didn't mind there was no meal ready. She didn't mention she'd forgotten to pick up Daniel, an awfully negligent thing to do. She'd feel guilty when the hangover wore off. Sylvia had gone to Liverpool by taxi, because she was too drunk to drive. She was coming back for her car.

Lauri was peeling the potatoes, because his wife had forgotten how to use the peeler, when Sylvia came bursting through the back door. She pulled off her white fur coat and threw it on the floor.

'What d'you think?' she cried, wiggling her hips.

Annie blinked as the brief purple dress shimmered. She blinked again at the violent purple and black striped tights. Sylvia also had a black velvet band around her forehead with a jewel in the centre.

'You look . . .' Annie searched for words, ' . . . truly ghastly.'

'Good!' Sylvia smacked her lips.

'Are you going to a fancy dress?' Lauri asked innocently.

'No, I'm going to play charades with Eric.'

She only stayed long enough to re-introduce herself to Sara and remark how incredibly tall she'd grown. The little girl turned out to have never forgotten her Auntie Sylvia. Then she departed in a cloud of expensive perfume and a final shimmy of her purple frock.

Annie watched the gold mini drive away. She returned to the kitchen, where Lauri said, 'I'm glad you two have made up, but is Sylvia all right? She looked rather manic to me.'

'She's desperately unhappy. I'll tell you about it later.' Daniel clung to her legs demanding a story. Sara was patiently waiting in the armchair, her favourite Noddy book on her knee.

'You read to them, love,' Lauri said. 'I'll do the sausages.'

'Are you sure you don't mind?' Annie asked anxiously. 'I've been a terrible housewife today.'

He kissed her. 'It does no harm to go off the rails occasionally.'

Annie squeezed into the armchair with the children. This was her favourite time of the day; her husband home and two little bodies snuggled against hers. Lauri was singing something tuneless in the kitchen. He was a husband in a million – Kevin Cunningham would raise the roof if he came home and found Valerie with a hangover. But was it enough to be married to someone prepared to cook sausages and let you pick the wallpaper, yet who put his foot down when it came to really vital things like having children? Kevin wouldn't make the dinner, but he and Valerie had a joint bank account and she could write cheques whenever she pleased. Annie had no idea how much money was in the bank and Lauri had laughed, as if it were a big joke, when she suggested *they* had a joint account, just as he'd laughed when she'd asked if, like Valerie, she could take driving lessons.

If it wasn't for him, they'd have four children, Joshua and Sophie, as well as Sara and Daniel. Sara mightn't be so withdrawn if she had a sister or brother close in age, but Lauri had insisted they wait. He claimed she would be 'overworked' with two small babies.

'If Valerie can manage, so can I,' Annie argued at the time.

'But Valerie doesn't manage, does she, love? I don't want to come home every night and find you exhausted.'

'But it's *me* who would have been exhausted,' Annie thought, several years too late. Could it be that Lauri was selfish, that he didn't want the smooth running of his home disrupted by too many children and an exhausted wife?

'You've lost your place, Mummy,' Sara said accusingly. 'You've missed out where Noddy crashes his car.' She knew the book off by heart.

'Sorry, sweetheart. I was miles away. Where am I up to?'

By the time she'd finished, Annie decided, because it seemed the safest thing to do, that Sylvia had been talking nonsense. Just because *her* marriage was a mess, she had no right to suggest there was something wrong with Annie's.

'Bloody cheek!' she murmured.

'You've gone wrong again, Mummy. That bit's not in.'

It was June, and something of vital importance was happening in the Labour Party. People kept ringing up to speak to Lauri. One night, several members, including Uncle Bert, came to the house. They stayed in the breakfast room all evening, arguing furiously. Lauri argued loudest, and it was strange to hear his normally pleasant voice raised in anger. At one point, he came into the lounge and asked Annie if she would kindly make them a cup of tea.

'I don't know how you stand living with this man, luv,' Uncle Bert said jocularly as he was leaving. 'I bet you're fed up having politics pushed down your throat the whole time.'

Annie smiled politely. People had said more or less the same thing before, but Lauri scarcely mentioned politics at home. 'What was the meeting about?' she asked when everyone had gone.

'Nothing, love,' he said absently.

It was a national issue, she'd gathered that much. Harold Wilson, the Prime Minister, had been mentioned. She started to watch 24 *Hours* on television when Lauri was out, and bought the *Daily Telegraph* several times. There were some weighty articles that gave her the facts.

She hadn't realised there was such high unemployment in the country – the highest since the war. Prices were rising, wage demands soaring out of control. The Employment Minister, a woman called Barbara Castle, was trying to push through a White Paper called *In Place of Strife*, to curb the power of the unions, but the Trades Union Congress and the left wing of the Labour Party were totally opposed.

A few days later, Uncle Bert and the same crowd turned up again just after Sara and Daniel had gone to bed. Annie left the lounge door open and listened. She gathered they were opposed to *In Place of Strife* and were drawing up a resolution to send to Transport House for the eyes of the Prime Minister himself. She was impressed.

'How does this sound?' said a voice, 'The Party is letting down the entire Trade Union movement with the proposed White Paper and . . .'

'Not letting down, betraying,' said Lauri. 'And point out the Labour Party grew out of the Trade Unions.'

Annie was innocently watching *The Avengers* when Lauri poked his head around the door and asked if she would make tea.

The tea served, they returned to their resolution. Annie hung round, wondering if she could bring herself to stick her oar in and ask what the Trade Unions intended doing about the really poor people; the ones who worked in very low-paid jobs and didn't have a union, or had no power to strike, like nurses. Did the unions care about the people who didn't have a job at all? And what about women? What had the transport union done to help the woman who'd become a bus driver and had been forced to quit by the other drivers, all men?

Lauri looked up and said, 'Did you want something, Annie?'

Her courage failed. 'I . . . er, would you like some biscuits?'

'Not for me, luv,' said Uncle Bert. The others were too involved with the resolution to notice that she'd spoken, just as they'd been too involved to thank her for the tea.

The meeting dispersed and everyone went home. Lauri came into the lounge rubbing his hands with satisfaction. 'Did you finish the resolution?' enquired Annie.

'Yes, love. Dan's having it typed.'

'Lauri,' she said eagerly. 'If I had a typewriter, a portable one, I could type things for you. Not only that,' she had an even more brilliant idea, 'if I went to meetings, I could take the minutes down in shorthand. I'm sure I'd get my speed back in no time.'

Lauri passed the back of the settee where she was sitting and ruffled her hair. 'No thank you, love. We don't want your pretty little head bothered with politics.'

Annie's brain must have turned to cotton wool. It took an age for the words and all that lay behind them to sink in. Her husband was deep in a newspaper when she said furiously, 'How *dare* you say that!'

He stared at her, mildly astonished, 'Say what, love?'

'How dare you suggest I'm too dim to be bothered with politics?'

'I never suggested any such thing. You've never shown the least interest, that's all.' He shrugged and returned to the paper.

Annie snatched the paper off him and flung it to the floor. 'That's because I haven't had the opportunity. All we talk about is wallpaper and children and what flowers to plant.'

Lauri was getting agitated. 'This isn't a bit like you, Annie. What's got into you tonight?'

Annie glared at him. 'Why couldn't *I* be at that meeting?'

'Because you're not a member of the Party,' he said easily. He tried to put an arm around her shoulders, but she moved out of his reach. 'Anyway, you hadn't the faintest idea what it was about.'

'I know exactly what it was about,' she said cuttingly. 'Barbara Castle's *In Place of Strife*, which I thoroughly approve of. The country will never get back on its feet if we give in to the unions.'

Lauri groaned. 'That, Annie, is a perfect example of why I have never wanted to bring politics into my home. Nothing is more divisive.' He looked at her beseechingly and for once there was no suggestion of a twinkle in his brown eyes. In fact, everything about him was different, not just his eyes, but the expression on his face, the way he spoke, his gestures. With a shock, she realised for the first time he was addressing her as an adult, not a young girl. He continued, 'I totally disagree with what you just said – people nearly came to blows over that very thing at the last ward meeting.'

'Why do you go, then, if it's so awful?' Annie sneered.

Lauri winced. 'It's not awful, I love it. But I like to leave it all behind when I close the front door. Here, this room, this house, is my sanctuary, the place where I expect peace and quiet, not violent arguments about politics.'

Then Annie understood what Sylvia always had, that behind his charming, easy-going persona, Lauri Menin was a very selfish man.

'In other words,' she said quietly, 'your wife must never bother her pretty little head over anything that might disturb your peace and quiet.' She resisted the urge to bring up the children she'd wanted, Joshua and Sophie, children who'd never been born for the sake of his peace and quiet. Perhaps some things were best left unsaid, otherwise the words would create a barrier that might never be breached. Suddenly, without warning, she resented he was so much older and settled in his ways. Dot said marriage was an adventure and Annie wondered what it would be like to be married to someone her own age, because nothing about her marriage had been adventurous. It had been safe, comfortable, secure, the things she'd wanted once, but wasn't sure if she wanted now.

The thought seemed so traitorous that it almost took her breath away. She was conscious there'd been silence for quite some time and she glanced across the room at her husband.

Lauri looked poleaxed. He had his hands on his stomach and his mouth slightly open as if someone had just delivered a terrible blow. Despite everything, Annie felt a pang of love that almost hurt, and with it came the awareness that things had changed; not massively, perhaps not even noticeably, but life would be slightly different from now on. Lauri might never be aware of it, but a barrier had been erected after all. Only a tiny one, but a barrier all the same.

Their eyes met. He said brokenly, 'I never dreamt you were unhappy.'

'I'm not unhappy.'

He held out his arms and she went to him. 'All I've ever wanted is for you to be happy.'

Annie knew that wasn't true, or there would be four children sleeping upstairs, but no doubt Lauri meant the words sincerely.

They never referred to the row again. A card came from the Labour Party. She was a member, though she never went to a meeting. Nor did she bring up the subject of more children. She'd wanted them close together, not years and years apart, so it was too late.

Two weeks later, men landed on the moon and Neil Armstrong took 'one small step for man, but one giant leap for mankind', and the whole affair of Lauri and the Labour Party seemed rather trite.

4

The August sun beat mercilessly down out of a lustrous blue and cloudless sky. The gardens of Heather Close were at their peak, bursting with flowers and bushes in full bloom. As the years passed, the creamy bricks were gradually turning golden brown. The children were on holiday; their voices could be heard, slightly muffled in the thick, humid air, as they played in the back gardens. A dog chased butterflies, barking in frustration, and birds sang joyfully in the trees.

On such a glorious day, no-one was prepared for the hearse, followed by a single black car, which drove slowly into the cul-de-sac and stopped at number six, the Travers'.

In Bootle, a crowd would have gathered. Here, there was an agitated twitch of net curtains. The Travers' had always kept very much to themselves. There was no coffin in the hearse, yet no-one was aware a coffin had been delivered, that death had visited Heather Close for the first time.

Annie made the Sign of the Cross when she saw a coffin carried by four pall-bearers emerge from behind the tall hedge that hid the old couple from the world. Then Mrs Travers followed, alone. She was dressed entirely in black and her face was hidden behind a heavy veil. The coffin with its single wreath was carefully stowed into the back of the hearse, and the miniature procession drove away.

'Did you see that, Annie?' Valerie Cunningham shouted.

Annie hurried into the back garden, relieved to have someone to talk to. There had been something inherently depressing about the scene: not so much the death of a very old person, but the fact it had occurred without anyone knowing. Mrs Travers must have been alone with the dead body of her husband for several days.

Valerie was leaning on the fence. She looked upset. 'They mustn't have any children.'

'Or relatives.'

'Or friends.'

'They didn't want friends,' Annie said. 'I tried talking to them over the years, but they always snubbed me.'

'I mean, I would have sent a wreath if I'd known.'

They stayed talking, anxious for company on a morning when death had cast its shadow over their comfortable and more or less contented lives.

'Just think, Annie,' Valerie said soberly. 'One of these days, we'll be as old as the Travers'. Either that, or we'll be dead.'

Annie shivered. 'I'm not sure which I'd prefer.'

They decided to call on Mrs Travers that night and offer their condolences. After a while, Valerie went indoors. She'd bought a new cookery book and wanted to make something nice for Kevin's tea.

The Cunninghams rarely rowed these days. They had sown their wild oats early and emerged unscathed, so Valerie claimed. Years ago, Kevin had confessed to an affair. 'It was when I was pregnant with Tracy,' she confided. 'He felt weighed down by the responsibility. It made him feel young again.' He refused to name the woman, said it was someone Valerie didn't know. 'I was so hopping mad, I had an affair myself with this nauseating chap from the TV rental shop. Kevin blew his top when he found out. But everything's all right now,' she added complacently. 'In fact, our marriage is stronger after all the ups and downs.'

When Valerie had gone, Annie sat on the patio and watched the children play. Sara was idly pushing herself to and fro on the swing Lauri had recently made, and Daniel was sitting in the plastic paddling pool playing with a blow-up boat, a bit half-heartedly, she thought. She hoped it was the heat and he wasn't coming down with something.

There'd been no ups and downs in the Menins' marriage, nothing to make it stronger. There was no way she could bring herself to be unfaithful to Lauri. It would show on her face, and she'd give the game away if she had to tell lies. She was no good at lies, apart from little white ones. Anyroad, not a single man had made anything remotely like a pass since she got married, so who would she have an affair with?

How could it be, she wondered, that you could love someone as thoroughly as she loved Lauri, yet be so . . . Annie searched in her mind for how she felt; not exactly fed up, not exactly bored, not really unhappy, maybe a bit of all these things. Last year, the Cunninghams had dumped their progeny on Valerie's mother and gone on holiday to Paris. Next month, they were off to Spain, this time taking the children with them. Other families in the close took holidays.

But when the children broke up last month and she suggested the Menins went away, Lauri protested they couldn't afford it. 'It could cost hundreds, love, and you know work's been dropping off.'

This was true. Inflation was soaring upwards in a dizzy spiral. With prices rising, people were reluctant to buy a new house and building firms were closing. Lauri had been working shorter and shorter hours.

'We could hire a tent and go camping,' she suggested hopefully. 'The Shepherds in number two go camping every year to this lovely site in North Wales. It wouldn't cost much more than staying at home.'

According to Connie Shepherd, it was really back to nature. The site was on a farm with only half a dozen tents. First thing each morning, they would cross the wet fields to buy fresh milk and eggs from the farmhouse. On fine days, they ate outdoors. The children loved exploring the Welsh woods and valleys, playing in streams and catching tadpoles.

'What happens when it's raining?' Lauri asked.

'You can still go walking in the rain.' Annie lifted her head and could almost feel the clean, invigorating rain falling on her face. 'Oh, it would be lovely! Sara and Daniel would have the time of their lives.'

'Quite honestly, love, it's not my cup of tea. When I'm off, we can go to New Brighton or Southport for the day, as we've always done.'

She couldn't very well put her foot down. You couldn't *force* someone to take a holiday they didn't want. She said, 'When Daniel starts school a year from now, I'll look for a part-time job. Then we can have a proper holiday.'

He shook his head emphatically. 'I don't want you working, Annie. You've enough to do, what with the house and the children.'

'*I'm* the one to judge what I can and can't do, Lauri,'

she said sharply. 'I'm quite capable of doing a part-time job and looking after things. It won't inconvenience you at all.'

'I wasn't thinking of myself, love. I just don't want you taking on too much.' His voice was pleasant. He never lost his temper.

But Annie knew he was thinking solely of himself. There was nothing vindictive about it, not like with Eric. Without realising it, he wanted his wife to be dependent on him. Maybe it was why he'd refused to let her learn to drive, though when she threatened to use the housekeeping for lessons, he'd agreed. She was down to take the test in December.

She said no more, though was inwardly simmering, when Lauri redeemed himself completely. 'I've been thinking, why don't you go to London for a weekend with Marie?' he said. 'You haven't been since we got married and it's ages since you've seen her.'

'You mean, by meself?' Annie gasped.

'Well, it wouldn't be much good with the children! I can manage them on my own for a few days. Dot will lend a hand if necessary.'

'Oh, Lauri!' She didn't throw herself into his arms as she would have done once, because of the invisible barrier that had been erected. 'Oh, Lauri,' she said again, 'that would be the gear.'

From the Travers' garden, the sound of clippers could be heard.

She's back! God, she must feel terrible!

But Mrs Travers was dry-eyed when the women called that night to express their sympathy. She didn't even ask them in.

'Thank you,' she said coldly. Her parchment-coloured face was a cobweb of deeply etched wrinkles. Through the door, an umbrella stand made from an elephant's foot could be seen, and there were ugly wooden masks on the wall. She closed the door in their faces.

'Well, what do you make of that!' Valerie remarked indignantly.

'I don't know,' Annie said slowly. 'I really don't know.'

A week later, Chris Andrews called. He still taught at Grenville Lucas, and Annie found it incredible that she'd once regarded him as old. At thirty-four, he was only a few years older than herself. Lottie had left him the previous year, and for a while he was devastated, but pulled himself together with a vengeance. He lost weight, had contact lenses fitted and grew a pigtail – Annie showed him how to plait it. He wore flared trousers, embroidered waistcoats and Indian shirts. The current fashion of platform soles added to his height. The transformation was amply rewarded when a procession of glamorous young women started to descend upon his house, some quite brazenly staying the night.

'If Lottie could see you now, she'd be back like a shot,' Annie told him admiringly, but Chris said he didn't want her.

He hadn't come on a social visit. His house adjoined the Travers' and there'd been no sound, nothing, for the past two days. He'd knocked and there'd been no reply, but even when the old man was alive, the Travers' had not always answered. He wanted to know if Annie had seen Mrs Travers in the garden.

'You can't see much for the trees, but now I think about it, I haven't heard her, either.' Annie panicked. 'I hope she's all right.'

'Why don't you call the police?' Lauri suggested.

'I'll take a look around first.'

Lauri went with him. He told Annie afterwards that

they looked through the windows and the letterbox, but could see nothing, so went round the back. Mrs Travers was sitting upright on a rustic bench in the garden. She had a pruner in one hand and a single red rose in the other. According to the doctor, she had been dead for two days.

An ambulance came and the body was removed. Nothing was heard about a funeral. Later, a van arrived and removed the foreign-looking furniture and a 'For Sale' sign went up. Rumour had it the Travers' had left their money to an orphanage in India.

The house was sold almost immediately to a middle-aged couple, the Barclays, from Smithdown Road. They had three teenage children, and the whole family spoke with a pronounced Liverpool accent and weren't the sort of people usually found in Heather Close. Sid Barclay ran a fruit and veg stall in various markets; Great Homer Street, Ormskirk and Birkenhead. His wife, Vera, was never seen without a cigarette hanging from her mouth. Their car, the latest Ford Granada, went in the garage, and a big shabby van was left on the drive for the whole world to see.

The first thing the Barclays did was to remove the hedge, lop the trees, and clear most of the plants out of the back garden so they could lay a lawn. Soon, there was no indication the Travers' had ever lived there. Indeed, as far as anyone knew, there was no indication that the Travers' had ever lived at all.

'I don't know why you find it depressing,' said Sylvia. 'They probably led a gloriously exotic life in India. Think of the clothes they used to wear in those days; the women in pure silk, dripping lace and precious stones, the men in military uniforms, and everywhere smelling of spices and musky perfume. I bet she had an affair with an army colonel who drank champagne from her slipper and Mr Travers shot him to redeem his honour. Imagine white-clad servants with dark handsome faces oozing sex appeal, fanning them with bamboo leaves as they lay naked and perspiring sensuously in their net-covered beds.'

'Wow!' said Annie. 'And here's me thinking they were just a lonely old couple who died within a few days of each other.'

'They'll have lived on their memories, Annie. I'd like to think *my* husband would die quickly because he couldn't live without me. Eric's more likely to laugh uproariously and get married again within a week.'

'Are things no better?'

'Things will never get better. We had our nastiest row ever last night. I think he might have killed me if his mother hadn't turned up. It was my fault. He told me I wasn't a whole woman because I couldn't become a mother, so I said he wasn't man enough to father a child.'

'Why is that your fault? It sounds childish, but *he* started it.'

It was Monday, and Sylvia was following Annie around upstairs as she stripped the beds; dirty sheets and pillowcases were heaped on the landing ready for the wash. The children had returned to school and playgroup the week before.

'I know, but men can't stand slights on their sexual prowess. Tell them they've got BO, squinty eyes or warts on their bottom, and they don't give a damn, but insult their manhood, and they're likely to explode. Wouldn't Lauri?'

'I've no idea, Syl. I wouldn't dream of insulting his manhood.'

Annie went into the main bedroom and pulled the clothes off the double bed where, apart from when she had been in the maternity hospital, she'd spent every

265

night with Lauri for the last eight – nearly nine – years. 'I wouldn't mind getting those duvet things,' she said. 'They're so much more convenient – you could make the bed in a jiffy.'

Sylvia said, 'You never talk about sex, do you, Annie?'

'I suppose it seems rather private.'

'I tell you everything that happens between Eric and me.'

'That's your choice,' Annie said primly. 'You tell me because you want to, not because I've asked.'

'You can be a proper Miss Goody Two-Shoes sometimes, Annie Menin.' Sylvia sat down at the dressing table, opened Annie's jewellery box and began to try on earrings.

'Our Marie used to call me that.' One occasion came back in a sharp memory; their dark bedroom on Christmas Eve after seeing her sister in the Grand pretending to be grown up when she was only thirteen.

She forgot the beds and opened the wardrobe door. 'What shall I take to wear in London? I'm going on Friday.' One of the women Marie shared a house with would be away and Annie could have her room.

'Don't ask me. I wouldn't be seen dead in anything you own.'

'Thanks very much,' Annie said tartly. She sorted through her frocks. They did seem rather drab.

'Hey, here's that orchid pendant I bought you in George Henry Lee's all those years ago. Poor little thing, it's all tarnished.'

'It was only nine and eleven.'

'What happened to the rose you bought your mother?'

'I've no idea. Perhaps it was left on when she was buried. She always wore it.' Annie abruptly sat down on the bed.

'I'm sorry, Annie.' Sylvia was instantly contrite. 'That was tactless. As you've nearly finished, shall I make us a cup of coffee?'

'Please.' Annie shuddered away the picture of Mam lying in her coffin wearing the little pink rose.

Sylvia sang at the top of her voice as she ran downstairs. Her relationship with Eric was a mixture of tragedy, comedy and farce, but she was determined to keep her spirits up. 'I won't let him turn me into a victim. If I become a victim, I'm lost. Anyway, everything will be over soon. Either he'll murder me, or I'll murder him.'

It was like a film, Annie thought. Trust Sylvia to have a marriage that was like a highly dramatic film. She shook the cases off her pillow, then picked up Lauri's to do the same. There were two hairs on his, rich brown and wavy. She removed them, then sat staring at the hairs, held between the thumb and first finger of her right hand.

No, she never talked about sex. There wasn't much to talk about. Lately, they made love less and less, and then it was not exactly a chore, but just something she put up with. There must be more to it than she knew. Sometimes, with Lauri asleep beside her, she could hear little desperate, delighted cries coming from the Cunninghams' bedroom. Nothing she'd experienced had made her want to cry out loud like that.

'There's no real *intimacy* between us,' she whispered. 'I don't mean sex, just intimacy.'

Valerie used a cap as birth control. Once, she told Annie laughingly, she'd been unable to get the cap out that morning. 'Kevin had to get it out for me. He had a terrible job.'

Annie had flushed red with embarrassment. She could never, *never* have asked Lauri to do such a thing. Never!

'Coffee's ready, Annie.'

'Coming.' She hastily collected the sheets and pillow-cases together and carried them downstairs.

On Friday, Fred Quillen arrived in the van. Lauri was about to leave, when he did one of the endearing things that made her love him so much.

'Have a nice time in London, love.' He kissed her cheek and put something in her hand. 'It'll be your birthday soon. Buy yourself some new clothes while you're there. Don't worry about the children. Dot and me will manage between us.'

After he'd gone, Annie looked down to see what she'd been given. Twenty-five pounds!

'Oh!' She opened the door. He was just climbing into the van, looking rather stooped and dejected she thought. 'Lauri!' She ran down the path and threw her arms around his neck. 'I'll miss you,' she cried.

He patted her on the back. 'I'll miss you, love. We all will.'

'Perhaps I shouldn't go!'

'Don't be silly.' She was pleased to see the twinkle back in his eyes. 'You deserve a break. It'll do you good.'

'You're definitely coming back, aren't you, Mummy?' Sara asked gravely when Annie left her at the school gates.

'Sweetheart, as if I'd ever leave my little girl!'

Daniel seemed unconcerned that his mother was going away. Annie told the playgroup leader his auntie would collect him at mid-day. The woman looked dismayed. On the few occasions Dot had done this before, she was apt to arrive early and tell them how to run things.

5

If Liverpool had ceased to be the place where everything happened, then London had taken over. London was the swinging city, and the very air seemed to buzz with excitement. Annie could feel it the minute she stepped off the train at Euston Station and saw a pretty girl wearing flared brocade trousers, a tight maroon velvet jacket and a big velvet hat covered with cabbage roses. She felt over-conscious of her own neat navy-blue frock and white cardigan, and wished she'd brought her red mini dress, but always felt uncomfortable showing too much leg.

'Hallo, sis,' said the girl, and gave Annie an enormous hug.

'Marie! Oh. I didn't recognise you. You look so young and so . . . so way-out! You look terrific – and you've had your ears pierced!' Black stones dangled from Marie's ears. 'I've always wanted me ears pierced.'

'You don't look so bad yourself. You'd never guess you were an old married woman with two children.'

The sisters hadn't met for nearly five years. Sometimes, Annie worried they might never meet again, that Marie was one of those people who didn't need a family. It was a waste of time telephoning: Marie was never there and whoever answered the communal phone either didn't pass on the messages, or Marie ignored them, just as she ignored her sister's letters. It had taken a telegram to persuade her to ring up and arrange the weekend.

She linked Annie's arm. 'Let's go for a coffee.'

Annie was about to enter the station café, but Marie steered her outside. 'There's a nice little place along here.'

The coffee bar was in a dark basement, surprisingly

full for the middle of the afternoon. They found an empty table next to two men playing chess. After ordering two cappuccinos, Marie said eagerly, 'How is everyone?'

'I've brought some photos,' Annie said shyly. 'We took most of them at Daniel's fourth birthday party in July. Just look at Sara. She'll be six next week. She's dead slim, like you, but I think she's going to be tall. She's got my eyes and almost my hair. And this is Daniel.'

'Shit, Annie! He's growing to look just like . . .' Marie bit her lip.

'I know, he's the image of our mam. No-one's noticed except me, not even Auntie Dot. I wondered if you'd see it.' The similarity was most marked when Daniel was asleep.

'He's incredibly good-looking, but then so was our mother.' Marie sighed. 'Lauri looks well. Who's this?'

'That's Valerie from next door with her children.'

'She's the one whose husband made a pass at me at that party!'

'Kevin. Did he really?'

'Jaysus, Dot looks old. Her hair's completely white.'

'She'll be sixty next year. She's been a bit down lately, all her lads are married except Joe, the littlest, and he's joined the Paras. There's only her and Uncle Bert left. He's retiring at Christmas.'

'I can't imagine Dot being down,' Marie smiled.

'She's already planning a huge do next August on her birthday. Uncle Bert's the same old Uncle Bert. He never seems to change. His hair's a bit thinner, that's all.'

'He lives in Dot's shadow, but he's like the Rock of Ages, Uncle Bert. Dot would be lost without him.'

'I think she realises that.'

A man on the next table shouted, 'Checkmate'. Marie

sighed as she put the photos away. 'I'm missing everything, aren't I? Particularly Sara and Daniel growing up.'

'You don't have to, sis. Sara's making her First Holy Communion next month. Why don't you come? There's always room for you with us.'

'I know, sis, it's just that it's all so frenetic here. I hardly think about Liverpool most of the time.'

Annie felt hurt. Her sister was always at the back of her mind.

'I'm terrified of leaving for even a short while in case something comes up, in case my agent rings to say I've got a part or there's an audition that day, and if I'm not here, I'll miss out. Even hanging round in pubs, you hear useful gossip.'

'Not much has come up so far, has it, Marie?' Annie said gently. It was a decade since her sister had left Liverpool, and stardom was no nearer now than it was then.

'I didn't expect overnight success,' Marie said defensively, though Annie distinctly remembered she had. 'Don't forget *The Forsyte Saga*.'

Everyone at home had watched *The Forsyte Saga* to see Annie Menin's sister play a maid. Marie had done the non-speaking part adequately, but it wasn't exactly a platform for displaying her acting talent. Annie sometimes wondered if Marie *had* talent. Perhaps she was flogging a dead horse and would be better off getting married or pursuing a career with more chance of success.

Marie had guessed her chain of thought. 'I'll never give up you know, sis.' Her small pointed chin jutted out stubbornly in a way Annie remembered well. It used to drive the nuns wild when she was chastised for some very real misdemeanour. 'I'm not doing so bad. A repertory company in Portsmouth want me next spring, and I've another bloody pantomime at Christmas. When I'm "resting", I do office work. Did I tell you I'd learned to type?'

'Yes, years ago.'

'I'm not very good, not like you.' She pulled a face.

Annie squeezed her sister's hand. 'Never mind, sis. I've a feeling in me bones you'll take the world by storm one day.' Inwardly, though, she was worried her sister was wasting her life. Marie had her eyes set on a far distant star, possibly too distant. It wasn't worth the effort.

She had the same thought when she saw where her sister lived: 'Is it worth it?' Her heart sank when she entered the dark Victorian terraced house in Brixton. The kitchen had an old-fashioned sink which was badly chipped and without a plug, and the grubby floor had several tiles missing. There were no curtains on the window. It was a million times worse than the flat in Upper Parliament Street.

Marie's room was at the back, overlooking the yard. The situation of the window and the dismal view were exactly the same as the room they'd shared in Orlando Street, but there the similarity ended. The walls could hardly be seen for theatre posters, and a brightly checked blanket covered the single bed on which Annie sat, as there was only one chair.

'Welcome to my happy home,' cried Marie. She removed her hat. Her hair was a cloudy mass of little curls and waves.

'You've had a perm!' Annie wasn't sure if she altogether liked it.

'What d'you think?' Marie pirouetted. 'I hope you're impressed. It cost twenty quid in Knightsbridge.'

'Twenty quid, for a perm!'

'You could do with spending a few bob on your own

hair. I don't know how you can stand having it always the same.'

Annie glanced at herself in the dressing-table mirror. The top was littered with pots of different shades of foundation, eye-shadow and lipsticks. 'I've been meaning to have it cut short for years.'

'Shall I cut it for you? I'm quite good at cutting hair.'

'I'm not sure. What's this?' Annie leaned over and poked her finger in a bright red pot. It looked too greasy for rouge.

'It's lipstick. You put it on with a brush.'

'Really! Can I try some?'

'If you let me cut your hair. Come on, sis,' Marie said coaxingly.

'Oh, I dunno. I've only been here five minutes.'

'What does that matter!' Marie picked a pair of scissors up off the dressing table and approached her sister, clicking them threateningly.

Because she was enjoying them being together and it was so much like old times, Annie gave in. 'Don't be too ruthless. I only want a trim.'

'But then you'll look no different than before.' Before Annie could say another word, Marie seized a lock of hair and snipped the lot off.

'Marie!'

'Shush. Don't look in the mirror. Close your eyes till I've done.'

Annie closed her eyes and gritted her teeth and prayed she wouldn't look a sight.

'You can look now,' Marie said after what seemed like an age.

'Jaysus! I look like Topsy.' Her hair was in tiny curls all over her head. It was a shock at first, but the more she stared, the more she liked it. It made her look rather sophisticated.

'You've got a lovely long neck, sis.' Marie stroked her

sister's neck then left her hands on her shoulders. They stared at each other in the mirror. Marie rested her chin on Annie's curls. 'This is like old times. I almost feel like coming back to Liverpool with you.'

'Then why don't you?'

Marie turned away. 'I can't, sis. I can't ever. Come on, wash your hair and it will look even better.'

They had dinner in an inexpensive restaurant off the King's Road. As soon as they were back, Annie phoned home. Dot informed her that yes, the children were still alive, Annie wasn't to worry about a single thing, and if anything happened they would call her instantly, and of course she knew Annie would come home like a shot if it did.

Annie went to bed, feeling peculiar, in a room belonging to an actress called Shelley Montpelier whose real name was Brenda Smith. There was a life-size head and shoulders photograph of Shelley/Brenda on the dressing table. After a while, she had to get out of bed and turn the photo round because it felt as if Shelley/Brenda was watching the stranger in her bed with her slightly pop eyes.

Saturday was sunny and warm. Straight after break-fast, the sisters went to Carnaby Street, bustling with brisk activity, the very hub of the swinging city, though not nearly as exciting as the Cavern used to be. It was too commercial. There were too many people on the make rather than just enjoying themselves, and the clothes were expensive.

After a hamburger lunch, they caught the tube to Camden Market, where Annie bought a full-length skirt in flowered corduroy, and a skinny ribbed jumper which matched the green leaves perfectly. Marie insisted she must have a pair of clunky-heeled sandals because ordinary shoes would look silly with a long skirt, after which Annie only had five pounds left of the twenty-five. She bought Sara a rag doll and a brightly painted soldier wearing a real busby for Daniel.

She was wondering what to get for Lauri, all she could think of was a tie, when she found herself drawn towards a stall glittering with cheap jewellery. Unfortunately, the earrings were for pierced ears.

Marie pointed to a notice. EAR PIERCING, INCLUDING GOLD HOOPS – £2. 'How about it, sis? It can be your birthday present from me. I've a feeling I completely forgot about it last year.'

'All right,' said Annie recklessly. A few minutes later she was sitting on the sunny pavement of a strange street in Camden having her ears pierced by a bearded man with arms a mass of colourful tattoos.

They went to a pub for a drink so she could recover. 'Sylvia will be dead envious. It's not often I do things before she does. It's not just my ears, she hasn't got a long skirt, either.'

'How is the high and mighty Sylvia Delgado?' Marie asked acidly.

'Not so high and mighty at the moment.' Annie briefly described the situation between Sylvia and Eric. 'She puts on a brave face, but she's desperately unhappy.'

Marie pursed her lips. 'I'm sorry. I never liked her, though I think it was more a case of her not liking me. I'll never forget the way she completely ignored me when Bruno drove us to that clinic in Southport.'

The final stall was heaped higgledy-piggledy with dusty books. Annie passed by without a glance. 'I'll get a tie for Lauri somewhere else.'

'Just a minute.' Marie picked up a tatty paperback. 'Lauri collects these. I noticed them in your bookcase. They were published by the Left Wing Bookclub before the war. Has he got this one?'

The title meant nothing to Annie. 'I don't think so.'

'I bet Lauri would prefer this to a tie. How much is it?'

The old man behind the stall shrugged. 'A tanner.'

'Fancy you remembering such a thing,' Annie said as she paid. It seemed rather mean to have spent so much on herself and a mere sixpence on her husband, though as Marie said, it was the thought that counted.

Wearing her new clothes, it was a very different Annie Menin who stared back from the full-length mirror in Shelley Montpelier's room. The long skirt made her appear taller, slimmer, and it was true she had quite a nice neck which she'd never really noticed before. Her ears hurt like mad, but the pain was worth it because the gold hoops made her look like a gypsy. She'd always liked to be fashionable in the days when she was single and it seemed to matter more than when you were a housewife, but now she looked – what was the word Sylvia used? – *outré*!

Annie took a final satisfied glance in the mirror before going to show her sister. Marie said she looked terrific, and on no account to take the clothes off as she could wear them for the theatre that night.

There was something familiar about the man playing the villain. He had smooth black hair and a swarthy complexion, but it was his walk that convinced Annie she'd seen him before, and something about his voice.

The play was a highly enjoyable thriller and she wondered how Marie could have afforded such good seats, right at the front. In the interval, she checked the programme to see if the villain was someone she'd seen on television.

'Clive Hoskins!' she exclaimed. 'Why didn't you tell me?'

'I wondered if you'd recognise him,' Marie said smugly. 'Isn't he brilliant? He did his best to get me the part of Constance, but the producer wanted someone older. Clive got us the tickets for free.'

When the play was over, they went backstage and found Clive in his dressing room, in the process of wiping off the dark make-up. He beamed when he saw Marie. 'Hallo, darling. As soon as I've got this muck-up off, I'll give you and your gorgeous sister a nice big kiss.'

He asked after Lauri and insisted on seeing the photos of the children. Sara was going to be a very beautiful young lady. 'And is this the chap who was giving you so much trouble when I stayed? You were expecting him, remember?'

Along with several other members of the cast, they went to a club in Soho, where Annie drank only a single glass of wine, but innocently took a puff on a big fat cigarette which was being handed round, mainly because everyone else was doing it. Her head instantly left her body and still hadn't returned when it was time to leave. For some reason, Clive Hoskins was in tears and refused to be parted from Marie. They took a taxi back to Brixton and between them helped Clive indoors.

'Poor pet,' Marie crooned as they laid him on the bed. 'He's just been jilted.' She kissed his cheek. 'I love him so much.'

'Isn't that a waste of time?' said Annie. 'Being in love with him, I mean.' In the taxi, her head had returned to its proper place, but everywhere looked slightly askew. Marie had never mentioned a man in her life. Perhaps, as well as wasting herself on a futile career, she was wasting her affections on a futile relationship with a homosexual.

'I'm not *in* love with him, Annie. I said I loved him,

which is a different thing.' She looked down at the sleeping figure. 'Me and Clive cling to each other like creatures drowning in this cruel world.'

'I see,' said Annie, though she didn't see at all. 'I think I'll make a cup of tea and go to bed. Do you want one?'

Marie had already started to remove her clothes. 'No thanks.'

'Would you like to sleep with me? We could sleep top to tail, the way we used to do when we were little.'

'It's all right, sis. I'll cuddle up beside Clive.'

Annie was careful only to use things out of the sparsely stocked wall cupboard marked, 'Marie', when she made the tea. There was no fridge, the milk was sour and little shreds of white floated to the mug's surface, but she didn't care. The other two cupboards were marked 'Shelley' and 'Tiffany'. Tiffany lived in the downstairs room and worked in a nightclub. There'd been no sign of her as yet.

She sat up in bed feeling exceptionally relaxed, staring at Shelley/Brenda's carefully posed portrait which she'd turned round again that morning. The face seemed almost real, almost alive. A street lamp shone through the thin curtains and everything in the room was unnaturally clear, the shadows sharply defined. A long woollen dressing gown hung behind the door like a headless monk.

It seemed odd, wearing earrings in bed, but the man had said to leave them in for six weeks and just turn the rings round from time to time. Her ears throbbed and her heels smarted where the strap of her new sandals had rubbed, yet neither seemed all that unpleasant, almost as if it was happening to someone else.

She'd actually smoked a drugged cigarette! Although she hadn't realised it at the time, she was quite glad she'd done it. Wait till she told Sylvia! It made her feel very much part of swinging London. How strange to think that on the nights she and Lauri were staidly watching television or fast asleep in bed, Marie was flitting round Soho smoking cannabis or whatever it was called. And what a peculiar set-up with Clive – how could you love a man, yet not be in love?

The front door opened and voices whispered in the hall, one male. Someone used the bathroom, then all was silence. An occasional car drove by, briefly illuminating the room with a flash of yellow light.

Annie sighed and wondered if Sara and Daniel were missing her, just as another car went by, and as the headlights swept the room, everything became clear. *She wasn't in love with Lauri, but she loved him!* It had been so right from the start. Dot's words after her twenty-first came back distinctly. 'Ken was never much of a dad, was he? You're looking for a father figure and Lauri Menin fits the bill perfectly.'

'Oh, God!' She put the mug on the bedside table and leaned forward with her arms around her knees.

After all those years of responsibility, how nice to be treated like a child and let Lauri take all the decisions. But she'd grown up without him realising, without realising herself, and he resented her becoming independent, just as she resented not being treated as an adult. It explained all those confused, mixed-up emotions she'd had recently.

Her head was spinning, but it had been an exhausting day and she quickly fell asleep. When she woke, her mind was as clear as crystal. It was early, not yet light outside. Everywhere was very quiet and she missed the sound of birdsong, usually the first thing heard in Heather Close. A radio was switched on next door and she could hear hymns and remembered it was Sunday.

She would never know what she'd missed by not

falling in love. 'I've made me bed, and I'll have to lie on it.' She had the children, and it wasn't an uncomfortable bed to spend the rest of your life on.

Clive Hoskins was still asleep when they left for Mass at Westminster Cathedral – Marie admitted she rarely went nowadays. Afterwards, they lunched in Lyons Corner House then window-shopped, arm in arm, in the nearly deserted West End. The weather had changed dramatically and it was dull and overcast. A sharp breeze whipped the air.

'Have you enjoyed yourself?' Marie asked as they tore themselves away from Liberty's window.

'I've had a lovely time. What I like most is just being with you. Sometimes, I worry you've forgotten me.'

Marie laughed. 'Sis! You're like an arm or a leg. I don't think about them all the time, but I'd be devastated if I didn't have them.'

'It's funny,' Annie said thoughtfully, 'I've got a family, yet I miss you more than you do me. You've got no-one except Clive.'

'Ah, but I've got an obsession – acting. Everything pales into insignificance beside that.'

'That time you were pregnant, you wanted a baby to love.'

'That was then, sis, this is now.'

They walked in silence for a while. 'I want to tell you something I've never told another soul, not even Clive.' Marie released her arm and began to walk ahead so her face was hidden behind the velvet hat. 'I was offered a big part in a play once. It was to go on in the West End, but the leading man died and it came to nothing. I was ten weeks pregnant at the time. I had an abortion – the law's changed, it's legal now.'

'Oh, Marie!' Annie breathed.

Marie didn't turn around. It was as if she were

talking to herself. 'When I first realised, y'know, I thought of giving up acting, perhaps coming back to Liverpool. Till then, I was getting nowhere fast. Then came the play and I was presented with two choices. The baby didn't stand a chance.'

A bus trundled along Regent Street and Annie wondered if she should have bought Daniel a bus instead of a soldier. He loved buses. 'What about the father?' she asked.

Marie shrugged her shoulders carelessly. 'Roger? Oh, he never knew.'

'Was he an actor?'

'He *is* an actor. He was in *The Avengers* the other week, playing a good guy for a change.' She paused outside a shop which sold Indian ware. 'I quite like that carved box with mosaic round the edge.'

'Did you feel upset afterwards, like you did the other time?' Marie's face was reflected in the window. She looked quite calm, yet . . .

'It didn't affect me a bit.' Marie's voice was brittle. 'I had to have that part, you see. Even when it turned out to have been a waste of time, I didn't care. It had made me realise what my priorities were. Kids weren't on the agenda, acting was.'

'Marie!' Annie touched her sister gently on the shoulder.

'Ah, but I haven't forgotten the other, my little boy.' Marie spun round. Her eyes were unnaturally bright and Annie was shocked by the naked misery there. 'He'd be fourteen, a year older than I was then. If I try hard, I can see him. I've watched him grow up over the years. He's as tall as me and, for some reason, he's got straight fair hair and blue eyes.' Her face twisted bitterly. 'Oh, Annie, sometimes I don't half hate our mam and dad.'

A man and woman passed, tourists, with cameras

slung around their necks. They stared curiously at Marie's impassioned face.

'Come on, luv.' Annie linked her arm. 'Let's have a cup of tea.' She felt she understood her sister better. Acting wasn't an obsession, but an escape from the past.

That night was Annie's last in London. Marie seemed to have recovered from her outburst and they went to a party in someone's attic. Annie might have enjoyed herself had she been able to stop thinking about her husband and her sister. There was little she could do about Marie, but she would look upon Lauri differently when she got home. Now she knew where she stood, perhaps they could get off to a fresh start.

It was dreadful, the thought of leaving Marie. Just as Annie was fastening her suitcase next morning, the phone rang.

'It's for you, Marie,' someone called, presumably Tiffany.

Annie wasn't sure whether to cringe or smile when she heard Marie's voice downstairs. It was loud, pretentious, false. 'Fantastic, darling,' she gushed, 'I'll be there in an hour.'

'Sorry, sis, I won't be able to come to Euston with you,' she said breathlessly when she returned, her face radiant. 'That was my agent. I went for an audition last week and they want to see me again.'

'That's all right, luv.'

Marie scarcely heard. She stared at herself in the mirror. 'I'd better get changed and do something with my hair.'

'I'll be off or I'll miss me train.' Annie felt in the way. Perhaps this was the real Marie, and the chummy, companionable sister was false.

'Right.' Marie said abstractedly. 'Oh, I'll come

downstairs and see you off. Can you remember the way to the tube?'

'Yes, just round the corner.'

'Sorry about this, but it's an opportunity I can't miss.'

'I'm glad your agent called before we'd left,' Annie said politely. 'I hope you get the part.'

'So do I. Oh, so do I.'

They embraced briefly on the step. Annie hadn't taken a step when the door closed. She was about to turn the corner of the cheerless street, feeling indescribably sad, when she heard her name called. 'Annie! Annie!' There was a hint of desperation in the sound.

She turned. Marie was standing outside the house blowing kisses with both hands. She looked as if she were crying. 'Goodbye, sis. Goodbye.'

Annie backed around the corner blowing kisses in return.

Heather Close looked peaceful in the late September sunshine, and the yellow door of number seven shone welcomingly at the end. Annie sighed with relief. She'd enjoyed the short holiday, but it was good to be home.

Daniel had spied her from the window. He came running out, followed by Auntie Dot. 'We were just about to collect Sara. Oh, you've had your hair cut! It looks nice. I always said you'd suit it short, didn't I?'

Annie couldn't recall a single time, but readily agreed. 'I've had me ears pierced, too,' she said proudly. She scooped her son up in her arms. 'Did you miss Mummy, sweetheart?'

'A bit,' Daniel conceded, twisting her nose.

'I've just put the kettle on, least I think I have. You can never tell with them electric ones.' Dot looked slightly moidered. 'There's time for a quick cuppa and you can catch up on the news.'

'What news?' She quickly learned that in the space of

four days Sara had lost a tooth, Lauri had cut his finger sharpening the lawnmower and had to get it stitched at the hospital, and Sylvia had left Eric and was living with Bruno at the Grand.

Sara's face lit up when she saw her mother waiting at the school gate. 'I missed you, Mummy,' she said gravely. 'Please don't go away again.'

'Next time you can come with me,' Annie promised. It meant visits to Soho clubs would be out, but that wouldn't be such a bad thing.

When Lauri came home, she made a big fuss of him. The first finger of his left hand was heavily bandaged.

'You should have taken a few days off,' she cried.

'We can't afford it, Annie.'

She thought he didn't seem at all well. His cheeks looked heavy and grey and he moved slowly, as if it was an effort. 'I think you should have an early night,' she insisted. 'Perhaps you're run down.' She felt guilty. It was he who should have had a holiday, not her. 'I'll get you a tonic from the chemist tomorrow.'

'I might turn in a bit sooner than usual.' He went upstairs at half nine and Annie took him up a cup of cocoa. He was sitting up in bed reading the book she'd bought and appeared slightly better.

'Your hair looks nice,' he said. 'And you suit the earrings.'

Annie sat on the bed. 'You always said you preferred it long.'

'I did, but as you reminded me, it's *your* hair.'

She felt guilty again, but only a little, for going against his wishes. 'So it is,' she said.

Their eyes met, and Annie saw fear in his. He'd always been able to read her mind. Perhaps he sensed their roles had changed.

She telephoned her sister to say she'd arrived safely home. Whoever answered, Tiffany, or possibly Shelley/

Brenda was back, promised to pass the message on. If they did, Annie never heard. Marie didn't turn up for Sara's First Holy Communion in October.

Nor did she come when Auntie Dot threw the best party ever to celebrate her sixtieth birthday. As she was surrounded by her husband, her lads and their wives, her grandchildren, Dot said emotionally, 'I'm the luckiest woman in the world.'

'And I'm the luckiest man,' said Uncle Bert. Love for his flamboyant wife glowed as fresh in his eyes as the day they were married.

No-one allowed the fact that the Conservatives had won the recent General Election to ruin the great day, even though the new Prime Minister, Edward Heath, declared it was his intention to denationalise everything that moved and do something about the Trade Unions.

Annie received a little scribbled note to say her sister had a part in *Dr Who*, but no-one would recognise her because she played an alien and the make-up was really weird. Although reconciled to the fact that their paths had parted for ever, Annie couldn't help but wonder if there was *anything* that would fetch her sister back to Liverpool!

6

'Thirty!' Sylvia said gloomily. 'Thirty! It wouldn't feel so bad if my divorce hadn't come through the same day.'

Parliament must have had Sylvia and Eric Church in mind when they changed the law to allow divorce by mutual consent after two years' separation. The Decree Absolute had arrived that morning. Eric's family were horrified, but had to concede it was the only way out. If they stayed together, either Eric would kill Sylvia, or she would kill him, and divorce was more socially acceptable than murder.

'How does it feel?' Annie enquired.

'Being thirty or divorced?'

'I know how thirty feels, don't I?' It had been her own birthday the month before, and it hadn't exactly seemed a landmark, but things were different for her. 'I mean divorced.'

'Odd,' Sylvia said reflectively. 'Peculiar. Very sad.'

'If you'd had children it might have been all right.'

'I doubt it. We would have found something else to fight about, at least Eric would. He's a sadist. He likes hurting people. I feel sorry for that woman he's going to marry.' Eric was already sort of engaged to the daughter of a friend of the family.

'I think you've been dead brave,' Annie declared.

'Thanks,' Sylvia said briefly. 'I'm glad you were around.' She'd vowed never to fall in love again. She'd had enough of men to last a lifetime. 'Perhaps the worst thing is that the Beatles have broken up,' she said tragically. 'It's the end of a great era. There'll never be another decade like the sixties.' The Fab Four had gone their separate ways. When he wasn't studying mysticism with Paul McCartney and George Harrison in the Himalayas, John Lennon was in America with his new wife, Yoko Ono, making records of his own.

They were in Sylvia's bedroom in the Grand, still the same as when Annie had first come on that bitterly cold night when Ruby Livesey had pushed Sylvia into a holly bush. The two women were lost in youthful memories, until Sylvia said brightly. 'I won't be staying in Liverpool now that I'm a free woman again. I cramp Bruno's style. He's dying to screw that new barmaid.'

'Where will you go?' asked Annie.

'I might give London a try. There's more openings when it comes to work, and far more to do socially.'

Annie had suspected this would happen. There seemed little to keep a single woman of thirty in Liverpool. 'I'll miss you,' she sighed.

'It goes without saying I'll miss you too.' Sylvia rolled off the bed. 'Tell me seriously, Annie, do I *look* thirty?'

'You don't look a day over twenty-nine.' Annie stared at her friend's beautiful face. Sylvia looked no different from when she started at Grenville Lucas sixteen years ago.

'You're a great help.' Sylvia patted her cheeks worriedly. 'Say if I go like Cecy! She's beginning to resemble a wrinkled, dried-up prune.'

'You haven't changed, some people never do. Others grow old before your very eyes.'

'I hope I'm the first sort,' Sylvia said frantically. 'I hope I take after Bruno. He still rakes in the women at fifty-six.'

Annie supposed charming, flirtatious Bruno *must* have changed a bit since they first met, but she still nursed a secret yearning for him, with his dark laughing face. She thought about Lauri; he was one of the second sort. Of course, he wasn't changing before her eyes, that was ridiculous, but he was nothing like the man with the warm twinkling smile she'd met at Auntie Dot's. It wasn't just that he'd grown so bulky or his hair had thinned – after all, Uncle Bert no longer had the sandy halo she remembered – but Lauri's whole attitude had altered. He was always depressed, rarely smiling. He'd never been the same since he cut his finger on the lawnmower two years ago when she was in London. It was stupid to think someone's personality could alter because of a cut finger, but the finger had never regained its feeling. It remained numb, unbending. Then the numbness spread to the next finger, and the next, until Lauri could hardly move his left hand. Although he'd been to see a specialist and had a variety of different treatments, the hand remained the same, completely dead, yet the specialist could find nothing wrong.

There was a knock on the door and Bruno came in. He grinned at Annie. 'How much do I pay you to keep my daughter company?'

'I clocked off mentally at half past two.' She'd been working lunchtimes at the Grand since Daniel started school last year. Lauri had been totally opposed, but it was fortunate she'd gone ahead regardless, as her small earnings had helped to subsidise the house-keeping ever since. There'd been no holiday, as originally planned.

'I came to say Cecy's just telephoned,' Bruno said to Sylvia. 'As it's your birthday and my night off, she's invited us both to dinner. I promised to ring back. What shall I tell her?'

Sylvia pulled a face. 'Yes, I suppose, but fancy having nothing else to do on your thirtieth birthday than go to dinner with your parents!'

After several visits to the hospital over nearly a year, it was concluded the cause of Lauri's frozen hand was psychosomatic. Annie was with him in the specialist's office when the diagnosis was made.

'What does that mean?' she asked.

'It's all in the mind.' The specialist was a pleasant man, but rather distant, with a narrow white face and deep-set eyes.

'But I can't feel it,' Lauri said a touch impatiently. 'I can't bend my fingers. How on earth can it all be in my mind?'

'I'm afraid that is a mystery medical science has so far been unable to solve. Some people go blind or lose their power of speech for no apparent reason.'

Lauri's brow creased. 'You mean there's no cure?'

'The cure is within yourself. Only you can make your hand better.'

'Bloody ridiculous!' Lauri said when they were outside. He rarely swore. When they reached the Anglia, Annie said, 'Shall I drive?'

'Don't you trust me?' he snapped.

'Of course I do.' He managed to change the gears by pushing the lever with his wrist, though he couldn't use the hand brake. She was sorry she'd asked. She'd offered to help because he was upset, but he couldn't stand it when she drove. 'I don't want to be seen driven by a woman, even if she is my wife,' he had said soon after she'd passed her test.

As Annie made her way to school to collect the children, she recalled the journey back from the hospital. She kept trying to start a conversation, but Lauri merely answered with a grunt. It wasn't until they were going into the house, that he patted her arm and said, 'Sorry, love. I'm finding this business with my hand hard to take.'

That was the night Fred Quillen came, uninvited, and asked if he could speak to Lauri privately. Annie shooed Sara and Daniel into the garden and left the men in the lounge whilst she got on with the ironing. Fred didn't stay long. After about fifteen minutes, she heard the front door open and went to say goodbye. Fred was letting himself out, there was no sign of Lauri.

Puzzled, she went into the lounge. Lauri was sitting stock still on the settee. His face was pale.

'What's the matter?' Intuition told her what the answer would be.

'They want me out of the co-op. They claim I'm not pulling my weight,' Lauri said dully.

'Oh, love!' Annie breathed. She felt as if her heart could easily split in two on his behalf. She sat down and laid her head on his shoulder. 'What are we going to do?'

She winced at the bitterness in his voice as he replied, 'They've given me a month to pull my socks up.'

But how could he? Lauri had always been the strongest and most conscientious of workers. She sensed how degraded he must feel. 'Why not tell Fred Quillen what to do with the co-op and find another job?'

Lauri looked at her as if she were mad. 'I'm fifty, Annie, and I've only got the use of one hand. What other job?'

The children came running in. Lauri reached for Sara. 'Come to Daddy, darling.' He adored his daughter. Sometimes, Annie wondered if Sara had taken her own place in Lauri's heart, to the detriment of boisterous Daniel who got on his father's nerves.

She ruffled Daniel's dark hair. 'Help me fetch the rest of the washing in, there's a good boy.'

Annie joined the mothers outside the school gates. Valerie Cunningham wasn't amongst them. As soon as Zachary started school, Valerie had taken a full-time job. Her children were what the newspapers referred to disparagingly as 'latchkey kids', though they spent the hours between school and their mother coming home at the Menins'.

It was a blowy November day and russet leaves danced across the playground. A bell went and suddenly the double doors flew open and children came bursting out like wild animals. Daniel was one of the first. He was a fine looking boy, Annie thought tenderly, as her son raced another boy to the gate, a look of determination on his handsome face that reminded her of Marie. The shirt that had been clean on that morning was grubby and the buttons were undone, or possibly lost.

'Hi, Mum,' he grunted when he reached her.

'Hi, Daniel.' She chucked him playfully under the chin. It would have been more than her life was worth to kiss him in public.

Sara followed more sedately. Annie watched lovingly as she paused to catch a falling leaf. A slim, serious girl with gold blonde hair and light blue eyes, at eight years old, her head already came up to her mother's shoulder. 'I've lots of homework,' she said importantly. 'I shall go straight up to my room and get started.' Annie would have to make sure that neither Kelly nor Tracy invaded her room to play.

The Cunninghams gathered round. 'Have we got orange squash at home?' Gary demanded.

'Yes,' said Annie drily. They regarded number seven as home until their mother put in an appearance.

With the children settled in front of the television and Sara in her room, Annie began to make pastry for a steak and kidney pie. She used to feed her own two at four o'clock and she and Lauri would eat later, but since the advent of the Cunninghams, all four Menins ate late. Annie wasn't prepared to subsidise Valerie's wages by providing her children with a meal, and it didn't seem fair to feed just Sara and Daniel.

It must have been the conversation with Sylvia about people changing, but her mind kept going back to the day she'd gone to the hospital with Lauri and Fred Quillen had said he must pull his socks up.

The children had gone to bed and Lauri had still scarcely moved from the settee, when Annie said tentatively, 'Y'know, love, I could take a refresher course and get a job as a secretary. I wouldn't earn as much as you, but it would be enough to live on.'

'I don't understand,' said Lauri.

Annie could tell from the black look on his face that he understood only too well. She plunged deeper into the mire of his anger. It was important that she make the offer, then it was up to him. 'It's not a law that the man has to be the breadwinner. I'm perfectly willing . . .'

He broke in coldly. 'Do you think I would allow my wife to keep me?'

'I thought I'd mention it. It can be one of the options we discuss.'

'I don't intend to consider such an option, let alone discuss it.'

Annie was secretly relieved. The last thing she wanted was to return to secretarial work.

She said no more and neither did Lauri. He went to bed early with a curt 'Goodnight'. He was usually asleep by the time she went up. She tried to forget they hadn't made love since she'd returned from the weekend with Marie in London.

The 39 Steps with Robert Donat started on television. She'd been mad on Robert Donat for quite a while until she discovered he was dead. But good though the picture was, she was unable to concentrate. The specialist had said the matter of Lauri's hand was – she searched for the word – psychosomatic, all in the mind, and she was struck with the horrific thought, *'Perhaps it's all my fault.'*

It was essential she talk to someone; not Sylvia, who'd say tell Lauri to get stuffed. Tomorrow, she'd go and see Auntie Dot.

'I have never,' Dot scoffed, 'heard such a load of ould cobblers in me life. Lauri's hand's seized up just because you had your hair cut! Come off it, girl, talk sense.'

'You're exaggerating, Auntie,' Annie said stiffly. She was rather put out when Dot's face turned more and more incredulous as she came out with her tortured explanation for Lauri's hand. 'It's not just me hair. It's everything. I'm no longer the girl he married.'

'I should hope not,' Dot expostulated. 'You were only twenty-one. If Lauri didn't think you'd change, he needs his bumps feeling. People change all the time. It's only natural. What do you want me to say? Grow your hair long again like Samson and Lauri's hand will be all right?'

'I wish you wouldn't concentrate on me hair. I told you, he didn't like me learning to drive, either. And I don't automatically assume everything he says is right. I argue with him all the time – he can't stand it when I talk about politics . . .' Annie's voice faltered at the sight of Dot's outraged expression.

'In other words,' she said, 'he's not the lord of the manor any more! I've no time for these feminists who say men are crap, but women have a right to their own identity. Lauri doesn't *own* you. Be yourself, luv, and if he can't take it, that's his problem, not yours.'

'I thought, if I acted differently . . .'

'You're not to change a jot, Annie,' Dot said firmly. 'I think the whole thing's daft, but if it's true, your husband's not much of a man.'

She went into the kitchen to make a cup of tea. Annie sat in the same place from where she used to watch her aunt when the Harrisons had lived there, though the kitchen was very different now. Five years ago, the Gallaghers had bought the house off the landlord, and bamboo-patterned units lined the walls. Beside the freezer, a new door led to the former washhouse, now a bathroom and toilet.

Annie transferred her gaze to Dot's current pride and joy, the fireplace fitted last Christmas, along with a gas fire which glowed with imitation coals. Her aunt's taste was very different from her own, and she thought the wooden surround truly ghastly, with its two-tier mantelpiece, the top supported by brass pillars. She had to concede that the warm wood went well with the hessian wallpaper on the breastwork, which in turn toned beautifully with the coral painted walls.

Dot came in with the tea. 'This business with Lauri's job, now that's something worth worrying about.' Her sharp nose twitched with pride. 'I wonder if our Mike's got a vacancy that would suit him.'

'Lauri's a carpenter, Auntie Dot. It's engineers and electricians that your Mike needs.'

Within the space of two and a half years, Mike's business had taken off and now employed eight people. The firm was still expanding and had recently taken over larger premises in Kirkby. They no longer dealt with vintage cars after getting several important long-term contracts from much larger firms. But Mike and Ray weren't satisfied. In the even longer term, the contracts offered no security; the firms, however big, might fold, cut back, take on staff of their own to do the work.

'It's a bit like singing someone else's songs, compared to singing your own,' Mike declared in reference to the group he and Ray had once belonged to. 'I always preferred our own.'

So they'd developed, of all things, a burglar alarm, much to Dot's dismay as she couldn't imagine anyone in their right mind sticking a burglar alarm outside their house. So far, only Mike and Ray worked on the prototype, but it would be ready for production and marketing soon when Michael Ray Security would be born. Glenda, Mike's wife, had prepared a brochure for the printers.

Dot was forced to concede her judgement of Glenda had been totally wrong. Glenda had turned out to be a wife in a million, working overtime to help get the business off the ground. Then she taught herself to type and did all the office work.

'Mike was talking the other day about taking on a salesman to go round with these alarm things,' Dot said. Her chest expanded with the magnitude of the fact she had a son who was an employer. 'Of course, he wouldn't be able to pay as much as Lauri's used to.'

'Mike'll want someone younger than Lauri.' Her husband was the opposite of her idea of a pushy salesman.

'I'll ring him later. I was going to, anyroad. Glenda, poor lamb, has been feeling a bit rough lately. I'd like to know how she is.'

It was Annie who answered the phone when Mike rang that night. 'How's Glenda?' she enquired.

Mike sounded worried. 'Not so well, Annie. She's tired all the time, which isn't a bit like her. I'm having a heck of a job persuading her to see the doctor.' He asked if he could speak to Lauri.

'What have you been saying to Dot?' Lauri demanded when the call finished. Annie had shut herself in the lounge so she wouldn't overhear.

'I'm not sure what you mean,' she said innocently.

'Did you tell her about me, about the co-op?'

'I think I did mention it this morning. Why?'

Lauri looked irritated. 'Mike's just offered me a job, that's why.'

'Doing what?'

'As a salesman.' He shook his head. 'I'd be no good at that sort of thing. What's more, I don't want charity.'

'Is that what you told him?' Annie asked sharply.

'I told him I'd think about it.'

'Honestly, Lauri,' she said, exasperated. 'Mike wouldn't offer a job out of charity. Anyroad, what's dole money if it's not charity?'

'He did say he'd interviewed a couple of chaps but they were too young, too brash,' Lauri conceded. 'He'd thought someone older might give a better impression.'

'Mike's an astute businessman. He must know best.'

'The basic wage isn't so hot, but I'll get commission on each sale, and there's a car, a secondhand Capri.'

'You're very lucky,' Annie said. 'Unemployment's going up, and last night you said you'd never get another job at your age. You've just been offered a soft job on a plate. If I were you, I'd be jumping for joy, but you look as if you'd just lost a pound and found a sixpence.' Personally, she couldn't have been persuaded to buy a baby's rattle, let alone a burglar alarm, off someone with such a miserable face.

The children were squabbling over the television. Daniel was almost certainly the cause. He probably wanted it changed to another station. Annie cursed Valerie Cunningham. She never offered a word of thanks for looking after her kids for two hours every day, yet seemed to consider herself superior because she had a full-time job and Annie hadn't. 'I'm getting as bad as Lauri,' she thought. 'Nothing but moans.'

It was strange, but over the last fifteen months Lauri had turned out to be a good salesman and Mike was very pleased. Perhaps potential customers felt sorry for him and bought an alarm to cheer him up. Far more likely, Lauri was his old self once outside the house and away from the wife who no longer hung onto his every word.

The steak and kidney pie smelt delicious. She felt her taste buds stir and looked at the calendar to remind herself where Lauri was today; Rochdale, which meant he might be late and she could eat with the children as soon as Valerie honked her horn to signal she was home.

The horn went when she was making the gravy and the Cunninghams came hurtling through the kitchen without a 'thank you' for Annie's pains. Valerie made no attempt to teach her brood good manners.

She was reading to the children when Lauri arrived.

There was quite a gale blowing. The garden fence groaned and the willow tree swished wildly. She worried about him negotiating strange towns and unfamiliar roads in the dark, but he seemed to enjoy driving long distances and was adept at manoeuvring the gears with his numb hand.

To her astonishment, his face was beaming when he came in. He looked ten years younger. 'I sold eighteen alarms today,' he said immediately. 'Eighteen!' The usual total was two or three and some days he sold none.

She did a quick calculation. 'That's ninety pounds in commission!'

'I know, marvellous, isn't it!' The words tumbled over each other in his excitement as he tried to explain. A few weeks before he was due to arrive in a town, Michael Ray Security would advertise in the local press for leaflet distributors. Only business premises and wealthy homes were targeted. That morning, Lauri had arrived at an estate of mock-Tudor properties and discovered there'd been a spate of burglaries and the leaflet had sparked off a residents' meeting. 'Nearly every house wanted an alarm, fifteen in all. I nearly came home at that point, but decided to press on and sold another three. I'll give Mike a ring later. He'll have his work cut out fitting that lot.' His enthusiasm was catching. Annie couldn't possibly have been more pleased. He looked rejuvenated, like the Lauri of old. The children had been listening, wide-eyed. He pulled them down, one on each knee.

'Next year, you might earn that much every day when the business goes national,' she said. He would be selling in bulk to stores, not just to individual customers.'

'Listen to us!' he said, aghast. 'We sound like capitalists.'

'What's a capitalist, Dad?' Daniel enquired.

'A person who makes a lot of money off the backs of others,' his father explained. 'But Mike's okay, he pays fair wages, and the alarm is good value for money. It's not as if it's something essential that people have to buy to live. I don't mind exploiting the rich.'

'Can we have an alarm, Dad?' Daniel piped up. 'A yellow one to go with our front door?'

'No, son. We don't need protecting from burglars in Heather Close. But I tell you what you can have, a nice day out in town on Saturday. I'll buy you both a present. What would you like?'

'*Robinson Crusoe*,' Sara said instantly.

'The person or the book?' Lauri asked jovially. It was ages since he'd been heard to crack a joke.

'The book, of course, Daddy.'

'I'd like a toy burglar alarm for my room.'

'There's no such thing, son, but we'll find something else.'

'It's terrible to admit,' Lauri said later, 'but I got a real buzz today at the thought of making all that money.'

'Just because you're a socialist, it doesn't mean you're not human. Socialists still have to pay mortages and feed their families.'

'I suppose so. On reflection, it wasn't just the money. It was the feeling of achievement, excitement almost, at the idea of belonging to a company that might become a great success. I realised how much I enjoyed being on the road. I'll be going further afield from January. I'll have to stay away overnight, perhaps several days. Will you mind, love?' He looked at her anxiously.

'No, Lauri. I'll miss you, but I won't mind as long as you're happy.' Annie felt as if they'd turned a corner.

He took her hand. 'I'm sorry, love. I've not been easy to live with over the last few years. I kept thinking of you on the way home, how pleased you'd be, and how lucky I was, having you and two lovely kids.' He sighed with satisfaction. 'I'll ring Mike now.'

He came back a few minutes later, his face grave. 'Wasn't Mike pleased?' said Annie.

'He wasn't much interested. Glenda's gone into hospital again. She's in a coma. Mike thinks this is it.'

'Oh, no!'

Mike had taken Glenda to the doctors by force. She had leukaemia, and it was too late to do anything about it. Glenda got sicker and sicker. As the company thrived, Mike's wife began to die.

Lauri held up his left hand and stared at it with contempt. 'Pathetic, isn't it? Getting worked up over a hand, when a relatively young woman's about to die from something a hundred times worse.'

Annie didn't answer. That night, for the first time in years, she fell asleep in her husband's arms.

Glenda fought on until Christmas Eve, rarely coming out of her coma. She died with Mike and her children at her side.

Dot was inconsolable. She would never forgive herself for the things she had said when Mike got married. 'I'll never make judgements on people again. I couldn't have been more wrong with Glenda.'

The feeling in Lauri's hand gradually returned. 'It was awful while it lasted, but it's been a blessing in disguise. I wouldn't have left the co-op and got the job with Mike.'

Michael Ray Securities continued to expand. Lauri was provided with a new Cortina. Some weeks, with commission, he earned twice what he'd done as a carpenter. Despite this, he never suggested Annie give up her job at the Grand. He seemed to accept she was entitled to make her own decisions. Annie enjoyed her few hours with Bruno behind the bar; it broke up the day and gave her a few pounds of her own to spend as she liked. Now Valerie was at work and Sylvia had moved to London, she had fewer visitors and Lauri was sometimes away for an entire week.

She was happy. Her marriage was not as perfect as she'd once thought, but she and Lauri jogged along contentedly and she knew she would never stop loving him. Sara and Daniel were her main joy; watching them develop and grow. It wasn't often nowadays that she thought about Joshua and Sophie, the children who'd never been born.

'Tenth anniversary!' gasped Sylvia. 'Isn't the tenth special?'

'It's tin or aluminium, take your pick. We're having a party. It's weeks off yet, but do you think you'll be home?'

'Of course. I wouldn't miss it. I'll be home for Christmas, anyway. I'll come early.'

It was almost a year since Sylvia had gone to London, where she found herself a cushy job in an advertising agency. She telephoned Annie from work several times a week.

'Will your boss let you off?' Annie enquired.

'I've got him eating out of my hand. He's dying to get me to bed.'

'What's he like?'

'Hideous!' Sylvia giggled. 'I wouldn't sleep with him if my life depended on it. I'm happy with my handsome Arabian prince.'

'I still can't believe he's a proper prince,' Annie said doubtfully.

'He's as real as they come,' Sylvia assured her. 'We've fallen for each other like a ton of bricks, gold bricks! Ronnie's made of money.'

'I thought you swore never to fall in love again?'

'I don't expect anything to come of it. He's returning

home next year. We're having a mad, bad fling whilst we have the chance.'

'Ronnie seems an odd name for an Arabian prince.'

Sylvia clucked impatiently. 'I can't pronounce his real name. He's happy with Ronnie. By the way, I saw your Marie the other day.'

'Really!' She was becoming increasingly fed up with her sister, who never answered a letter and only wrote to boast she'd got a part.

'Did she tell you she's in *Hair*?'

'*Hair*! Isn't that the show where they're all naked?'

'Yes! Poor Ronnie was terribly embarrassed.'

'She hadn't told me, no, but then I'm not surprised.'

The guest list was pretty much the same as the one for their second anniversary party, though she wouldn't be asking anyone from the co-op. They'd made new friends since then. The Barclays, who lived in the Travers' old house, were genuine salt-of-the-earth scousers. Some in the close still didn't like the idea of rubbing shoulders with market traders, but it would be hard to find a nicer couple than Sid and Vera Barclay. Having scarcely any education themselves, they were making sure things were different for their children. Ben, their eldest, was hoping to go to university next year, a fact that irritated Valerie Cunningham no end. She thought universities should be reserved for the middle and upper classes. The Cunninghams considered themselves very much middle.

For days beforehand, Annie baked trays of sausage rolls and mince pies. She was looking forward to Friday. Ten years! The fact that they were so happy together after all that time was a confirmation of their wedding vows, and it was only right to celebrate with a grand do.

Lauri was away, covering the Home Counties from his base in the London hotel where he always stayed.

He promised faithfully to leave at mid-day on Friday so he'd be home in time.

Annie bought herself a new outfit; a black ribbed-jersey suit. The top had tight sleeves and a cowl neck, and the skirt was long and narrow. She'd have to remember to hold her stomach in all night.

On Friday, she fetched the decorations from the loft. It was earlier than she usually put them up, but it seemed appropriate with the party so close to Christmas. Bruno said there was no need to come to work that day, but she went to calm herself down because she was so excited.

The children came out of school, Cunninghams included, excited themselves because they'd broken up for the holidays. She gave stern instructions not to touch the food in the breakfast room, already set out for tonight. Sara had made a pretty centrepiece of cones glued to a small log, sprayed with gold, and finished off with a red ribbon.

At half five, Valerie sounded her horn and her children made their departure. Annie had hoped the horn was Lauri's. Glancing at the clock, she saw he was late. Maybe he'd found it difficult to leave at mid-day.

'Is there time for a story?' Sara asked. They could both read well, but it wasn't the same as squeezing in the armchair with their mother.

'Just a quick one.' She was about to turn the television off when the announcer said something about an accident on the M6; a lorry had overturned. No-one had been hurt, but there was already a tailback of traffic. 'That probably accounts for why your dad's not here.'

The children were still addicted to Noddy. Annie read the one about Father Christmas getting stuck in the chimney and Noddy coming to his rescue with a tow hook and a rope on his little red car.

When she finished, Sara said in an awed voice, 'Look, Mummy, it's almost snowing.'

Through the French windows, little particles of ice were floating like fireflies against the black night air, and the lights of the Christmas tree were reflected; blurred smudges of red and yellow, blue and green. They could see themselves, very far away, as if they were at the bottom of the garden in the cold, their bodies joined together, but three distinct heads, one copper, one golden, the other dark.

Annie had a sense of perfect happiness as she sat with her children and imagined Lauri waiting impatiently in a traffic jam, longing to get home to his family, to the party which was being held to celebrate the fact that they had been married for ten whole years. There was that special atmosphere in the house, the thrilling, anticipatory feeling there always was when something particularly nice was about to happen, as if the bricks and mortar were aware a party had been planned.

Sara and Daniel had felt it, too. They were silent, staring at themselves in the garden whilst tiny dazzling fireflies flew around.

'Well,' Annie broke the spell, 'I'm getting nowhere fast at this rate. People'll be here soon. I'll trust you two to get washed and changed on your own. I reckon your dad's going to be late.'

Cecy was the first to arrive, she always was. Annie sent her next door to remind Valerie to bring her wine glasses. Then Chris Andrews came and wanted to know if Marie would be there.

'Pigs might fly,' Annie said sarcastically.

'It's just that I've written a play. I wondered if she'd read it. I say, you look nice, Annie. I've never seen you in black before.'

'You don't look so bad yourself,' she said. He wore a brocade waistcoat over a long, loose shirt and floppy trousers. 'I'll give you Marie's address and you can send the play to her.' She put him in charge of the music. 'I'm afraid it's all sixties stuff; the Beatles and the Rolling Stones. I haven't bought a record in ages.'

More people came. The Barclays brought two bottles of best sherry. Sid gave Annie a smacking kiss on the cheek and wished her, 'Happy Anniversary, luv.' Everyone wanted to know where Lauri was. Dot hollered, 'I heard about the M6 being blocked. I said to Bert, didn't I, luv? I said, "I wonder if poor Lauri's bogged down in that." And you can't let people know, can you, when you're stuck in a car?'

Mike Gallagher arrived in the fringed jacket he'd got married in, his red hair in a pony tail, and wearing the round metal-framed glasses that had become fashionable. Despite his freckles and still impish face, Mike had acquired an air of gravitas since becoming a successful businessman. Tonight he looked rather subdued. Annie remembered it would be a year next week that Glenda had died.

Every time she heard a car, she looked to see if it was her husband, but it was more guests; more cousins and their wives, people from the Labour Party. Then Sylvia in a taxi, even though the Grand was only ten minutes walk away.

Mike opened the door to let Sylvia in. They allowed each other a cold smile. Sylvia grabbed Annie's arm and began to drag her upstairs.

'Syl!' Annie protested. 'There's a party going on.'

Sylvia ignored her. She pushed her friend into the bedroom. 'I'm pregnant!' she sang. She threw herself on the bed. 'It's due in July – I'd give anything to see Eric's face when he finds out!'

'Oh!' Annie breathed. 'I couldn't possibly be more glad. When are you getting married?'

'Who's getting married? Ronnie's already got several wives. I've no intention of joining a harem.'

'But that means the baby will be illegitimate!'

Sylvia laughed merrily. 'Don't be so old-fashioned, Annie. This is the seventies, remember! Being illegitimate doesn't matter any more.'

'What's Ronnie got to say?'

'Oh, *him*!' Sylvia snorted. 'I've run away from Ronnie. I'm back in Liverpool for good. He had the nerve to suggest the baby was *his*!'

'Isn't it?' Annie said faintly.

'Yes, but he wanted me shut in a nursing home for the next six months, then the baby would be sent to his mother. Cheek!' She began to comb her hair in the mirror. 'I've chucked in my job. I suppose I'm a fugitive in a sort of way.'

'Bloody hell!'

Dot screeched, 'Annie, where's the corkscrew?' and she remembered the party and the fact there was still no Lauri at almost nine o'clock.

She wasn't quite sure when her feelings changed from worry to the almost certain knowledge something was wrong. Lauri's continued absence was beginning to concern everybody. People began to recall times when they had been stuck in a traffic jam for three hours, four hours, five. Dot said stoutly that if anything serious had happened, Annie would have heard hours ago. Chris Andrews suggested Lauri might have broken down.

'But he would have phoned,' Annie said, trying to sound sensible. 'They have telephones on the motorway, don't they?'

It was gone ten when the doorbell rang, and Gerry & The Pacemakers were singing, 'You'll Never Walk Alone'. Lauri wasn't very keen on music, but this was one of the few songs he liked.

Uncle Bert had opened the door. He held out an arm and Annie could feel it heavy on her shoulders when she saw the two policemen outside. She noticed how pretty the frost looked, glinting on the pavements, the blue light flashing on the car parked down the close.

'This is Mrs Menin,' Uncle Bert said. His arm tightened. The music came to a sudden halt and everyone gathered silently in the hall.

'I'm sorry, madam,' a policeman said. Annie thought dispassionately what a terrible job some people had. 'I'm afraid we have bad news . . .'

7

Lauri must have arrived at the hold-up on the M6 just before an exit. He left the motorway just past Manchester to take an alternative route home. Perhaps he got lost, perhaps he thought the country lane would take him home more quickly to his family and the party being held to celebrate the tenth anniversary of his marriage to Annie. No-one knew except Lauri himself, and Lauri was dead. His car skidded on the ice as he was about to drive over a little humpbacked bridge. Instead, the car had plunged into the stream below. The water wasn't deep enough to drown in, but the impact killed him instantly. He'd been there several hours before the headlights of a passing motorist revealed the Cortina, nose down in the stream.

Annie felt as if someone had removed a warm, comfortable blanket from her body. She was cold all the time. She couldn't stop shivering, and although she did her level best not to cry in front of the children, she wept when she lay in her cold bed at night and thought about the future without Lauri.

People couldn't have been kinder. Because they were there when the news arrived, they felt as if the tragedy was partly theirs. It helped to be surrounded by so much love, everyone saying what a fine man Lauri had been, such a devoted husband and father.

Fred Quillen came, looking uncomfortable, bringing condolences from the co-op. 'He was always on about you, Annie. He idolised his family.'

Mike Gallagher was the greatest help of all. 'You're thinking the world will never be the same again, but it won't last for ever, luv. Bit by bit, everything will return to normal. Lauri will always be part of you and the day will come when you'll be able to look into the future and it won't all be black. I know, it happened to me with Glenda.'

There was so much to do: the police came several times and she had to get confirmation of the death so a Death Certificate could be issued and she could arrange the funeral. Lauri had lodged a Will with the bank, leaving everything to her. The manager offered to release funds in the meantime to pay the undertakers.

Dot thought it terrible the coffin wasn't being brought back to Heather Close so everyone could say prayers around it.

'Lauri would hate that,' Annie said stubbornly. 'It would frighten the children, a dead body in the house, even if it is their dad.'

On the morning of the funeral, Annie woke up shivering, wondering how she would get through the day. It was still dark. She sat up, switched on the bedside lamp and pulled the duvet around her shoulders. Although she was used to Lauri being away, the empty space beside her seemed unbearable now she knew he would never sleep there again. She began to weep.

There were light footsteps outside, the door opened and Sara came in. Annie did her best to smile as her daughter crept into the bed.

'Sylvia's gone to make a cup of tea,' Sara whispered. Sylvia had scarcely left the house since the night of the party. She'd slept in the spare bed in Sara's room. 'Daniel's still asleep. I looked.'

It was odd, but Sara, Lauri's favourite, seemed far less affected by his loss than Daniel. Daniel wasn't upset. He was angry. 'Why won't Daddy be coming back?' he demanded when Annie tried to explain.

'Daddy's gone to heaven, sweetheart.' She couldn't bring herself to use the stark word, 'dead', not to a seven-year-old child, though 'heaven' was a lie, because Lauri was an atheist and should by rights be burning in hell if everything she'd ever learnt about religion was true.

'How *dare* he go to heaven and leave us?' Daniel burst out furiously.

She felt totally inadequate. More than anything, she wanted the children to be upset as little as possible by Lauri's death. Christmas was only a few days off. Their presents had been bought. She would do all she could to make it happy for them.

'I hate him. I bloody hate him.' Daniel stomped up to his room and, before Annie could follow, the telephone rang for the umpteenth time.

Sara snuggled underneath her mother's arm. 'Why can't me and Daniel go to the funeral, Mummy?'

'Because young children don't normally go to funerals, luv. Cecy's coming to look after you.'

To Annie's relief, Sylvia came in with three cups of tea. She sat on the edge of the bed. 'How do you feel?' she asked.

'As well as can be expected.'

Sylvia was too happy within herself to look sombre all the time. Every now and then she would burst into song, then stop when she remembered what had happened. Annie didn't mind. In fact, it was far preferable to Dot, who collapsed into paroxysms of tears every time she came, upsetting the children no end. Even Valerie Cunningham was distraught. She'd always had a soft spot for Lauri, she confessed. Sylvia had never liked Lauri. Although it didn't make sense, it was almost a relief to be in the company of someone whose eyes didn't fill up with tears at the mere mention of his name.

'Auntie Sylvia's expecting a baby,' said Sara. 'The daddy is a prince. He wears a gold turban with a jewel in the middle, and lies on a couch while beautiful ladies feed him with purple grapes.'

'You're filling her head with nonsense,' Annie said mildly.

'I thought I'd turn it into a fairytale,' Sylvia patted her flat stomach. 'It *is* a fairytale in a sort of way.'

'Has Cecy got over the shock yet?'

'She'd got over it by next morning when she realised she could ring Mrs Church and tell her I was pregnant. I've no idea how she'll explain the lack of a husband. Eric's got a wife, but I'll have a baby, which means the Delgados have come out on top.' She grinned slyly. 'Talking of husbands, I really dig Mike Gallagher in those glasses.'

'Sylvia! You're to leave Mike alone. He's terribly vulnerable at the moment. It's only a year since Glenda . . . you know.'

'What was she like, this Glenda?'

'Very nice. Much nicer than you'll ever be.'

Daniel came into the room looking very grim and clutching the Teddy he'd discarded years ago. Annie patted the bed. 'Come on, luv.'

'I'd sooner sit the side Daddy used to sleep,' he said gruffly.

Sara obligingly climbed over her mother. Daniel got into bed and sat stiffly in Lauri's place. When Annie put her arm around him, he shrugged her off. 'I'm fed up Daddy's gone to heaven. Why couldn't he stay here?'

'Because heaven is a much nicer place than Heather Close, silly,' Sara admonished him.

Sylvia frowned and said, 'I think you should be a bit more honest with the children, don't you?'

Annie was about to explain she didn't want them hurt, when the doorbell rang and Sylvia went to answer it. She supposed she'd better get up. She glanced at Daniel. His brow was furrowed and his bottom lip trembled as if he were about to cry. She nudged him. 'Cheer up.'

'Don't want to,' he muttered.

'You've got a visitor, Annie,' Sylvia shouted.

It must be someone like Auntie Dot or Valerie, or Sylvia wouldn't have let the visitor come upstairs. Annie wasn't prepared for her sister to come into the bedroom. 'Marie!' she gasped.

'Dot rang yesterday wanting to know why I wasn't coming to the funeral. I told her I knew nothing about it. I'm terribly sorry to hear about Lauri.' Marie looked stricken. 'Oh, sis, why didn't you tell me?'

Annie's voice was very slow and deliberate when she answered. 'Because if I had, and you'd ignored it like you ignore everything, then I would never have forgiven you. I thought it best to say nothing.'

Marie looked deeply hurt. 'What sort of person do you take me for? I may not turn up for parties and stuff, but do you honestly think I'd turn a blind eye to the death of my sister's husband?'

Annie glanced sharply at the children, but the word 'death' didn't seem to have penetrated. Instead, they were staring, fascinated, at the strange young woman in the curly fur coat that Marie mustn't have realised was just like the one Mam used to have. 'This is your Auntie Marie,' she said. 'She was in *Dr Who*, remember?'

'You look different,' Sara remarked.

'I should hope so!' Marie made a funny face and the children giggled. 'I looked ghastly in that make-up.'

'Did you meet the Daleks?' Daniel asked eagerly.

'Every single one.'

'Would you like a cup of tea, Marie?' Sylvia called.

'Thanks.' Marie jerked her head. 'What's she doing here?'

'Keeping me company.'

'I'm your sister. I would have been prepared to do that.'

'Really!' Annie smiled sarcastically. 'What about *Hair*?'

Marie shrugged uncomfortably. 'Who told you?'

'Sylvia saw it a few weeks ago.'

'I'm only in the chorus. I'll easily be replaced.'

'Would you still be here if you were the star?'

'For goodness' sake, Annie,' Marie said wearily. 'You always expect things to be perfect. You have this rose-tinted picture in your mind of what sisters should be like, for ever in each other's pockets. Why can't you accept me for what I am? I'm an actress, a hopeless communicator, but I'll always be here for you when you really need me.'

Sara had slipped out of bed and was stroking the fur coat. Marie smiled. 'Try it on, darling.'

Sylvia came in with the tea. 'How long are you staying?' she asked.

'Till Boxing Day.'

'In that case, I'll take my stuff away and you can have the bed.'

'There's no need, Syl,' Annie put in. 'Marie can sleep with me.'

'I'd sooner go. Bruno will welcome the extra help over Christmas.'

Marie made a face at Sylvia's departing back. 'She still hates me.'

Downstairs, the doorbell went and the telephone rang, both at the same time. Annie threw back the duvet. 'I'd better get up. It's going to be one hell of a day and I'm not looking forward to it a bit.'

Daniel crawled across the bed and grabbed Marie's skirt. 'Will you tell us about the Daleks?'

Marie leant and clasped his face in both hands. 'Of course. You know, you remind me very much of someone I knew a long, long time ago.'

'Has he gone to heaven?'

'It was a lady and I've no idea if she went to heaven.' She glanced wryly at her sister. 'What do you think?'

Annie supposed it was no different from any other funeral. Sylvia loaned her a black coat to save buying one and she bought a black beret, because it seemed silly to spend a lot of money on a hat she'd never wear again. She looked a bit like a refugee, but what did it matter?

A cold wind blew across the cemetery and it was impossible to accept that Lauri lay inside the coffin when it was lowered into the grave. A lump came to her throat when she thought she would never see him again.

A small crowd came back to Heather Close, to the refreshments that Cecy had prepared. Most didn't stay long. Perhaps Sylvia felt in the way, because she left early, and by one o'clock only Marie, Dot and Bert remained. As Mike Gallagher was leaving he handed Annie an envelope. 'We'd just started a pension fund. That's due for Lauri.'

Annie knew nothing about a pension fund. She opened the envelope later and found a cheque for five hundred pounds. Like Lauri, she didn't want charity. Next time she saw Mike she'd give him the cheque back.

*

Christmas came and Christmas went. Marie got on well with the children. She seemed able to come down to their level without being patronising. Annie thought wistfully she would have made a wonderful mother. Daniel wanted to know everything about *Dr Who* and she promised to send a photo signed by Dr Who himself, Patrick Troughton.

On Boxing Day morning, it was Marie who came into the room and got into bed with Annie. They sat up, hugging the duvet around them.

'You won't forget that picture, will you?' Annie pleaded. 'Otherwise Daniel will be bitterly disappointed.'

Marie promised to post it as soon as she got home. 'I won't leave it so long before I come again,' she vowed.

'I've a feeling you said something like that before.'

'I'm sorry, sis, but everything's so frenetic down there.'

'You said that, too.' Annie smiled. 'It doesn't matter, luv. You came when I really needed you. That's all I care. How's the acting going, anyroad? We've scarcely had time to talk since you came.'

Marie paused before answering. 'Lousy, sis,' she sighed. 'I think I'm the oldest female in *Hair*. I'm thirty, and the others are at least ten years younger. I was surprised they took me on at my age.' Her face twisted bitterly. 'I'm *old*, Annie, and I've got nowhere.'

'I don't suppose you've thought of giving up?' Annie prayed the answer would be 'yes', but Marie shook her head.

'If I give up now, I'll have wasted thirteen years. No, sis, I'm keeping on. I'll be a success if it kills me.'

Chris Andrews came over later to see Marie. He blushed when she told him he looked adorable with his pigtail. 'I've written a play,' he said nervously. 'It's the

313

first I've done since *Goldilocks*. I wondered if you'd read it and let me have your opinion.'

'Of course,' Marie said grandly, as if budding playwrights regularly pressed their work on her. She left that afternoon to return to the chorus of *Hair* and her dream of becoming a famous actress.

Marie had gone, Christmas was over. Tomorrow, things would be back to normal. People would get on with their lives, including Annie, though it wouldn't be normal for her. She had to learn to live without Lauri.

She'd never looked in the drawer containing Lauri's papers before. He'd taken care of everything; written cheques for the bills which he left on the windowsill beside the front door for her to post.

'Crikey!' she muttered when she sorted through the bank and building society statements, the bills for gas, electricity, rates, telephone, insurance. 'I never realised the central heating cost so much.' She'd never realised *anything* cost so much, and felt resentment that he'd kept her so much in the dark, not shared things the way other couples did. The resentment was immediately replaced by guilt, as it seemed awful to feel even mildly angry with someone who'd so recently died.

She immediately turned the central heating down. It was New Year's Day and snowing heavily, but Sara and Daniel were next door.

The papers were spread on the table and she saw that, according to the last statement from the building society, two thousand pounds was owed on the house, yet the initial loan hadn't been for much more. The monthly payments had been taken up in interest charges.

'Bloody hell!' She multiplied the quarterly bills by four, the mortgage payments by twelve, added the yearly bills, and divided the total by fifty-two.

'Bloody hell!' she said again. It came to nearly twice what she would get in widow's pension coupled with Family Allowance for Daniel. She might be allowed other benefit from the State, but it would never be enough to meet the bills – and there were food and clothes to buy on top. She searched for the latest bank statement. It was irritating that she had no idea how much money was in the bank.

'Well, *that* won't last long,' she thought when she found it was four hundred and eighty-two pounds, but the statement was dated the first of December and would be taken up by funeral costs. 'I think I'll keep that cheque from Mike, after all. It will last until I get a job. We should have taken out one of those insurance things me dad used to sell.' People paid coppers a week towards a lump sum when someone died. 'But it never crossed me mind one of us would die.' She screwed up her face, determined not to cry. 'Anyroad, funerals cost a fortune nowadays, it would have taken more than pennies to save four hundred pounds.'

As soon as the children were back at school, she'd look for a job. Bruno said she could return to the Grand, but the wages weren't nearly enough. Even so, the job would have to be part-time. There was no way she'd let Sara and Daniel become latchkey kids like Valerie's.

It was strange how life seemed to repeat itself. Annie found herself again searching through the Liverpool *Echo* for work. Chris Andrews let her borrow his typewriter to practise on, and after a few hesitant starts, she found her fingers as nimble as ever. It was the same with shorthand. Machin & Harpers were good teachers. If she were asked to take a test during an interview, she would pass with flying colours.

If she ever went for an interview! Only a few of the

jobs advertised were part-time. Annie wrote after every single one, but by the time February arrived all she had received was letter after letter of rejection. In desperation, she discussed the matter with her neighbour. Valerie had found a job. What magic formula had *she* used?

'No-one will take you if you've got young children,' Valerie said flatly. 'They think you'll be off every five minutes if they've got a cold or something, that you'd always put the kids before the job.'

'I would,' said Annie.

Valerie shrugged, as if this proved her point.

'How did you manage it?' Annie asked curiously. 'You've got four.'

'I told them my mother lived with me.' Valerie had the grace to blush. Mrs Owen had been persuaded to stay in Heather Close during the holidays, but that was all. Tracy had suffered from a bad cold the whole of last term, but she'd still been sent to school.

School holidays were something Annie hadn't allowed herself to think about. She was concerned only with the immediate future. The money in the bank was shrinking alarmingly. If she wasn't fixed up by Easter, she had no idea what would happen.

That night, she walked round the house to see if there was anything to sell, but all she found was the children's old cot which might fetch enough to pay for half a week's groceries. Of course, she could sell the Anglia which was old, but it ran well and she wanted to keep it. It would save time hanging round for buses if she ever got a job, though that seemed more and more unlikely, and when Sara started at Grenville Lucas next year, she could give her a lift when it was raining.

'Oh, Lauri,' she whispered. She tried to imagine him, wherever he was; perhaps his spirit still existed, looking down on her, offering advice, telling her what she should do. They'd never talked about death, they'd never really talked about anything serious. No doubt he thought he'd always be there to look after her and the children.

Annie sighed. It was story-time. The hour spent together in the chair had become very precious lately. When she finished reading, Daniel always wanted to know about heaven, what was it like? Tonight, he twisted his face earnestly. 'Will Dad get on well with God?'

'Your dad got on well with everybody.' Except me, she thought.

She'd gone to see the headmistress, Mrs Dawson, and told her about Lauri the day the children returned to school. 'We'll keep an eye on them,' Mrs Dawson promised. 'The loss of a parent affects different children in different ways, but in my experience, they always pull through.'

The children went to bed. Marie had sent the signed picture of Dr Who, and it was stuck with a drawing pin to Daniel's wall.

Sylvia was coming round later. She was happily househunting, looking for somewhere with a garden for children to play in. 'I'm not stopping at one,' she said cheerfully. 'Once this is born, I shall look round for a suitably gorgeous man to sire the second. D'you think Mike would be interested?' she added teasingly. 'I'd quite like a red-haired baby.'

Lucky old Sylvia, Annie thought moodily. She's never had to worry about money.

She made tea ready for when Sylvia came, and was sitting in the breakfast room, thinking tearfully about Lauri, and wondering what the hell she was supposed to do, when the back door opened.

'It's only us,' Valerie Cunningham shouted. She came in followed by Kevin. 'We'd like a little word.'

'Sit down. I'm expecting Sylvia any minute.' Annie felt a moment of hope. Perhaps Valerie had told Kevin about her unsuccessful search for work, and he'd come to offer her a job in his bank!

They looked at each other expectantly, then, when her husband made no attempt to speak, Valerie began in a rush, 'I've been talking to Kevin about your little problem.'

It didn't exactly seem a *little* problem, Annie thought, and her expectations of a job offer soared slightly higher.

'The thing is, we wondered if you'd thought of selling the house?'

'Selling the house!' The idea had never crossed her mind.

Kevin was becoming jowly. His throat wobbled when he spoke. 'It's just that we've got these friends, it's a chap I work with, actually, and when I told him there was a possibility next door might become vacant, he was immediately interested.'

'No-one told me there was a possibility my house might become vacant.' Annie's head felt very hot, as if the blood were rushing through at top speed and becoming over-heated. She told herself they were only being kind in attempting to solve her 'little' problem.

'I don't know if you realise how much these houses are worth, Annie,' Valerie said eagerly.

'My friend is prepared to pay five thousand – cash, that is.' Kevin's pale eyes blinked behind his glasses. 'So you wouldn't have to wait until he got a mortgage. He wouldn't want a survey. There's nothing wrong with our house, so yours is bound to be all right.'

'Five thousand!' Annie gasped. 'But Lauri only paid . . .' What was it? She'd only looked at the building society papers a few weeks ago.

'Two thousand, seven-fifty,' Valerie said promptly. 'Property is the best investment you can have.'

'My friend is even prepared to pay the solicitor's costs,' Kevin went on. 'It would be over and done with in a few weeks, and you'd have a few thousand to play with once you've paid off the mortgage.'

'And where do me and the children live then, on the streets?'

Valerie laughed. 'You can get a nice little place for a couple of thou or less. Some of those terraced houses look quite cosy done up.' She glanced around the room. 'You have an eye for decoration, Annie. I've always thought your house looked far smarter than ours.'

A nice little place like Orlando Street, Annie thought bleakly. A place without a garden, so there'd be no willow tree, no shed with a verandah, no swing. If she'd stayed with Auntie Dot, that sort of house might hold no terror, but there was no way she'd return to somewhere like Orlando Street now.

'Heather Close is such a desirable place to live,' Valerie said.

'I know,' said Annie. 'Which is why I intend to stay.'

Next morning, Annie phoned an estate agent and said she was thinking of selling her house in Heather Close and how much was it worth?

'Whereabouts in Heather Close?'

'The far end, number seven.' She hoped he wouldn't ask to put a board up, as she had no intention of parting with Lauri's house.

'The best part!' the man said warmly. 'I can see it in my mind's eye. We handled next door, the old couple who died. You've got an exceptionally big garden. Are you the one with the willow tree?'

'That's right.'

The estate agent hummed a little tune. 'Well, I'd need to look round, but I'd say, roughly, mind, six and a half thou. You could ask a few hundred more, then wait and see how the cookie crumbles.'

'Thank you,' Annie said faintly. She assured him she'd be in touch immediately she'd made up her mind.

Six and a half thousand! She cast aside the suspicion that the Cunninghams had been trying to deceive her, because it scarcely bore thinking about. She supposed she *could* sell and buy somewhere cheaper and live on what was left, but although she didn't know much about this sort of thing, she had a feeling the building society would never give her, a widow without a job, another mortgage, which meant she'd have to buy the 'somewhere cheaper' for cash. By the time she'd repaid the two thousand pounds owing, the rest wouldn't last all *that* long. The cost of living was rising, despite the fact Edward Heath had promised to 'cut prices at a stroke', and the new Value Added Tax didn't help. Food prices were set to rise even further now the country had joined the European Community. Lauri had always said joining the EEC was a terrible mistake. Nearly everyone in the Labour Party was dead against it.

Annie touched the smooth cupola-shaped knob at the bottom of the stairs which Lauri had made specially. She couldn't stand the idea of another family living here. It was intolerable to imagine a strange woman using *her* kitchen, strange children playing inside the willow tree, an entirely strange family sitting in front of the fireplace that Lauri had built. It may only be a rather ordinary semi-detached in a suburb of Liverpool, but the house was part of Lauri, part of her. It was the only home the children had ever known. The time might come when she'd have no option but to sell, but until that time came, Annie vowed she would do all she could to cling on to the home she loved.

*

She wasn't sure where to turn next. She typed out a dozen cards for shop windows offering typing at ten shillings an hour, and was thrilled when a girl, a medical student, brought a thesis to be typed. The writing was execrable and contained numerous Latin terms. Annie typed till past midnight for two nights in a row. The girl looked startled when asked for three pounds, although it should have been more.

Days later, an elderly man turned up with a novel he'd written in a neat, crabbed, though legible hand, but when she began to type, there were lines and circles everywhere, moving words, sentences or entire paragraphs from one place to another, and she'd be halfway down a page, only to discover she hadn't included something from the page before. It took two weeks of solid work to complete the nearly five hundred pages. Annie totalled up the hours; it came to over a hundred. She couldn't possibly ask for fifty pounds! She asked for thirty, and the man looked even more startled than the student.

'I hope I get it published after all this expense,' he grumbled.

She doubted it. It was the worst novel she'd ever read.

Although a very nice man from a garage brought several invoices and insisted on giving her a pound when she only asked for ten shillings, she realised she wasn't going to make a fortune as a typist. A few weeks later she gave Chris Andrews his typewriter back.

She economised on everything, kept the central heating turned down during the day, cancelled some of the insurances, bought the cheapest mincemeat and made pies and stews. The children remarked on how often they seemed to have jelly and custard for afters.

They had no idea how hard up she was. She still gave them dinner money for school, although they could have had free meals, because she didn't want them thinking they were different. No-one knew the difficulties she was having, except the Cunninghams. She would have had the telephone disconnected, but people might guess why. When Dot or Bert asked how she was coping, she assured them, 'Fine.' They had a few pounds put away, and would insist on helping if they knew she was in trouble. But it would be degrading to take money off two old people who enjoyed splashing their tiny amount of wealth on their grandchildren.

In May, the balance in the bank had shrunk to double figures, and the electricity bill was due any minute. 'I should have stayed at the Grand, there would have been a few pounds coming in.' But Bruno had hired someone else months ago. 'If only I had someone to *talk* to,' Annie fretted. 'If only our Marie would get in touch!' Marie was impossible to get hold of, never there when she phoned. Chris Andrews, though, had received a letter. Marie thought his play 'wonderful', and promised to show it to a director she knew.

One Sunday after Mass, she was in the garden, digging at the weeds in a desultory fashion, conscious of the sun warm on her back, when she heard Vera Barclay come into her garden. Vera helped on the fruit and veg stall all week and could only do her washing on Sundays. Annie straightened up, relieved to give the weeds a rest for the moment.

'Morning, Vera,' she shouted over the Travers' old shiplap fence.

Vera was hidden behind a sheet she was pegging on the line. Her rosy, weatherbeaten face appeared, the inevitable cigarette hanging from her mouth. She bade Annie a cheerful 'Morning, luv.' She was a small, outgoing woman with short curly brown hair. 'How's things?'

'Fine,' Annie said automatically.

After Vera had pegged out another sheet, she came over to the fence and looked at Annie searchingly with her bright blue eyes. 'You're always "fine",' she said.

'Well . . .' Annie shrugged.

'I wouldn't be fine if my Sid had passed away and I was left with two young kids to bring up on me own.'

'Well,' Annie said again. She'd always known that Vera and Sid were kindness itself. They were good neighbours, and had sent a lovely wreath for Lauri's funeral, but the two women had never become close. They talked mainly, as now, over the fence. Annie was more friendly with Valerie, whom she'd never particularly cared for, than with Vera.

Sara and Daniel came wandering into the garden, looking rather lost. 'Why don't you go and play next door?' Annie suggested. Shouts and screams could be heard from the Cunninghams.

Sara shook her head. Daniel took no notice and headed for the swing. They sat on it together, Sara pushing slightly with her foot.

'I've got something that'll cheer you two up.' Vera disappeared into the house and came back with two big Jaffa oranges. 'They're lovely and sweet and juicy – and there's no pips!'

To Annie's embarrassment, Daniel made no move to get the orange, but Sara came across and took them both. 'Thank you very much,' she said politely. 'It's ages since we had an orange.'

'Is it now!' Vera leant her brown, sunburnt arms on the fence. 'Finding things difficult, are you, Annie? And if you say "well" again, I'll fetch another orange and chuck it at you!'

It was awfully difficult not to cry with Vera regarding her so understandingly. Annie nodded without speaking.

'Look, luv, I've another load of washing to hang out, and there's dinner to cook, but I'll pop round to see you this avvy, about three. I think what you need is a shoulder to cry on.'

'I would have come before,' Vera said, 'but folks are dead snooty round here, and I didn't want to appear as if I was intruding. Back where we used to live in Smithdown Road, I wouldn't have hesitated. That's what I miss most since we left, me neighbours. Have you got an ashtray, luv?'

Annie shoved an ashtray in her direction, and described the pickle she was in, holding nothing back. Vera said she thought she'd be mad to sell the house. 'It's going back when you want to go forward.'

'But what else can I do?' Annie said desperately. 'I'm down to eighty pounds.'

Vera puffed furiously on her cigarette and thought hard. 'What about dressmaking?' she suggested. 'I could hardly believe it when you told me you made your own clothes. They look dead professional.'

Annie glanced at the sewing machine on the small table in the bay window. 'I don't know,' she said doubtfully. 'I've never had a lesson and I'm hopeless at turning collars.' She remembered the awful time she'd had with typing, but supposed dressmaking was different as you could give a firm quotation beforehand.

'Women are always on the look-out for a good dressmaker,' Vera said encouragingly. 'You could take a course, finish yourself off, as it were. I'd be only too happy to recommend you to me mates.' She tapped her teeth with a tobacco-stained fingernail. 'In the meantime, you need to get a few bob together, don't you?'

'The electricity bill's due any minute, and the mortgage has to be paid at the beginning of June.'

Vera snapped her fingers as if she'd had a brainwave.

'Look, why not have a good clear-out? Get rid of the kids' old toys, the odd dishes and cutlery you never use, tools, knick-knacks like ornaments you hate which have got shoved to the back of a cupboard, and I bet your wardrobe's stuffed with clothes you'll never wear again.'

'And what do I do with them?' asked Annie, mystified.

'You sell 'em,' Vera grinned.

'Who to?'

'Have you never been to Great Homer Street market, luv?' When Annie shook her head, Vera went on, 'Traders are always on the look-out for good stuff to sell; bric-a-brac and secondhand clothes, mainly. Once you've got the stuff ready, I'll take it and see what I can get.'

'There's no need for you to go to so much trouble. I'll take it meself.' There was still tax and insurance left on the Anglia.

'Lord Almighty, luv, when they see an innocent like you, they'll offer peanuts. No,' Vera said firmly, '*I'll* take it, and make sure you get a good price. There'll be enough for the electricity bill or my name's not Vera Barclay.'

After Vera had gone, Annie thought, 'Dressmaking!'

She'd do it. She'd do anything to keep the house and get herself out of the hole she was in, but she wasn't keen on making clothes for other people. Customers would want things made to a pattern, but she rarely used a pattern. She made things up out of her head, adding little imaginative touches, like a pleated bodice, an embroidered flower on a pocket. She actually got a little thrill when the garment was finished, though nothing had given her such pleasure as the costumes she'd made for the pantomime at Grenville Lucas. It wouldn't be possible to use your imagination on other women's clothes.

The children joined in the great sort-out, as if it was a game, delving in cupboards and drawers. Annie was pleased. Daniel loved going in the loft, though he wasn't willing to part with a single item of his own. He glared at her mutinously when she opened the cupboard in his room in search of baby toys.

'But you haven't played with it in years,' Annie cried, when he refused to give up the plastic telephone he'd got on his first birthday.

'Want to keep it,' he mumbled. 'It's mine.'

'All right, sweetheart. I wouldn't dream of taking anything you want to keep. Where did all these come from?' She pointed to the neat row of Matchbox cars at the back of the shelf.

'Dad gave them to me.' He burst into tears. 'Don't take the cars that Daddy bought.'

'Oh, Daniel!' Annie knelt and took him in her arms. He felt hot. He'd been very sullen since Lauri died, but she was at a loss what to do. All she could think of was to make as much fuss of him as possible. 'I didn't realise Dad had bought so many, that's all.' Lauri brought a Matchbox car for Daniel and a book for Sara each time he went away.

It was nice to have a good clear-out, she thought later, when the table was full of old cups and saucers she'd never use again and several Pyrex bowls that she'd never used at all. How on earth had she managed to acquire three tin-openers and so many pairs of scissors? She was glad to see the back of that hideous set of three monkeys which was a wedding present from she couldn't remember whom, and where on earth had the bronze lion which Daniel had found in the loft come from?

Uncle Bert had taken Lauri's clothes for a seamen's

charity in town, though there was no way she would have sent them to a market. Annie found herself stopping from time to time, remembering, as she ruthlessly cleared her wardrobe. The ivory polka-dotted dress she'd made for her twenty-first, the night Lauri proposed. The brown coat she wore to Stickley & Plumm. Her wedding dress, which wasn't a proper wedding dress at all. In fact, it was a miserable garment which she'd never worn again. She paused over a green dress with a pleated skirt which she'd forgotten she had. The first time she'd worn it was when she'd gone to see *Psycho* with Sylvia. God, what an awful night! *Psycho* had been on television months ago, but she still couldn't bear to watch.

The bed was heaped with clothes when she finished, most in very good condition. She and Sylvia had been mad on clothes, and Annie had thrown little away. It was always in her mind to re-model things, though she rarely did. She recalled meaning to turn the green dress into a suit, and the ivory taffeta would look lovely as a skirt with a black top.

But there was no chance of that happening now. In a few days, the things would be gone, and what would she get? Enough to pay the electricity bill, along with the stuff downstairs. It wasn't that she cared about losing a few old clothes, but the manner of their going upset her.

'Damn you, Lauri!' she swore. It was terrible, but with the non-stop worry over money since he'd gone, the main emotion she felt for him was anger; anger that they'd never had a joint bank account, that he resented her having any responsibility so she didn't know how much electricity and gas cost, that they'd never talked about death. Valerie Cunningham boasted that Kevin had a massive insurance policy. 'Me and the kids will be better off with Kevin dead than alive.'

Annie burrowed under the clothes and began to cry. She cried until she felt as if her heart would break; for Lauri, for Sara and Daniel, a little for herself. She emerged what seemed like hours later, but a glance at the alarm clock showed it was only ten minutes. The telephone was ringing, but she ignored it and began to fold the clothes neatly.

She wasn't sure where the idea came from; it arrived quite out of the blue. If someone was prepared to pay for all these things, they must be planning to sell them at a profit.

In which case, *she would start a secondhand clothes stall herself*!

Great Homer Street

I

Vera Barclay said Great Homer Street market only operated on Saturdays which was a relief, as there would be no problem with the children.

However, Vera went on, getting a stall wasn't easy. There was a list of people waiting for a place. She tapped her nose and winked. 'Leave it to Sid. He'll put in a word on your behalf. His ould ma had a stall in Paddy's Market all her life, so he's quids in with the powers that be.'

All Annie could do was wait. She put her clothes back in the wardrobe, and Vera got just over seven pounds for the bric-a-brac.

Of course, she couldn't just sit and do nothing in the meantime. Money was needed to live on. Yet again, she returned to the jobs section of the *Echo*, but this time she didn't bother with office vacancies. With relative ease, she found employment as a cleaner-cum-kitchen worker in a residential hotel in Blundellsands, a short distance away. From Monday to Friday, she stripped and re-made beds, cleaned bathrooms, and vacuumed till one-thirty. Then she went down to the kitchen to wash dishes and mop floors. At half past three she went home, just in time to meet the children coming out of school.

She told no-one what she was doing, not because she was ashamed, but because she didn't want their comments. When anyone asked, she told them she was in Reception. 'It's only temporary. Soon, I'm going into business on me own.' On Saturdays, she left the children with Valerie and took herself in the Anglia to jumble sales in Southport to acquire stock. The garage was full of stuff which she had yet to wash and iron.

'What sort of business?' Dot demanded. Annie said she'd explain when she was ready.

She earned enough to keep her head above water until she started the market stall. Although she didn't expect to become rich, she hoped and prayed she'd earn enough to pay the mortgage and the bills and keep the children, if not in the manner to which they were accustomed, at least so they didn't go short of the things other children had.

Annie was almost asleep when the phone went. She glanced at the clock, just gone midnight. She threw back the bedclothes and ran downstairs, praying it wasn't bad news.

'Sylvia's had the baby.' Cecy was exultant. 'I'm a grandmother!'

'But it's two weeks early!' Annie gasped.

'I know, but the first contraction came at ten o'clock tonight. Bruno got her to hospital just in time. It's a little girl, Annie, a beautiful little girl with jet black hair.'

'Has she decided on a name yet?' Sylvia had thought of a hundred names over the last few months.

'Yasmin.'

'Yasmin!' Annie had never heard that mentioned before.

'Actually, Annie,' Cecy's voice sank to a whisper, 'I wouldn't say this to another soul, but I've a strong suspicion the baby is coloured. Has Sylvia ever discussed the father with you?'

'No, she hasn't,' Annie lied.

When she went to see her friend in hospital the next day, Sylvia was sitting up in bed wearing a frilly blue bedjacket over a matching nightie, her face made up and her blonde hair perfectly groomed. She looked unreasonably glowing and unbearably smug.

'Have you seen Yasmin?' she crowed the minute Annie appeared.

'Yes. Cecy pointed her out in the nursery. She's gorgeous.' Apart from Sara, Annie had never seen such a pretty baby. Yasmin's skin was a creamy coffee colour, and she had thick glossy hair.

'You know,' Sylvia hissed, glancing surreptitiously around the ward, 'some of the babies are actually *bald*!'

'They don't stay bald.'

'And some are hideously ugly.'

Annie made an impatient face. 'They don't stay ugly, either.'

'You know something else? I can't understand all the fuss you made over Daniel. Having a baby is as easy as pie.'

'It would be wise not to say that to the other women, Sylvia,' Annie snapped, 'else you won't be very popular in the ward. Daniel was three and a half pounds heavier than Yasmin.' Sylvia's air of self-satisfaction was irritating. 'I hope your next affair is with a man built like Mr Universe and the baby weighs at least twelve pounds.'

Annie could have a market stall in August, three weeks off. 'But if anyone asks,' Sid Barclay said, 'you've been waiting six months.'

'Oh, Sid. What can I do to thank you?'

He winked. Sid was a small man with unnaturally broad shoulders and muscled arms from hoisting thousands of boxes of fruit and veg over the years. 'If I wasn't married, luv, I could think of a hundred things.'

Annie blushed. The message had come just in time. She'd given her notice in at the hotel as the children were about to break up for the summer. If the stall failed, she'd look for another job in September. 'But it *won't* fail,' she vowed. 'I'll make it work if it kills me!'

That night, she washed the remainder of the clothes which had been stored in the garage. She wondered if Valerie was ever curious about the never-ending assortment of strange garments hanging on her neighbour's line, but Valerie was probably too busy to notice.

It was amazing what people threw out. Some things were virtually new. Perhaps they didn't fit, or the owner decided she didn't like the frock or blouse or skirt when she got home, and couldn't be bothered returning it. There were items that seemed to have been thrown away merely because a seam was undone or the hem was coming down, which were easily repaired. There might be a button missing and, occasionally, there was actually a spare button inside. Otherwise, she sorted through her button box and could always find one that matched reasonably well.

The washing finished, she did some ironing. Fancy chucking out a white silk Marks & Spencer's shirt blouse that looked as if it had never been worn! It was the sort of thing that would never go out of fashion.

She hung everything in the garage when she'd finished. She'd made two clothes-racks out of broom-handles. They were rough and ready, but would do until she could afford the professional sort. The wire hangers she'd got a shilling a dozen in a shop in Bootle which was closing down.

The children were as thrilled as she was when she told them what she had planned. They'd come to the last few jumble sales. Sara had bought loads of books, and Daniel acquired the oddest things; an old toaster, a clock with no hands, and last week an ancient wireless that he was carefully taking to pieces in his room.

She could hardly wait for August. Mike Gallagher had said that the day would come when she would look forward to the future, and Annie was astonished that it had arrived so quickly.

'A *market* stall! Jaysus, girl, have you no shame? Your mam and dad'll turn in their graves.' Dot Gallagher's face had turned white with shock. 'What will people think?'

'Oh, you're a terrible snob, Auntie Dot,' Annie said crossly. 'I don't give a damn about what people think.'

Dot looked quite faint. '*Me*, a *snob*!'

'You're a working-class snob, which is the worst sort. Cecy thinks it's dead exciting, and she's got far more to be snobbish about than you.' After all, if Bruno was a Count, then Cecy was a Countess. 'She's given me loads of lovely things to sell.' She'd even offered to go to jumble sales on Saturdays when Annie was busy, or look after the stall if she preferred to go herself. Bruno too was full of admiration for Annie's entrepreneurial spirit.

Dot muttered there was no need for Lady Muck to put on her airs and graces now there was an illegitimate baby in the family. She offered to turn out her wardrobe. 'I'll let you have all me old things.'

'Thanks, Auntie Dot,' Annie said gratefully, though she couldn't imagine anyone wanting to buy the stiff, violently patterned Crimplene frocks her aunt usually wore.

For some mysterious reason, Sylvia had bought a thatched cottage down an isolated country lane just outside Ormskirk, miles away from Waterloo. Perhaps she'd been influenced by the big, wild garden with its mature trees, that would be ideal for children to play in. It was awkward to get to and she complained bitterly that no-one came to see her.

'I'm not surprised,' said Annie the second time she went. 'Why didn't you buy somewhere nearer? Anyroad, Cecy comes every day.'

'I wish Cecy would stay away, she drives me mad!' Sylvia looked harassed. Yasmin had turned out to be a fractious child – Annie tried hard not to be glad. 'She keeps reminiscing about when I was a baby. If you must know, I find it distasteful to be reminded I was breastfed. She even had the nerve to suggest I give Yasmin a dummy!'

'What's wrong with that! A dummy dipped in Virol might stop the poor child crying so much.'

'And spoil the shape of her lips for ever, not likely!'

Yasmin started to cry, and her anxious mother raced upstairs to fetch her beautiful five-week-old daughter from the Victorian pine cradle draped with old Nottingham lace. Most of the furniture in the cottage was genuine antique pine. Even the lovely, floppy three-piece with its feather cushions was old, and had been re-upholstered in dusky pink velvet. Annie dreaded to think what would happen when Yasmin started walking and touched everything with her sticky fingers.

The early morning sky was black, threatening rain. Annie made sure she had the tarpaulin before she set off at six o'clock for her first day as a market trader. The boot had been packed the night before, the clothes neatly laid on top of each other until it would barely close. There were smaller things on the passenger seat and Sara and Daniel were in the back with more stuff piled on their knees.

'Ready for off!' she cried cheerfully, though she felt anything but cheerful. Now the moment had come, she was petrified. A market stall seemed a stupid idea. What on earth had made her think of it?

'Ready!' the children said gleefully.

What if it rained? What if she didn't sell a thing? Were her prices too high? Too low? Vera said she should mark each item with old and new currency because some folk hadn't got the hang of the new decimal currency yet.

'Neither have I!' Annie confessed, but it turned out Sara had. She'd written the labels attached to each garment.

She had to drive slowly because her legs felt like jelly, and the market site was crowded by the time she arrived. Scores of traders were already busy setting up their stalls. She stopped the car on the pavement and went in search of someone who knew which pitch was hers. After a long while, during which she began to feel quite frantic, she found a man who looked as if he might be in charge.

'Menin?' he said, as if the name meant nothing to him, '*Menin*? Oh, yes, you're over there. Looks like rain, don't it, luv,' he added conversationally. The sky was slightly brighter than when they had left, but the brightness was a fearsome yellow more ominous than black.

She managed to manoeuvre the car through the stalls. 'You're late,' grumbled the man who turned out to be her neighbour. He had to remove his tables to let her in. Incredibly, there were already several people wandering around with bags of vegetables and meat.

Her hands were shaking too much to fix the broom-handles together. Sara took them off her. 'We'll do it, Mummy. Which bit goes where?'

Her neighbour came to help. He was in his sixties, huge, with a bluff red face and mutton-chop whiskers which went perfectly with his old-fashioned collarless shirt and stained chalk-striped waistcoat. His blue jeans seemed rather out of place. 'These are a bit flimsy, luv. A breath of wind and your lovely clothes will be on the ground.'

'I'll get better ones if I make some money,' Annie said weakly. She was glad he'd turned out to be friendly, even though he'd had to move his tables to allow her in.

He extended a large red hand. 'Ivor Hughes, fine antiques.'

'Annie Menin, secondhand clothes.'

She actually sold a frock before she'd begun to fill the second rack. It was one of Dot's, a horrible purple and yellow thing she'd almost not brought with her.

Sara and Daniel's eyes glowed as the woman tucked the frock in her bag. 'We're in business,' whispered Sara.

Another two frocks and a blouse went before there seemed to be a lull, during which the early customers went home and more arrived, many with children, obviously come for a day out. She got angry when some women carelessly yanked her precious things off the rack. Some made offers which she firmly refused. After this had happened several times, Ivor said, 'You should mark your prices up a bit, luv, allow for bargaining. Some customers won't buy if they don't get a reduction.'

'But that's not fair on those who don't make offers!'

Ivor shrugged. 'It's the way of the world, luv. A market's not a market if you're not prepared to barter.'

From then on, Annie took offers if they seemed reasonable. She'd get Sara to price the tickets up for next week.

She'd sold a few more things when Cecy arrived with a plastic carrier bag, a pleased expression on her prematurely wizened face. 'See what I found in a rummage sale.' With an air of triumph, she pulled a long blue dress out of the bag and held it up by the shoulders. It was sleeveless, with a heavily jewelled bodice and a floating gauzy skirt lined with taffeta. 'Look at that label! It must have cost the earth.'

The label meant nothing to Annie. She was about to say she couldn't imagine anyone wanting to buy such a posh frock in a market, when a well-dressed woman approached. 'Is that dress for sale?'

'It certainly is.' Cecy winked at Annie. 'Five quid and it's yours!'

'I'll take it.'

'Cecy!' gasped Annie when the woman had gone, obviously delighted with her purchase. 'You missed your vocation. You should have been a market trader. I would never have dared to ask so much.'

'I'm enjoying the whole experience.' Cecy looked pleased, as if she'd been paid a great compliment. She began to go through the clothes. Despite Annie's protestations, she insisted on paying for the Marks & Spencer's silk blouse. 'It will go with all my suits,' she claimed.

She took Sara and Daniel for a drink and a bun, and Annie was left to herself. There being no customers to keep an eye on, she surveyed the nearby stalls. On her other side, an elderly woman was selling odds and ends of pretty china. The woman smiled and remarked she hoped the rain would keep off. Opposite, a bookstall was safe from the threatening rain beneath a striped awning. 'I wouldn't mind something like that,' Annie thought. 'And a van would be useful. If I make enough money . . .' There were watches and jewellery on one side of the bookstall, and secondhand radios and televisions on the other.

The things on Ivor Hughes' stall looked more like rubbish than fine antiques. Even so, he was doing brisk business. To her amazement, she recognised the bronze lion she'd found in her loft. 'How much is that?' she enquired.

'Eight quid,' Ivor said promptly. 'Very rare piece of work, that is. Got it off one of the landed gentry.'

'Really! I'll think about it.'

'Here's Grandma back with the kids,' Ivor remarked.

'He thinks you're my mother,' Annie said when Cecy came up, Sara and Daniel skipping happily beside her.

Cecy's blue eyes grew wistful. 'I sometimes wish that were so, dear. You're a far nicer person than my own daughter.'

Two women had begun to sort through the clothes. 'You've got a good assortment here, luv,' one said. 'Will you be here next week? There's lots of things me daughter might like.'

'I'll be here every week from now on,' Annie promised.

After the women had bought a blouse each, Cecy suggested Annie have a break. 'It's almost noon. I expect you've been up since dawn.'

She hadn't realised the market had an indoor section, and supposed you had to have been there for years to become entitled to such a choice pitch. The goods were a repetition of those outside. She waved at the Barclays when she saw them behind their fruit and veg stall.

Sid made the thumbs up sign. 'How are you doing, luv?' he called.

'Not bad.' They looked too busy to stop and talk.

She came to a clothes stall where everything was piled on top of each other on two old tables, like jumble. The stuff didn't look very clean. Annie was about to walk past, when a gruff voice from behind the tables drawled, 'Well, if it isn't Annie Harrison!'

Annie tried to place the tall woman, almost six foot, with a hard, lined face and small eyes. Her brown hair was cut short like a man's, and she wore a shabby leather bomber jacket and jeans.

'Don't recognise me, do you?' she chortled. 'It's Ruby, Ruby Livesey, though it's Crowther now, I'm married with five kids. We knew each other at school.'

'Ruby!' Annie swallowed. She'd always dreaded coming across Ruby Livesey one day. 'What are you doing here?'

'Running this stall, obviously. Me and me sister inherited it from our mam. And what are you doing, slumming it?'

Annie bridled. 'I happen to have a stall meself,' she said shortly.

'Come down in the world, have we?'

'I never thought of meself as up. I only lived in Orlando Street and me dad collected insurance on his bike.'

'Maybe so,' Ruby sneered, 'but you always looked like you had a bad smell under your nose at school, as if you thought us all beneath you.'

'Well, it's been nice meeting you again, Ruby.' Annie made no attempt to keep the sarcasm out of her voice. 'I'd best be getting back.' She vowed never to enter the indoor section again.

When she returned, Dot had arrived and was talking stiffly to Cecy. Her face shone with relief when her niece turned up. 'I was just saying, I'll always lend a hand, luv, if you're stuck.'

'She won't ever be stuck whilst I'm around,' Cecy said pointedly. 'I took another couple of pounds whilst you were gone, Annie. I'll just go and see if I can buy one of those apron things you keep the money in. All the other traders seem to have one.'

The minute Cecy had gone, Dot pounced on a cream jacket. 'I didn't want her ladyship to see me buying secondhand. How much is this, luv?'

'For you, Auntie Dot, nothing.'

But Dot also insisted on paying. Annie didn't mention the jacket was Cecy's and hoped the women would never meet whilst Dot was wearing it.

Auntie Dot left. She was taking two of her grandchildren to the pictures. A few minutes later, Annie could have sworn she felt rain. 'Get that tarpaulin out,' she said to Daniel. A huge black cloud loomed menacingly overhead.

'So, this is where you are!' Ruby Livesey looked even bigger and more unpleasant close up. She was accompanied by a plain girl of about twelve. 'And you're selling clothes, too. Is this stuff new?' Ruby fingered Annie's polka-dotted dress.

'No, it's all secondhand.'

Ruby's small eyes glinted in disbelief. 'It *looks* new.'

'Well, it isn't.'

'Can I have this jersey, Mam?' The girl pulled a fluffy white sweater off the rack.

'How much is it?' Ruby growled.

'Fifty pee or ten bob, I'm not sure,' the girl said.

'Ten bob for an ould jersey, not fucking likely. C'mon,' Ruby jerked her head at her daughter. 'Let's sod off.'

As everyone had been predicting since early morning, the heavens opened and the rain came thundering down. Annie shoved the racks together and, with the help of the children, managed to get everything safely beneath the tarpaulin. They huddled in the car, listening to the rain beating on the roof. Sara and Daniel counted the money. 'Sixteen pounds, seventy-five pence, Mummy,' Sara cried triumphantly. 'We should be able to live on that for weeks.'

Annie shook her head. 'Not really, sweetheart. We need to make rather more.'

The rain didn't last long. The skies quickly lightened

and a pale sun had appeared by the time they emerged from the car. A great pool of water had gathered in the middle of the tarpaulin. Annie gently lifted it by two corners so the rain would pour away without touching the clothes, but the weight was too much for the clumsily made racks. There was a crack as one rail snapped and collapsed, taking the clothes with it.

'Oh, no!' she cried. Half the things had fallen outwards, onto the dirty wet concrete. The others were precariously suspended on the broken pole, the end of which was caught in the sleeve of a coat.

Sara and Daniel seized the pole whilst Annie removed the clothes before they could join those on the ground – they'd all have to be washed and ironed again. She cursed herself for her lack of carpentry skills. Lauri could have made a couple of stout rails with perfect ease, but then, if Lauri were around, there would be no need for a market stall to keep a roof over their heads. If Lauri were around, they'd be at home, and he'd be pottering in the garden, or the garage if it was raining. But Lauri *wasn't* around, and she *did* have a market stall to run. Annie sighed and threw the dirty clothes into the boot. She managed to squeeze the rest onto the remaining rack. She'd just have to buy proper equipment for next week.

The rain seemed to have washed most of the customers away. It was a quarter to three, and a few traders began to pack up ready to leave.

'Will you be going soon?' she asked Ivor. He was puffing contentedly on a cheroot and didn't seem to care that his fine antiques were wet.

'No, luv. I always stay till the end. I often do good business at the last minute. If folks arrive late, they'll buy almost anything. No-one likes to leave a market empty-handed.'

'In that case, I'll stay, too.'

Cecy was shocked to find half of the stall had disappeared when she returned with a canvas apron. Annie explained she'd have proper racks by next week – Ivor had told her where they could be acquired second-hand. Cecy patted her arm affectionately. 'You're a brave girl, dear. Indomitable, that's what Bruno calls you.'

No-one bought a thing for the next hour. Even Ivor was gazing at his fine antiques as if wondering whether to pack them away, when a crowd of at least twenty coloured men appeared, chatting excitably amongst themselves in a foreign language.

'Lascar seamen,' Cecy hissed. 'You saw hundreds of them on the Dock Road before the war. I doubt if they'll be wanting women's clothes.'

But she couldn't possibly have been more wrong. Half a dozen of the men descended on the stall and began to pull the garments out. They showed them to each other, dark eyes flashing.

It didn't take long for them to make up their minds. Within the space of ten minutes, Annie was presented with a huge bundle. She carefully added up the total. 'Eighteen pounds, ten shillings,' she said weakly. 'But eighteen pounds will do.'

One of the men carefully counted the money out. 'Eighteen pound, ten shilling,' he said, grinning widely.

She tried to give the ten shillings back, but he refused. 'No, nice clothes for ladies back home. You take all.'

'Thank you.'

'Thank *you*, nice lady. Like her.' He tapped his head and winked.

'Like who?'

'He likes your hair,' Cecy whispered.

The men departed as quickly as they'd come. 'I told you it was worth while staying,' said Ivor. 'One of them bought that bloody brass lion. I thought I'd never get rid of the damned thing.'

'I gave you a brass lion like that when you first got married,' Cecy said. 'You said you needed a doorstop between the kitchen and breakfast room. Have you ever used it?'

Annie's exhausted brain searched in desperation for an answer; in other words, a lie. Assistance came from an unexpected quarter. 'We kept stubbing our toes on it,' Sara said sweetly.

'So it got put in the loft,' Daniel added.

'You should never normally tell lies,' Annie said seriously on the way home, 'but a white one doesn't matter occasionally if it saves hurting people's feelings. Thanks. You got me out of a hole. Cecy would be dead upset if she'd known I'd sold her lion.' She glanced at their bright faces through the rear mirror. 'Did you enjoy yourselves?'

'It was smashing, Mummy,' Sara enthused. 'You'll have to go to lots more jumble sales next week.'

'I hope I can find some on weekdays. How about you, Daniel?'

'It was okay,' Daniel said grudgingly.

As Daniel was not usually given to exaggeration, Annie assumed he'd had a good time. On the way home, she stopped at a fish and chip shop and bought three cod and chips for their tea. 'I'll open some fruit for afters, that's if I've got the strength to use the tin opener. I don't know about you two, but I could sleep for a week.'

She had never felt so weary. Her legs, her arms, her entire body throbbed with tiredness. It had been the longest day of her life, physically and emotionally draining. The children needed no persuading to go to bed. When Annie looked in a few minutes later, both were sound asleep. Despite her exhaustion, she made herself unpack the clothes before they got creased, then assembled the rail and hung them up. She carried the muddied garments into the kitchen and loaded the washables into the machine. The heavier things would have to be brushed when the dirt dried. It wasn't financially viable to have them dry-cleaned.

Financially viable! Annie grinned. Lauri would have been amused at the phrase. She sat down and began to count the takings, but her brain felt light-headed and refused to work. She put the money away, the children would enjoy counting it tomorrow.

Her mind slowly travelled through the day. It had been worse than starting a new job, but she'd get used to it. It was a pity about Ruby Livesey. Hopefully, she'd keep out of her way in future. Annie frowned. Where was the white sweater Ruby's daughter had tried to persuade her to buy? It wasn't in the garage or the washing machine, and it definitely hadn't been sold. Someone must have pinched it! She recalled Ruby had been the ringleader when the gang used to shoplift from Woolworth's.

'Bitch! I bet she took it. I'll appoint Daniel stall detective and he can keep an eye on things from now on.'

The phone went. It was Sylvia, full of apologies for not turning up on Annie's first day as a businesswoman. They were in the middle of making arrangements to see *The Godfather* next week, because Chris Andrews said it was the best film ever made, when Annie fell fast asleep, still clutching the receiver. Sylvia thought she'd died and nearly rang for an ambulance.

Annie began to recognise her regular customers. She gave them names: there was the Handknitted Lady, who would buy anything crocheted or knitted in a complicated pattern; the Lady With The Veins, always after a skirt or frock long enough to hide the bright purple veins in her legs. After a while, she began to keep a look-out at jumble sales for items that would suit particular women, like the Lacy Lady or the Velvet Lady.

The well-dressed woman who'd bought the evening dress off Cecy returned several times to look for another. 'My husband's a councillor,' she said, 'and we're always being invited to functions where we have to wear evening dress. I hate turning up in the same outfit, but I can't afford to buy evening frocks I'll only wear a few times.'

'I'll keep an eye-out for you,' Annie promised. A few weeks later, she unearthed a long dress with a blue and green tartan skirt and a velvet bodice from beneath a heap of clothes in a jumble sale. She washed it carefully in Lux soapflakes and replaced the broken zip, which seemed to be the only reason it had been thrown away. She kept the dress in the car until the woman returned and felt a bit put out when she tried to beat her down to half the asking price.

'It's worth two pounds fifty,' Annie said stubbornly. 'I had to sew the new zip in by hand.'

'One pound fifty, then.'

'Two pounds.'

'All right, two pounds, but I hope it fits.'

The children, particularly Daniel, were beginning to get bored with spending all day in the market. Cecy was only too pleased to take them into town. She liked being taken for their grannie.

Annie thoroughly enjoyed running the stall. It was hard work, but gave her a tremendous sense of satisfaction. She'd never dreamt herself capable of making her living in such an unconventional way. Throughout the week, she travelled far and wide to jumble sales, and spent the evenings washing, ironing and mending. She found it helped to put two, or even three, items on the same hanger; a cardigan over a matching blouse, a sweater with a toning skirt, or a jacket, blouse and skirt altogether, which often persuaded customers to buy the lot. The money earned was enough to pay the bills and live reasonably. If she'd had more rails, she might have made more profit, but the Anglia was already packed to capacity, and she doubted if she'd earn enough to buy a van. Her heart had been in her mouth when the car had gone for its MOT, but apparently the rust was in places that didn't really matter. She'd had to buy two new tyres and the brakes needed tightening, or was it loosening? She wasn't quite sure.

A sense of camaraderie prevailed amongst the stallholders and Annie swiftly made friends. If business was bad one week, it was bad for them all. They would bemoan their misfortune and hope things would be better next Saturday. Ivor Hughes would look after Annie's pitch if she wanted a break, and she in turn looked after his.

Ruby Livesey turned up occasionally to make a nuisance of herself and Annie always kept a sharp eye open for her daughter in case something went missing. Clothes *did* go missing from time to time, but the culprit or culprits were never caught in the act.

When winter came, it was a touch less enjoyable being on her feet in the cold for nine or more hours, so she bought herself a pair of fur-lined boots and thick jeans and came across a well-worn sheepskin jacket for ten pence at a jumble sale, but it still took several hours to unfreeze when she got home. On the coldest days, she made the children stay in the car until Cecy arrived.

'I honestly don't know what I'd do without you,' she said one freezing day in December when Cecy came bustling up in her sable coat, cossack hat and smart suede boots, rather incongruously laden down with old clothes she'd acquired from a friend. Sara and Daniel immediately got out of the car, delighted to see her.

'I'm only too pleased to help, dear. It makes me feel needed. I always look forward to Saturdays, to seeing these two darling children.' She put an arm around each. Sara nestled her face in the expensive fur.

'Frankly Cecy, I think I need you far more than you need me.'

Cecy flushed with pleasure. 'That's what everybody craves, isn't it, to be needed? I've always felt rather superfluous since I've been on my own.' She beamed at the children. 'I think a shopping trip's in order. It's only two weeks off Christmas.'

Daniel's eyes shone. 'Can I have an army outfit for my Action Man?'

'Daniel!' Annie said, horrified. 'Don't be so greedy.'

Cecy smiled. 'I think it's only natural for little boys to be greedy. Ah, look! You've got a customer wanting to buy that lovely red coat. Such a bargain, isn't it?' she cried when the woman came up. 'I've seen coats like that in George Henry Lee's for fifty pounds.'

The woman paid the asking price without a murmur. Cecy would have made a fortune on a market stall.

It was a very different Christmas from the sort she'd grown used to since she married. All Lauri had wanted to do was watch television. He declined to leave the house, even though they were often invited to Christmas dinner, and there was always something happening on Boxing Day or New Year's Eve.

Annie still missed his reassuring presence, but after Mass on Christmas morning, it was a joy to drive through the frost-tipped countryside to Mike's new detached house in Melling, a village not far from Kirkby Trading Estate where Michael Ray Security had taken over even larger premises as the demand for burglar alarms grew and grew.

Every member of the Gallagher clan, thirty in all, had gathered for their Christmas dinner. Mike had engaged professional caterers to provide the food. The children ate first, and the sixteen adults just fitted around the long table, extended to its fullest. The meal was delicious and wine was liberally distributed throughout the meal.

When the tables had been cleared, Mike stood, a trifle unsteadily. He banged the table and everyone fell silent.

'I've never made a speech before, but I suppose there's a first time for everything.' He paused and took a deep breath. 'We've come a long way, us Gallaghers,' he said emotionally. 'There's our Tommy, a foreman in A C Delco; Alan, a chef at one of the poshest hotels in Liverpool. Our Pete's not doing bad with Bootle Corporation, and Bobby's coming to work for me in the New Year. Last, but not least, there's Joe. Who'd have thought our baby brother would end up a corporal in the Paras?'

Joe's heavily pregnant wife, Alison, leaned over and kissed his cheek. Dot glowed with pride at her six lovely lads.

Mike paused and sighed. 'I won't go on about meself, just to say I'd far sooner me pop group had taken off, rather than me business, and I'd give the whole lot up in a minute if I could have Glenda back.' His face grew sad and his eyes sought out Glenda's children, Kathy and Paul. 'But this is not the time for being maudlin. The reason I got up is to say "thanks" to our mam and dad.

Thanks for having us, for bringing us up the way you did, for giving us so much love. I know things were hard when we were little, but we never went without. You've always done your best by us, and we'll always be grateful. I'd like you all to raise your glasses and drink a toast to Mam and Dad.'

There was a loud murmur of appreciation and shouts of 'Hear, Hear'. The company rose and drained their glasses willingly. Dot's daughters-in-law found her hard to take at times, but there was no denying her heart was made of solid gold, and if it wasn't for her, there wouldn't have been a Gallagher for them to marry.

Dot burst into tears. Bert patted her shoulder and stood up himself. His face was red with perspiration. He undid the top button of his shirt and loosened his tie. 'I'd like to say a few words if you don't mind, Mike. I won't mention me ould wife here, or she'll only cry even more, but I want to say you lads have done us proud, and you've done it on your own, without any help from those useless geezers in Westminster. I won't go on about politics, not at Christmas. You won't want to hear me ranting on about the mess the Tories are making, the three-day working week, the country plunged into darkness, all because the miners have banned overtime. Everyone, including the government, knows the miners deserve more money.' Dot recovered enough to nudge him sharply with her elbow and hiss that he wasn't at the Labour Party. 'No, no, I won't go on about politics,' Uncle Bert said hastily. 'I'd like to make a toast meself to another member of the family, your cousin, Annie.'

Annie looked up in surprise. Perhaps she'd drunk too much wine, because instead of Bert with his fading blue eyes and wispy hair, she saw the soldier who'd returned after fighting in the war, and recalled how much she and Marie had resented his presence in the little house in

Bootle. She'd never dreamt how quickly she would grow to love him.

'Our Annie's had a hard time of it since Lauri went to meet his maker,' Bert was saying, 'but she's come through with flying colours. Annie's living proof of the resources we have within us, but fortunately not many of us have to call on.' Bert raised his glass. 'To Annie!'

The assembled Gallaghers chorused merrily, 'To Annie!'

Mike came out with her when it was time to go. The children climbed into the car, laden with presents and Christmas cake.

'How are you doing, luv?' Mike asked. 'I've been meaning to ask all day, but there never seemed to be a minute.'

'I'm fine,' Annie said happily. 'We all are.'

'Good,' he smiled.

She was fastening her safety belt when Mike knocked on the window. She rolled it down a few inches, which was as far as it would go.

'How's Sylvia?' he enquired. 'Me mam told us about the baby.'

'She's okay. Yasmin's five months old now. She's beautiful.'

Mike grinned. 'I've always fancied that girl!'

'You thought she was conceited.'

'I suppose she had plenty to be conceited about, with them knock-out looks. Mind you, she thought I was boring.'

Annie started up the engine. 'Actually, Mike,' she shouted, 'I think Sylvia quite fancies *you*!'

New Year's Eve was spent quietly with the children in Ormskirk. Sylvia's lounge was warm and cosy, with logs spitting in the inglenook fireplace and the peach-shaded wall lights glowing softly. Delicately patterned gold and silver decorations hung from the black beamed ceiling, shimmering gently in the draught. They played word games, watched TV, and Annie and Sylvia drank too much. Both were more than a little inebriated by the time Big Ben chimed in 1974 and Sara and Daniel went to bed. Yasmin, adorable in her long white nightie and lacy boots, lay asleep in her mother's arms. Cecy rang, then Bruno, followed by Auntie Dot, to wish them a Happy New Year.

'Well, that was nice!' Sylvia said tartly at half past twelve, the phone calls finished.

'I thought the evening very enjoyable.'

'Jaysus, Annie! It was as boring as hell. I kept wishing we were at some crazy party.'

'You can't expect life to be exciting when you've got kids, Syl,' Annie said practically.

'I don't see why not!' Sylvia looked down at her daughter's lovely face. 'I'm not sure if having Yasmin was such a good idea.'

When Annie looked horrified, she said irritably, 'I wouldn't be without her now she's here, but I get lonely, stuck on my own all day.'

'Why don't you get a job?'

Sylvia snorted. 'Oh yes, and take Yasmin in her carrycot!'

'No, make two people happy and leave her with Cecy.'

'I suppose I could.' Sylvia looked quite tearful. 'I love her so much it hurts, then I hate myself for not feeling happy. I suppose I only had her to spite Eric.' She stared moodily into the log fire. 'Did I tell you Eric came the other day?'

'No!' Annie gasped. 'You canny bugger! What did he want?'

'His second marriage didn't last five minutes, he's

getting divorced. He wants us to get back together. He's prepared to accept Yasmin as his own.'

'Bloody hell! What did you say?'

'I was so desperately fed up, I nearly agreed. At least we'd be a proper family, and the sex between us is still as good.'

'Sylvia, you didn't . . . !'

'I did,' Sylvia said smugly. 'I've been feeling frustrated along with everything else. He said wife number two was tame in bed compared to me.' She wrinkled her nose. 'Oh, Annie, all those plans we had when we were single! Now we're thirty-two, you're a widow and I'm divorced, and we've got three kids between us. What's to become of us, eh?'

'I don't know,' Annie said slowly. 'I'm too busy coping with the present to worry about the future. I won't think about it until Sara and Daniel don't need me any more.'

Sylvia said curiously, 'Don't you ever get the itch, Annie?'

'The itch? Where?'

'Honestly, you're too naive for words! Don't you ever feel sexually frustrated?'

'I'm not sure. I miss things . . .' She missed a shoulder to cry on, the occasional unexpected kiss, someone warm in bed beside her. It would be heaven to be kissed by Robert Redford or Sean Connery or the man on television who advertised cigars, but her imagination stopped there. She couldn't visualise going the whole hog. 'I'd feel as if I was being unfaithful to Lauri if I slept with someone else,' she said. 'Perhaps I'm undersexed, who knows?'

In February, faced with a miners' strike, Edward Heath called an election with the cry, 'Who rules Britain, unions or government?'

The voters were divided over the issue. Labour emerged as the largest party, but without a majority in the House of Commons. Harold Wilson was once again Prime Minister, and struggled on until October, when another election was called.

Annie had been attending Labour Party meetings since Lauri died. She was one of the few women there and rarely opened her mouth in case she said something stupid, though the men said stupid things all the time. She still felt uncomfortable when she remembered her first meeting. A resolution was put forward about the National Health Service which seemed a very good idea. Then someone proposed an amendment which sounded even better. When the time came to vote, Annie put her hand up straight away. For some reason, they had to vote a second time, so she raised her hand again. A man sitting behind roughly pushed her arm down.

'Idiot!' he hissed. 'You just voted for the amendment. You can't vote for the original resolution as well.' Since then, she'd sat in a corner and said nothing, though she had got the hang of things eventually.

In both elections, Annie delivered leaflets and addressed hundreds of envelopes. The children helped. Sara wrote addresses in her small, square writing, and Daniel folded the election address and stuffed it inside. When, in October, Labour won a working majority, the Menins had been politically blooded. 'Your dad would be proud of us,' Annie said contentedly. She had visions of Lauri happily waving a red flag.

To her surprise, Chris Andrews asked her out to dinner to celebrate, although he was a Liberal and his party had come nowhere. When they arrived home, he surprised her even more by kissing her cheek and confessing that he loved her. They were both un-attached. Was there a chance she might feel the same about him one day?

Annie let him down gently. She liked him very much, but couldn't imagine falling in love. 'Anyroad,' she said to herself, 'it's too soon. I feel as if Lauri only died yesterday.'

On a bleak, stormy day the next January, with snow gusting against the windows, Sylvia triumphantly descended on Heather Close, and announced that she and Eric Church were getting married again.

'You must be mad,' gasped Annie. 'He's already proved he's a brute; once bitten, twice shy. Fancy getting involved with him again!'

'Thanks for the good wishes!' Sylvia said acidly. 'Eric's turned over a new leaf. He's utterly charming whenever he comes round, and he adores Yasmin. He's going to move into the cottage with us.'

Annie went into the kitchen to put the kettle on. 'But there's no need to get married,' she said when she came back. 'Why don't you just live together? Couples live together quite openly nowadays.'

'Oh, really! Cecy, of all people, said the same thing.'

'Why don't you?' Annie persisted. 'Then you can kick him out if things go wrong.'

'I'm surprised at you, Annie Menin!' Sylvia snorted. 'What a way to go into a relationship! We're getting married mainly to please Eric's parents. You know the Churches, everything must be official, though it'll be a register office this time.'

Annie shook her head despairingly. 'I don't understand you, Syl. You're continually getting involved with the most unsuitable men.' Ted Deakin, that weird dentist, the Arabian prince, were just a few she could bring to mind. Eric Church was the worst of the lot.

Sylvia wrinkled her nose thoughtfully. 'I suppose everyone's in search of happiness – except you.'

'What d'you mean, except me?' Annie said, outraged. 'Are you suggesting I don't want to be happy?'

'No, but you sit back and wait for it to happen. When you get a proposal, it's from someone across the road. Me, I look for happiness. That's why I often end up in a mess. And we're different in other ways.' Sylvia warmed to her theme. 'You're content to go on in the same way, year after year. I can't stand one year being the same as the last.'

'Does that mean Eric will be swopped for a new model next January?'

Sylvia merely grinned. 'At least I'll have a decent social life for a change. I hate being a single woman at dinner parties – you wouldn't know, because you never go. I'll give up that loathsome job.'

'You said the job was brilliant!' For almost a year, Sylvia had been working as personal assistant to the manager of a stockbroking firm, whizzing around in tailored suits whilst Cecy looked after Yasmin.

'All I do is wait on this chap hand and foot.'

'That's what personal assistants are for.'

Sylvia looked at her slyly. 'There's something else, I'm pregnant.'

'Jaysus, Syl!' Annie gulped. 'Is it Eric's?'

'No, he's seen a doctor, he's sterile. It must be that Norwegian naval officer I met last November.'

Annie sighed. 'You make me feel extraordinarily ordinary.'

'Annie, dear friend,' Sylvia cried affectionately. 'Thank God there's people like you in the world. If everyone behaved as I did, anarchy would prevail.' Before Annie could ask, she said that Eric knew all about the baby. 'That's why he pleaded, implored me on his bended knee, Annie, to marry him, so everyone would think it was his.' Only Cecy and Annie knew the truth.

355

It seemed incredibly complicated, Annie thought when she went to make the tea. With luck, the wedding would be on a Saturday which meant she wouldn't be able to go because of the market. The last thing she wanted was to see her friend married to Eric Church a second time.

Chris Andrews' play was being put on in London. He came over to see Annie, his face red with excitement. 'A producer's just telephoned. Marie had given him my play. He wants to put it on at Easter.'

'I'm ever so pleased, Chris.' It wouldn't be the West End, merely over a pub in Camden, where it would run for three nights.

For the next few weeks, he kept her abreast of developments. The actor in the main role had once been in *Z Cars*. Marie had phoned her congratulations and promised to be there on the first night. He asked Annie's advice on what he should wear. Since becoming Assistant Head at Grenville Lucas, his pigtail had gone and he'd reverted to glasses, and was also growing plump again. 'Should I look formal or casual?' She advised casual.

He was a bag of nerves by the time Easter came. 'Give Marie my fondest love,' Annie said when she saw him off. She would have loved to see the play herself, but Easter Saturday was one of the busiest and most profitable market days of the year. She hadn't seen her sister since Lauri's funeral. There'd been a few postcards since to say she'd got parts – she'd appeared briefly in *Upstairs, Downstairs* – and there was mention of a film in Spain, but nothing so far this year. Annie had got used to her letters remaining unanswered, and, as usual, Marie was never there when she phoned.

Easter Saturday was warm and sunny. Crowds poured

into the market and Annie had her best day ever. Her stock was hugely diminished by the time five o'clock arrived and it was time to pack up. Cecy had taken the children to a fête in Ormskirk and would be bringing them home later.

The trouble with the stall was, Annie mused as she drove home, although she loved it, you could never take time off or you lost a whole week's income – she hadn't missed a Saturday in nearly two years. During the week, she was for ever flying off to jumble sales, and although some people said she was too finicky and there was no need to wash and iron the clothes and do all the necessary repairs, it made her feel she was earning her money more honourably.

It left no time for other things, however. She'd not stopped thinking about Chris Andrews and his play. Tonight would be the final performance. She would have given anything to be there, and the children would have enjoyed a weekend in London. They'd never had a holiday in their lives. 'I'm missing out,' she thought. 'If I had a conventional job, even a conventional business, I would have had the weekend off.'

Sara and Daniel had enjoyed their day out. Sara had won a jar of home-made jam and a bottle of shampoo on the hoop-la, and Daniel had come first in the sack race. The first prize was a pound.

'A measly pound,' he said disgustedly. 'I mean, what the hell can I buy with a pound?'

Annie felt too tired to remonstrate. Daniel had become very aggressive lately. Dot said her boys had got too big for their boots when they went into long trousers. 'I just gave them a clock around the ear and it soon brought them to their senses.' Annie felt this was a bit extreme. She'd have a talk with Daniel to-morrow.

'Was Auntie Sylvia there?' she asked.

'Yes, and Yasmin,' Sara replied. 'Uncle Eric bought us ice-creams.'

Uncle Eric! Annie grinned. Eric had been nothing but sweetness and light since the wedding.

Chris Andrews arrived home on Sunday evening. He reported to Annie immediately. 'It went beautifully,' he beamed. 'The actors were superb. They put everything they had into it.' He babbled on breathlessly. A woman from the BBC had been there. She thought the play ideal for television and asked for a copy of the script. 'She warned me not to get my hopes too high. Even if it's accepted, these things can take years. She asked if she could read *Goldilocks*. As soon as I get home, I'll start typing it out afresh.' He gave Annie a copy of the duplicated programme with his name on the front as a memento.

'I'm so pleased for you, Chris.' She felt even more sorry she'd missed all the excitement. 'How's our Marie?'

'Well,' Chris paused and Annie felt a twinge of alarm. 'She seemed a bit low, rather depressed.'

As soon as he'd gone, Annie telephoned her sister. There was no reply. She called again an hour later. A man with a foreign accent answered and told her Marie wasn't in.

'How do you know?' Annie demanded.

'I saw her go out, that's how I know.' He slammed the receiver down.

Annie left it a further two hours before ringing a third time. The same man answered and said brusquely, 'She's still not in.'

'Do you mind slipping a note under her door saying to ring her sister? It's an emergency, a real emergency. I've got to speak to her.'

'I might,' he said, and rang off.

At ten o'clock when she called and the voice with the foreign accent answered, she put the receiver down herself.

It was past midnight when the phone rang. Annie was getting ready for bed. She raced downstairs. To her relief, it was Marie.

'Sis, what's wrong?' Her sister's voice was slightly slurred.

'Nothing. I just wanted to speak to you, that's all.'

'But there's a note under my door to ring my sister, there's been an emergency. I thought something had happened to one of the children.'

'The children are fine, except that the school doctor says Sara has to have glasses. She's at Grenville Lucas – I think I told you in a letter. Anyroad, it was a terrible blow. She's so pretty, and . . .'

Marie interrupted crossly. 'It's scarcely an emergency, sis.'

Annie decided to plunge straight in. 'Chris said you seemed depressed. I was worried . . . are you drunk? Your voice sounds odd.'

'Chris doesn't know what he's talking about,' Marie said listlessly. 'And no, I'm not drunk, I'm tired. I've just taken a sleeping tablet.'

'Why do you need a sleeping tablet if you're tired?'

'Oh, for Chrissakes, sis. I'm not in the mood for this.'

There was a pause and Annie said gently, 'What's the matter, Marie?'

An even longer pause followed, and Annie could hear a snuffling sound and realised her sister was crying. 'Oh, Annie,' she whispered. 'I had another abortion last year. There was this movie in Spain. I only had a small part, but you never know what may come of these things.' Her voice sank so low that Annie had to press the receiver against her ear. 'Afterwards, I had non-stop periods. I've just had a hysterectomy.'

'Marie, luv, why didn't you tell me? I can't stand the thought of you being in hospital all by yourself.'

The programme for Chris's play was on the window-sill in the hall. In a way, it was all his fault. If it hadn't been for *Goldilocks* Marie would never have caught the acting bug. She'd probably be married with a family by now. Annie imagined him feverishly re-typing the play that had caused so much havoc in their lives. *Goldilocks* had been the cause of the terrible scene the night Mam and Dad died.

Marie said, 'You've got enough to worry about, what with the children and this famous market stall.'

'Oh, so you read my letters?'

'I read them over and over, sis. One of these days I might reply.'

'In that case, I might drop dead.' Annie transferred the receiver to her other ear. 'Seriously, sis, why don't you come home?'

'I hope you don't mean for good,' Marie said coldly.

'Of course not,' Annie said hastily, though she had. 'I meant for a holiday. Are you working at the moment?'

Her sister sighed. 'I'm on the dole. I was told to rest for three months after the hysterectomy, but I've got a summer job in a holiday camp.'

'That's good.' There'd been a repertory company in the camp she'd gone on holiday to with Sylvia.

'I'll have to give my room up. I suppose I could stay with you then go straight to Skegness.'

Marie arrived a few weeks later with two suitcases containing the possessions of a lifetime. Annie was shocked by her appearance. She didn't look so bad with her make-up plastered on, but without it her skin was grey and she looked haggard. She had little patience with the children and spent a lot of the time in bed.

Mike had bought his mam and dad a car, so Dot and

Bert came several times to see their errant niece. The first time, the conversation turned to reminiscing over the years they'd spent living together in Bootle.

'I used to think you were my mother.' Marie's expression was wistful. 'It was a terrible blow when we left for Orlando Street.'

'My main memory is of Dot throwing the cup against the wall after she'd burnt the custard,' Annie put in.

'I remember that day,' Uncle Bert said. 'It was raining cats and dogs. Father O'Reilly came and got me out of bed.'

'It was Father Heenan,' Dot corrected him.

'No it wasn't, luv, it was Father O'Reilly.'

'I distinctly remember it being Father Heenan.'

'Actually,' said Annie, 'it was Father Maloney. You didn't see him, Uncle Bert. He'd gone by the time you came downstairs.' The morning had been a turning point in her young life, vividly etched on her mind.

Marie went upstairs to the bathroom and Dot hissed. 'Is she all right? She looks bloody terrible.'

'She's just a bit run down,' said Annie.

'Doesn't Dot look terrible!' Marie remarked when they went back into the house after waving goodbye.

'Dot! Why she looks exactly the same,' Annie said, astonished. 'Her face has scarcely changed, there isn't a wrinkle on it.'

'No, but she hobbles around like an old woman, and why was she waving her hands about all night?'

Annie laughed. 'She's got a touch of arthritis, that's all. She waves her hands to exercise them. You know Dot, she'll overcome it.'

'Can you overcome arthritis? I always thought it came to stay.'

Sylvia was seven months pregnant. She came lumbering

along one afternoon with Cecy and Yasmin in tow. Cecy embraced Marie fondly. 'I still regard you as my third little girl.'

Behind her mother's back, Sylvia made a face which Annie ignored. Cecy's presence was only tolerated in Ormskirk because she looked after Yasmin whilst Sylvia rested. This pregnancy was more tiring than the first. Cecy would have both children when their mother found another job. Eric, graciousness itself, thoroughly approved.

Marie was fascinated by Yasmin. Almost two, she was a beautiful, exotic child with glossy black hair cut in a fringe and curling slightly under her ears. Her long-lashed velvet brown eyes glinted mysteriously. Annie was never sure whether it was mischief, or some secret knowledge that she found amusing. Marie sat on the grass and showed her how to make daisy chains until the little girl was covered with them.

'Sylvia's got everything, hasn't she?' Marie remarked after the visitors had gone.

Annie glanced at her sharply. There'd been a touch of envy in Marie's voice. 'What do you mean, everything?'

'A husband, a kid, a mum and dad. She's not hard up for a few bob, either, *and* she's pregnant.'

'You sound as if you're jealous.'

'I'm not jealous of the mum and dad or the husband, and I don't care about the money, but I'd give anything for a little girl like Yasmin.'

Annie was preparing a salad for the tea. She continued laying ham on each plate, took four tomatoes from the fridge and began to slice them neatly with the breadknife and lay them decoratively around the edges.

'Cat got your tongue?' Marie said lightly.

'Possibly.' Annie turned exasperatedly on her sister. 'I was thinking what a stupid remark that was! You've been pregnant three times. The first abortion was unavoidable, but no-one forced you to have the others.'

'You're all heart.' Marie tossed her head and went into the lounge.

Annie followed, waving the breadknife. 'You can't expect sympathy if you go all dewy-eyed over another woman's child, when you could have had two of your own.'

Marie flounced through the French window. Annie went after her. 'It was you, nobody else, who decided to put your career before a family.'

'Thanks for reminding me,' Marie snapped.

'You shouldn't need reminding. We're all authors of our own destiny.'

'What pretentious twaddle!' Marie disappeared into the willow tree.

Annie knelt on the grass outside. 'Another thing, have you never heard of birth control?'

'Of course, but the pill disagrees with me and nothing else works. I must be the most fertile woman in the world. Least I was. I'm not now.'

'Oh, Marie,' Annie sighed. 'I don't know what to say.'

'I think you've said enough already.'

Annie did her best to think of something encouraging. 'At least you've got a nice acting job lined up for the summer.'

'I don't know where you got that idea from.' Marie's voice was cutting. 'I'm working in the bar.'

'But I thought you were in the theatre!'

'Well, I'm not.'

Annie opened the curtain of leaves and crawled inside. 'Must I climb the tree to escape from you?' her sister groaned.

'Remember when we used to go to the Playhouse? Some of the actors were brilliant, but I've never heard of most of them again.'

'Is there a message hidden there, sis?'

'You're working in an over-crowded profession, luv. Even I know only a tiny percentage of actors become successful.'

Marie glared at her belligerently. 'Well, I've no intention of dropping out and making it less crowded.'

'In that case, stop bloody moaning and get on with it.'

To her relief, Marie smiled. 'I don't often moan, sis. It was the hysterectomy that did it. They took away my womb, and I felt as if I was no longer a proper woman. All I had left was acting. What had I given up two babies for? I've spent more than half my life trying to become an actress, and I'm no nearer now than the day I left Liverpool.'

'You *are* an actress, Marie,' Annie said comfortingly. There probably wasn't another person in the world who'd feel sorry for her sister, so ruthlessly pursuing this ephemeral success. 'Anyroad, something might come of the picture you made in Spain.'

'It isn't released until next year and it was a crap movie, sis. It was made on a shoestring, and the director was hardly out of nappies. He hadn't a clue what he was doing.'

Annie patted her hand, 'You'll make it, sis. I feel it in me bones.'

Sylvia's new daughter, Ingrid, was pale and fair, the absolute image of Eric, according to his parents. 'I feel a bit lousy about it,' Sylvia confessed when Annie went into the expensive nursing home to see her, 'but it was Eric's idea to fool them, not mine.'

'I'm glad I don't get into pickles the way you do. I'd give meself away in no time.' Annie played with Ingrid's tiny fingers as she lay sleeping in the frilled cot beside Sylvia's bed. She was like a little ice maiden, skin pure white and hair the colour of milk. 'I'd give anything for another baby.'

'There's nothing stopping you, Annie.'

Annie laughed. 'In case you haven't noticed, I've no husband.'

'Who needs husbands?' Sylvia said airily. 'Seduce Chris – he'd be a knockover. Then we could walk our babies in the park together the way we said we'd do. It'd be ten years later than planned, but so what!'

'I'm too old-fashioned.' Annie made a face. 'I'm not the type.'

3

She felt slightly despondent when winter approached, the hour went on the clocks and the nights grew darker. People began to talk about Christmas when it seemed scarcely any time since the last.

'What have I done with meself during 1975?' Annie asked herself one miserable grey day in November. She was surrounded by clothes which she was supposed to be mending. Instead, she leant on the sewing machine and stared gloomily out of the window at the damp pavements and limp gardens of Heather Close.

'Absolutely nothing,' she replied. 'Nothing of any significance.' Whilst Marie had got another small part in a film, Valerie Cunningham had been promoted to office manager, and Sylvia's life was once again a whirl of dinner parties, her own life was nothing but hard work followed by more hard work. She never went anywhere, not even the pictures. There wasn't the time, and anyroad, she had no-one to go with, apart from Chris Andrews. If the stall were more profitable, she could have taken on a partner and had every other Saturday off, but she didn't take enough to share with someone else. She'd had to ask the bank manager for a loan to get the Anglia through its last MOT. The garage had suggested it was time she bought something else, but the car seemed like a member of the family and she couldn't bear to part with it. Anyroad, she would have had to borrow even more for a replacement.

She sighed, told herself to stop wasting time, and picked up a skirt which had a button missing. 'I'm fed up washing and mending other women's cast-off clothes,' she said aloud. 'If Sara goes to university, as Chris thinks she should, I could be at this for the next decade.'

But what else could she do? By this time next year, Daniel would be at Grenville Lucas and Sara would be thirteen – a teenager! Perhaps she could have another stab at getting a job. Though the same problem still remained, young children: not as young as last time, but young all the same. She still wasn't prepared to leave them at a loose end during the holidays. Another thing, she didn't fancy taking orders after running her own business. It was nice being independent, your own boss.

It was a relief when the phone rang. She hoped it would be Sylvia, she felt like a good gossip, but it was Auntie Dot. 'Are you watching telly, luv?' Dot asked eagerly.

'No, I find it a distraction when I'm working.' She stared out of the window instead.

'The Conservatives have elected a woman leader, Margaret Thatcher. I'd never vote for them, but I think it's great. God forbid it should happen, but if they get in again, we'll have a woman Prime Minister.'

Annie agreed that a woman, Tory or otherwise, could only do the country good. 'How are your aches and pains?' she asked.

'Not so bad, girl, not so bad.' Dot chuckled. 'I got stuck on the lav this morning and Bert had to help me off. We've been married forty years, and it's the first time he's seen me on the lavvy.' The arthritis was spreading at a terrifying rate. Bert said she was often close to tears with the pain. She went on, 'The trick is not to give in or you're done for. One day, I'll wake up and the pain'll be gone.'

'I hope so, Auntie Dot.' Annie prayed nightly this would happen.

After Dot rang off, Annie phoned Sylvia. Cecy answered and said she was lunching with Eric. 'Sorry, dear, I can't stop, Ingrid's crying.'

Annie gloomily envisaged her friend, done up to the nines, driving into town in the new Volvo estate and lunching in an expensive restaurant, whilst she was stuck in this dead quiet house with heaps of clothes to mend. She switched the lamps on, hang the extravagance, and played a Freddy and the Dreamers record to cheer herself up. It would be today that both the children planned to be home late; Sara was having tea with her friend, Louise, and Daniel was playing snooker. One of the boys from school had a six-foot table in the garage. Daniel desperately wanted one himself. 'You could leave the car outside, Mum,' he pleaded.

'If I could afford it, son, you could have a table tomorrow,' Annie told him. Daniel had turned away, disgusted. He refused to believe they were hard up. 'We're not *really* hard up,' she thought. 'There's always enough food, the house is warm, and I've never had to buy their clothes secondhand – and Daniel's shoes cost a mint.' His feet were so broad, she had to get Clarks. 'It's just there's never enough for luxuries.'

'I'm getting nowhere at this rate.' She searched for a black button for the skirt, but could find none the right size. Determined not to use the lack of a button as an excuse to do nothing, she fetched the box of odds and ends in from the garage, stuff she'd bought because she liked the look of the material. She'd always meant to do something with them one day, she wasn't sure what.

She tipped the box upside down and the clothes spilled out onto the floor. Her eyes were searching for a garment that might have a black button, when she noticed an olive-green frock sprinkled with little dark roses had fallen on top of something made of glossy plum velvet.

'Oh, don't they look lovely together!'

She picked the velvet up. It was an old dressing gown, and the material ran through her fingers like silk. Underneath the arms was completely frayed and the collar was hanging off, but the rest was whole. Perhaps it was the years of wear that made it feel so soft. She examined the frock, which was crepe with square padded shoulders, and vaguely remembered thinking it too old-fashioned to sell. The roses were exactly the same colour as the velvet.

Annie laid the things side by side on the arm of the settee and stared at them for a long time. Then she closed her eyes and in her head she designed an outfit; a plain dirndl skirt with an elasticated waist from the dressing gown, a loose, shapeless top out of the dress with scalloped velvet trim on the sleeves and hem. Baggy sleeves, a low round neck that wouldn't need a fastener. Both garments already had their own tie belts. She would decide which one to use when she finished – no, she'd open up both belts and sew them together so they could be used either way.

Excitement mounting and mending forgotten, Annie picked up her scissors and got down to work. The skirt took no time, she already had several yards of wide elastic. Making the top took slightly longer. She had to face the neck and put a dart in the bust. The scalloped trim required the patience of Job. She ironed it lightly before attaching it to the top. She could hardly wait to see the whole thing finished, and impatiently began to pick at the stitches on a belt.

It was almost five o'clock and she'd forgotten all about Daniel's tea by the time she'd done. Her hands were shaking when she put the suit on a hanger and suspended it from the door. She tried the two-sided belt one way, then the other, before deciding to leave the green uppermost. The plum velvet was revealed when she tied the knot.

She took a step back and regarded her handiwork with a gasp of pleasure. It looked *beautiful*!

When Sara came home, Annie asked what she thought. 'You're not going to wear it, are you, Mummy? It's horrible.'

Dismayed, Annie took her precious suit next door to show to Valerie. 'It's certainly different,' Valerie said dubiously. 'It looks expensive – I can see you or Sylvia in it. How much will you ask for that?'

'I wasn't thinking of selling it.'

'Actually,' Valerie cocked her head sideways, 'it grows on you. I bet it's comfortable to wear, and stylish at the same time.'

Perhaps she could put it on the stall, Annie thought when she got home, but she wasn't prepared to take a penny less than ten pounds, and not many women came to Great Homer Street market prepared to pay that much for an outfit, despite the fact it was completely unique. If no-one bought it, she'd keep it herself.

When Saturday came, she put the two-piece at the front of a rack. Several women approached and looked at it longingly, but pulled a face when they saw the price. It was mid-day when the woman who was always on the look-out for evening wear came up. Annie was serving someone else. Out of the corner of her eye, she saw the woman pounce on the suit and hold it against herself. Then she looked at the price tag. 'Will you take six pounds for this?'

'Sorry, no.'

'How about eight?'

'I'll not take a penny less than ten,' Annie said stubbornly. 'It's an original. You'll never see another woman in the same thing.'

'All right, ten it is. Are you likely to have any more? We've been invited to all sorts of functions over Christmas.'

'I might have one next week.'

By the time next Saturday came, Annie had made another suit. She'd kept her eye open at jumble sales for things made from suitable material, regardless of the style, and had converted a cream Viyella frock and an old-gold silky bedspread, threadbare in places, into a thing of beauty, according to Chris Andrews who saw the finished outfit. Following the same pattern as last week, she made a skirt from the bedspread. This time, she attached big gold diamond shapes down the front of the baggy cream top, and cut the hem so it hung in points. Then she covered several tiny buttons with the gold material and attached one to each point. Once again, she made a reversible belt.

'This is the sort of thing you should have been doing years ago, Annie,' Chris said admiringly. 'It's a work of art.'

She was still setting up her stall when a customer bought the suit.

'I saw the one you had last week,' the woman said breathlessly. 'I only wandered off to make me mind up, but when I came back it was gone. I came early this time in case you had another. This one's even nicer. Will you be having more? I'd love to send one to me sister in Canada.'

Annie was pleased when she was able to tell her regular customer, whom she'd never much liked, that, yes, she'd had one of her 'unusual outfits', as the woman called it, but it had gone hours ago.

'I thought you'd have kept it for me.' The woman looked annoyed. 'I wore the other to a dinner dance on Wednesday and everyone asked where I'd got it. Of course, I didn't say it came from a market.'

'I'll have another for next week.' She thoroughly enjoyed creating her 'unusual outfits'; it was a pleasant and easy way of making money. If she managed to sell one a week until Christmas, there'd be enough to buy Daniel a snooker table.

It was New Year's Eve, no, New Year's Day. Annie held her watch up to the light which filtered through the white curtains of Sara's room. Ten past four and she hadn't slept a wink.

This year, the Cunninghams had thrown a party. Annie had taken Daniel but they hadn't stayed long as it began to get rather wild. Fortunately, the children were playing Monopoly in the breakfast room and didn't seem aware of what the adults were getting up to elsewhere – you daren't open a door lest you found a couple involved in some sort of hanky-panky. Kevin had pinched Annie's bottom and suggested they go out to the garage. Lord knows where Valerie was, she disappeared for ages.

Annie had a good excuse to leave at eleven because her daughter was due home. Sara had been to her first proper party. When the invitation arrived, Annie began to plan a party dress, but Sara insisted on a skimpy black skirt and a black polo-neck jumper.

'For a party, luv?' Annie said, dismayed.

'Yes, Mummy, and I know we can't afford it, but I'd love a pair of pixie boots.'

Annie had bought the pixie boots for Christmas and Daniel had got his longed-for snooker table. Bruno kept it in the Grand, then brought it round after the bar closed on Christmas Eve and helped to erect it in the lounge. As soon as Christmas was over it was going in the garage.

'Merry Christmas, Annie!' Bruno had kissed her warmly on the lips before leaving and her stomach gave a pleasant little lurch. He was sixty, but still gorgeous. Cecy must be stark raving mad!

She turned over for the umpteenth time. She hadn't been sleeping well for weeks, ever since she'd made that first outfit. Her mind buzzed with ideas and she had to keep a notebook by the bed to jot them down in case they'd been forgotten by morning. It wasn't exactly true to say her outfits had sold like hot cakes, because there hadn't been enough, the most she'd managed was three a week, but word seemed to have spread. On the last Saturday before Christmas, a woman had asked, 'Are you the lady who makes the patchwork frocks?' Annie had to tell her she'd sold out, but would have more in the New Year.

Then a terribly haughty woman, beautifully dressed, had offered to buy two suits a week on a regular basis at seven pounds fifty each.

'I'll think about it,' Annie said, dazed.

'What did she want?' Cecy asked.

'Do you know her?'

'I know who she is. She runs an expensive boutique in Chester. You can't buy anything there for less than fifty pounds.'

'Fifty pounds? She offered to buy two outfits off me every week for seven pounds fifty.'

'Cheek!' Later, Cecy said thoughtfully, 'You know, Annie, it wouldn't be a bad idea for you to start a shop yourself.'

A shop of her own! It was another reason for not sleeping. She'd seen a lot of Cecy over Christmas – Sylvia, Eric and the children had gone to Morocco for the holiday, so she was at a loose end. They talked all the time about opening a shop.

'The thing is,' said Annie, 'I couldn't possibly make enough clothes to fill a shop.'

Sylvia telephoned as Annie was about to go to the Cunninghams'. They'd just arrived home and had enjoyed themselves tremendously. 'We went to the Casbah every day. I bought heaps of lovely things.'

'What are you doing tonight?' Annie enquired.

'We're spending the evening quietly as a family. I'll be thinking of you, friend, when the clock strikes twelve.'

Annie remembered glancing at the Churches' Christmas card as she put the phone down. Only Sylvia could send something so ostentatious; a photo of the family taken in the cottage, Sylvia in the pink armchair looking queenly, with Ingrid on her knee, and Yasmin leaning against her mother, staring at the camera with her dark, mysterious eyes. Both girls wore frothy white dresses. Eric was sitting on the arm of the chair, his arm laid casually on his wife's shoulder. There was a Christmas tree, lights glowing, in the background. They must have put the tree up exceptionally early, as the card had been one of the first to arrive.

'I'm never going to sleep tonight.' Annie carefully eased herself to a sitting position, so as not to disturb Sara, though the house could fall down and Sara wouldn't wake up. Even when the doorbell rang about two hours ago, she'd slept right through.

The doorbell had rung on and on, as if someone were leaning against it. Worried it might be a drunk come to the wrong house. Annie shouted 'Who's there?' before answering.

'It's me,' a voice said huskily.

Sylvia! Annie opened the door. 'Oh, Jaysus!' she exclaimed. Sylvia's jaw was swollen and there was blood trickling from her nose. She was in her night-clothes, as were the children. Ingrid was fast asleep in her arms. Yasmin, looking scared, clutched her mother's dressing gown.

'What happened, Syl?' Annie picked Yasmin up and carried her inside.

Sylvia sank onto the settee. 'Eric had one too many,' she said dully. 'We were just about to go to bed, when something seemed to snap. He said he loathed me more than ever because I'd been with other men. He particu-larly hates . . .' she nodded at Yasmin, 'because she's coloured. According to him, people snigger behind his back and regard him as a cuckold. I didn't think that word was used nowadays, Annie. Cuckold!'

'Oh, luv!'

'You were right, after all.' Sylvia closed her eyes briefly. 'I should never have got involved with him again. They say the leopard never changes its spots, don't they?'

After several cups of tea, Sylvia went to bed. Annie put all three in her room, emptying the wardrobe drawer for the baby.

'You're the only person in the world I could turn to,' Sylvia said gratefully as Annie tucked her in. 'Cecy would have had hysterics, and Bruno'd have driven to Ormskirk and slaughtered Eric in his bed.'

'You know I'll always be here for you, Syl.'

'And me for you, Annie.'

Annie slid back under the bedclothes, feeling envious of her daughter's regular breathing. Despite what had happened, her thoughts went back to the shop. Cecy had asked what she would call it, should the dream turn into reality. '"Annie's" would be nice,' she mused.

But this was something Annie had already decided. 'No, I've already thought of a name. If me shop gets off the ground, I'll call it "Patchwork"!'

Patchwork

I

Uncle Bert bent on one knee beside Dot's wheelchair and began to sing 'If you were the only girl in the world . . .' in a surprisingly steady baritone, considering the amount of beer he'd drunk that night.

There was scarcely a dry eye in the room over the pub where Tommy and Dawn's reception had been held twenty-four years ago. The place was packed, the music loud, the August night stuffy. The windows were even more difficult to open than in 1956.

All the Gallagher lads were there with their families. There were eighteen grandchildren at the last count – twenty if you counted Mike's stepchildren, Kathy and Paul. Great-grandchildren had begun to arrive, two so far and two more on the way. Mike, elegantly handsome in a dark grey silk suit, his red hair cut short, had become a sort of grandfather when Kathy had a son the previous year. Kathy and her boyfriend were living together in Melling. It was, thought Annie, incredible how things had changed. Young people no longer required a piece of paper to formalise their relationship.

Bert wheeled Dot to the side of the room. He did everything for her nowadays; washed and dressed her, carried her to the lavatory, did the cooking, the cleaning. The lads, their wives, Annie, came to give him a break, to sit with Dot whilst he went for a pint or to the Labour Party. Otherwise, Bert dedicated his waking hours to the care of his beloved wife. 'He even wipes me botty for me, poor feller,' Dot told Annie with a chuckle that turned into a sigh. 'I can't reach round that far.'

Despite being severely crippled and wheelchair-bound, Dot had still insisted on a party on her seventieth birthday. Her infirmities did nothing to dampen her indomitable spirit.

Annie had never seen her aunt look beautiful before. Perhaps it was because she could no longer use her body that Dot's face appeared so wonderfully alive. Her skin glowed taut and silvery over the angular bones and her eyes glittered behind her new pearl-rimmed spectacles. Even the fact Bert had applied her lippy crookedly did nothing to detract from the brilliant radiance of the seventy-year-old woman with the cruelly twisted body. She wore a white gossamer knitted shawl, Annie's present, over a pale blue dress and pretty slippers with pom-poms on the toes, because Bert could no longer get shoes on her feet.

Her lads fussed over her all night, terrified their mam might not see another birthday. After all, there was a limit to what a body could stand. Steroids had given her diabetes and now she had angina, which meant awful pains in her chest, which, Dot said with a grin, was the only place the arthritis hadn't reached.

The pianist was playing all the old tunes; 'Amongst my Souvenirs', 'The Old Lamplighter', 'There's a Small Hotel' . . . He ran his fingers up and down the keys and began, 'Goodnight Sweetheart', as Mike came over and asked Sylvia to dance.

Annie had a strong feeling of *déjà vu*, as Mike's girlfriend, Delia, an attractive blonde in her thirties, glared at him from across the room. He hadn't been so rude as at Tommy's wedding with poor Pamela, but Annie noticed he'd had eyes for no-one but Sylvia all night. And as if a circle had taken twenty-four years to form, he was dancing with her again, holding her closely and scarcely moving to the music played on the same old piano as before.

Annie went into the kitchen in search of a cup of tea. The room was empty and a giant kettle steamed gently on the antique gas stove. She put a teabag in a cup, filled it with water, added powdered milk and drank it leaning against the sink. Wouldn't it be marvellous if Sylvia and Mike got together! It was about time Sylvia settled down; after all, they'd both be forty next year. Annie recalled the New Year's Eve when Eric had gone berserk and his wife and children had landed on her doorstep. Next morning, Eric turned up, having already been to Cecy's and roused Bruno from a hangover, utterly contrite, swearing he'd never do anything like that again. Annie refused to let him in.

Bruno's hangover was not so bad that he didn't begin to wonder why his son-in-law was searching for his family so early on New Year's Day. He came storming round to Heather Close to see if Annie had an explanation, and found Eric on the doorstep almost in tears.

'What's going on?' he demanded.

Sylvia came down in her bloodstained nightdress. A big purple bruise had appeared on her swollen chin. Bruno's horrified glance went from his daughter to her husband, then, with a growl, he took Eric by the scruff of the neck, dragged him down the path and threw him on the pavement. 'You're never to come near Sylvia or the girls again!'

Annie, though glad it was too early for the neighbours to witness, quite enjoyed the scene.

Eric disappeared. Cecy heard he'd been transferred to the Churches' new London office. Divorce proceedings commenced a second time.

Sylvia stayed a month with Annie, then she put the

cottage on the market, bought a house in Waterloo and announced that, from now on, she was going to write poetry and devote her life to the children. She wore dirndl skirts and baggy sweaters and let her hair flow free and wild. She often turned up at Annie's to read her latest poem.

'What do you think?'

Annie's opinion was usually more or less the same. 'If you want the truth, I think it's awful. It doesn't rhyme and it doesn't make sense.'

'It's not supposed to make sense. Life doesn't make sense.'

'Anyone could write poetry that doesn't make sense. Even *I* could.'

'You haven't got a poetic bone in your body, Annie Menin.'

'No, but I've plenty of practical ones. I need to make a living.' Annie was in the throes of an inner debate; should she give up her small, regular income from the stall and take the risk of opening her own shop? It was the most difficult decision she'd ever had to make. Sylvia and her poetry were getting on her nerves.

'One day,' Sylvia said haughtily, 'my poems could make my fortune.'

'Huh!'

After a year, the dirndl skirts and baggy sweaters were thrown away and the poetry forgotten. Cecy was pressed into service to look after the girls whilst her daughter changed her image for the umpteenth time and went to work for an employment agency in Southport.

'It's not what I want, Annie,' Sylvia confessed. 'What I want more than anything is a happy marriage. I would have made a go of it with Eric, but I wasn't prepared to be a punchbag for the rest of my life.'

'I don't blame you,' Annie murmured.

'What do *you* want, Annie?' Sylvia asked seriously.

'I'm not sure.' Annie thought hard. 'Same as you, I suppose. I never planned on having a market stall or a shop. I still miss Lauri, but can't visualise marrying again, not that anyone but Chris has asked.'

Sylvia shuddered. 'One day the children will be married, and we'll be stuck with each other. We can go to whist drives and play bingo.'

'Oh, don't, Syl! That sounds too depressing for words.'

'Mummy, there you are! I've been searching for you everywhere.' Sara came into the kitchen. 'We're going into town to a disco.'

'Who's "we"?' demanded Annie.

'Becky, Emma and me.'

'Will you be all right, three girls on your own?' Becky and Emma were Alan Gallagher's daughters.

'Of course we will,' Sara assured her.

'Give Auntie Dot a nice big kiss before you go. Where's Daniel?'

'He's in the pub.' Sara wriggled her tall, slim frame uncomfortably. 'He's drinking an awful lot of cider. I think he's showing off.'

Annie made a face. 'All right, luv, I'll see to him.' She gave her daughter an affectionate shove. 'Enjoy yourself – don't be late home.'

'I've told Becky and Emma I have to be in by half eleven.'

Sara left. She was still a model child, awkward and gangling, and childishly innocent for seventeen, despite being so clever. Annie worried men would take advantage of her naivety. Her glasses emphasised the babyish curves of her face and the wide blue eyes that seemed incapable of seeing wrong. How on earth would she cope at university?

Annie sighed and transferred her thoughts to Daniel. He shouldn't be in the pub, but the landlord was unlikely to guess the handsome six-footer with the deep voice was only fifteen. If she yanked him out he'd claim she'd made a show of him in public, which apparently she'd done when she found him smoking behind the gym at Grenville Lucas last year.

'What will me mates think?' he said angrily as she marched him home. 'No-one else's mother turns up to spy on them.'

'I was there to see Mrs Peters about something to do with Sara,' Annie said defensively. 'I only came across you by accident.'

'I won't be able to hold me head up in class tomorrow.'

She recalled Marie had been found smoking when she was only nine or ten and supposed it was something most kids got up to, particularly boys. She made him promise never to smoke in the house and said no more.

Since then, Daniel had grown another six inches and took size ten shoes. Like Marie, he seemed adult before his time. He badly needed a father to keep him in line. How would Lauri have dealt with his over-sized son? Annie had a feeling he would have left everything to her.

She was rinsing the cup when Dawn Gallagher came into the kitchen. No longer thin and darkly dramatic, Dawn had grown stout and grey over the years. She looked Annie up and down enviously.

'I bet you could still wear that bridesmaid frock. My wedding dress wouldn't go near me.' She patted her wide hips. 'How's your Marie?'

'She's making a film in America.' According to the critics, the young director Marie had been so contemptuous of had turned out to be a youthful genius. He'd used her in his subsequent films, as he liked having the same actors in supporting roles. Unfortunately, the films were uncommercial and had never gone out on general release, so Annie had never managed to see one.

'America! You've both done well for yourselves; Marie in films and you with your shop. Dot said it's really taken off. What's it called? I keep meaning to come and buy something off you one day.'

'Patchwork, but I'm afraid things are rather expensive.' Nowadays, her dresses and suits cost upwards of thirty pounds.

Dawn sighed and glanced around the shabby room. 'I remember coming in here on me wedding day to take two aspirin, me head was splitting.'

'Everyone cried their eyes out at your wedding.'

'Perhaps they sensed how it would turn out,' Dawn said bitterly.

'What do you mean, luv?' Annie asked astonished. Dawn and Tommy had always seemed very happy.

'Don't say a word to Dot, I don't want her to know until it's absolutely necessary, but me and Tommy are getting divorced.'

'I don't believe it!'

'Annie, luv, he's had another woman for years. He promised to stay with me until the kids were off our hands. With Ian getting married at Christmas, he reckons it's time he went.' Dawn glanced at her reflection in the darkening window. 'They're a flighty lot, the Gallaghers. I'm being exchanged for a younger version of meself.'

Annie sat with Dot and Bert during the last waltz. She had no-one to dance with. She could have brought Chris, but it seemed wrong to use him just because it was convenient. Anyroad, he might get ideas . . .

'I see our Mike's at Sylvia again.' Dot's eyes gleamed wickedly. 'He's a much better catch these days. He'll be a millionaire soon.' She gave a triumphant cackle. 'That Delia's gone home in a huff, I'm pleased to say. Never did like those peaches-and-cream, butter-wouldn't-melt-in-me-mouth women like Mrs Thatcher.'

'Now, luv!' Bert said warningly. 'Don't get yourself all worked up.'

'Not Mrs Thatcher again, Auntie Dot,' Annie groaned.

'Well, I can't stand the woman. Said she'd reduce taxes when she got in, and what did she do? Put that VAT thing up double. Going to tame the unions, is she? Well, let's see her do it.'

'She'll do it, luv.' Bert shook his head sadly. 'Unemployment's going through the roof. The unions'll be on their knees before long.'

'The whole country'll be on its knees if Mrs Thatcher has her way, apart from the nobs and the bosses.' Dot's voice rose.

'Auntie Dot, remember your heart!'

'Sod me bleedin' heart. If I can't pass an opinion on someone I loathe and detest, then I might as well be dead. Not that I've any intention of going before that woman. They're making such a cock-up, they'll never get in at the next election.'

Bert made a face at Annie behind his wife's back. In a bid to distract her attention, he said, 'Aren't Sylvia's kids a picture? One's as dark as the other's fair.'

The bid worked. 'Is the eldest one coloured, Annie?' Dot enquired. 'She looks as if she's got a touch of the tar brush in her blood.'

'I don't know,' said Annie. Seven-year-old Yasmin and Ingrid, two years younger, were as striking as their mother.

Dot lapsed into silence as she watched the dancers. Although Annie wouldn't have dreamt of saying so, she thought Labour deserved to lose last year's election.

Over the winter, the unions had gone completely crazy – the gravediggers had gone on strike in Liverpool and ordinary people were unable to bury their dead. Of course, she'd canvassed and leafleted as usual, but felt it was in aid of a lost cause.

The last waltz ended. The pianist played a few final crashing chords. Tommy demanded three cheers for the birthday girl. 'Hip, hip . . .'

'Hooray!' roared the entire Gallagher clan.

And Dot burst into tears as her party came to an end.

Valerie Cunningham had spotted the empty premises in South Road, a few minutes' walk from Heather Close, four years ago. Annie had gone round straight away to peer through the double-fronted windows. It turned out to be where she'd bought Mam the pink dress for Tommy Gallagher's wedding. Empty, the place looked bigger. It needed decorating and the carpet was hideous, shades of green, squares within squares. She'd like a plain carpet so as not to detract from the clothes; a warm oatmeal.

After making enquiries, she found the rent was reasonable, though the agent wanted a year in advance. A ten-year fixed rate lease was available if she wanted. She dithered for another month, trying to make up her mind. What had she got to lose? She could always go back to the market. Actually, there was quite a lot to lose; the advance rent, the cost of decoration, the carpet . . .

Annie discussed it with the children. Daniel didn't care one way or the other, but Sara thought she should go ahead. 'You love making clothes, Mummy. You should do what you enjoy. You've only got one life.'

So Annie had taken the plunge. The bank manager was forthcoming when asked for another loan, 'Your own shop! What an enterprising lady you are, Mrs Menin,' he said, a trifle patronisingly she thought.

The problem of being unable to turn out sufficient stock was solved. She wouldn't just sell her own clothes, but other things with the same patchwork theme. Cecy knew a woman whose sister made beautiful patchwork quilts and cushion covers. When Annie approached Susan Hull, she was pleased to have an outlet for her work.

'I'd take twenty-five per cent,' Annie told her.

Susan pulled a face. 'Twenty-five!'

'You've got nothing to lose. I'll have all the outgoings; rent, rates, advertising, as well as the upkeep of the shop. It's costing the earth for a new carpet and the place is being decorated throughout.'

'I suppose that's fair,' the woman said reluctantly.

'If it doesn't suit you, I'll find someone else.' Annie wasn't keen on Susan Hull, with her thin rhubarb face and long red hands, but her quilts were glorious and she'd quite like them in her shop.

'There's no need for that,' Susan said hastily.

'Do you know anyone with a knitting machine?'

'Sorry, no.'

But Auntie Dot did. 'There's this ould feller in Frederick Street who turns out smashing jumpers.'

'A man!' Annie only imagined women having knitting machines.

'He took over his wife's machine after she died. He's far better at it than Minnie ever was.'

She'd gone to see Ernie West, a wizened little chap who looked at death's door. He lived in a tiny terraced house, furnished as it might have been in the last century. 'I can turn out a jumper in a night,' he said boastfully when she explained what she wanted.

'Yes, but as I said, I don't want them dead plain. I'd like at least two different colours.'

Ernie looked at her indignantly. 'I got you the first time, missus.'

'I'll take twenty-five per cent.'

'Take what you like, luv, I don't give a toss about the money. I just like knitting on ould Minnie's machine.'

She asked for a couple of samples. Two weeks later, Ernie turned up at the house with an old sack, bulging. Annie's heart was in her mouth, worried they'd be awful. Instead, she gasped. 'They're lovely!'

There was one black and white, the squares the exact size of a chess board, with a single red stitch in each centre. Another, red at the hem, gradually turning to blue, green, yellow at the neck; one maroon and navy, the sort of colours she would have chosen herself, though she'd never dream of combining lemon with mustard, but it looked really effective.

'I'm dead pleased with these,' she said.

'I knew you'd be.' Ernie preened himself. 'I'm an artist in me own way.'

'You certainly are,' Annie conceded.

She was sad at giving up the market stall which had seen her through the worst times after Lauri's death. On her final day, she reduced the remaining stock to half price and bought two crates of beer to share with her fellow traders when she said her goodbyes.

'You'll have us caught for drunk driving,' Ivor Hughes protested, downing his third bottle. 'Well, good luck with the shop, girl.'

Annie made a special point of going into the indoor section to say goodbye to the Barclays on their fruit and veg stall. Sid and Vera had recently sold the house next door and gone to live in Woolton.

'I don't know what it was, Annie,' Vera confessed, 'but I never felt right there. It was as if the place was haunted, which is a stupid thing to say about a place so newly built.' She shuddered. 'I always had the feeling the old couple who used to live there resented us.'

Number six had been bought by the Dunns, a childless couple in their forties. They were an unsociable pair, who complained about the noise from the children. Annie was glad her two no longer played in the garden. The Dunns had recently planted a tall hedge at the front.

There were shouts of, 'Good luck, Annie', as she began to pack up early. Ruby Livesey appeared. Annie gave her a beer and asked if she'd like the remaining clothes as she was giving up.

'I knew you'd never stick at it,' Ruby sneered. 'And you can keep your clothes. They're not the sort I sell.'

'Suit yourself,' said Annie.

On the Monday morning after Dot's party, Annie paused outside Patchwork. A signwriter had painted the name, each letter a different colour. Even after four years, she still got pleasure from looking at her shop.

A single outfit hung in the left-hand window, a white voile two-piece with a wide band of soft blue satin bordering the hem. Inserted between the blue and white was a strip of white lace threaded with blue ribbon. The top had a blue shawl collar tied in a knot. A handwritten card indicated the price was £35. In the other window, a brightly patterned quilt was draped over a pine box, and one of Ernie's jumpers lay casually on the floor.

Annie unlocked the door. Two rails of clothes, one following the other, were to her left, and a rail of jumpers and waistcoats to the right. A small cane settee was heaped with patchwork cushions. Three more quilts, folded on their special racks, hung from the wall. The place looked uncluttered without appearing bare, though the wall above the clothes bothered her. It needed pictures.

She sat down at the Regency desk at the rear of the shop and wrote out an order for Mr Patel in Bolton. Mr Patel owned a small mill that turned out exclusive cloth for the very best shops in London. Although Annie was one of his smallest customers, he always made a great fuss of her when she went to look at his latest designs; the silky velvets, the soft jerseys, coarse knobbly cottons, delicate voiles, all dyed the most unusual colours. It was the sort of stuff you never saw in shops like Lewis's or Owen Owen's. Once she'd turned professional, it was no good relying on jumble sales for material.

The order written, Annie stood the envelope on the desk ready to post. It was ten minutes before the shop was due to open, but she changed the sign from 'Closed' in case she forgot, and went into the minuscule kitchen to put the kettle on.

On the way, she paused in front of the fitting-room mirror. Dawn was wrong, that bridesmaid frock would never fit, she'd only been fourteen then. On the other hand, she'd get into her wedding dress, except it had been sold in the market. Her figure had scarcely changed since she got married. She was lucky to be uninterested in food. In times of stress, she ate less, whereas other women were inclined to gorge.

Annie peered closely in the mirror. Hardly any wrinkles. She didn't look so bad for a woman not far off forty. Her crimson and tan dress, one of her own creations, set off her red hair. She could do with more earrings – she could sell jewellery in the shop!

'I'd love to grow me hair long.' It was as short as the day Marie had taken the scissors to it all those years ago. She ruffled her curls. 'I don't half fancy one of those thick plaits that start at the scalp.'

She took a step back and regarded her full reflection thoughtfully. 'I wonder what Lauri would think of these gold sandals?' They consisted of merely a few straps with high, spindly heels, and were torture to wear. Her eyes went from her feet to her face. 'I still give Sylvia a good run for her money, but am I wasting me life like Cecy said?'

Two years ago, Cecy was convinced she had cancer. The day before she was due to see the specialist, she told Annie tearfully how much she regretted leaving Bruno all those years ago. 'You don't know the details, dear, but I should have stayed and made the sacrifice.'

Annie didn't let on she'd known the details from the start. Sacrifice! Sleeping with Bruno, a sacrifice! She clutched Cecy's hand, terrified she'd die. It would be like losing her mother.

'I'm only half alive. Women need men. Men don't need us, except for one thing,' Cecy blushed, 'but we're wasted without them. Marry again soon, dear, before you become a useless, dried-up old woman like me.'

'Frankly,' Annie said to her reflection, 'I feel more alive now than when I was married to Lauri. Am I useless just 'cos I'm a widow? And would I be less useless if I became Mrs Andrews instead of Mrs Menin?' Chris proposed on average once a month. 'He's a lovely chap, but not one I'd pick to spend the rest of me life with, and I'd definitely prefer the telly in bed!' She'd bought a colour portable for the bedroom and stayed up till all hours watching old films. She smiled at herself, 'Maybe I'm already a dried-up youngish woman!'

The specialist had diagnosed kidney stones, not cancer, and Cecy had been as fit as a fiddle since the operation, but it had given Sylvia a terrible fright. 'I didn't realise how much I loved her till I thought she could die. Bruno's the same. He visited the hospital every day.'

A woman opened the shop door and shouted, 'D'you sell tights, luv?'

'Sorry, no.' Annie hung up the clothes she'd made over the weekend. She put two suits behind the sign that said 'Maternity', to replace those sold last week. The skirts had narrow braces so they wouldn't slide below the bump, and were perfectly wearable after the baby had been born.

It had been twelve months before Patchwork had 'taken off' as Dawn put it, but nowadays it provided her with a more than respectable income. Lots of customers came recommended by others, some dropped in drawn by the window display. The white outfit, for instance, was very likely to sell before the day was out.

As if to prove the point, the door opened and a woman came in to ask if she could try on, 'That lovely white and blue thing in the window.'

She ended up buying an entirely different outfit. 'I've a friend who'd love a two-piece like this. Have you got a branch in town?'

'No, this is the only one.' People often suggested she open a branch in Liverpool or Southport – or both.

'I might one day,' she usually replied. Perhaps she wasn't very ambitious, because one shop seemed enough.

Annie returned the white suit to the window. Her fingers itched to get on with more sewing; she had some lovely stuff at home, but she'd have to wait until Barbara turned up at one o'clock. She'd been obliged to take on an assistant when it became impossible to be in two places at once – in Patchwork selling clothes, and at home making them. There'd been five replies to her advert, but she had only interviewed Barbara Eastleigh. She recognised the name immediately. She and Barbara had worked together in the English Electric and they'd got on well. She was a bubbly cheerful woman, ten years older than Annie, with two young children. Now the children were married and she was anxious for a part-time job. She was delighted to find Patchwork belonged to her old friend. Annie had no hesitation about leaving the shop in her capable hands every afternoon from one o'clock.

Barbara arrived early and Annie went home. The children were on holiday and Daniel would be wanting food. Sara was out for the day with her friend, Louise. They did the same things Sylvia and Annie used to do; wandered round the shops, caught the ferry to New Brighton, went to the pictures – though only a fraction of the cinemas remained.

As she walked unsteadily down Heather Close on her spiky heels, she saw the garage door was open. Daniel was playing snooker with a lad from school. Two girls lounged against the Anglia, which was parked outside. 'If you scratch me car, I'll kill you!' she said lightly when she passed. The Anglia had been thoroughly overhauled and re-sprayed turquoise. It looked like new.

The girls giggled. Daniel looked up. 'Hi, Mum. Is there grub going?'

She assumed he meant grub for four, so opened two tins of soup and buttered half a loaf of bread. She cut four wedges of boiled fruit cake and hid the rest in the bread bin – if she left it out, the whole lot would go, and it was Sara's favourite. They ate noisily – the girls seemed unable to stop giggling. Annie left them to themselves and was glad when they returned outside. She went into the kitchen to clean up, but to her surprise found it already done, though someone – it could only be Daniel – had taken the cake from the bread bin and every crumb had gone.

'Bloody hell!' she swore, and threw fruit, butter and sugar into a pan, and added half a cup of water to make another. The mixture was simmering nicely when the phone rang.

'This is it!' Sylvia's voice throbbed with excitement.

'Syl! I tried to call you yesterday, but there was no answer. What's "it"? What are you on about?'

'Me and Mike. This is it, Annie. I can't understand how you ever thought him boring.'

'*I* thought him boring! I did no such thing, you idiot. It was you.'

'He's the least boring man who ever lived. Me and the girls went back to his house from Dot's party and we've been here ever since. They love him, I love him, and he loves us.' Sylvia drew in a deep rapturous breath. 'I've moved in permanently, Annie. I've chucked in that lousy employment agency. We're getting married in September.'

'Isn't that a bit quick?' Annie sat down suddenly.

'Quick!' Sylvia snapped. 'Jaysus! It's a quarter of a century since we first went out. I think me and Mike have been in love all along.'

Annie didn't think it wise to point out that Sylvia would never have fallen in love with a mere toolmaker. As his mam had said, Mike was a far more attractive proposition nowadays.

'I see congratulations aren't forthcoming,' Sylvia said grumpily. 'Honestly, Annie, every time I get married you disapprove.'

'Oh, Syl, I couldn't possibly be more pleased. You took me by surprise, that's all. If Mike wasn't me cousin, I'd be green with envy. He's a super bloke.' As the news sank in, Annie felt quite emotional. Sylvia was happy at last! 'Are you getting married in church?'

'We can't. As far as the Catholic Church is concerned, I'm still married to Eric. It'll have to be a register office – you'll be my matron of honour, won't you?'

'Of course.'

'But,' Sylvia said crisply, 'you're not to wear a ghastly Patchwork creation. Something a bit more stylish, if you don't mind.'

'What do you mean, ghastly!' snorted Annie. 'I thought you liked them – you bought one the day I had me Grand Opening.'

'Yes, but have you ever seen me wear it? It's been hanging in the wardrobe ever since. In fact, you can have it back if you like.'

An unspoken truce was declared when Cecy Delgado's only daughter married Dot Gallagher's second son.

'It's awkward arguing with a woman in a wheel-chair,' Cecy grumbled. 'I let her have her own way over all sorts of things, the guest list, for one. There's over forty of them Gallaghers, and she insists that every last one come. I hardly know anyone to ask.' Her aunts and uncles had long since died, and her only sister in Bath was fed up being invited to Sylvia's weddings and had refused to come.

'I let her take care of the flowers and the cars, Annie,' Dot said condescendingly, 'but I couldn't very well insist on the usual place for the reception when they've got the Grand.'

'That's very kind of you, Auntie Dot, but the bride's mother is supposed to make those sort of arrangements.'

In the past, Dot had driven the mothers of several Gallagher brides to the verge of gibbering insanity by the time the wedding arrived. 'I'll leave most of it to Cecy this time. She's got the dosh. If she wants to waste it on posh flowers, it's up to her.'

Sylvia wore a simply styled calf-length dress of the

palest pink lace, and a coronet of matching roses on her gleaming blonde hair. Annie's dress was deeper pink, soft, slippery crushed velvet. The bridesmaids, Yasmin and Ingrid, wore darker pink still, a lovely warm rose.

'Gosh, I was pregnant last time I was Sylvia's matron of honour.' Annie turned round, half expecting Lauri to be there with Sara on his knee. Instead, Sara was sitting between Chris Andrews and Daniel. Her son looked bored and had threatened not to come. He wore the Grenville Lucas navy blazer and his grey school trousers. It had seemed extravagant to buy a suit which he might never have the opportunity to wear again.

When the time came for Mike to kiss his new bride, he put his finger under Sylvia's chin, tipped her face towards his and kissed her softly on the lips. Their eyes smiled at each other.

Behind them, Annie had a quite unexpected thought. 'I wish someone would look at me like that! I wish . . . I wish . . .'

She turned round again. Chris Andrews gave her an encouraging smile. 'No, not Chris, never Chris. Just someone. I don't know who, perhaps I'll never meet him, but oh, I do wish . . .'

2

Sylvia did a pirouette and threw herself onto the cane settee full of patchwork cushions, which Annie had taken ages to arrange and weren't there to be sat on. 'I shall feel far more cheerful on my fortieth birthday than I did at thirty,' she cried gleefully. She and Mike had been married six months and the doctor had just confirmed she was pregnant. She'd come straight to the shop to impart the good news. The baby was due two days before her birthday.

'Does Mike know?'

'He's over the moon. Twice he's married a woman with two children, but never had one of his own. We're going to try for another before I'm too old. The doctor wrote "Geriatric Mother" or something on my notes.'

They'd been a long time coming together, Mike and Sylvia, but now nothing could disguise their love for each other. 'I can actually see us growing old together, Annie,' Sylvia confided. 'I never thought about the future with Eric.' The urge to lead a frantic social life had gone. She and Mike stayed in, watched TV or talked. 'I've discovered I really enjoy cooking.' He liked old-fashioned food, like stew with dumplings, and Dot had shown her how to make treacle pudding and scouse. Lately she'd been in her element furnishing their new home, an eighteenth-century manor house set in wooded grounds in Ince Blundell. It had eighteen rooms, and an *oak-panelled banqueting hall*! She'd bought two of Susan Hull's quilts and four cushions.

'You'll be having your baby just as I'm losing one of mine,' Annie sighed. Sara had been accepted by the University of Essex in Colchester, and would be leaving in October.

'I'll be going on for sixty by the time this one gets itchy feet.' Sylvia patted her stomach.

'But you'll have Mike!'

'That's right, I'll have my darling Mike.'

There was silence, until Sylvia said softly, 'I hate you being unhappy, Annie.'

'It's your fault for telling me about the baby.' Annie smiled. 'I never visualised you having more chldren than me.'

'It's not too late. Why not marry Chris and start a second family?'

'That would be too easy.'

Sylvia shrugged. 'You shouldn't avoid things because they're easy.'

'It would be like giving up, taking the soft option. I mean,' Annie spread both hands, palms upwards, as if she were weighing something, 'when you compare Chris with Mike . . .'

'I get the picture.' Sylvia nodded understandingly.

On the first Sunday in October, a day she'd been dreading for months, Annie drove her daughter to Colchester. The car was packed with Sara's belongings; her record player, her favourite doll, text books – she was taking Sociology – and almost every item of clothing she possessed.

'I got you a nice new set of towels, twelve pairs of those bikini pants you wear, and there's enough tinned food to last for weeks.' Annie's list had been several pages long. She mentally ran through it; soap powder, plasters, coffee, deodorant, toothpaste, spare spectacles, needle and cotton . . . 'I don't think I've forgotten anything.'

'Okay, Mum.'

'If you feel like a weekend at home, phone and I'll come and fetch you. Barbara will look after the shop. I'll catch up with your washing.'

Sara nodded, white-faced. She hardly spoke during the journey. Annie chatted away about nothing, anxious to keep her mind busy so she wouldn't dwell on the parting which grew closer with each mile.

They reached the university, crowded with young people and their parents. It took ages to transfer Sara's things from the car to her bare, grey room on the fifth floor of a tower block on the campus.

'The view's nice,' said Annie from the window. All that could be seen was green parkland and fields. A river shone like ribbon. Colchester was out of sight on the other side of the building. Sara would have been better on that side. She was a city person, not used to a vast empty space devoid of people, no matter how pretty it might be. Annie prayed it wouldn't make her feel lonely.

Everything had been put in its place. The doll on the window sill, the books on the shelf. A fresh notebook, pens, and a matching stapler and punch were set neatly on the desk. The room still looked bare.

'You could do with some posters,' Annie said.

'I'll buy some,' Sara said in a thin voice. She was sitting on her hands on the narrow bed, shoulders hunched. She looked fourteen.

The thought of her daughter wandering around Smiths or Athena by herself looking for posters was too much. Annie felt her throat tighten.

Shouts could be heard from the corridor, 'Cheerio, darling. Look after yourself.'

'Bye, Mum.'

'Bye, son, stay cool.'

'Bye, Dad.'

'I think everyone's going,' said Annie. 'I suppose I'd better be on me way.' She sat on the bed and put her arm around Sara's shoulders. 'Tara, luv. Take care.'

'Mum!' Sara turned to her mother, her face stricken. 'I don't want to stay. I want to go home with you.'

There was nothing, absolutely nothing, that Annie wanted more than to return Sara's things to the car and whisk her back to Heather Close. She swallowed hard, but the tightness in her throat remained. 'You'll soon settle in, sweetheart. You'll make new friends in no time.'

Sara began to cry and threw her arms around her mother's neck. 'I'd sooner be home and get a job, like Louise.'

It was time to be hard, and being hard was something Annie had never been good at. She took hold of Sara's hands and firmly removed them from her neck. 'No, luv.'

'*Please*, Mum!'

Annie felt as if her heart would break. She gritted her teeth, determined not to cry. If she did, they'd both be lost. Sara would be back in Liverpool and would probably regret it for the rest of her life. 'No, luv,' she said sharply. 'You must stay. This is what you've always wanted. You'd never forgive me if I took you home.'

Sara removed her glasses and the sobs continued. 'Shall I make some tea?' Annie offered desperately. 'The kitchen's along the corridor.'

'No thanks, Mum.'

'Perhaps you can make one after I've gone. Don't forget, the food's in the top drawer – I made two of your favourite fruitcakes.'

'I won't forget.' Sara pulled a handkerchief from her sleeve, wiped her eyes and her glasses and blew her nose. The sobs subsided.

They both stood. Annie embraced her daughter one final time. She was conscious of Sara's heartbeat, and remembered how frequently she used to check her heart was beating when she was a baby just in case she'd died.

'Tara, Sara, luv.'

'Tara, Mum.'

Annie left her eldest child standing wanly in the middle of the bare, strange room, in a strange town she'd scarcely heard of before. She flew down the stairs. When she reached the second floor, a woman was sitting at the bottom, her body racked with sobs. Annie touched her arm. 'Are you all right, luv?'

'I will be. Oh, isn't it terrible! He looked so cheerful

when I left, and all I wanted to do was die. Children! Why do we have them, eh?'

'Don't ask me,' said Annie. She managed to reach the car before dissolving into tears herself, but quickly drove away, just in case Sara came looking for her, wanting to come home. It was one of those days that provided a marker in her life, like the day Mam and Dad died, the day she met Lauri, got married, the times the children were born. Then there was the day Lauri died. Now Sara had left home and things would never be quite the same again. Annie had left part of herself in that miserable tower-block room.

'This is the first time,' Sylvia said proudly, 'that I've had a baby and the father's been around.

'That's nothing to boast about,' Annie said scathingly. 'Most women'd be ashamed.'

Sylvia nuzzled her fine nose against the baby's little snub red one. 'Don't take any notice of your Auntie Annie, darling. She's quite nice when you get to know her.' She grinned. 'I'm calling her Dorothy.'

'Toad!'

'I know, but it's a way of getting in your Auntie Dot's good books for ever, and she's got Dot's ginger hair. Mike said the girls will look like liquorice all-sorts when they're together.'

'I bet he's thrilled.' Annie held out her arms for the baby.

'He's tickled pink. He's letting all his two hundred and fifty-eight workers home early today, and giving them ten pounds bonus each.'

Annie hadn't realised Mike employed so many people. 'Isn't that rather paternalistic?' she frowned as she traced Dorothy's pale gold eyebrows with her finger.

'Seems generous to me.'

399

'I mean, it implies *his* baby is more important than any of theirs.'

'No it doesn't.'

'Yes it does.'

'I'll have my baby back if you continue.'

Annie took no notice. 'She's got three chins.'

'As long as she hasn't got three eyes or three noses, I don't care.'

Sara was too busy to come home during her first term. Annie pored over her frequent letters, trying to read between the lines. *I think I've made a friend*, Sara wrote.

'She only "thinks",' fretted Annie. 'I thought she'd've made stacks of friends by now.'

Some people on my floor play loud music all night long.

'It must be deafening if it keeps our Sara awake,' Annie said to Daniel. 'Perhaps I should write to the university authorities?'

'She wouldn't thank you if you did.'

'I expect not,' Annie sighed.

'When's she coming home?'

'Not till Christmas, luv.'

Daniel missed his sister more than Annie had expected. They'd never seemed close, yet he moped about the house, lost, now she'd gone.

'How's the sixth form?' Annie asked him.

He pulled a face. 'Okay.'

'You know, you could always go to university like Sara. You'd need three good A levels, though.' His O level results had been abysmal. His teachers claimed he was intelligent, possibly more so than his sister, but he seemed determined not to do well.

'There's no chance of that, Mum.'

Annie stared worriedly at her son. He had no ambition, no aims. There was nothing he was good at except snooker. Physically, he was becoming more like a young Lauri every day, big, broad, handsome, but he had none of his father's commitment to hard work. She was constantly concerned about him. 'What are you going to do with yourself when you're eighteen?' she asked casually. She'd already asked several times before.

Daniel scowled impatiently. 'Shit knows.'

Barbara gave in her notice at the beginning of December. 'I'm dead sorry, Annie, but me husband's been made redundant. I need to work full-time.' She deeply regretted having to leave Patchwork for a factory. 'I love working here. It's a bit much, having to go on an assembly line at my age, but there you are. Stan's not the only one to lose his job. People are being made redundant like nobody's business.'

Unemployment had passed an incredible two million. There were riots in Toxteth, a few miles away. For the first time, CS gas was used on the citizens of Britain. A protester in a wheelchair died. Auntie Dot acted as if the world had ended. 'It's that woman's fault,' she croaked.

Annie regretfully advertised for another assistant. Instead of five replies, this time she received over fifty. She interviewed half a dozen, and decided on Chloe Banks, a small, plain girl with narrow, deep-set eyes and brown hair parted in the middle, giving her the look of a Victorian waif. She'd just finished a course in fashion design and showed an expert interest in Annie's clothes. Despite being only eighteen, she had an air of maturity unusual in one so young.

'I'd like it here so much, I'd work for nothing,' she said at the interview.

'I wouldn't dream of such a thing! It's three pounds an hour. I'll need you full time occasionally.'

Cecy and Valerie dropped in when Annie wasn't there and reported that Chloe managed perfectly well on her own. She didn't press the customers, but left them to browse as she'd been instructed to.

A week before Christmas, Sara came home by train with a haversack full of washing. She seemed more confident and self-assured than when she left. 'I'm glad you made me stay,' she said when Annie collected her from Lime Street station. 'I'm beginning to enjoy university.'

Annie squeezed her hand. 'If you only knew how much I wanted to bring you back! Now,' she said happily, 'let's get you home. Daniel can't wait to see his sister.'

After Mass on Christmas Day, they went to Mike and Sylvia's for dinner. It had become a tradition that the Gallaghers collect together on this one day of the year, and Sylvia was determined it should continue, particularly as they now had a room where everyone could eat in one sitting. Cecy and Bruno were there, and Tommy Gallagher brought his girlfriend, Trish, twenty years his junior. They were getting married as soon as his divorce from Dawn came through. Dawn had been invited but refused, saying she would feel uncomfortable.

After the meal, Dot nursed her latest grandchild. Cecy hovered anxiously nearby in case Dorothy might drop from the twisted arms.

'She's the spitting image of her gran,' Dot boasted loudly. 'Bert, where's that photo of me when I was two? I bet you forgot to bring it.'

'It's here, luv.' Bert fished a faded black and white photo out of his pocket. 'We were thinking of getting it coloured.'

There was no denying the resemblance between two-year-old Dot and Sylvia's new daughter. Dot's head swelled to monumental proportions.

'Never mind,' Annie whispered to Cecy. She was Dorothy's other grandmother, but was being kept very much in the shade. 'Ingrid's very much like you.'

'Do you think so, Annie?' Cecy said pathetically. 'I keep expecting Dot to lay some claim to Sylvia and I'll have had no part in this gathering at all.'

Annie hid her hurt when Sara refused a lift back to Colchester. 'I'm meeting some friends in London, Mum.' She'd been looking forward to the long drive with her daughter. The holiday had flashed by and there'd been little time to talk. She smiled. 'At least let me take you to the station.' Later, she watched, appalled, as Sara carelessly stuffed the freshly washed and ironed clothes into her haversack.

'I wonder if children ever feel the same about their parents?' she thought as Sara hauled her tall, slight form onto the train. She wore jeans and a scruffy anorak she'd acquired from an Oxfam shop. 'Would she have this same, sad feeling if it was me leaving her?'

Sara found a seat and opened the window. 'Look after yourself, Mum.'

She looked so happy to be going back! 'Don't worry, luv, I will.'

The train started. Annie hurried alongside. 'Eat properly, now.'

'Okay, Mum.'

'And keep warm. I put your vests in with your things.'

Sara laughed. 'Mum! I wouldn't be seen dead in a vest.'

Annie was almost running as the train picked up speed. 'There's Vick in your toilet bag. There's nothing like Vick for a cold.'

'Thanks, Mum.' Sara held out her hand, but the train was going too fast for Annie to reach it.

The police rang one afternoon when Annie was busy with a new design; a plain shift dress, no sleeves, no collar, just two pieces of material sewn together, but with a dazzling patchwork jacket to go over. She was only making a few and would see how they sold.

Outside, a gentle wind rustled the trees in Heather Close. She stopped for a moment, watching. 'They were only titchy when we first came. Now they're fully grown, just like the kids.' Except the trees couldn't leave!

To think it was March already! 'The year's flown by,' she thought. 'I can hardly believe it's twelve months since Sylvia came into the shop to say she was expecting Dorothy.'

When the phone went, she wondered if it was Sylvia and she was pregnant again. She and Mike were trying hard for another baby. Instead, it was the police. A male voice demanded that Annie come immediately to Seaforth police station.

Sara's been murdered, was her first thought, until she pulled herself together. Seaforth the man had said, not Colchester.

'What's happened?' she asked dazedly.

'We'd like you to collect your son.'

'Daniel? But he's at school.'

'No, Mrs Menin. He's at the station. Now, if you wouldn't mind . . .'

'I'll be there straight away.'

Daniel was lounging nonchalantly on a bench just inside the door. He looked up when his mother entered. His expression didn't change, but she sensed fear behind his eyes.

Annie ignored him. 'What's he done?' she asked the desk sergeant.

'As far as we can gather, nothing, but he was with a group of lads who mugged an old man for his wallet on Liverpool Road this afternoon.'

'*Daniel!*'

He got to his feet and stuffed his hands in his blazer pocket. Annie noticed the hands were shaking. 'I didn't know what they were up to, honest, Mum. One minute we were walking along, next they ran off and there was this old chap on the floor. I know I should have helped him, but as soon as we saw what had happened, the rest of us just scarpered.'

'He'd never do anything criminal,' Annie assured the policeman.

'That's what every parent says,' the man said drily.

'But he wouldn't!'

'Luckily, the attack was witnessed. Only three boys were involved. Take your son home, ma'am. He needs a lecture on the company he keeps.'

'Why aren't you at school?' Annie demanded as soon as they were in the car. Now that it was over, her heart was thumping with fright.

'What's the point? I'm not interested in A levels. I'm only wasting me time.' He was already his old arrogant self.

'And you feel your time is spent more usefully mugging an old man?'

'I had nothing to do with it. Even the police believed that.'

Annie believed it too. It had happened to her. She'd been with a gang of girls when Sylvia had been pushed into a holly bush. She hadn't known about it until after the act was done.

Daniel said, 'If you don't mind, I'd like to leave school, Mum.'

'But what's to become of you, son?' Annie said

anguishedly. 'You'll never get a job in this climate. Unemployment's going up all the time.'

'I don't want a job.'

'But you've got to do *something*! How about a course?'

'On what?' Daniel asked sarcastically.

'Electronics!' Annie cried after a pause. 'You used to love taking clocks and radios to pieces when you were little. I'll ask Mike Gallagher. He'd find an opening for you. Your dad worked for Mike.'

'I told you, I don't want a job. I'm not working for some cruddy employer, even if it is Mike Gallagher. There's no point.'

'You can't see any point in school, either.'

'I don't see any point in anything.' Annie was taken aback by the unexpected despair in her son's voice. 'It's a fucking lousy world. No-one gives a sod for anybody else. The politicians, all politicians, not just the Tories, are only out for what they can get. It might be power, it might be money. It's not making things better for the people.'

'Where did you get all this from, luv?' Annie asked quietly. She'd never dreamt he felt like this.

'From inside me own head.'

As soon as they were home, Daniel went upstairs. Annie made tea and took a cup up to him. He was lying face down on the bed. The little cars Lauri had bought were arranged in their usual neat line on the window sill. 'You can leave school,' she said. It seemed wrong to let the teachers waste their time on someone who had no wish to be taught.

He didn't raise his head. 'Ta, Mum.'

'Perhaps you should talk to someone about . . . about all that stuff you were saying before.'

'Who?'

'What about Bruno?' Bruno seemed to have an answer for everything.

'He wouldn't understand,' Daniel said in a muffled voice. 'No-one understands.'

Annie twisted her hands together worriedly. 'I wish I did, son.'

'So do I, Mum.'

A few days later, Annie switched on the television to discover foreign troops had landed at Port Stanley, in the Falkland Islands. In no time, Great Britain was at war with Argentina.

Dot blamed it all on the British diplomats who'd let the Argentinians think we were no longer interested in maintaining control of the islands. Now, Mrs Thatcher was bent on war and it didn't matter how many lives were lost to save face. Dot was particularly concerned. Sergeant Joe Gallagher, thirty-four, still had two years to go in the army – and the Paras had been mobilised.

'I mean,' Dot argued, 'lads don't join the army expecting war.'

But Uncle Bert disagreed. 'They're fascists, them Argies. We can't let them get away with invading one of our possessions.'

A task force set sail, the Argentinians were routed. The British flag again flew over the Falkland Islands, though much blood was spilt in the campaign, including that of Joe Gallagher, husband of Alison and father of two, who lost his life at Wireless Ridge on the 28th May, 1982.

Dot's youngest lad was dead, but against all the predictions, she herself was still around a year later when the Conservatives were swept back to power with a majority of 144 seats. Unemployment had passed three million, but Labour was in disarray. The party had split and many MPs had switched to the new Social Democrats. The Labour leader, Michael Foot, was a sweet old man, but, Annie thought sadly, it was no longer a world in which a sweet old man became Prime Minister.

It was the afternoon after the election, a lovely sunny Friday. Annie was sewing and watching television at the same time. Experts were analysing the result as final figures came in for the far-flung seats in Scotland. Dot had telephoned earlier. 'It looks like my poor Bert's stuck with me for another five years,' she groaned. 'I'll see that woman out, I swear it.'

There was laughter from the garage. Daniel was playing snooker with a couple of old schoolmates, out of work like him, and totally uninterested in the election. They'd disenfranchised themselves.

'We're powerless,' Daniel said. No matter who got in, nothing would change. 'Politicians and multi-nationals have got the world sewn up. There's nothing people like you and me can do about it.'

'What's to become of him – of them?' Annie wondered aloud. She cheered herself up by remembering Sara was due home shortly for the long summer holiday. In October, she would return to university for her final year.

Annie abandoned her sewing and went upstairs to her daughter's room. It still had the same wallpaper as when she was a baby, which had faded badly over the years. She felt overcome with the urge to redecorate – it would be a lovely surprise for Sara.

She went into the garage to check if there was wallpaper paste and a decent brush. There was. 'I'm popping round to South Road for wallpaper,' she told Daniel. 'I'm going to decorate Sara's room.'

'I'll help,' he offered. He was anxious to have his sister home.

Annie chose a pattern of tangled golden flowers and ordered four yards of matching curtain material. She'd get new duvet covers at the weekend. Yellow, Sara's favourite colour.

Seeing as she was here, she supposed she might as well call in Patchwork and see how Chloe was getting on.

Her assistant was displaying a quilt to a woman customer. It was a startlingly beautiful thing; octagonal patches of black, red and green on a cream background. Annie tiptoed past, mouthing 'Hi'. She sat at the desk, waiting for Chloe to finish, and glanced around the shop.

Sadly, Ernie Ward had gone to meet his maker, God bless him. His replacement, Pearl Sims, didn't have his imagination, his way with colours, but her sweaters sold well. Annie had found two elderly sisters at a craft fair who made pretty silver jewellery. They were pleased to leave a selection with her. Pendants and earrings were pinned to a black velvet board inside the door. She must find an artist and have pictures for sale. The blank wall above the clothes still niggled her.

She wondered why Chloe was so jumpy. She kept glancing nervously in her direction, and had twice dropped the quilt. Annie turned away in case she was embarrassing the girl. It was then she noticed the thick spiral artist's pad on the desk. The pad was open, and her latest outfit, the blue and lilac twopiece she'd made the other day, was half drawn on the page. She flicked through the book. All her designs were there, going back for months. They were drawn well, in the elongated, unnatural style of fashion magazines, the colours filled in with crayon.

The customer decided not to buy the quilt after all. 'I'll think about it,' she said, which meant she'd never be seen again.

The door closed. 'What's this?' Annie asked, pointing to the pad.

Chloe no longer looked nervous. She laughed, 'Oh, I draw them for my mother. She'd love to come to the shop, but she's stuck at home, an invalid. I got fed up trying to describe your lovely clothes, so decided to draw them for her. I show her the book every night.'

'I didn't know your mam was an invalid.' She and Chloe never chatted the way she'd done with Barbara.

'She's got multiple sclerosis.'

'Oh, luv, I didn't realise.' Before leaving, Annie took one of the prettiest pendants off the wall. 'Give this to your mam with my love.'

Chloe's eyes shone with gratitude. 'Why, thank you, Mrs Menin.'

Walking home, Annie wasn't sure what she'd thought when she saw the drawing pad. It was unlikely some big London fashion house had bribed Chloe for her designs. 'I must have a suspicious mind,' she decided.

Six rolls of wallpaper was a fair weight. She was glad when the house came into view. After a cup of tea, she'd start stripping the old stuff.

Daniel's friends seemed to have gone. He was standing on the path, waiting for her, which wasn't a bit like him, and it was even less like him to come and meet her. 'Sara's just phoned,' he said breathlessly.

'Oh,' Annie cried delightedy. 'Is she coming home early?'

'No, Mum. She called to say she's just got married.'

3

Annie knew immediately that this was the man her daughter had married. Sara was sitting next to him for one thing, and he was in his late twenties, older than the dozen other students around the long wooden table outside the riverside pub.

Sara looked incredibly proud, as if she'd done something unique and remarkable. She wore a yellow dress that had been made a long time ago for somebody else's wedding. A gold ring glinted on the third finger of her left hand. The ring was proof, not that Annie needed proof by now, that it was true. Sara was married!

Her daughter's husband seemed to be the only one with anything to say. He was sounding forth confidently in a loud, harsh voice, and she could actually hear the occasional word, although it was noisy outside the pub and she was standing some distance away. He wore a too-big white shirt, like a cavalier, with the collar turned up, and heavy, horn-rimmed glasses. Every now and then, he would brush back the dark, untidy hair which fell onto his forehead. She could tell he thought very highly of himself. It was obvious, from his voice, his sharp confident gestures, the conceited way he tossed his head, that this man considered himself a cut above everybody else.

Annie hated him immediately.

Students were only allowed to live on campus in the first year. From then on, they found their own accommodation. During her second year, Sara had shared a small terraced cottage in Wivenhoe with three other girls. Although nominally a town, Wivenhoe was more like a large village. Within walking distance of the university, it stood on a river, the one visible from the tower-block room where Sara had first lived, and had a picturesque quay packed with sailing craft.

Annie had taken a walk to see the sights when she brought Sara down to help her settle in last October. On that occasion, the journey had taken roughly five and a half hours each way. Today, she'd done the same journey in just over four hours.

After numerous attempts to get through to the house where Sara lived, she'd given up. The pay phone at the other end must be out of order, somebody must have tried to use a foreign coin and it was blocked. It had happened before.

Annie tried to contact her daughter via the university, but after being transferred from department to department, apparently no-one had the faintest idea where Sara was.

'Is it an emergency?' one woman demanded.

'Well, yes,' Annie stammered.

'By an emergency, I mean has someone died?'

As she had no intention of explaining to the crisp, disembodied voice that her daughter had got married without telling her mother, Annie made up her mind to go to Colchester herself.

'Did she sound drunk?' she asked Daniel.

'No, she just sounded excited.' He looked sulky. Perhaps he, like Annie, felt deeply, horribly, hurt.

She kept her foot on the accelerator the whole way, dodging in and out of traffic, overtaking, things she wouldn't have dreamt of doing normally. The Anglia wasn't a high performance car; the engine was taxed as it had never been before. It rocked crazily at seventy.

The contents of Sara's letters flashed through her mind. 'We went to the debating society, Derek is a brilliant speaker.' 'Sam and I went to London to see The Boomtown Rats.' 'Nigel drove us to Norwich.' 'Joanna's in love for the umpteenth time.' Joanna had stayed in Heather Close last summer. Annie tried to think of other boys' names; Gareth, Jonathan, Paul – no, Paul had given up last term and gone home. Sam came from Australia, or was it Derek? Nigel was a postgraduate student. There'd never been any suggestion that one of the names was special.

It was half past nine when she stopped in the narrow street where Sara lived. The car groaned with relief when she turned the engine off.

Annie hammered on the door with her fist. When there was no reply, she hammered with both fists. Upstairs, a window opened and a girl's voice said crossly, 'Who's that? Have you forgotten your key again? There's some of us got revision to do.'

'I'm sorry to disturb you.' Annie stepped back. The window was open a few inches and she couldn't see whoever was there. 'Is that Joanna?'

'No, it's Sam. Joanna's out.'

The window moved to close. Annie said quickly, 'It's Sara I wanted.'

'Oh!' The voice changed, became kind. 'You're Mrs Menin, aren't you? Sara's down on the quay in the Rose and Crown.'

'Is she – I mean . . . ?' Perhaps, after all, it was a joke, or Daniel had got the wrong end of the stick. 'Is she married?' Annie blurted out.

'Yes.' The word was uttered in a clipped, disapproving way.

'This probably seems a stupid question, but who to?'

'Sara's completely flipped her lid and married Nigel James. He's a creep, Mrs Menin, a total creep, but then you'll soon find that out for yourself.' With that, the window shut and the girl disappeared.

Annie left the car where it was and walked the short distance to the quay. From memory, it was impossible to park there.

It was a beautiful evening. Dusk had fallen and the sky glowed pink and red. There were lots of people about. Several doors were wide open, the occupants sitting on the step, the way they had in Bootle when she was a child. She passed a house where a party was going on; laughter, music, the hum of conversation came through the open window.

'Of course, it's Friday. Friday always seemed special when me and Sylvia were young.' It was the start of the weekend, and who knew what sort of adventures they might have over the next two days!

She arrived at the quayside. Crowds were gathered outside the Rose and Crown, standing, or sitting at the wooden tables outside, only a few feet from the water. The boats moved gently in the lapping tide, and there was a faint jangling sound from the masts.

Annie shoved her way through the throng, searching for her daughter. She was at the door of the pub itself, when she saw her sitting at an outside table next to Nigel James. She stood stock still, in everybody's way, just staring, whilst the hurt ate away at her body like a cancer.

'I had such plans for you, Sara! I was going to make your wedding dress meself. We talked about it, remember? Organdie, you wanted. I said I didn't think you could still get organdie, but Mr Patel would have something just as nice. We'd have the reception in the Grand – where else? Uncle Bert would give you away because he's the nearest thing you've got to a dad. You said you weren't getting married for ages yet, and Daniel would be old enough to do the honours by then.'

A man stood on her foot and apologised profusely. 'It's all right,' Annie said. She began to edge closer. As soon as she felt calmer, more controlled, she'd let Sara know she was there. She didn't feel angry, just this deep, gnawing hurt.

A girl's voice said, 'Excuse me,' and Annie stood aside to let her past. Then the girl gasped. 'Mrs Menin!' It was Joanna, small, cheerful, friendly. She grabbed

Annie's arm. 'Don't bawl Sara out, will you? It was all Nigel's idea. She's completely under his thumb.'

'Do you mind saying I'm here? I'd like a word in private.'

'Okay.' Joanna, obviously relishing her role, crept up behind Sara and whispered in her ear.

'Oh, God!' Annie murmured when her daughter's face lit up and her eyes searched happily for her mother in the crowds. It was almost dark by now. 'She doesn't think she's done anything wrong.'

Sara hurried towards her. 'Mum! You shouldn't have come all this way, we're coming to Liverpool on Monday. I tried to phone again, but the number was engaged. Oh, Mum!' She flung her arms around Annie's neck. 'You don't mind, do you? It seemed so romantic to get married on the spur of the moment. Anyroad, we didn't have that much time.'

'Surely you could have waited, luv, and got married from home?' Annie's voice was stiff. Was she being unreasonable? Sara was almost twenty. But didn't all mothers want to be there when their children got married? 'What do you mean, you didn't have that much time?'

'Nigel's finished his Doctorate, Mum, and he's already got a job. He's due back in Australia a week on Monday.'

Annie felt faint. Her daughter wasn't merely married, but was going to live on the other side of the world.

Nigel must have noticed his wife was missing. He arrived suddenly and put his arm protectively around her shoulders. This was no ordinary T-shirted, jean clad student. As well as the oversized shirt, he wore baggy, pleated trousers and lace-up shoes. His eyes were shrewd and intelligent behind the heavy glasses, and he had a large bony nose and wide mobile lips. Annie resented the way he faced her, as if she were the enemy.

Sara said, 'Darling, this is my mother,' just as Nigel muttered, 'We don't want any fuss.'

'No-one's making a fuss,' Annie said mildly. She didn't like his words, or his warning tone. She wished Lauri were there to punch his smug, arrogant face. He wasn't as tall as she thought he'd be, an inch or so shorter than Sara. 'Perhaps I could take him on meself,' she thought hysterically. 'I'd love to shove him in the water.' With luck, he wouldn't be able to swim.

She stayed another hour and refused the offer of Sara's room to sleep in – Sara, slightly embarrassed, explained she had moved in with Nigel. All Annie wanted was to get back to Heather Close. She made the return journey through dark, empty villages and along the deserted motorway, in even less time than it had taken to come.

Sara and Nigel arrived by car at tea-time on Monday. Chloe was looking after the shop until further notice, so Annie could spend every available minute with her daughter who was flying to Australia with her new husband on Friday. Over the weekend, the Gallaghers, the Delgados and the neighbours had been given the news.

'Isn't it marvellous!' Annie told them excitedly. 'Nigel James, his name is. He's twenty-nine, and has just got his Doctorate in Physics. Everyone says he's brilliant.' Even Joanna had conceded Dr Nigel James was exceptionally clever. 'I'm so pleased,' Annie trilled. 'There's so many opportunities in Australia – Nigel's already got a job in a top-class laboratory in Sydney. There's a lovely flat for them to move into.'

Only to Sylvia did she express her real thoughts. 'He's a prick, Syl,' she said flatly. 'I hated him on sight, but Sara's totally besotted. She doesn't realise how much she's hurt me, though he does, I can see it in his eyes. He persuaded her to get married straight away because he knows I might have talked her out of it.'

'Oh, Annie,' Sylvia breathed. 'I hope you're exaggerating.'

'I'm not,' Annie said savagely. 'See for yourself next week.'

Nigel was mainly boorish to everyone who came to congratulate Sara and wish the young couple luck. He clearly couldn't be bothered being polite to people he considered inferior, which, as far as Annie could see, comprised the entire human race. After the first day, Daniel swore he'd never speak to him again. He hurt Cecy's feelings and was rude to Valerie when she asked a quite reasonable question about his country.

'Of course we make our own cars,' he answered cuttingly. 'I'm from Australia, not the Third World.'

'I thought you imported most factory made goods,' Valerie stammered.

'That was a long time ago.'

The Gallagher lads came in a bunch and weren't inclined to let Nigel put them in their place. When he made a sarcastic remark, they mocked him gently, whereupon he sulked and said no more until they'd gone.

Sylvia thought he was pathetic. 'Have you noticed he wears built-up shoes? He doesn't want people to think he's small.'

Annie nodded. 'I've noticed.'

'Doesn't Sara care he gets on everybody's nerves?' Sylvia asked. The young couple had gone into town for last-minute shopping.

'Sara thinks the sun shines out of his arse,' Annie said bitterly. 'The way she runs after him! "Fetch me this, Sara. Fetch me that."'

'Why not have a quiet word with her, Annie?'

'I've already tried.' It was impossible to get Sara on her own. Nigel never left her side. Only that morning Annie, unable to sleep, had been up at six, and taken her tea onto the patio. Sara appeared shortly afterwards, rubbing her eyes. Annie indicated a white plastic chair. 'Sit down, luv. I'll fetch another cuppa.'

She'd gone into the kitchen. At last, the chance to talk! Though what would she say? 'I'll try and make her realise what a giant step she's taking, going to a strange country with a chap she hardly knows.'

But Nigel was already in her chair when she returned. She could have sworn he looked at her triumphantly, as if Sara were a prize he'd managed to snatch from under her mother's nose.

To Annie's amazement, Auntie Dot quite liked him. The first thing she did when Uncle Bert trundled her into the house, was grab him by the collar and pull him down until their noses touched. 'Let's take a look at you, young feller,' she said in her piercing voice. 'I hope you're going to take good care of our Sara.'

'You can count on it,' Nigel said meekly. Perhaps even he realised he couldn't be rude to a sick old woman in a wheelchair.

Dot proceeded to question him closely about his job. 'You're not going to cut rats and mice up in that there laboratory, are you?'

Nigel actually laughed. 'No, it's a physics lab, no animals.'

Annie wondered guiltily if she should have tried harder to get on with her son-in-law, but remembered how he'd faced her when they met, as if she was an enemy. He didn't kiss her, shake her hand, apologise for stealing her daughter. 'We don't want any fuss,' was all he said.

'He seems a nice lad, Annie,' Dot whispered as she was leaving.

Nigel was equally impressed. 'What a feisty old lady!' He squeezed Sara's hand. 'Only one more day . . .'

Sara looked at him adoringly. 'I can't wait,' she said.

Four large, strapped suitcases stood in the hall when Annie went to bed on Thursday. They looked ominous, as if they contained terrible things like bloody, dismembered limbs, not Sara and Nigel's belongings.

She woke up next morning with a jolt, knowing something awful was about to happen. After several seconds she realised what it was – Sara was going to Australia! They were leaving at ten to drive to Heathrow. The plane took off at seven that evening. Someone from the university had bought Nigel's car and would collect it from the airport later.

'I'm not sure how I'll get through the day. It's worse than Lauri's funeral.' The house would seem dead quiet, for one thing. There'd been endless visitors all week who'd come to say goodbye to Sara.

Suddenly, there was a bump, a crash and a cry, followed by the sound of loud weeping. Annie leapt out of bed and onto the landing. The sounds came from Sara's room. She knocked on the door and went in.

Sara, in a brief, frilly nightdress, was lying face down on the bed, sobbing as if her heart would break. Nigel, clad only in white shorts, was kneeling on the floor beside her.

'Sara,' he was saying helplessly. 'Sara.'

'What's the matter?' Annie demanded.

At the sound of her voice, Sara raised her head. 'Mummy, oh, Mummy, I don't want to go to Australia. I want to stay with you.'

'Jaysus!' Annie muttered. 'Would you mind leaving us a minute,' she said to Nigel.

'But . . .' he protested.

Grasping his arm, Annie virtually flung him out. Daniel, in shorts and T-shirt, came out of his room. 'What's wrong?'

'It's your sister. She doesn't want to go.' Annie slammed the door and turned to her daughter. There was something she had to know first. 'Sara,' she said firmly. 'Did Nigel pressurise you into marrying him?' If he had, then as far as she was concerned, Sara could stay. She stared at the heaving back and prayed, willed the answer to be, 'Yes.'

It was a while before Sara replied. Eventually, she took in a long, shuddering breath and said, 'No.'

'I see,' Annie sighed.

Sara turned over. Her eyes were bloodshot and red-rimmed, her face blotchy. 'He proposed, but it was my idea to do it straight away. He wanted to wait till Liverpool. He was worried you'd be upset and make a fuss, but I said you wouldn't mind.'

'I've spawned an idiot,' Annie thought. It was worse than the first day at university. Then, Sara had only been a car ride away, but was Annie supposed to persuade her to go to the other side of the world?

'Do you love Nigel, sweetheart?' she asked awkwardly.

'I'm not sure,' Sara sniffed. She sat up and hugged her knees. 'I loved him until yesterday, but when I woke up I knew I didn't want to go.' She looked at her mother wretchedly, 'Oh, Mum! What shall I do?'

'I don't know, luv.' Annie shook her head. 'Y'know,' she said reluctantly, 'you've got a responsibility to Nigel. You shouldn't have married him if you felt like this.' The words stuck in her throat. 'It's not right, him going back and leaving his wife behind.'

Sara bent down and picked something up from the floor; Nigel's glasses. A sidepiece had come off. 'I broke them. They fell off when I pushed him. I'll fix them for him. You know, Mum, he's ever so sweet when you get to know him. Oh, Nigel!' She began to cry again.

Annie sat on the bed, took the shaking body in her arms and began to rock her daughter back and forth. 'Sara, only you can make the decision. I've no intention of saying you should go or stay.' She stroked the pale golden hair that still felt as soft as a baby's. 'Why not have a nice bath and I'll make some tea? Perhaps it'll help make up your mind.'

Sara nodded tiredly. 'Okay, Mum.'

Annie opened the door and found Daniel pacing the landing like a father expecting his first child. Nigel was sitting at the top of the stairs. He stood up when she appeared. Without his oversize clothes, built-up shoes and glasses, he looked extraordinarily small and very young. His features were much softer than she'd realised.

'How is she?' he asked hesitantly.

'She's about to have a bath. I'd let her alone if I were you. Daniel, lend Nigel your dressing gown.' He must feel uncomfortable half-dressed with Daniel towering over him. 'I'll make a cup of tea.'

Daniel took his tea into the lounge and switched the television on. Left with her son-in-law, Annie searched desperately for something to say. He'd lost all trace of his brash, confident manner, and huddled nervously within the towelling dressing gown. He was the first to break the uncomfortable silence.

'I'm sorry I was rude when we first met,' he said thinly. 'I thought you'd start a row, not that I would have blamed you.'

Annie made a face. She admired him for not putting the blame on Sara. 'I wanted to kill you. I contemplated pushing you in the water.'

He managed a weak smile. 'I'm a good swimmer.' He rubbed his eyes, as if they felt odd without his glasses. 'I love Sara, Mrs Menin. If she comes, I'll take good care of her, I promise.'

'You better had,' Annie said fiercely. Her intuition told her Sara would be leaving for Australia at ten o'clock. She put her hand over his slight one. 'If you don't, I'll be on the first plane to sort you out.'

Sara entered the room, already dressed in jeans and T-shirt. Her eyes caught Nigel's, and for the first time, Annie felt totally excluded from her daughter's life.

'I'm coming,' Sara said quietly.

Several people from the close came out to wave the couple off. Most had known Sara all her life. She hugged and kissed them all. Gary Cunningham seemed especially sad to see her go. They'd been babies together, gone to playgroup, then school. Valerie had always hoped they'd fall in love. But it was not to be. Gary was getting married in November to a girl from Knotty Ash, and Sara was off to Australia with Nigel James.

'Bye, Daniel.' Sara threw her arms around her brother.

'Tara, sis, take care.' Daniel's face was hard, as if he were doing his best not to cry.

Finally, Sara turned to Annie. 'Mum!'

'Sara!' Oh, what did you say at times like this! Look after yourself, take care, have a nice journey. Not, 'See you soon,' because she wouldn't be seeing Sara again in a long while.

'I've left our Daniel's eighteenth birthday present under my bed. I wish I could have been here, but never mind . . .'

'No, never mind,' said Annie. 'Tara, luv, look after yourself, have a nice journey.'

Then they were in the car, and Nigel had started up the engine, and the car was slowly moving down

Heather Close. It paused at the end and everyone waved frantically, then the car turned the corner and was gone.

There was no sign of Daniel when Annie went back into the house. She called upstairs; no answer. Having just lost one child, she badly needed the other. She found him in the garden, moodily kicking an old football.

'That's that then,' she said with an attempt at cheeriness. It wouldn't do to let him see she felt as miserable as sin.

Daniel kicked the football savagely into the willow tree and the leaves swished wildly. 'Why did you let her go?'

Annie was taken aback by the accusing look on his face. 'It wasn't up to me, luv. It was Sara who decided to go.'

'No, it wasn't,' Daniel said in a grating voice. 'You talked her into it. I heard you. All that guff about "responsibility". If you'd played your cards right, she would have stayed with us. Instead, she's gone to the other side of the world with that . . . that utter wanker!'

'Nigel's not so bad. I think we misjudged him.'

'He's a wanker!'

Annie went back into the house. She'd expected comfort from her son – not words or actions, merely an unspoken awareness of how they both felt – but he seemed to think Sara's leaving was *her* fault.

'Don't you think I would have given anything on earth to keep Sara?' she asked when Daniel followed her in.

'You had the opportunity and you muffed it,' he said coldly. 'Most mothers would have leapt at the chance, but not you! You let our Sara go because you don't give a damn about anything.'

'Daniel!'

He threw himself into an armchair. Annie stared, horrified, at his dark brooding face. For a moment, he looked exactly like her mam, sullen and unforgiving. 'I'll not forget when Dad died,' he sneered. 'You didn't cry, not once. You told us he'd gone to heaven. For years, I thought he'd just walked out on us.'

'I'm sorry, perhaps that was wrong,' Annie said carefully. She felt confused and had difficulty putting the words together. 'I wanted to make it easier for you, that's all.' She was about to tell him that she'd cried for Lauri, secretly, in bed, that she still cried for him occasionally, but that she didn't want her children to know their mother was unhappy. Her own parents had caused too much unhappiness when she was a child. But Daniel didn't give her time to speak.

'When Sara left for university, you didn't give a toss,' he went on bitterly. 'Now it's Australia, and all you can say is, "That's that then!" in this stupid, cheerful voice, as if she'll be back tonight.'

Annie said slowly, 'I think it's you that's being stupid, luv. I'm tearing apart inside for Sara. I didn't want to make you feel worse by letting you see me cry.'

'For fuck's sake, Mum. I'm eighteen soon. How old do I have to be to see me mother cry? I've never seen you lose your cool, let alone cry.'

The phone went. It was Sylvia, wanting to know if the young couple had left and how did Annie feel? 'I'm not sure,' said Annie. She glanced at Daniel. He got out of the chair and left the room. 'Can I ring you back?' she asked her friend.

Minutes later, the roll and clip of snooker balls could be heard in the garage. Annie went into the kitchen and began to peel potatoes, though she'd never felt less like food. It was as if a hive of bees were buzzing angrily in her head, and her thoughts veered wildly from Sara to Daniel, Daniel to Sara. 'What have I done wrong?' she asked herself.

About mid-day, her son appeared in the kitchen

doorway. 'That time the old man was mugged, Frank Wheeler's dad gave him a good leathering, yet Frank had no more to do with it than I did.'

'In that case, Mr Wheeler was unfair.' Annie said shortly.

Daniel gave a sardonic laugh. 'At least it showed he cared.'

'Are parents supposed to beat their children to show they care? Your dad would never have leathered you, and you're half a head taller than me, Daniel, so I couldn't if I wanted to.'

'And Frank's dad wouldn't let him leave school, either.'

Annie didn't answer, and after a few seconds he returned to his snooker. She fried a piece of cod and shouted that his dinner was ready.

'I'm not hungry,' he shouted back.

'Well, it's here whenever you feel like it,' she said tiredly. She made a cup of tea, took three aspirins and went to bed.

Surprisingly, she fell asleep straight away. It was five o'clock when she woke. There was activity in Daniel's room and she wondered if he'd had the meal. 'What I'd like,' she whispered, 'is for the door to open and Lauri to come in with a cup of tea and tell me everything's going to be all right.'

The door opened and Daniel came in. She'd never known her husband at eighteen, but this is surely what he would have looked like; the same easy walk, the same brown hair curling onto his neck, broad shoulders, but he had Mam's face. He would never have his father's twinkling eyes. She wondered why he had Sara's old haversack thrown over his shoulder.

'I'm off, Mum.'

Annie sat up so suddenly it hurt her head. 'What do you mean, son?'

'I'm off to find meself – or lose meself, I'm not sure.'

She scrambled out of bed and nearly fell. 'Where are you going?'

'I don't know. I might drop in on Sara.'

'*Daniel!*' She was conscious of the raw fear in her voice.

'Oh, you won't let my going bother you, Mum. You won't cry. You'll just say, "That's it, then", and get on with your life.'

He closed the door. Annie opened it and ran after him down the stairs. 'Daniel, please stay, and we'll talk.' She'd tell him about Mam and Dad and about how dangerous it was to lose your cool because you said things you regretted for the rest of your life.

'There's nothing to talk about,' Daniel said and slammed the front door.

Annie collapsed on the stairs. She didn't watch him go, because each step would have driven a nail into her heart. She felt tears stream down her cheeks, warm, salty when they touched her lips, and she lifted her arms towards the door. 'I'm crying now, son, I'm crying now.'

After a few minutes, or it might have been an hour, perhaps several hours, Annie got stiffly to her feet. She took the telephone off the hook, locked the doors, drew the curtains, and wondered what she was to do with the rest of her life now that both her children had gone.

4

It was a nightmare, a black nightmare. She wandered round the house, made tea, took aspirin, and then more aspirin, slept fitfully. The doorbell rang several times, but she ignored it. There was no-one she wanted to see except Sara and Daniel. She heard a baby cry one night and found herself in Daniel's room; it could only be him, because Sara never cried. Instead of a baby, she found an untidy, empty bed, and a neat row of Matchbox cars on the window sill. The nightmare enveloped her again and despair flooded the furthest depths of her spirit.

On Sunday afternoon, she heard laughter from next door's garden. She peered through the bedroom curtains; Valerie was in a deckchair and the children were lolling on the grass. Gary and his girlfriend whispered together. Kevin appeared with a tray of drinks. He put the tray down, threw himself at his wife's feet and began to read the paper.

'What a perfect scene!' she thought. Yet the Cunninghams had never seemed a contented family. Valerie and Kevin had been unfaithful to each other, and Valerie had lashed cruelly at her kids when they were little. It was Annie who'd looked after them when their mother went to work.

'Why are they so happy and I'm not?'

She was unable to find an answer. She stayed with her arms resting on the sill, remembering the day Lauri had first brought her to the house. It was the only time he'd ever talked about his childhood. She mostly forgot he wasn't from Liverpool. He'd pointed out the River Mersey from this very window. To her dismay, the river could no longer be seen. She'd never noticed before, but a new building blocked the view. Annie shuddered, drew the curtains together, and turned to face the dark, silent room. After a while, when she could stand the noise from next door no longer, she went downstairs and played all her favourite records at top blast. She sat on the floor with her eyes closed, whilst the Beatles sang, 'Penny Lane', 'Eleanor Rigby', 'Can't Buy Me Love', 'Yesterday' . . . When it came to 'The Long and Winding Road', the song she liked best of all, she sang along in a cracked, tuneless voice. Without too much effort, she transported herself back to the flat in Upper Parliament Street, the Cavern, the Locarno, the places where she and Sylvia had had such wonderful times. 'And I was mostly happy with Lauri. There was only a little patch when things went wrong.' Even after Lauri died, the market had been hard work but fun. Patchwork, her very own shop, would always be a source of pride.

But Annie knew that everything real, everything of worth, had already taken place. Nothing of significance would happen again. From now on, it would all be second best.

Sylvia came on Monday afternoon. Annie knew who it was when the doorbell rang and rang and didn't stop.

'I know you're there, Annie,' Sylvia shouted through the letterbox. 'If you don't come soon, I'll call the police.' Then, seconds later, 'Dorothy's about to wee-wee on your front garden.'

Annie opened the door. 'Jaysus, you look a sight!' Sylvia said briskly. She came in, rushed upstairs with Dorothy, returned, yanked the curtains back, and put the kettle on. Then she shoved Annie onto the settee and said, 'Now, what's up with you?'

'Nothing,' said Annie.

'In that case, why didn't you ring me back? Why has your phone been off the hook for days? And why do you look twice as old as you did last week?' She turned exasperatedly on her twenty-month-old daughter. 'Lord, Dorothy, do you *have* to crawl under your Auntie Annie's rug? I had to bring her,' she explained. 'I think I told you we're between au pairs.'

'I think you did.'

'Annie, friend,' Sylvia said gently. 'What's wrong?'

Annie sighed. She'd cried so much over the last few

days that her body felt completely dry. In a dull, emotionless voice, she told Sylvia what had happened. Sara had gone, Daniel had gone, she was alone.

'Daniel might be home in a few days.'

'No.' Annie shook her head. 'I know my son. He'd consider it a sign of weakness if he came back too soon. He might not come back at all.'

'As for Sara,' Sylvia went on, 'she's been trying to ring since yesterday to say she's arrived safely in Sydney. She ended up calling me at six o'clock this morning, worried stiff because she couldn't get through to her mum. I've got her number in my bag.'

Annie leapt to her feet. 'I'll call this very minute.'

'It's three o'clock in the morning there. Why not wait until tonight?' Sylvia grasped Annie's shoulders and sat her down again. 'I'll make that tea.' On the way, she put the receiver back in its place.

Dorothy came crawling towards her Auntie Annie with the rug draped over her head. 'I'm a little bear,' she roared.

'You're a little madam!'

Dorothy Gallagher the second was a wearing child, hyperactive and intelligent beyond her years. Her bright blue eyes missed nothing and she was every bit as bossy and inquisitive as her paternal grandmother.

Annie said, 'You'll get all dirty from that mat.'

'Why you got a dirty mat?' Dorothy asked curiously.

'It's not exactly dirty, luv, more dusty.'

'Auntie Annie clean it so Dorothy can be a bear.'

'I'm not in the mood, luv. You'll just have to be a dirty bear.'

Sylvia came in with the tea and orange juice for her daughter. 'I know it's no comfort right now, Annie,' she said, 'but you should feel proud having two such independent-minded children. It shows how well you brought them up.'

'That's not what Daniel said,' Annie moaned. 'He thinks I'm a hopeless mother.'

'He'll see sense one day,' Sylvia said comfortingly. 'Now look, you must snap out of this. You've got a living to make and a shop to run. You're bound to feel down in the dumps, but open the shop and get down to making clothes again. It'll take your mind off things.'

There didn't seem much point, the money had been mainly to make life better for her children. 'The shop's still open,' Annie said. 'Though I suppose I'd better go in tomorrow and see how things are.'

'Cecy said Patchwork was closed when she passed on Saturday,' Sylvia exclaimed. 'She came to see you, but no-one answered the door.'

'But Chloe was looking after it,' Annie said, puzzled.

The phone rang and she went to answer it, just in case, you never know, it might be Sara. Instead, it was Susan Hull, who didn't waste time on formalities. 'I've been trying to get through to you for days,' she said angrily. 'What's happening with Patchwork? I had that girl, what's-her-name, on the phone on Friday, asking if she could take my quilts and cushions to new premises in St John's Precinct. Are you closing down, Annie? It would have been polite to let me know.'

'I'm not closing down,' Annie said, astonished. 'Was it Chloe?'

'The one with the narrow eyes,' Susan explained impatiently. 'The new shop's called Pasticcio, which sounds like an ice-cream to me. She said it's sited in a good position, right in the middle of town, the others were going with her and I'd do much better than with you.'

'Bitch!'

'That's what I thought. I told her she was a traitor, but when I tried to call you, the operator said your phone was off the hook.'

Annie bit her lip. 'Things have been a bit upside down here – my daughter went to Australia on Friday.'

'Really! I've got one girl who's a secretary in Japan, and the other's hitch-hiking across India with her boyfriend at the moment.'

They rang off on a friendly note, agreeing that children were a worry, and when they left home, you worried even more. Annie assured her Patchwork would open normally tomorrow.

She returned to the lounge, where Dorothy appeared to be taking a serious interest in last week's *Radio Times*. 'What does pasticcio mean?'

Sylvia wrinkled her nose. 'Isn't it a nut?'

'It can't be.' According to the dictionary, pasticcio was a medley of bits and pieces, rather like patchwork. Pistachio was a nut. She explained what had happened with the shop. 'The other week, I found Chloe had a notebook full of drawings of my clothes. She's opened her own shop with a similar name and *my designs*!'

'You should sue her, Annie,' Sylvia was outraged.

'I can't be bothered.' Annie was angry, very angry. At any other time, she would have at least come face to face with Chloe and told her what she thought, but in a way she was almost glad it had happened. For fifteen minutes, she'd thought about something other than the events of the last few days. The sense of muggy despair had lifted. Tomorrow, she'd assess the damage, get other people to supply knitwear and jewellery, build up the shop so it was better than before. She'd find an artist and sell paintings. And she'd need a new assistant, one she could trust this time.

Dawn Gallagher! Dawn had felt very low since her divorce from Tommy. She'd been on the look-out for a job for ages. 'But who wants a woman going on fifty, when able-bodied men are being thrown on the scrapheap,' she'd said despairingly last time they met. She'd ring Dawn later.

But, deep down, Annie wasn't much interested in Patchwork any more. 'Y'know,' she said slowly, 'I'd like to do something dead selfish.'

'Such as?'

'I'm not sure. Something absorbing, not sewing, when me mind's all over the place. I'd like to use me brain instead of me hands.'

Sylvia looked dubious. 'You'd never stop thinking about the kids.'

'I know,' Annie said soberly. She would never get over the suddenness of Sara leaving, or the brutality of how Daniel had gone. She would still cry for her children, but couldn't mope for ever. She was forty-two. For the very first time, she had no-one to consider but herself.

Sara was unhappy in Australia. The flat was small and poky and she was lonely. Nigel had no family, no friends. Unemployment was high and she couldn't get a job. She pleaded with her mother to come for Christmas.

Annie's first inclination was to rush out and buy a ticket, Dawn could look after the shop, but common-sense prevailed. It wouldn't do Sara's marriage any good if she knew she only had to pick up the phone and her mam would come running.

'Sorry, luv, I can't,' she said, hoping she didn't sound too harsh. 'Anyroad, your Auntie Marie's coming on Christmas Eve.'

Marie had spent eight years in America, but the young director who'd wanted her in his films was no longer all that young. Now Hollywood had wooed him away from the low-budget, critically-acclaimed movies that had become his trademark, and he was about to embark on a major project with a twenty-million-dollar budget. Casting control was no longer his. Marie Harrison had been shown the door.

To Annie's relief, her sister didn't seem to mind. 'It was good while it lasted, I did some TV work over there. The thing is, sis, I was getting nowhere.'

Annie felt she'd heard those words before. Marie smiled, as if she guessed her thoughts. 'I've no illusions any more. The penny dropped when I reached forty. I'm not sure what it is; no great acting ability, not exactly great good looks, no charisma, or a bit of all three, but I know I'll never see my name in lights. I'm not giving up. You can make a fairly good living in supporting roles. I earned enough in the States to buy my own place in London. My agent's got a small part lined up in a new TV comedy series. We start shooting in the New Year. I play the dizzy American next-door neighbour – I've got the accent off pat.'

'Chris will be pleased to see you. His plays came back from the BBC years ago. He was too disheartened to write more.'

'That's stupid!' Marie said contemptuously. 'If you want to succeed, you've got to keep on and on and on. Even then, you might not make it.'

There was something different about her. Her hair was just the same, thick and dark, curling up slightly at the ends and, as usual, she was perfectly made up. The difference was something to do with her remarkably unlined girlish face. After a while, she burst out laughing. 'You'll never guess what it is, sis!'

'Sorry, luv, I didn't realise I was staring.'

'I had a nose job a few years ago. See!' Marie turned sideways. 'It now tips up when it used to tip down.'

'It never did tip down,' Annie said indignantly. 'It was a perfectly good nose before.' She felt ill at ease with her sister. They'd drifted too far apart. She was reluctant to say how shattered she felt when the children left.

'I'm surprised Daniel isn't home for Christmas,' Marie remarked.

'He's travelling round with a group of youngsters the same age as himself. They wanted to stay together.'

'Will he telephone? I'd like to speak to my one and only nephew.'

'He called to wish me Merry Christmas yesterday,' Annie lied. She had no idea where Daniel was, or who he was with. There'd been one card which had arrived months ago, the day after his eighteenth birthday, with a smudged postmark which might have been Cardiff or Carlisle. 'Thinking of you, Mum. Daniel,' was all the card said. Since then, there'd been no more word.

'You haven't put the decorations up.'

'I thought the tree was enough, me being on me own.' Perhaps she should have brought at least a few decorations down from the loft, because it didn't seem remotely like Christmas Eve.

Marie glanced at her sharply. 'Are you all right, sis? It must have been a blow, both of them leaving about the same time.'

'It was a bit, but the shop keeps me busy.' She'd managed to get used to being alone – no, not used to it, to accept the fact that this would be her lot from now on – but the run-up to Christmas had been painful. To think of all the food she used to buy! She'd always got far too much, and some years there'd still be special biscuits or figs or nuts left in January. Now there was no need for mountains of groceries, little gifts for the tree, crackers, cans of fizzy drinks or Christmassy serviettes. She'd stopped going to the supermarket, anyroad, because passing the cornflakes, the fish fingers and

434

beefburgers she wouldn't have dreamt of buying for herself only made her want to weep. She felt uncomfortable at the checkout with her miserable basket of groceries, when there were women with trolleys packed to the gills. Nowadays, she bought everything from a little corner shop that was open all hours.

Marie yawned. 'What will this dinner be like at Sylvia and Mike's tomorrow?'

'It's bound to be more cheerful than last year. Joe had not long died and Mike left an empty chair at the table as a sign of respect. No-one could take their eyes off it all day.' This year, for the first time, Sara and Daniel wouldn't be there, but only their mother would regard that as a reason to be sad.

5

The miners sang defiantly as they marched back to work. As with Dunkirk, defeat was being celebrated in a carnival atmosphere, despite the cold rain of a dark March morning. A pit band led the triumphant procession and the streets were lined with onlookers, clapping and cheering. Annie felt a lump in her throat. These men were the salt of the earth, beaten by a government backed by multi-millionaires.

The newsreader appeared on the screen and introduced another topic. Annie switched the television off and turned to Auntie Dot.

Her aunt was in tears. 'Such stout lads, only fighting for their jobs, but you know what Thatcher called them, her own people? – "the enemy within".'

It was the end of one of the bitterest disputes in trade union history, as miner fought miner. For a year, TV screens had shown the ugly violence on the picket lines and vicious battles with the police.

Annie patted Dot's hand with its swollen knuckles and bulging wristbone. 'Don't upset yourself, luv.'

'I can't help it, Annie, when I see what that woman's doing to the country.' Dot made a move to dry her eyes. Annie dried them for her.

'Would you like me to put your make-up on?'

Dot sniffed. 'Would you mind, luv? Bert does the lippy all crooked. Go easy on the rouge, I don't want to look like a tart.'

It was heartbreaking to see such a once-vital, energetic woman so completely helpless. Dot rarely left the house these days. The parlour had once again been turned into a bedroom, and a double bed stood in the place where Annie's mam and dad had slept during the war. Dot lay propped against a heap of pillows, her stick-like arms and twisted hands resting on the eiderdown. A row of bottles were lined up on the bedside table; pills for this, pills for that, pills to maintain almost every bodily function, as well as a variety of other medical aids which kept her aunt alive. Despite the fact it was a sick room, the atmosphere was usually one of gaiety and fun, and Dot's hoarse, infectious laugh could be heard halfway down the street.

Annie dabbed powder and blusher on the wax-like cheeks and drew the lipstick outline carefully. 'Close your eyes,' she murmured. She smeared a suggestion of blue shadow on the almost transparent lids, then gently combed the silver hair, inserted pearl stud earrings and helped her aunt into a frilly pink nylon bedjacket. Then the final adornment, a pair of horrible zebra-striped spectacles.

'There, you're done! What scent are you in the mood for today?' Everyone seemed to think an appropriate present for a bedridden woman was perfume. Dot had an assortment worth several hundred pounds.

'Poison!' Dot cackled.

436

Annie sprayed her aunt and herself, then held up a mirror so Dot could see the finished result. 'You look dead beautiful!'

Dot turned her head from side to side. 'I don't look so bad, do I?' she said conceitedly. 'I've far fewer wrinkles than Cecy, and she's years younger than me. The Harrisons and the Gallaghers were at the front of the queue when the Lord handed out good looks.' She peered over the mirror at her niece. 'It's about time you got yourself another feller, Annie. You're a fine looking woman, in the prime of life.'

Annie made a face. 'Chance'd be a fine thing.'

'How long is it since Lauri died?'

'Thirteen years.'

'And you've never met anyone over all that time?'

'No-one special. I was always too wrapped up in the children.'

'Sara's married and Daniel's on his travels, so you can get yourself a feller.' Her eyes narrowed. 'Have you heard from Daniel lately?'

'Yes, Auntie. He rings every week.' Annie began to pack the make-up away in its little zipped bag.

'You know, luv,' Dot said softly, 'I may be old, but I've got a dead good memory. You said that in exactly the same voice as you told me your mam played Snakes and Ladders and made cakes.'

Annie stood the mirror on the mantelpiece. 'You didn't cross-examine me then, Auntie Dot, and I'd sooner you didn't now.' Only Sylvia, and she'd had to tell Sara, knew the truth about her son. She couldn't stand the thought of people feeling sorry for her.

'If that's the way you want it, luv.' With an effort, she lifted her arms a few inches from the bed. 'Come and give your ould auntie a hug.'

'Oh, Dot!' Annie buried her face in the bony shoulder.

The parlour door opened and Uncle Bert came in with three cups of tea. For a man two years off eighty, he was the picture of rude health. 'It smells like a knocking shop in here.' He looked at his wife in amazement. 'Bloody hell! I left an ould woman in me bed, and I come back to find Rita Hayworth!'

'I'll have to go soon.' Annie took the tea. 'I've a lecture at eleven. I thought I'd drop in on the way. I knew you'd be upset when you saw the news.'

Bert nodded at the television. 'I couldn't bear to watch. The Government might have won the battle, but they didn't win many hearts. Most people were on the miners' side.'

Dot had perked up and her blue eyes shone as brightly as a young girl's. She said, 'Perhaps you'll click at university, Annie.'

Annie grinned. 'As I said, chance'd be a fine thing. Anyroad, all I'm interested in is getting me degree.'

'Your dad was a clever lad. He passed the scholarship. Me mam always thought he'd end up at university. 'Stead, he met Rose . . .' Dot shrugged. 'Your dad'd be proud of both his girls. It's a pity Marie's programme ended – what was it called? She was a scream in that part.'

'*His and Hers*,' supplied Uncle Bert.

'They're making another series,' Annie said. 'Next time, Marie's part will be bigger.'

She said goodbye. Every time she left, she was convinced she would never see her aunt again. Dot had lost her appetite completely. She hardly ate. Only willpower, and a determination to see the back of Mrs Thatcher, kept the scraggy, undernourished body alive.

After seeing the miners, it was equally depressing to drive into town along the Dock Road and witness another major industry laid to waste. When she was young, the Docky had been jammed end to end with traffic; lorries, horses and carts, handcarts. The funnels of great ships had once loomed over the high walls of the docks, whilst a noisy bustling mass of humanity thronged the busy pavements – you could hear a dozen languages being spoken in the space of a few minutes, as ships from all over the world came to the great port of Liverpool. The Germans had done their best to destroy the docks during the war, but since then 'progress' had done what Hitler had failed to do, and all that now remained was mile after mile of dereliction and neglect. Annie was glad to reach the Pier Head and see signs of life.

Sylvia had expressed herself astounded when one of Mike's employees gave in his notice. 'You should see him, Annie. He's thirty-five and is covered in tattoos, yet he's going to university to study Philosophy.'

'There's nothing wrong with that.'

'I thought that's what you'd say. In which case, why don't *you* go to university. You're always on about wanting to use your brain.'

'Me!' Annie burst out laughing. 'I'm totally ignorant, Syl. I left school at fifteen and I haven't got a single qualification.'

'Ignoramuses can take an Access Course at night school. It brings your brain up to condition. That's what Nick, the would-be philosopher did.' Sylvia seemed to have everything worked out. 'You wouldn't have to go away, Liverpool University is one of the best in the country.'

'I dunno.' The idea appealed enormously, but she couldn't for the life of her imagine someone like her being accepted.

'It wouldn't hurt to try,' Sylvia said encouragingly. 'We're both awfully ignorant. We've known each other thirty years, yet we've never once talked about anything deep or intellectual. It used to be boys and clothes and the Beatles, now it's kids and food and general gossip. We're a very shallow pair.'

'You used to write poetry,' Annie reminded her.

'Yes, but it was crap poetry, nothing about it was profound.'

'I'm not even sure what "profound" means!'

'See! It's about time one of us had a decent education.'

'Why can't it be you?' Annie raised her eyebrows.

'Don't be silly, Annie, I'm pregnant, aren't I?'

'So you are!'

Annie parked the Anglia on Brownlow Hill and walked to the building where the lecture was to be held. Sylvia's fourth daughter had been born last July. Lucia had chestnut brown hair and Bruno's clever mind.

'That's my lot!' Sylvia announced when Annie went to see her. 'I've gone through all the hair colours, I don't want any more kids.'

'It seems odd, you having a baby when I'm about to become a grandmother,' Annie said. The older she got, the more peculiar life seemed.

The lecture room was already crowded. Annie waved to everyone she knew as she slid behind a desk. She put on her glasses and took a pen and notebook from her bag.

Sara's son, Harry, had arrived just before Christmas. Again, she pleaded with her mother to come and stay. She was still lonely. Things weren't going well between her and Nigel, even though they'd moved into a detached bungalow with a swimming pool in a nice part of Sydney.

'I've just started university, Sara, luv,' Annie said reasonably. 'It's hardly worth me while coming all that way for only a few weeks. Anyroad, I can't afford it.'

Dawn Gallagher worked full-time at Patchwork, and two women machinists made the clothes to a few standard patterns. Annie did nothing, except somewhat guiltily take the profit, which wasn't much once the bills and wages were paid. She still had a mortgage and needed to support herself over the next three years. Nevertheless, she started to put money aside for Australia.

Annie knew she was being selfish, but not for obvious reasons. She'd got used to being without the children, the wound no longer festered, but still hurt. She didn't want to open up the wound by going to Australia, then returning, alone, to Heather Close, and the agonising worry over Daniel. There'd been another card, this time from London, just after his nineteenth birthday. The message was the same as the first; 'Thinking of you, Mum.'

Being accepted at university was easier than she'd thought. Mature students, particularly women, were especially welcome. After discussing it with Sylvia, she decided to take American literature. On the Access Course, she learnt how to discipline her mind and assemble her thoughts, how to write a paper using other writers' work to support her thesis.

The lecturer had arrived, Euan Campbell. The students fell silent and directed their gaze towards his sad, beautiful face. Euan's dark hair was parted in the middle like a saint in a stained glass window, his velvety liquid eyes had the same blank stare. He'd come to Liverpool from Glasgow University at the same time as herself. The younger students made fun of his morose manner, but it was whispered that he'd left Glasgow after his wife and two young children had been killed in a car crash. Annie wasn't the only woman who felt the urge to take him in her arms and comfort him.

He began to speak in his gentle voice with its soft Scots burr. Gradually, enthusiasm for his subject – Ernest Hemingway – took over and his tone became firmer. 'On close scrutiny, Hemingway's work doesn't stand up to his reputation. He's overrated, a good writer, but not a great one. Much of his work was written in Paris, an advantage to any artist. Paris is the most beautiful and inspiring city in the world.'

'Have you ever been to Paris, Annie?'

The lecture was over and the class were shuffling out of the room for lunch. Annie turned to the questioner. Binnie Appleby was a divorcee with three grown-up children. It seemed sensible to attach themselves to each other when surrounded by students less than half their age.

'I've never been abroad,' Annie replied. 'We couldn't afford it when the children were young, and I was too busy when they got older.'

'That's always the way, isn't it?' Binnie giggled. She linked Annie's arm. 'Fancy a sarnie and a beer for lunch?'

'Perhaps you and me could go to Paris sometime,' Binnie suggested as they strolled along Hope Street towards the Philharmonic pub.

'That would be nice,' Annie said politely. She wasn't sure if she cared too much for Binnie. They'd been thrown together, and she felt about her as she did about Valerie Cunningham, someone she'd lived next door to for more than half her life, yet never truly liked. Binnie was pretty, flirtatious and man-mad. Annie had got used to going to places and being deserted the minute Binnie saw a man she only faintly knew, something she and Sylvia had never done to each other. Today, she was quite likely to end up eating her meal alone, not that she minded. She'd get on with the Hemingway novel they'd been set.

The ornate Victorian pub was crowded. They bought a sandwich and half a lager each and searched for a seat. Binnie eyed up the male customers with an expert eye. She was, she had confessed to Annie, desperate to get married again. It seemed any man would do.

They sat at the end of a long table of dark-suited businessmen who were far too preoccupied discussing office politics to notice two middle-aged women. Annie produced a photograph of her grandson which had arrived from Australia that morning. 'He's ever so like me son,' she said proudly. 'I shall send Sara a photo of Daniel at three months so she can compare them.'

Binnie shuddered. 'I don't know how you can stand being a grandmother, Annie. I shall keep it to meself if it happens to me. Oh, look!' She waved to a man who'd just entered. 'There's Richard Cross. I used to work with him. Richard!' she hollered. She picked up her bag. 'I'll be back in a minute.'

'Like hell you will!' Annie muttered. She took *The Sun Also Rises* from her bag and began to read.

'Is anybody sitting here?'

Annie looked up and saw Euan Campbell standing politely in front of her, a plate in one hand and a glass in the other. 'No,' she said. He obviously didn't recognise her. She returned to the novel, only vaguely conscious of the young man settling beside her.

Some minutes later, he spoke. 'Were you at the Hemingway lecture this morning?' He nodded at the book.

When Annie confirmed she was, he continued, 'I'm afraid I haven't familiarised myself with all the faces yet, let alone the names.'

'I'm Annie Menin.' Close up, his skin was olive, smooth and clear, his eyes deep, dark wells of sadness. He had full, rather feminine lips. She searched for something to say that wouldn't rake up unpleasant memories. 'How are you settling in Liverpool?'

'Not so bad. It's a lively place, lots to do.' He finished off his sandwich. 'What do you think of the book?'

'It's lovely,' Annie said enthusiastically. She bit her lip. Perhaps 'lovely' wasn't the right word to use to a university lecturer. She should have said 'intellectually stimulating'. 'I never had much time to read in the past, what with the children. After me husband died and I became the breadwinner, I had less time than ever. I never dreamt that books by reputable authors could be so, so . . .' she searched for the word, 'so *enjoyable*! I thought they'd be beyond me,' she finished a trifle lamely.

Euan Campbell gave a sweet, gentle smile. 'That's good. Wait till we come to F. Scott Fitzgerald, you'll like him even more.'

Annie sighed with pleasure. 'I can't wait.' She actually found it exciting to read novels *properly*, not just skim the surface as she'd done the occasional books she'd read before, but search for nuances and hidden meanings, admire metaphors and clever turns of phrase, try and diagnose the author's own personality from his or her words. She found herself quite good at it and her marks so far had been high.

The businessmen had gone. Binnie Appleby returned, and winked when she saw Annie's companion. 'Tell us all about Paris,' she demanded.

Euan winced. 'That's impossible. You need to see it for yourself.'

'Annie and I thought we might go.'

'I hope you enjoy yourselves,' he said stiffly. He finished the remainder of his drink and left abruptly. Annie cursed Binnie inwardly as she'd been enjoying their talk.

Binnie looked hurt. 'I must have BO! You made a conquest there.'

'Don't be stupid,' Annie said irritably. 'Women are the furthest thing from his mind at the moment. Anyroad, I'll be forty-four this year, and he's what – twenty-nine, thirty?'

'Toy-boys are all the rage. I'd go for a twenty-nine-year-old, particularly one that looked like Euan.'

'Well, I wouldn't.' There was only one boy Annie wanted. Daniel.

The usual card arrived in July a few days after Daniel's birthday. He was twenty. 'Thinking of you, Mum. Daniel.' The card bore a Swedish stamp, Annie tore it in two in a rage. 'What the hell's he up to in Sweden! What did I do to deserve this? Doesn't he realise he's crucifying me, staying away all this time?'

A few days later, Sara phoned and implored her mother to spend the summer holiday in Australia.

Annie was implacable. 'I can't, luv. I'm going to the Isle of Wight with Sylvia and Cecy and the girls, then I'll be staying with your Auntie Marie in London for a while.'

'You don't *want* to see me, that's it,' Sara said sulkily. 'You've turned your back on your own daughter.'

'Sweetheart, as if I would! I'll come, I promise, as soon as I've finished me degree – I'll stay three whole months, six, if you like.'

'But that's two years off!' Sara wailed. There was a pause. 'I'm pregnant again. The baby's due in November.'

'Congratulations, luv,' Annie said warmly. 'That's marvellous news.'

Sara rang off and Annie went into the lounge clutching her head in both hands. Children! There were times when she wished she'd never had any – and to think she'd actually wanted four!

The hotel overlooked the cliffs in Ventnor. Sylvia, Cecy and the two youngest girls shared one room, whilst Yasmin and Ingrid slept in a three-bedded room with Annie. The weather was perfect. They woke every morning to find sunlight flooding through the windows and a cloudless blue sky. Most of the time was spent in a little sandy cove, where the children built castles and made channels to the water – Dorothy stared, entranced, as the tide came rushing into the little ditch she'd dug. 'Dorothy made a river,' she announced grandly.

Cecy rolled up her skirt and led Lucia, who'd just started walking, into the sea, where the tiny girl kicked and screamed in delight.

'I loved it when mine were that age,' Annie said wistfully. 'In the summer, I used to take them to the sands in Waterloo.'

'Yes, but they don't stay that age, do they, Annie?' Sylvia replied sagely. 'Time rolls on. See how those boys are eyeing Yasmin? She's only twelve and her breasts are almost as big as mine.'

Annie hadn't noticed the way Yasmin's young body curved enticingly in the skimpy swimsuit. Her black hair was in bunches, her mysterious, exotic face screwed up in concentration as she covered a sandcastle with shells, entirely unaware that half a dozen lads, fifteen-, sixteen-year-olds, were watching her every movement with considerable interest. Ingrid knelt on the other side of the castle, equally engrossed. Her face already held the promise of an icy beauty.

It was a lazy, relaxing holiday. Nights, they drank wine and watched television in the hotel lounge. On the final evening, Annie and Sylvia stumbled their way in the dark down to the little cove, where they sat on a rock beside the inky water and watched the reflection of the full moon dancing further out on the waves.

'Remember when we used to sit on that little scrap of sand in Seaforth and talk about the future?' Sylvia said. 'It was there you told me Marie was pregnant, she was only thirteen, a year older than Yasmin.' She picked up a handful of sand. 'Actually, Annie, I've been meaning to say this for ages. I was horrible to Marie. I pretended to be shocked, but really I was jealous. Oh, not because she was pregnant,' she said quickly in response to Annie's gasp of surprise. 'I was jealous of her being your sister. I wanted you all to myself. I couldn't bear the thought of Marie having so much of your attention.'

Annie picked up a handful of sand herself. It was moist, and she moulded it into a ball and threw it into the water where it landed with a loud plop.

'Are you shocked?' said Sylvia.

'No.'

'Then why don't you say something?'

'I've just said, "No", I'm not shocked.' Annie picked up more sand.

'Mind you, it was years before the penny dropped and I realised my true feelings. By then, it was too late and Marie hated me.'

'I don't think she hates you,' Annie said mildly. 'I think it's more a case of thinking you dislike her.'

'I'll try and make up with her next time we meet.' Sylvia slipped off her shoes and made for the water. 'I think I'll have a paddle.'

Annie watched her friend silhouetted against the moonlit sky. 'I've a feeling we should have a row about what you just told me,' she called.

'We'll have one if you like.' Sylvia kicked water in Annie's direction. Annie threw a ball of sand and missed.

'Why is it I never get angry with you?' she asked.

'Because you understand me, probably better than I understand myself.' Sylvia giggled. 'You've always known I'm not very nice.'

'You're too honest to be nice,' Annie said. 'You didn't have to come out with all that stuff about being jealous of Marie.'

'And you're too nice to be honest. Oh, this water's lovely and cool. Why don't you join me?'

'I'm not in the mood. Shall I be honest for once?'

Sylvia stopped paddling. 'I'm all ears.'

'Just then,' Annie said calmly, 'when you turned your head against the sky, I saw quite clearly that you're getting a double chin.'

'*No!* Is it really bad?' Sylvia frantically began to slap her chin.

Annie shook her head sorrowfully. 'It does sag quite a bit. I don't know about these things, but perhaps you can have plastic surgery. Whilst you're at it, you could get those bags done under your eyes.'

'Bags under my eyes! Oh, Annie, you're joking!' She was so relieved, she sat down in the water. 'You horrible thing!'

Later, they walked back arm in arm, Sylvia soaked to the waist.

'It's been a lovely week,' Annie said. 'I've really enjoyed it.'

'Me too, but I can't wait to see Mike.' Sylvia uttered a blissful sigh. 'I'm so lucky, Annie. I don't deserve such happiness.' Her face grew dark. 'It's too good to be true. I have nightmares that something will happen to Mike or one of the girls, and it will all be spoiled.'

Annie didn't say anything, because she knew how cruel fate could be. Nor did she say that she hadn't been joking about the double chin.

*

448

Marie's flat was on the top floor of a four-storey house in Primrose Hill. The lush greenery of Regent's Park was visible from the wrought-iron balcony that Annie was too scared to sit on. 'It looks too precarious,' she claimed.

The walls were white and the furniture new; plain bleached wood, and grey and white upholstery. It looked cold and unlived in. Annie's house-warming present, a red and blue vase, might have looked too bright in such colourless surroundings, if it hadn't been for Marie herself.

Her sister dazzled like a too-bright light bulb. Her eyes were brilliant, her face glowed. At last, her dreams were close to being realised: she was almost, nearly, a star.

A second series of *His and Hers* had already been recorded and would be on television that autumn. Audience research had shown that Marie Harrison had scored a hit as Lorelei, the wise-cracking American neighbour. Her part had been expanded – to the detriment of the two main characters, whose roles were inevitably reduced.

'They hate me,' Marie chuckled on Annie's first day there.

'Don't you care?' Annie enquired. 'I couldn't stand it meself.'

'I don't give a shit,' Marie said icily. 'Avril Paige was horrible at the start, really condescending. I'm glad she lost pages of script to me. There's talk of an entirely new programme, *Lorelei*, based on my character. Avril will spit tacks when she finds out.'

'I hope it comes off,' Annie murmured. 'Dot will be thrilled.'

Marie squeezed her palms together as if she were praying. 'Oh, so do I, sis, so do I. Guess what I did last week?' she boasted. 'I opened a supermarket in

Birmingham. The mayor was there, and all the local dignitaries. I got paid two hundred and fifty quid.'

'Good for you,' said Annie. It was difficult to believe this was the same cheeky, frightened little girl she'd shared a room with in Orlando Street. They had nothing left in common except their roots. She began to dread the week ahead and longed for Saturday when she could go home.

'Can I have a bath?' she asked. She had to get away. Two babies had been sacrificed, for what? So another actress could spit tacks and her sister open a supermarket in Birmingham. It scarcely seemed worth it.

The strained week ended and Annie returned to Heather Close. To her astonishment, there was a For Sale board in the Cunninghams' front garden. Valerie came to see her that evening.

'I suppose you noticed the board?'

'Where are you off to?'

'Kevin's been offered early retirement,' Valerie said in a rush. 'We thought we'd buy something smaller now there's only Zachary at home.' Both Kelly and Tracy had got married the previous year. Gary and his wife already had a baby girl. 'Kevin fancies over the water, his brother lives in Greasby. He intends to take up golf.' Valerie paused, eyes gleaming. 'Guess how much the estate agent said we should ask for the house? Fifty-five thousand!'

'Jaysus!' gasped Annie.

'Incredible, isn't it, to be worth so much money?'

'It doesn't make much difference if you're buying another place. It just means estate agents and solicitors get a bigger cut.'

Valerie burst into peals of laughter. 'Oh, I'll miss living next door to you, Annie. I truly will.'

'And I'll miss you.' To Annie's surprise, she really meant it. You got used to people. You actually grew fond of them, even if you didn't like them all that much. The house would feel peculiar without the Cunninghams next door. 'I hope you'll be very happy over the water.'

Dawn Gallagher telephoned on Sunday. 'Can you come into the shop tomorrow, Annie? This chap from Yorkshire, Ben Wainwright, turned up the other day wanting us to sell his paintings. I told him it was up to you. He said he'd come back at nine o'clock on Monday.'

'What are they like?' Annie asked.

'Weird! I didn't care for them much, but then I'm totally ignorant about art. They could be works of genius for all I know.'

'I'm as knowledgable about paintings as you are,' Annie said drily.

'The thing is, luv,' Dawn said in a husky low-pitched voice, 'he's drop-dead gorgeous. If I hadn't got another feller, I'd have bought the lot meself, despite them being weird.' Dawn was getting married again in a few weeks' time to a six-foot-six-inch Detective Sergeant in the police force who she'd met at a Divorced and Separated club. 'Another thing, Annie. Our Marilyn went into town on Saturday. She said Chloe Banks' shop in St John's Precinct has closed. According to one of the other shopkeepers, she left owing thousands of pounds.'

Annie grimaced. 'I'm trying me best to feel sympathetic.'

'Don't try too hard, luv. She deserved all she got.'

On Monday morning, Annie was about to get dressed up to the nines to impress the drop-dead gorgeous artist, but changed her mind. He might be married and she mightn't think him gorgeous. Anyroad, she was too busy with her studies to become entangled with a man, but then she'd always been too busy with something or other since Lauri died.

She put on jeans, a baggy blue T-shirt and a pair of espadrilles. It was years since she'd covered her freckles with pancake. Nowadays, she merely used powder and a touch of lipstick, though she still rubbed her lashes with spit. In front of the mirror, she inserted gold hoop earrings and ran her fingers through her short red curls. There was no doubt about it, she still looked youthful. She turned sideways to check if there was any sign of a double chin – it had come as a shock to notice Sylvia's sagging jawline. Her own chin looked just the same, but then she should tip it down, not up. She made a face. Perhaps it would be best not to find out, because there was nothing she could do about it.

At half past eight, she walked round to the shop. Patchwork no longer gave her a thrill, it was just another dress shop, more attractive and unusual than most. She cast an expert eye over the clothes. They were well made to her own designs, but several styles were duplicated which had never happened when she'd run the place herself. Susan Hull's quilts and cushion covers were as lovely as ever, and the knitwear was almost as good as Ernie Ward's. She paused in front of the glass jewellery, wondering if Sara would like an earring and necklace set for Christmas.

Annie contemplated the paintings on the wall; water-colours, done by an elderly lady, a friend of Cecy's. Each was a precise reproduction of a single flower; a staid iris, a curved rose, a frilly carnation . . . Framed in narrow pine, they sold well, usually two or three a week.

The door opened and a man about her own age came in. 'I know it says "Closed", but I saw someone inside,' he said in a strong Yorkshire accent. 'Are you the owner? I'm Ben Wainwright. You're expecting me.'

'Annie Menin.' She shook hands. Dawn must need glasses. There was nothing remotely handsome about Ben Wainwright. He was tall, lanky, with a very ordinary face. His skin was dark and rough, as if it had been chipped out of stone. 'His eyes are nice,' she conceded, dark blue, almost navy, with stubby lashes. His hair was black and curly like a gypsy's. He wore shabby jeans and a knitted sweater covered in snags.

'How did you hear about Patchwork?' she asked, easing her fingers apart. His grip had been exceptionally strong.

'Through the local Labour Party. I presented them with a painting at last week's meeting in appreciation of their support during the miners' strike. You weren't there!' he said accusingly.

'I was away.' She hadn't been to a meeting in months.

'Someone said you exhibited paintings. I'm always on the look-out for an outlet for my work.' He glanced contemptuously at the neat watercolours. 'When I saw these, I nearly didn't come back.'

'No-one made you.'

He grinned. It was nice the way the skin crinkled around his navy blue eyes. 'I hoped your taste mightn't be as execrable as it seemed.'

Annie hooted sarcastically. 'Ta very much! Where are these wonderful paintings, anyroad?'

'Outside in the car.'

'Well, you'd better bring them in, hadn't you?'

He grinned again. 'Right away, ma'am.'

She watched through the window as he walked towards an old Cortina estate. His walk was confident, as if he were very sure of his place in the world. He came back carrying three unframed canvases.

'What do you think?' He held up a painting for her to see.

The picture was almost wholly black, with just the suggestion of four miners in the bowels of the earth, bare to the waist, bent double as they hacked at walls of coal. The lamps on their heads glowed dully. The paint was laid on thick and oily, with broad strokes of the brush. Close up, she could see straining muscles, beads of perspiration, tired eyes. It was so real, she was conscious of the acrid smell of coal.

Ben Wainwright put the painting down and picked up another, a pit head at sundown, the black wheel stark against a dull red sky tinged with purple and green.

The final painting showed half a dozen miners leaving the pit at the end of their shift, eyes shining with unnatural brightness in their coal-smudged faces. There was something joyous and free about it, as if the men couldn't wait to get home to their families.

'They're beautiful, but I can't see my customers buying them.'

He looked at her, aghast. 'They're not supposed to be beautiful.'

'What do you expect me to say?' Annie snapped. 'That they're ugly?'

'I'd prefer ugly to beautiful.'

'In that case, I can't see my customers buying ugly paintings.'

'I suppose they prefer this shit!' He gestured at the walls.

'Quite frankly, yes. We sell several a week.'

'Huh! Sorry to have bothered you.' He picked up his paintings.

'Just a minute,' Annie called. 'I wouldn't mind the first one meself, as long as it's not too dear.'

He stopped and looked at her, an expression of

amusement on his rugged face. 'You're just being tactful.'

'Tactful! You don't look the sort of chap who'd appreciate tact. No, I like it, but it depends on the price.'

'It's seventy-five pounds.' He regarded her challengingly. 'That's cheap for an original.'

'I know.' The watercolours were twenty-five. 'Will a cheque do?' She sat down at the desk and took her chequebook and glasses from her bag. 'Do you make your living as a painter?'

He lounged against the wall and shook his head. She was suddenly very aware of his powerful masculinity, and her fingers trembled slightly as she wrote his name. 'No,' he said. 'I give a lot of stuff away, to miners' clubs and unions. I can't abide artists who paint only for themselves. I've something to say about the working man's lot and I want to spread the word. I'm always searching for places to exhibit.'

'In that case, you must be a miner.'

'I was, but I watched my dad and two uncles die of fibrosis of the lungs and decided I didn't want my sons to see me go the same way. I gave up years ago. Now, I paint when I can and earn my living as a plumber.'

He was married! Annie felt slightly disappointed. She handed him the cheque. 'It won't bounce.'

'Ta.' To her astonishment, he tore the cheque in two and handed it back. 'Regard it as a gift, Mrs Menin.'

'But . . .' She realised it was no use arguing. 'Call me Annie.'

'I'd best be going, Annie.'

She followed him to the door. When he bent down for the paintings, she noticed how his black hair curled tightly on his weatherbeaten neck. His fingers, long and narrow, gripped the paintings, and he stood and faced

455

her. Annie opened the door. He paused on the threshold.

'I don't suppose you're free for dinner tonight?'

'I'm sorry. I've promised to visit someone.' Dot was longing to hear all about Marie. 'I'm free tomorrow.'

'I'm going home in the morning, back to Yorkshire.'

'Oh, well, never mind.' A voice inside Annie's head urged, 'Take him to see Auntie Dot, then have dinner. She'd like him, and he'd like her. Men like Ben Wainwright don't grow on trees.' The voice seemed to have forgotten he was married.

She'd opened her mouth to speak, when Dawn Gallagher arrived. She glanced curiously from one to the other.

'Bye, then,' said Ben Wainwright.

'Bye,' said Annie, closing the door.

Dawn looked at her eagerly. 'I've been stood across the road for ages, waiting for him to go. What d'you think, Annie?'

'You were right. He's drop-dead gorgeous.'

'He asked you out, I could tell. Oh, I had this really strong feeling in me water that he would. I just knew you two would get on.'

'I'm not in the habit of going out with married men.' Annie said primly, thinking what a hypocrite she was. If Dawn hadn't turned up, she would have gone out with Ben Wainwright like a shot.

'You bloody idiot!' Dawn's face twisted in disgust. 'He's divorced.' She gave Annie a shove. 'Catch him and say you've changed your mind.'

But another car was already backing into the space where Ben Wainwright had been. The Cortina had gone.

6

Annie pushed Ben Wainwright to the back of her mind and confidently returned for her second year at university. The course had become more difficult. It was no longer a matter of reading books and dissecting them; she had to work out why the novels of the great Theodore Dreiser, a communist, were so obsessed with capitalist tycoons and crooks; show where anti-semitism could be found in the poetry of Ezra Pound; what was the central theme behind the liberal works of William Faulkner.

Some nights she worked till the early hours, reading and making notes. Sylvia persuaded Mike to let her have an old electric typewriter when Michael Ray Security converted to computers. She became involved in some of the university's extra-mural activities, joining the debating society, the Fabians. If an old film was shown on television that related to the course, *Sister Carrie*, *The Sound and the Fury*, *The Great Gatsby*, Chris Andrews recorded it on his remarkable new video machine, and Binnie Appleby would come over and they would watch it at Chris's.

In the autumn, Bruno Delgado turned seventy and celebrated the fact in the Grand. He was still a magnificent-looking man, with a comfortably lined face that only added to his air of distinction and a fine head of jet black hair, which, Sylvia told Annie, he regularly dyed.

'Look at him, the old devil,' Sylvia said as she regarded her father fondly across the bar. Bruno was holding forth to an entranced audience consisting mainly of young women. He wore a red shirt, open at the neck, and black leather trousers. Dozens of cards were strung across the bar. 'He'll screw that blonde barmaid rotten when this is over.'

Annie glanced enviously at the fiftyish woman with dyed yellow hair and too much eyeshadow who was drawing pints of beer.

Later, someone took a photo of Bruno with Sylvia and Mike and his four beautiful granddaughters. 'Where's Cecy?' he called.

Cecy had been invited but hadn't come. The following morning, she rang Annie to ask how things had gone.

'We had a lovely time,' Annie enthused, 'but why weren't you there?'

'I would have felt in the way,' Cecy said with a sigh.

'Don't be silly – Bruno asked for you.'

'Did he? Did he really?'

'You're still his wife.' They'd never got divorced. Having a wife suited Bruno down to the ground. It was a good excuse for not letting other women get their claws into him.

'Yes, but in name only – just a minute, Annie, there's someone at the door.' Cecy returned, seconds later. 'It's Bruno,' she said happily, 'he's brought flowers. I'll speak to you another time, dear.'

Annie rang off thinking that Bruno needed two wives; Cecy, whom he loved with all his heart, and another he could go to bed with.

Nigel James telephoned early one Friday morning in November to say Sara had given birth to a little girl. 'She's seven pounds, six ounces, and she looks just like you. We're calling her Anne-Marie.'

'Oh, that's lovely!' Annie blinked back the tears. 'Congratulations, luv. Tell Sara to ring as soon as she can.'

Next day, the Cunninghams moved to Heswall and Valerie came to say goodbye. She made Annie promise to stay in touch. 'Even if it's only letters with our

Christmas cards.' Annie duly promised and wished her good luck with the move.

Valerie pulled a face. 'We'll need it, Annie. I've had to give up my job, it's too far to travel. I'm not sure how me and Kevin will get on, under each other's feet all day.' She looked at Annie, perplexed. 'It's funny, the children used to drive me mad when they were little, but I've been thinking how much I'd love to have those days back.'

'Let's hope Kevin likes golf – or you find another job.'

'Let's hope, eh!'

They kissed for the first and only time. 'Kevin'll pop in and say goodbye once the van's loaded.'

Annie watched as the Cunninghams' furniture was carried out. She was surprised how shabby it looked in the cold light of day. The back of nearly everything was covered in cobwebs. Zachary, a tall, drooping lad, as anaemic as his father, stood miserably on the pavement.

Hours later, the van drove away and Valerie and Zachary climbed into the car. Annie opened the door when she saw Kevin approaching. She extended her hand. 'Cheerio, Kevin.'

'D'you mind if I wash my hands, Annie?' His pasty face was sweaty.

She stood aside to let him in. 'You know where the bathroom is.'

'The kitchen will do.'

He washed his hands, dried them, then, to her everlasting astonishment, grabbed her shoulders and began to kiss her passionately.

'Kevin!' she spluttered, struggling free.

'You've not changed, Annie. You're still as stunning as when you first moved in,' he said in a thick voice and tried to kiss her again.

'Kevin! Valerie might come in.'

'Sod Valerie. When can I see you again?' His eyes

were wet with emotion. 'Please, Annie. We could meet in town one afternoon.'

'Absolutely not!'

Outside, a car door slammed and Valerie called, 'Kevin!'

Kevin adjusted his glasses with shaking hands. 'I'll phone, Annie. Some time when Valerie's out.' He backed out of the door.

Annie followed through the breakfast room. '*NO!*'

'We could book a room in a hotel.'

'No way, Kevin.' She pushed him into the hall. He stumbled backwards out of the front door and into the arms of his wife.

As the Cunninghams drove away, Annie dutifully waved goodbye. The minute the car disappeared, she collapsed in fits of laughter. 'Jaysus! I never thought that sort of thing would happen to me again at my age!' She staggered towards the phone. 'I must tell Sylvia.'

Her hilarity had subsided somewhat by the time she'd dialled and the ringing tone sounded in her ear. 'Poor Valerie,' she thought soberly.

The silence from number eight was ghostly over the weekend, but when Annie came home on Monday, she saw thick net curtains on the windows. She immediately called to introduce herself; Valerie had said an elderly widow, Mrs Vincent, and her unmarried daughter had bought the house.

A distracted, fiftyish-looking woman opened the door. She had short grey hair and round glasses that gave her an owlish look. Her clothes were twenty years out of date; a tailored woollen blouse, tweed skirt and flat shoes. She wore no make-up and her skin was finely lined, but flawless. Her only jewellery was a tiny gold locket on a chain.

'Hi, I'm Annie Menin from next door. I just came to say hallo.'

The woman blinked timidly behind her glasses. 'I'm Miss Vincent, I mean, Monica.' Her voice was faint and whispery.

'Who is it, Monica?' someone called.

'It's the lady from next door.'

'Well, ask her in, you silly girl.'

'Would you like to meet Mother?'

Annie stepped over the cardbord boxes in the hall and went into the lounge, which was already in some semblance of order. An expensive oak display cabinet, as yet empty, stood against the wall, and a matching dining-room suite with six chairs was in front of the french windows.

Mrs Vincent was sitting on a peach brocade settee watching television. She looked too young to be Monica's mother. Heavily made up, she wore a purple mohair sweater and a cream skirt. Her hair was a cloud of pure white. She greeted Annie effusively. 'Would you like tea or coffee, dear? Monica!' she snapped her fingers.

'Nothing, ta,' Annie said quickly, as Monica sprang to attention.

'Now, dear,' Mrs Vincent gushed. 'If we're going to be neighbours, we need to know all about each other. I can see you're married. What does your hubby do? Have you any children?'

Annie had never imparted so much information so quickly as during the intense interrogation she was subjected to. When she finished, Mrs Vincent told the story of her own life. Her hubby had died twenty years ago. 'So I was left a widow, like you. Fortunately, he had a pension so I was well provided for.' Monica was a nurse in those days, but Mrs Vincent's heart wasn't strong. 'I was terrified when she was on nights in case I

461

had one of my attacks.' Her daughter had given up nursing and was now a Health Visitor, though there was no need for her to work. She glanced with contempt at Monica, who was twisting the gold locket nervously.

'Mother seems to think we can live on fresh air,' she said in her little-girl voice. 'Dad's pension hasn't gone up with inflation.'

'She's actually going back to work tomorrow and leaving me with this mess,' Mrs Vincent said fretfully.

Monica gave Annie an imploring look, as if seeking her support. 'I've got several families I don't like letting down. I should have this place more or less straight by tomorrow.'

'You've done wonders so far,' Annie remarked. She said goodbye and made for the door. Monica came with her.

'You don't remember me, do you?' she said breathlessly. 'I was in the class after you at Grenville Lucas. I knew I recognised you, but it wasn't until you were talking to Mother I remembered who you were.'

Annie would never have dreamt the woman was younger than herself. 'I'm afraid we didn't take any notice of the kids below us.'

'You were friendly with that lovely Italian girl, Sylvia.'

'I still am. She's married to my cousin and has four daughters.'

Monica looked wistful. 'I always wanted a family, but things never seem to work out the way you want, do they?'

'Not always,' said Annie. 'By the way, if you remember me, you'll remember the English teacher, Mr Andrews. He lives across the road.'

'I used to have a crush on him.' Monica blushed.

'I think we all did in those days.'

It was gone midnight by the time Annie finished the

462

paper on Ezra Pound. She made a cup of cocoa and took it into the lounge. Noises were coming from next door; thumps and bangs, as if boxes were being humped around, drawers and cupboards opened and closed. Mrs Vincent's voice could be heard, shrill and complaining, 'Not there, you silly girl!'

There was a shattering of glass, something must have dropped, followed by Mrs Vincent shrieking, 'You're stupid, stupid, *stupid*! I've had that vase since before the war.'

Annie turned the television on to drown the noises out. She might feel low at times, but compared to some women, she was incredibly lucky.

The second series of *His and Hers* had come to an end, and no more would be made. It hadn't been a particularly good programme; the only attraction was the fizzy, extrovert Lorelei. Viewers were informed a new series, *Lorelei*, would be screened next year.

Marie was in seventh heaven when she called her sister. 'It's all happening, sis. My agent is besieged with offers of more work, and journalists are queueing up to interview me.'

'I couldn't possibly be more pleased, Marie,' Annie said warmly.

'Could you come for Christmas? I've been asked to tons of parties.'

Annie squirmed uncomfortably. 'I'd sooner not miss dinner with Mike and Sylvia, sis. Anyroad, you won't want me at the parties. They'll be full of your friends.'

'Yes, but . . .' Marie paused.

'But what?'

'Well, they're not really friends. I've been a rolling stone for too long. I haven't gathered any moss.'

'What about Clive Hoskins?' Marie hadn't mentioned him for ages.

'Clive died years ago, when I was in America. I thought I told you. I suppose,' Marie said slowly, 'I want my own flesh and blood.'

'I know the feeling.' There'd been numerous times when Annie had needed her sister, but Marie had been too embroiled in her career. Perversely, in her moment of triumph, Marie wanted *her*! 'Perhaps I could come for a few days in the New Year,' she suggested.

'It doesn't matter,' Marie said coldly. 'I'm sure you've got more important things to do.'

Mike Gallagher refused to entertain the notion of the ritual Christmas dinner without his mam and dad there. He hired a private ambulance to transport them from Bootle to Ince Blundell. Dot persuaded the driver to switch the siren on for most of the way.

'I felt really *urgent*!' she trumpeted gaily when she was carried out on a stretcher.

'What's that?' asked Annie, as Bert emerged with a complicated contraption of tubes and a cylinder.

'Oxygen, luv. Dot loves it. It makes her talk even more.'

All five of Dot's remaining lads were grandfathers, and fifteen of her grandchildren were married, most with children. The Delgados, Annie, and forty-two Gallaghers sat down to dinner, whilst Punch and Judy, the housekeeper and the Danish au pair entertained the children.

'I don't know what we're going to do next year,' Mike chuckled. 'Even the banqueting hall isn't big enough for us Gallaghers.'

It was incredible, thought Annie, that the womb of one frail old lady was responsible for too many people to fit a banqueting hall.

To Annie's surprise, early in January an air-mail letter

arrived from Australia. She'd only spoken to Sara on New Year's Day.

Dear Mum, Sara wrote, *I felt it best to put this down on paper, rather than tell you on the phone – I know how upset you are over Daniel. The thing is, Mum, he stayed with us over Christmas . . .*

'Oh, God! Annie clapped her hand to her breast. She read on.

He had our old address, but fortunately the people there knew where we'd moved. I didn't recognise him at first. He looked strange, terribly grown up and very thin. His eyes are incredibly wise, as though he's seen and done everything – as if he understands everything. I found it hard to accept that this was my little brother, Daniel.

'Did he ask about me?' Annie breathed. 'Did he ask about his mam?'

He seems to have been everywhere in the world, even the places that are dangerous – Cambodia was one, Iran, Iraq. He and Nigel got on reasonably well. Nigel, being Nigel, knows all about the various religions and that was mostly what they talked about.

Of course, he wanted to know all about you, Mum. Annie sighed with relief. *He was chuffed when I told him about university, and said he'd always thought you were clever. I think he's sorry he walked out so suddenly. 'I had to do it,' he said. 'I had to sort out my life.'*

No, Mum (I know you'll be wondering), he didn't say anything about coming home. He'd only just arrived in Australia and was about to hitch-hike round the coast.

Don't ring straight away, Mum. Get used to the news before you get in touch. The truth is, I'm still all choked up, and I'll only cry if you do. Every time I close my eyes, I see my little brother, so different from the way I remembered, waving goodbye on the day I left.

465

*I think that's all there is to say. This is not the sort of
letter where you try to think of a nice cheerful ending.
Your loving daughter, Sara.*

At Easter, the Anglia gave up completely. The engine
had clocked up a hundred and twenty-eight thousand
miles.

'I'm afraid it's a write off, Mrs Menin,' she was told
in the garage. 'The bodywork's more filler than metal,
and last year I had to patch the patches underneath to
get it through the MOT.'

Annie was forced to dip into her special account for
Australia. She bought an ancient red mini with low
mileage and a long MOT. She was allowed ten pounds
on the Anglia, which looked lonely and forlorn when
she left it on the garage forecourt, fit only for scrap.
Over the years she'd come to regard it as a friend.

She didn't go away that summer. Sylvia, Cecy and the
children were going to Italy for six weeks – Bruno still
had relatives there. He and Mike would join the party
for the last fortnight. Annie was invited but declined.
'I've got to look after Patchwork when Dawn's on
holiday, and there's a couple of projects to do for me
degree.'

Out of a sense of duty, she telephoned Marie and
offered to come and stay. Relations with her sister had
been frosty since Christmas.

'I'm sorry, sis, but I've been invited to this private
island in the Caribbean. It's owned by a lord.'

Chris Andrews was also away and she felt slightly
neglected as July turned into August, then became
September. There wasn't even someone she could ring
for a chat, Auntie Dot tired quickly on the phone.

She decorated Sara's room with the wallpaper bought
three years before, and tidied up the garden, which was
as neglected as herself. Next door's French windows

were usually open, and she often heard Mrs Vincent laughing as she played bridge with the friends who came several times a week. The situation reminded her slightly of Orlando Street, although Mrs Vincent was nothing like Mam, because Monica would come home in her navy blue uniform at six and prepare the evening meal. At weekends, Monica did the washing and cleaned the house from top to bottom. Annie suspected there was nothing much wrong with her mother and she was just taking advantage of her soft-hearted daughter.

To cheer herself up, she applied for a passport and went to a travel agent's to get details of flights to Australia. She would be free to visit Sara in less than a year; the final term at university finished early in June. She also picked up a brochure on holidays in Paris. Euan Campbell continued to mention it as a source of inspiration, and Binnie was for ever suggesting they should go. 'If it was good for so many writers, it might help us with our exams,' she said persuasively.

The cost of a few days' bed and breakfast was surprisingly cheap. Patchwork had done well lately and her bank balance was quite healthy – after all, she'd only need spending money in Australia.

'I'll show this to Binnie next time I see her,' she resolved.

'What shall we do when we've got our degree?' Sylvia demanded.

'Get a job,' said Annie.

'What as?'

'We could go to training college and become a teacher.'

Sylvia was lying on the rug in front of the fire. She sat up and poured herself more sherry. 'We might find that rather boring.'

'One of us might, the other wouldn't.' Annie

wandered over to the window. What an awful day! February was a hateful month. She'd never liked it. The willow tree looked bedraggled. The sky was as black as night and rain was coming down in sheets – there'd been hailstones on the way home from Mass and she'd got soaked.

Sylvia had arrived at mid-day claiming she felt depressed. Mike was locked in his study with his accountant; Michael Ray Security was about to be floated on the stock exchange. The children were getting her down, so she'd left Sunday dinner to the housekeeper, the children to the au pair, collected a bottle of sherry and driven to Heather Close.

Annie wasn't all that pleased to see her. She'd had a horrible dream the night before in which an enraged Lauri stood at the foot of the bed demanding to know what she'd done with his children. The dream was still there; she was unable to get Lauri's angry face out of her mind. She was about to lose herself in a novel when Sylvia turned up.

'Couldn't we do something more exciting than teaching?'

Annie refilled her glass and returned to the settee. The collective 'we' was getting on her nerves. 'Such as?'

Sylvia rolled onto her stomach and groaned. 'I'm so stiff, I can't sit crosslegged any more.' Her body was becoming thick and heavy, particularly round the waist, but her face was as radiantly lovely as ever, despite her slightly sagging jawline. She leant her chin on her hands. 'We could write a novel.'

'Could we really?' Annie was conscious of the sarcasm in her voice. 'And how much effort will your half of the partnership put in?'

'You write, I'll read and give my opinion.'

'Oh, ta! If you're so anxious to see your name in print, why not write a book yourself?'

Sylvia burst out laughing. 'Don't be silly, Annie. I've got a husband, four children, and a big house to run.'

'You've also got a housekeeper and an au pair,' Annie snapped. The remark had touched a raw nerve. 'Anyroad, do you have to rub it in?'

'Rub what in?'

'The fact I haven't got a husband and children, and my house is rather small.'

'I didn't mean it like that, Annie.' She looked hurt.

'You're for ever emphasising how full your life is compared to mine.'

'No, I'm not. Least, I don't mean to.'

'You've always had to be on top, haven't you? You couldn't stand me being happy with Lauri. Your own marriage was shit, so you had to convince me mine was shitty, too.' Working backwards, Annie was able to put the blame for last night's dream on Sylvia. Lauri never got angry until his wife turned bolshie, and she didn't turn bolshie until Sylvia suggested it was time she did.

'But it *was* shitty, Annie,' Sylvia said reasonably. 'Lauri was a misogynist of the worst kind.'

'I didn't know what a misogynist was in those days.' Annie got up and began to walk round the room, waving her arms wildly. 'At least my husband didn't thump me like yours did.'

'What's Eric got to do with this?' Sylvia's cheeks flushed red.

'What's Lauri?'

'I've no idea. You brought him up, not me.'

They glared at each other angrily. 'Even now, you're not content with what you've got,' Annie said hotly. 'You're trying to take credit for my degree, that's if I get one. It's *me* that's done all the hard work, but apparently it's *our* degree.'

Sylvia's bones creaked as she got up. 'You must have got out of the wrong side of the bed this morning,

Annie, and where's your sense of humour? I called it "our" degree as a way of encouraging you along.'

'I didn't need encouragement, thanks. I would, though, appreciate some time. What makes you think you can land on me without notice? I've stacks of work to do for *my* degree.'

'I didn't think you required notice,' Sylvia said coldly. 'I'll leave you to work and go and see another friend.'

'You haven't got another friend.'

Sylvia unexpectedly grinned. 'I know I haven't, Annie.' She spread her hands. 'Why are we rowing?'

The grin disconcerted Annie. She kicked the back of the settee. 'You started it by saying how empty my life was compared to yours.'

'No, you took offence at a perfectly innocent remark.' Sylvia looked amused. 'Shall we have another row over who started the first?'

They both jumped when hailstones rattled against the windows. The sound brought Annie to her senses. 'I'm sorry,' she mumbled.

'So am I.' Sylvia said warmly. 'I wouldn't crow over you for worlds. I won't deny I'm deliriously happy, but I do envy you sometimes.' She shook her head at Annie's incredulous face. 'I do, honest. I envy your freedom to do exactly what you want; Paris at Easter, Australia in June. I envy you being able to watch what you want on television, or read in bed until the early hours – Mike can't bear the light on. You're not beholden to any other person, your life is completely your own.'

'If you're not careful,' Annie warned, 'I'll get upset again.'

'But it's true, Annie,' Sylvia said earnestly. 'Being independent has its attractions.'

'I wonder why I flew off the handle like that?' Annie mused later.

'Perhaps you secretly resent me. Perhaps you always have.'

Annie thought about this for a while. 'Nah!' she said eventually. 'You were right the first time. I got out of bed the wrong side. Pass the sherry, Syl. We'll finish it off, then I'll make a cup of tea.'

Sylvia went home just as it was growing dark. The sherry had given her a terrible headache.

'But you never get headaches,' Annie said in surprise.

'I had one all last week. I wonder if it's the change of life?'

Sylvia phoned next evening. 'Guess what was on TV late last night? *Three Coins in a Fountain*.' She hummed a few notes. 'I recorded it. Shall I bring the video machine over sometime and we'll watch it? We'd never get any peace here and I'd hate the girls to spoil it.'

'I'd love to.' They'd been teenagers when they last saw it. 'I've no lectures on Wednesday, I was going to work at home.'

'Wednesday it is then, say early afternoon?'

'Great. How's your headache?'

'It's just returned with a vengeance,' Sylvia groaned.

'I hope it goes soon,' Annie said sympathetically.

'So do I!'

To Annie's surprise, Mike turned up just after lunch on Wednesday. 'I've brought a video and the film. Sylvia thinks you've just got to plug it in, she doesn't realise the TV has to be tuned.' He grinned. 'Women are no good with electronics.'

'I'm amazed a busy executive can spare the time to do such a mundane thing,' Annie said in mock surprise.

'I'm on me way back from a business lunch in town. Sylvia should be here any minute.' He knelt down beside the television and began to fiddle with the knobs. 'You can keep this machine, Annie. It's just one that was lying round the office.'

'Mike, I couldn't possibly!'

'Shurrup, luv, and take it. The richer you are, the harder it is to give things away. I'm for ever offering to move me mam and dad into a nice bungalow, but they refuse to leave that house in Bootle.' He inserted the video into the machine. 'I hope she recorded it on the right station. It's quite likely to be something different altogether.'

Minutes later, Frank Sinatra began to croon the theme song and *Three Coins in a Fountain* appeared on the screen. Annie closed her eyes briefly. She was fourteen, watching the same credits and feeling that excited little thrill that always came at the beginning of a film. 'We saw it the first time we went out together,' she said.

'I know, luv, Sylvia told me. If it hadn't been for you, we'd never have met. Look, here she is now!' He went over to the window. A dark brown BMW had drawn up and Sylvia got out. Her hair was loose and she wore a white padded fur-trimmed coat over a crimson dress. Her blue eyes danced when she saw Annie and Mike watching. She waved and Mike's gasp of admiration was audible. 'Isn't she a cracker, Annie? I thought that the minute I first set eyes on her at our Tommy's reception.'

'She's beautiful, Mike.'

Halfway down the path, Sylvia paused. She looked at them, a strange, puzzled expression on her lovely face. Her eyes glazed. Her hands lifted slowly to clutch her head and her blonde hair spilled through her fingers like strips of torn silk. Later, Annie supposed the whole thing took less than a minute, but watching, it seemed to last an age. Sylvia's body seemed to crumple, as if her bones had turned to jelly, and she collapsed into a distorted heap on the path.

*

472

'Why couldn't it be me?' Cecy wailed. 'No-one expects their children to die before them. Why did God take Sylvia when he could take me?'

'I've no idea,' Annie said calmly. She couldn't get her head around the fact Sylvia had gone, although she'd actually watched her die. She kept expecting the phone to ring and her friend to be at the other end, eager for a chat or to exchange a bit of gossip.

'You'll never guess what's happened, Annie!'

'Are you sitting down, Annie? I've got some incredible news.'

People didn't usually die unless they were very old or very ill or had an accident, like Lauri. For someone to be taken without warning, as Sylvia had been, from an unsuspected brain tumour, was unfair on those left behind; monstrously, stupefyingly unfair.

It wasn't fair of Mike, either, to have them play 'The Long and Winding Road' when everyone was filing out of the little chapel at Anfield Crematorium. It was enough to make you weep even if Sylvia hadn't been the best friend in the world. It was only then it hit Annie, forcefully and painfully, that she would never see Sylvia again. At this very second, her friend's body was being reduced to ashes. Sylvia was dead.

Everyone stood awkwardly in the fog outside, not knowing what to say, reading the cards on the wreaths which were spread on the damp grass. Mike stood alone, his eyes empty, his face expressionless; Uncle Bert and the Gallagher lads stood protectively nearby.

Cecy was inconsolable. Her sobs echoed like a banshee's wail around the rose bushes and the dark green trees. Bruno, oh, Bruno, he looked so old, old and shaken. He took Cecy in his arms and tried to comfort her. Then he led her away, though she could hardly walk in her distress.

Annie didn't go back to Mike's for refreshments. Instead, she drove to Auntie Dot's.

Dot was too ill to attend the funeral. Annie thanked the neighbour who'd kept her company and sat on the edge of the bed. Her auntie's body was nothing but skin and bone, yet her eyes still gleamed in her haggard face. 'How was it, luv?' she asked hoarsely.

'Terrible, auntie.'

'Our poor Mike,' Dot lamented. 'Two wives gone and he's only fifty. Christ, I wish it could have been me instead of Sylvia.'

'That's what Cecy kept saying.'

Dot's eyes clouded with sympathy. 'Poor lamb, she took it hard?'

Annie nodded. 'Really hard.'

'And you, luv? Sylvia was more like a sister than Marie.'

'I don't know how I'll live without her,' Annie said simply. 'We had some great times, me and Sylvia.'

'You were there the night the Cavern opened.'

'We saw the Beatles before anybody else.'

Dot squeezed her knee, though the pressure was so light you could scarcely feel it. 'You'll never lose that, luv. Memories, memories, they make your life so much richer. I don't know what I'd do without them, lying here night after night with Bert asleep beside me.' Her voice became fretful. 'I can hardly sleep at all, Annie, for the pain.'

'Oh, Dot!' Annie bent down and kissed her auntie's cheek. 'Would you like a tablet now? I'll make a cup of tea.'

'No, I'll wait till Bert comes. He sorts out me medicine. I take morphine for me aches and pains.' She cackled. 'I've become a drug addict. I haven't seen me arse in years, but I bet it looks like a Spotted Dick after all the injections.'

The phone was ringing when Annie got home. She picked up the receiver gingerly, half expecting it to be Sylvia calling from another world.

'Hi!' a man's voice said cheerfully. 'Remember me? It's Ben Wainwright. You've got one of my paintings.'

'I remember.'

'It's just that I'm in Manchester, and I wondered if I drove over if you'd be free for dinner tonight?'

'Sorry,' Annie said regretfully, 'but I'm just back from a funeral. Someone very dear to me died. I'd be terrible company at the moment.'

'I wouldn't mind terrible company, not if it was you.'

'I'd sooner not, but thanks for asking.'

She rang off. Maybe she should have gone. 'Not if it was you,' he'd said, as if he remembered her in a special way. Last time she had been sorry afterwards, but tonight she preferred to stay in and grieve for Sylvia. Until today, she'd been too stunned to take it in.

Three Coins in a Fountain was still in the video. Annie watched it from beginning to end. It wasn't nearly as good as she remembered. At fourteen, it had seemed deeply dramatic and romantic, but now it was rather trite. Rossano Brazzi, though, was still mournfully handsome.

Annie was dry-eyed when she turned the television off. What had been the beginning had become the end. As long as she lived, she would never have another friend like Sylvia.

A month after the funeral, Bruno and Cecy came to announce the Grand was to be sold and they were going to live in Italy.

'Together?' Annie said hopefully.

Bruno took Cecy's hand. 'Together.'

'I couldn't be more pleased, though I'll miss you

475

terribly.' Annie smiled tremulously. 'What about the girls?' She was amazed they could bring themselves to leave their granddaughters.

Cecy's face grew troubled. 'That's what made us decide to go, Annie. Have you seen Mike since the funeral?'

'I've rung several times, but his secretary or the housekeeper always say he's unavailable. There was no sign of him each time I've been to see the girls.' They'd clung to Annie, four little lost souls. Dorothy wanted to know what she'd done with their mummy.

'We found the same,' Cecy nodded, 'till last time, when Bruno forced his way into the study. Mike's changed, Annie. His face was set like concrete. He made it obvious he doesn't want us around. Maybe we remind him too much of Sylvia. He promised to send the children over once a year – Yasmin and Ingrid are almost old enough to fly alone. They're already looking forward to staying with us during the summer holidays. We thought it best to leave now and prepare a second home.'

'You must come, too, Annie,' Bruno said emotionally. 'I feel as if we're losing our other daughter.'

Annie watched them walk away, two people who had played such a major part in her life. Bruno wasn't as stooped as he'd been at the funeral. He was the first man she'd fallen in love with, though he'd never known.

She gripped the windowsill with both hands. Pretty soon, there'd be no-one left to leave.

7

Paris stretched before her, a glittering carpet of twinkling lights. How many miles could she see? Ten? Twenty? Places looked so lovely in the dark. The neon lights on the tall buildings blazed on and off as if they were sending out mysterious messages, and the sky was navy, shot with deep, ruddy orange.

She'd climbed literally hundreds of steps to reach the basilica of Sacré-Coeur – throughout the day, she kept glimpsing the white stone monument shimmering above the city. After getting her breath back, she went inside, admired the statues and the stained glass windows, then lit three candles. She knelt in a pew and prayed for everyone she knew.

Outside again, she sat at the top of the stone steps and marvelled at the glorious view. So many windows! Thousands and thousands of them. It made you feel dead funny, trying to imagine what people were doing inside those thousands and thousands of rooms. It also made you feel very small and rather unimportant, as if you were merely the tiniest speck on God's universe.

A black man approached; his face ebony smooth, he wore an embroidered gown and a round beaded hat and offered her a lizard skin clutchbag to buy. She shook her head. 'No, ta.' She wouldn't dream of carrying a poor dead lizard under her arm.

On the terrace below, someone was juggling with fluorescent sticks. A guitarist strummed idly and sang 'Volare' in a soft, husky voice. The steps were crowded; old couples hand in hand, young ones arms entwined. In front of her, a man and woman sat, each with a small child on their knee. Two teenage boys on her right kept leaving to explore and returning to their mam, faces shining with excitement. On her other side, about a dozen youngsters lounged, drinking Coke and gabbling away in a tongue she couldn't understand. Their haversacks bore tiny flags of many countries, and she wondered if they'd been to every one.

She seemed to be the only person alone. Now she knew what it meant to be isolated in a crowd. She had never felt so lonely in her life. The loneliness welled up

477

in her throat, a bitter, choking ball. She bit her lip, held back a sob, and smiled at nothing in particular.

Annie had come to Paris by herself. The holiday had been booked months ago, and when Sylvia died she'd considered backing out but hadn't liked to let Binnie down. The week before leaving, she and Binnie rang each other constantly.

'Shall we take jeans?'

'I'll take a hairdryer, you bring your travelling iron.'

They were travelling on a Tuesday. On the Monday, Binnie called, her voice thick with cold. 'I've got the flu,' she groaned. 'I feel lousy. I'll never make it. Do you know anyone who'd like a free holiday?'

Annie was filled with disappointment. 'No, but if you're sick, we could get a refund with a doctor's note and go to Paris another time.'

'The doctor's not coming till tonight. It's awfully short notice to cancel. You go by yourself, Annie,' Binnie urged. 'It's only five days.'

At the time, it hadn't seemed a bad idea. People often went on holiday alone. She called Binnie later to see what the doctor had said and was surprised at how chirpily she gave the number.

'It's Annie.'

There was a silence, then Binnie's voice, heavy with cold as it had been that morning. 'Oh, hallo. The doctor said I'll live.'

Annie knew the doctor had been nowhere near her so-called friend. There was nothing wrong with Binnie. Almost certainly a man had something to do with the change of heart, perhaps the one she'd spent a weekend with in Chester, the one who'd 'dumped' her as she put it, Roy. Roy had probably reappeared on the scene and she wanted Annie out of the way in case she came round to see how she was.

'I hope you're better soon,' she said shortly.

The first day was taken up with travel. It was late when the coach arrived and almost midnight by the time she was dropped off at the hotel and allocated her gloomy room with its tall, narrow window in the corner.

Until she'd come to Sacré-Coeur, the second day had gone reasonably well. She'd dutifully gone up the Eiffel Tower in the lift, visited the Louvre and Notre Dame, window-shopped in the Champs Elysées, though she felt rather like a sleepwalker, unable to appreciate anything she saw. It was difficult to believe that so many great artists had found inspiration here. Too nervous to use French restaurants in case she ordered the wrong thing, she bought frequent snacks in McDonald's.

But now! She wanted to shrivel up inside her anorak, hide herself, so no-one would notice she was alone. And there were two more days like this to get through! One of the youngsters produced a mouth organ and began to play. Of course, it had to be a Beatles' song, 'Yesterday', Sylvia's all-time favourite.

'Oh, no!' Annie moaned. She looked at her watch. It was only just after ten, and as she never went to bed at home before twelve, she had no intention of doing so in Paris. Was it safe for a woman to walk the streets late at night? Perhaps she could wander slowly back to her hotel in République and have a coffee on the way.

She was searching her bag for the map, when a surprised and vaguely familiar voice said, 'Mrs Menin, Annie!'

Almost any familiar voice would have been welcome. Her heart lifted as someone in jeans and a thick woollen sweater squeezed himself onto the steps beside her. Euan Campbell! They'd rarely spoken in Liverpool, but it was like meeting a long-lost and greatly loved friend. She grabbed his arm and gave a shaky laugh. 'Oh, am I pleased to see you!'

He was also alone, and Annie suspected he was as pleased to see her as she was him. There was relief and pleasure on his thin brown face. Two lost souls, she thought, brought together by accident in a strange city. He asked for her first impressions and she confessed she didn't know. 'I've felt a bit peculiar all day,' she said, 'as if I was seeing everything through dark glasses.'

After a while, they left the steps and began to stroll through the crowded Place du Tertre, where the trees were festooned with coloured lights. Artists, easels and charcoal ready, offered portraits at a hundred francs each. The pavement cafés were packed to capacity.

'I met my wife in this square,' Euan said in a dull voice. 'We were only eighteen, students. We came back year after year, including our honeymoon. I haven't been since the children were born.' He looked at Annie with his sad, dark eyes. 'I suppose everyone knows what happened?'

She nodded. 'Yes, luv.'

'I've been too scared to return by myself and there was no-one else I wanted to be with. I thought it was time to lay the ghost. I arrived yesterday . . .' He broke off and sighed.

'How's it working out?' Annie asked.

He gave the suggestion of a smile. 'Awful! Everywhere I go, I went with Eva. The memories are killing me. I was thinking of going home.'

'I'd toyed with the same idea meself. I was coming with a friend, but she took ill at the last minute.' Despite his obvious unhappiness, everything had changed since they met, although she knew it was only temporary. Her spirits had soared, for one thing, and Paris seemed an entirely different place; colourful, unusual, coursing with vitality. She wondered if he'd mind if she linked his arm. She did so, and he smiled, properly this time. 'I was never so glad to see a face I knew,' she said thankfully.

'Frankly, neither was I. I'm glad it was you and not your friend,' he added surprisingly. 'Have you eaten yet? Suddenly, I'm starving.'

'I've been in and out of McDonald's all day.'

His face brightened. 'Let's have dinner. Not here, it's too expensive. I know a little place not far away.'

'As long as you let me pay my share.'

They walked through the narrow, sloping streets, Sacré-Coeur behind them on the skyline. Euan turned into a cul-de-sac and they entered a café that was half as big as her lounge. The only illumination came from a flickering candle on each table.

Annie chose a herb omelette, Euan ordered coq au vin and a bottle of red wine. His French was good. The wine came first and tasted vinegary.

'Dilute it with water,' he advised when she pulled a face. 'That's a genuine Parisian working man's drink.'

The omelette was delicious and she soon got used to the wine. The bottle went quickly and he ordered another.

'Did you use to come in here with your wife?' she asked.

'Yes, I doubt if there's anywhere in Paris I haven't been with Eva.' He glanced around the dimly lit room. Only three of the six tables were occupied. 'We used to sit at that table by the window. We considered it *ours*. Eva used to get cross if it was occupied.'

'Have you got a photograph of Eva?'

He crumbled a piece of bread on the red and white checked cloth with long, lean fingers. 'I chucked them away after . . . after it happened, and those of Meg and Jenny – they were twins, mirror images of each other.'

Annie put her hand on his. She felt strangely light-headed. The wine must be very strong. Euan had drunk half the first bottle and was swiftly demolishing the second. 'Do you want to talk about it, luv?'

He looked at her, his face tragic. 'Do you mind? I've never spoken about it before, but it's all seemed unusually real today. The girls were conceived in Paris.'

'Then why don't you begin,' Annie said softly.

It came pouring out; the rage, the grief, the utter waste of three young lives. 'Eva was taking the girls to buy ballet shoes. We'd had a row over it. I thought they were too young, they were only three.' He'd wanted to kill the lorry driver who was responsible. Once, he'd actually gone round to the man's house with the express intention of doing that very thing. 'I don't know what stopped me – yes I do. I hadn't thought to take a weapon and he was considerably larger than me.' His eyes, no longer sad, burned into hers. 'You know what happened when it came to court? He was fined two hundred and fifty pounds, and his licence was suspended for six months. His lawyer pointed out he'd lose his job, as if that were a worse punishment than me losing my family.'

The wine was beginning to take effect. His speech became slurred and disjointed. Tears began to roll down his smooth, olive cheeks. Annie watched helplessly. After a while, she said, 'Come on, luv. I think we'd better get you back to your hotel.'

She sat up in bed, head spinning. 'Well, Syl. I've got meself into a fine old mess, haven't I?'

On the bed that should have been Binnie's lay the boyish figure of Euan Campbell, fully dressed except for his shoes. He was breathing heavily, but otherwise dead to the world.

There was no way she could have got him to a Metro station, even if she'd known where one was. The waiter had called a taxi, and as she hadn't liked to go through Euan's pockets looking for the name of his hotel, there seemed no alternative but to bring him back to hers. One good turn deserved another, anyroad; he'd rescued her from Sacré-Coeur.

'Jaysus, Annie!' Sylvia laughed. 'He'll feel embarrassed tomorrow.'

Annie slid under the clothes and continued her conversation with Sylvia. 'It's ever so strange, Syl. If we'd met in Lewis's or the Playhouse, we'd have just said "hallo". But abroad, it's different. I'd have been pleased to meet me worst enemy on those steps.'

'Such as Jeremy Rupert?' Sylvia said with a sly chuckle.

Annie shuddered. 'Well no, not him.'

'What about Kevin Cunningham?'

'Not Kevin, either.'

'Seems to me, Annie,' Sylvia said in an amused voice, 'that you quite fancy Euan Campbell.'

'He's too young to fancy, Syl. I mean, we'll be forty-six this year – we're old enough to be his mother.'

Sylvia giggled. 'That wouldn't stop me, friend.'

It was still dark when Annie woke. The window was open and the room smelt pleasantly of baking bread from the boulangerie opposite. The occasional car drove down the side street where the hotel was situated, and heavier traffic was audible, muted and distant, on the Boulevard de Magenta which ran along the top. Women's voices could be heard, penetratingly clear in the early morning air. Feeling wide awake, Annie slipped out of bed to see what was going on.

The boulangerie was brightly lit, the door wide open. Two women were outside, their bags crammed with sticks of bread. Their voices rose and fell in the lovely melodic way of the French. There was something fascinating about the scene. It looked so appropriately *foreign*!

A voice said, slightly incredulous, 'Annie?'

She turned. 'Sorry, luv, did I wake you?'

'No, it was those women. Oh, my head!' Euan Campbell groaned as he struggled to sit up.

'You drank a lot of wine.' Annie wished she'd brought a robe. They hardly knew each other, yet here they were, waking up together in a hotel bedroom in Paris. Still, her cotton nightie was quite chaste.

'I'm sorry. Did I make an exhibition of myself?'

'Not really. You could walk, but you couldn't tell me where you were staying, so I brought you back with me.'

He groaned again. 'I feel terribly embarrassed.'

'Sylvia said you would.'

'Sylvia?'

She could just about see his puzzled face. 'Me friend, Sylvia. She died two months ago, but we still have conversations in me head.' It must be Paris and their crazy situation, because she wouldn't have dreamt of telling anyone that under normal circumstances.

'I sometimes talk to Eva.' He stretched. 'Despite my head, I feel good this morning. I hope you didn't mind listening to all that stuff? I found it very cathartic.'

'Always glad to be of assistance,' she said lightly.

He sighed. 'I'd give my right arm for a cup of coffee.'

'I wouldn't mind a drink meself,' her mouth felt like the bottom of a birdcage, 'but breakfast's half seven and it's only just gone five.'

'Where exactly is this hotel?'

'République.'

'There's an all night café by the canal.' He swung his legs onto the floor. 'Gosh, you took my trainers off! Now I feel embarrassed again.'

'I've seen men's stockinged feet before,' Annie said drily.

He laughed for the first time since she'd known him. It was deep and rather attractive. He pushed his feet into his shoes. 'I won't be long.'

The door closed and she heard his quiet footsteps down the stairs. She wondered if the coffee was an excuse to escape and she wouldn't see him again until she returned to university. Would she mind? 'I'd be hurt him leaving so deceitfully. I'd sooner he told me to me face.'

She lay down. In a minute, she'd get dressed for when Euan came back – *if* he came back.

A shaft of yellow sunshine had penetrated the curtains by the time Euan returned, and Annie was fast asleep. She sat up, flustered.

'I meant to get dressed. I must be more tired than I realised.'

'It's lovely out!' His eyes were shining and his face was flushed. He was barely recognisable as the sad young man who'd lectured her on American literature. He sat on the edge of her bed quite naturally, as if they'd known each other for ever, and handed her a carton of coffee. 'The canal looks beautiful. We must go there later . . . if you want to, that is,' he added hurriedly. 'I'll make myself scarce if you prefer.'

'I'd love to spend the day with you, Euan,' Annie said gravely.

He looked relieved. 'That's good. I don't know what I'd have done if you'd told me to get lost.'

The coffee tasted lovely. Annie thought how envious Binnie Appleby would be if she could see her. How fortunate Binnie had been 'ill'!

She drained the carton and Euan threw it in the waste-paper bin, along with his own. 'I'll go back to my hotel shortly for breakfast and a change of clothes.'

'You can have breakfast here,' Annie said. 'It's been paid for.'

'Can I?'

'Yes.'

Their eyes met and the atmosphere in the room subtly changed. Suggesting he have breakfast seemed pretty innocuous, after all, they'd just spent the night together, but the words seemed to contain a double meaning she hadn't intended.

Euan said casually, 'Please tell me to stop if you find this offensive.' He leant down and kissed her softly on the lips.

The last thing in the world Annie had expected was for Euan Campbell to kiss her. At the same time, she wasn't the least bit surprised and not at all offended.

He kissed her harder. His hands slid round her waist and he pulled until she was lying flat on the bed. For the barest second, her body was stiff and unyielding, then, as if a brilliant flower was unfolding inside her, the inhibitions of a lifetime slipped away; her arms went round his neck and she began to kiss him back. She took her nightdress off, or perhaps Euan took it off for her, she wasn't sure. She only knew she was naked in his arms. With a gasp of delight, she felt his tongue on her breasts. Wild, ecstatic sensations swept through her, feelings she'd never experienced before. His mouth tore down her body to between her legs, and in the pit of Annie's stomach, something was building up, a swelling almost too delicious to stand.

Suddenly, he was no longer kissing her. 'Don't stop!' she screamed.

He tore off his clothes, knelt over her, then entered her, rock hard, and the swelling mounted sweetly to a point when she thought she must have died and gone to heaven. Despite his delicate build, he was surprisingly strong and at the back of it all, there was something urgent and desperate about the way their bodies tangled together. Annie knew she wasn't just making love, but attempting to purge herself of the misery of the last few years; of Sara's sudden marriage, Daniel leaving, Sylvia dying. The memories vanished as everything burst, and the explosion was gut-wrenchingly glorious and better than anything that had gone before.

'Aaahhh!' She gave a long, shuddering gasp of delight, followed by a brief sigh that she'd had to wait so long for her first orgasm.

Euan buried his head in the pillow and didn't speak. 'What's the matter?' she asked after several minutes of silence.

His voice was muffled when he replied. He didn't look at her. 'That's the first time since . . . I feel as if I've been unfaithful.'

Annie shook him impatiently. His tragedy was a million times worse than hers, but it wasn't right to let him think he had a monopoly on misery. 'Me own husband was killed in a car crash,' she said, although Lauri had been far from her mind when they were making love.

'Gosh, I'm sorry.' He raised his head and she felt a moment of unease when she thought how young he was. Was she taking advantage of his vulnerability? She remembered he'd made the first move. Perhaps it would help him, as it would help her, to indulge in two days of sheer madness in Paris. She stroked his arm, the skin smooth and unblemished, like satin.

'Don't be sorry,' she murmured. 'You know, luv, you can't grieve for ever. You've got the rest of your life to live. Eva wouldn't have wanted you to stay celibate, would she?'

To her relief, he gave the glimmer of a smile. 'I'm not so sure. She was very selfish. Even from beyond the grave, she'd hate the idea of me being with another woman. What about your husband, would he mind?'

'Lauri would wag his finger at me and look very disapproving, though if I'd gone first I'd've wanted him to get married again.'

'I would have wanted the same for Eva. It feels odd, criticising her. I haven't had a single bad thought since she died.'

'That's a good sign,' said Annie.

'I suppose it is.' He kissed her shoulder. 'I'm sorry. Before was wonderful. I hope I haven't spoiled it for you.' He ran his slim hand down her body, and within seconds they were making love again.

The trees that lined the Canal Saint Martin were bursting into pale green life. Numerous pretty bridges spanned the narrow width of rippling water, which was a glaring, dazzling yellow as it reflected the rising sun. The air was fresh and cool and smelt slightly salty. Some of the wrought-iron benches on the bank were already occupied: two very old men in deep conversation, a woman sketching, a couple of girls eating croissants and sharing a carton of milk.

'I would never have come to a place like this,' Annie said happily, as she strolled arm in arm with Euan. She breathed in the heady atmosphere. 'Paris seems entirely different today.'

Euan squeezed her arm. 'I nearly didn't go to Sacré-Coeur last night. I thought it would be too painful. At first it was, but then I saw you . . .' he skipped a few steps like a child and she had to hurry to keep up. 'You know, I've always liked you. I remember sitting by you in that pub, you were reading *The Sun Also Rises*. I wanted to talk to you again, but you were always with your friend.'

He veered her off the bank of the canal when

industrial buildings came into view. They stopped for coffee, then walked further and came to a wide boulevard full of shops. To Annie's pleased surprise, the clothes on the racks outside were cheap; everything she'd seen yesterday had been way beyond her means. She treated herself to a colourful Indian skirt, a blue embroidered T-shirt and a pair of gold-embossed sandals. The lot came to less than twelve pounds.

'I'll just look for something for me aunt and uncle,' she murmured. 'There's hardly anyone left to buy presents for nowadays.'

'What about your children?' Euan asked.

'Me daughter's in Australia. As for Daniel, I haven't a clue where he is. Oh, Lord!' To Annie's intense horror, she felt tears pour down her cheeks. 'It was terrible,' she sobbed. 'Sara got married and was gone within a week, then Daniel walked out on me the very same day. I still can't get over it, years later. I don't think I ever will.'

'Come on, Annie.' Euan took her gently in his arms in the middle of the crowded pavement. 'Let's go home.'

On the way, he bought a bottle of wine. Back at the hotel, Annie drank hers sitting by the open window. The boulangerie was still busy. In an apartment opposite, a family were eating their mid-day meal. A woman came down the street with a fluffy white poodle on a lead. As she passed a parked car, a black cat shot out and ran across the road and was narrowly missed by a van. Further down, where the street sloped towards the canal, purple roofs glinted in the April sunshine.

'It's lovely,' she said. 'There's nothing the least bit extraordinary about it. It's just lovely.'

'It gets under your skin, Paris.' Euan was sitting on her bed. He raised his glass, 'To Paris, the enchanted city!'

'To Paris!' She already felt slightly drunk. Perhaps it mightn't be a bad idea to stay that way until it was time to leave. She drained her glass and refilled it. 'I could get addicted to this wine.'

'Do you feel better now?'

'Much better. Thanks for listening.' She'd told him about Daniel and the fact he'd been gone for almost four years and all she'd received were a few postcards. It all seemed rather tame. At least Daniel was alive and there was every likelihood she'd see him again, whereas his girls were lost for ever.

'One good turn . . . ! Come here.' He patted the bed. Annie felt her stomach turn pleasurably when she sat beside him. He took her glass and laid it on the floor, then slid his hand beneath her T-shirt. Quickly, she succumbed to the touch of his fingers, the pressure of his lips, the final act of making love when he sank right into her and she felt he'd touched her very core. Her body was hot, as if the blood raged through her veins like burning oil. The shuddering, gushing climax was so exquisite that she screamed out loud.

Euan had been back to his hotel to fetch his clothes. Annie sat at the dressing table and watched through the mirror as he changed into a fresh pair of jeans and a clean sweater. His body was slim and lithe, without an ounce of surplus fat. His shoulders were neither narrow nor broad, and the planes on his back glistened when he pulled on the jeans.

He was so *young*! He was thirty-two, but looked less. Annie held up her arm and examined it closely. It didn't look a particularly *old* arm, but in the mirror she could see her elbow was wrinkled. She held up the other arm, which looked exactly the same. Still, so far no-one had looked at her and Euan peculiarly, as if wondering what such a handsome young man could see in an obviously middle-aged woman. Perhaps they thought she'd hired a gigolo for the week!

She patted her hair, inserted her earrings, and as an afterthought rubbed moisturiser on her elbows. 'Ready!' she sang. They were going to Montmartre for dinner.

Euan was still stripped to the waist. 'You look nice,' he said. She wore the clothes she'd bought that morning. The Indian skirt fell on either side to the floor, the gauzy material soft against her legs. He knelt behind her and put his arms around her breasts. Annie felt her body melt. 'Jaysus!' she groaned.

When eventually they left for dinner, it was very late.

He was the sort of young man Auntie Dot would call 'lovely'. Annie could find no fault with him, not that she looked for any. Despite the tragedy of his past, he was naive, unworldly, incredibly *nice*. He was also virile, with a healthy sexual appetite that had been suppressed for the last few years. She regarded it as lucky she'd been around when he snapped out of the long drawn-out mourning for his dead family. She assumed almost any woman in the right place at the right time, as she had been, would have done for Euan. And he was lucky to have found someone who'd make no claims when the perfect holiday was over.

She liked him. She liked listening to him, talking to him, laughing with him. She woke up in his arms on the second morning, their last full day, feeling as if the world had been touched by a magic wand. The room was golden with sunshine and the curtains lifted gently on the open window. Euan's hand stroked her belly then sank into the warmth between her legs. It wasn't just magic, it was heaven.

The outdoor market was full of tourists. Between the stalls it was packed and you could scarcely move. Annie clung to Euan's hand. It was a poor market, difficult to get near the stalls and once you did, the goods were new and expensive. 'Shall we go somewhere else?' she shouted, but he didn't hear. She tripped over someone's foot and her sandal fell off.

'Euan!' she called, releasing his hand. She bent down to look for her lost sandal. By the time she'd found it, Euan had disappeared.

Annie remained where she was, searching for his dark head in the crowds. She felt slightly panic-stricken as she was buffeted by eager bargain hunters. Perhaps she should go after him. Her panic rose as the minutes passed and he didn't reappear. She couldn't understand why she was getting in such a state; if he didn't come soon all she had to do was go back to the hotel.

It was twenty minutes before a voice called, 'Annie!' and she saw his arm raised several feet away. She was about to shove through the seething mass towards him when he shouted, 'Stay where you are.'

Suddenly he was there, his face flushed. 'I thought I'd lost you!'

Annie flung her arms around his neck. 'Euan, darling. I was dead frightened.' She was shaking and her stomach was knotted, but now he was back, she felt entirely at home in his arms.

He buried his face in her neck. 'Don't worry, Annie. I'm here. You'll never feel frightened again.'

Annie froze. She didn't just like him, she loved him. But it was a passing thing, a romantic interlude in an enchanted city. She had no wish to hurt this lovely young man, but she was going back to Liverpool tomorrow and that would be the end of her affair with Euan Campbell.

The wine had almost gone, as had the night. Pale yellow touched the grey sky, and one or two stars remained, blinking weakly. Annie poured the last of the wine and filled the glass to the brim with water. Her throat was sore. They'd talked for hours, argued bitterly most of the time.

'Can I have a sip?' said Euan.

She took the glass over to the bed and held it for him, as if he was a child. 'Finish it off, if you like.'

'No, thanks.' He put his arms behind his head and turned his face away from her.

Annie kissed his ear, let her mouth wander down to his chest . . . She'd learnt many things over the last two days.

'Don't do that!' he said hoarsely.

'I thought, just one more time. The coach will be here at eight o'clock to pick me up.'

'I couldn't stand it, knowing that it's all over.'

She finished off the wine and lay beside him, her arm loosely on his waist. 'Darling, it would be mad for us to see each other again.' She thanked God it was her last year at university. There would be no more lectures, only the final exams. 'We've got no future, you and I.'

'You've said that a hundred times.' His voice shook. 'The thing is, I love you and you love me. What future could be more perfect?'

'I don't think you do love me, Euan,' she said softly. 'It's Paris. It's been like a fairytale, with you my wonderful Prince Charming, except I feel a bit like the wicked Stepmother, rather than Cinderella.'

'Don't talk stupid!' he said angrily. 'And how dare you tell me I don't love you. Am I incapable of knowing my own mind?'

'No, luv. I think you're just fooling yourself. Once you're home, you'll soon see sense and realise I'm not the one for you. There's stacks of young women who'd jump at a handsome young man like you.'

He propped himself on an elbow and looked down at her. 'If you knew how pompous and ridiculous that sounds.' He laughed sarcastically. 'I don't want stacks of young women jumping at me, I want you.'

'Euan, I'm nearly old enough to be your mother.' Lauri had been old enough to be her father, but it seemed different when it was the man.

'You've said that a hundred times, as well,' he said coldly. 'I don't give a damn. What does age matter when two people are in love?'

Annie sighed. She was convinced he'd see things differently in the cold light of Liverpool. It was best to leave things on a high, rather than let it filter out with embarrassing excuses from him in a few months' time, when possibly she'd love him even more. 'I'd like to think you'll get married again and have a family one day.'

'Now you're beginning to *sound* like my mother. As for a family, there's no way I'd bring more children into the world.' He shuddered violently. 'I couldn't stand it!'

'Is that the attraction I hold, Euan?' Annie said gently. 'The fact I'm too old to have a baby?'

He groaned. 'The only attraction you hold is that you're *you*! Oh, Annie!' He took her in his arms. 'How can you be so cruel?'

'I'm not being cruel, luv. I'm being sensible.' He began to stroke her body and delicious sensations shivered through every nerve. In the midst of it all, Annie told herself he'd thank her one day when he met someone his own age. And she'd thank him. The memory of this holiday would stay with her until she was a very old woman.

The coach stopped at Victoria Coach Station for a twenty-minute respite. Annie got off to stretch her legs. She felt restless, unable to get Euan Campbell out of her mind. He wasn't due home until tomorrow, but had decided to leave today. 'What point is there staying without you?' he said bleakly. She dismissed the idea of going to Euston Station on the off chance that they'd meet. She'd said goodbye, and she meant it, though her heart contracted when she remembered closing the door on the dismal hotel room where she'd reached such dizzy heights of happiness, leaving behind the beautiful young man who claimed he loved her.

'Oh, Syl,' she whispered. 'I wish you were here to talk to.' There was no-one now, no-one. She noticed a row of telephones on the wall. 'I'll ring our Marie and say I'm in London! It's ages since we spoke.'

She dialled her sister's number. After three rings, the receiver was picked up, and a voice said, 'This is Marie Harrison.'

'Hallo, sis,' Annie began, but the voice continued as if she'd not spoken. 'I'm sorry I'm not in at the moment, but if you'd like to leave a message after the long tone, I'll get back to you as soon as I can.'

It was one of those weird answering machines. Annie waited for the long tone, then said, 'Sis, it's Annie. I was just passing through . . .'

'Annie!' Marie, the real Marie, broke in. 'Are you in London?'

'Only for a few minutes. I'm on me way home from Paris.'

'Oh, sis, why don't you come round? You can go home any time.'

'I'll see you in half an hour,' Annie said promptly.

Her sister was on the balcony when Annie turned the corner. She waved and disappeared. By the time she reached the house, Marie was waiting at the door. There was something different about her, but then there often was. Her face was smooth and serene. Perhaps she'd had it lifted!

'Hi, sis!' She kissed Annie warmly. 'You look wonderful. Your holiday in Paris did you good.'

'I had a lovely time.'

Marie took her bag as they walked upstairs. 'Who did you go with?'

'I went by meself. Me friend let me down at the last minute, but I met someone I knew, so it was all right.'

Fortunately, Marie didn't enquire into the identity of the someone; the memory was too precious to share just yet.

'Your flat looks nice,' Annie remarked as she went in. There were pictures on the walls and bright cushions scattered around.

'I made some tea. I knew you'd be gasping.' Marie went into the kitchen and returned with a tray. Annie settled herself onto the settee.

'I had no idea you were going to Paris,' Marie said. She looked slightly hurt, as if she felt she should be kept up to date with her sister's affairs.

'I didn't think you'd be interested.'

'I'd have invited you to stay over so you'd have an easier journey.'

'Would you?' Annie looked at her sister, eyebrows raised. 'The usual reaction when I tell you anything is no reaction at all.' Perhaps that was rather blunt, but she wasn't in the mood to be tactful.

Marie looked uncomfortable. 'I wouldn't say that.'

'Oh, luv! I'm not complaining, because you've had your career to think of, but over the years I've written and told you about all sorts of things, anniversaries, birthdays, weddings, and you've ignored them.'

'Oh, God!' Marie got up and went out onto the balcony. Annie poured herself more tea and waited for her to come back. A few minutes later, she returned, her expression sombre. 'I've been thinking about this sort of stuff a lot lately,' she said. 'It was when I heard Sylvia had died – you didn't write until a month after it happened!'

Annie sensed a slight accusation in the words. 'I didn't think you'd be much interested in that, either.'

'It meant it was too late to do anything about it. Cecy and Bruno would have appreciated a wreath.'

'You've never so much as sent a Christmas card before.' Annie wasn't quite sure how the conversation had so swiftly become acrimonious. 'Let's face it, sis. The Menins, the Gallaghers and the Delgados have played a pretty small part in your life since you left home.'

'I know,' said Marie.

The room was silent. Annie noticed the vase she'd brought as a housewarming present was on the hearth, full of dried bronze leaves. A clock shaped like a sunflower ticked loudly on the wall.

Marie threw herself into a chair. 'Oh, Annie, if you knew the way I clawed and fought and slept my way to recognition. Now I've achieved it. I'm a star. We've just wrapped up a third series of *Lorelei*, and they're planning a fourth, and I've been asked to make a film in Hollywood.'

'Congratulations,' Annie murmured.

Marie grinned mischievously. 'I've turned everything down. I'm retiring from show business, sis. I'm getting married.'

Annie regarded her sister in astonishment. 'You've got a prospective husband tucked up your sleeve and you didn't let me know!'

'I've only known a few days myself. I phoned on Tuesday but you must have been in Paris.'

'What's his name?'

'Justin Taylor. He's a doctor in Tower Hamlets. I met him at an AIDS concert in January – that's what Clive Hoskins died of, AIDS. You'll see him tonight, he's coming to dinner.' Marie leaned forward, her face twisted with the effort to explain. 'It was when I got your letter saying Sylvia was dead, that the penny dropped. I thought about all the people who would miss her, then thought, "Who the hell would miss me?"' She shook her head when Annie began to protest. 'Don't tell me not to be silly, sis. I know you miss Sylvia far more than you would me.'

Annie said slowly. 'I miss having someone to phone when there's no earthly reason for phoning.'

'That proves my point!' Marie nodded emphatically. 'When have you been able to ring me for a chat? I've always been too frantically involved in my career to return your phone calls. It paid off, the involvement, but only at the expense of the people who loved me; Dot and Bert, Bruno and Cecy, but most particularly you, my sister, not to mention my niece and nephew who I've never really got to know. The thing is, I was the one who lost out most.'

'Where does Justin Taylor fit into this?' Annie enquired curiously.

'Ah, Justin!' Marie's expression grew dreamy. 'I knew he was in love with me, but that he'd never ask the star of *Lorelei* to marry him. The other day, I decided to pop the question myself, and he graciously accepted. So, sis, I'm going to be a doctor's wife in Tower Hamlets, where there's an awful lot of very poor and very sick people.'

'When's the happy day?' asked Annie.

'The thirtieth of June. You'll be there, won't you?'

'I'm afraid not,' Annie said regretfully. 'I'll be in Australia, but my thoughts will be with you, you can be sure of that.'

She realised what was different about her sister. Marie hadn't had a face lift. She was truly happy for the first time in her life.

There was no sign of Euan Campbell during the examination period. Annie's nerves were ragged;

worried that she'd fail, terrified he'd be the invigilator and she wouldn't be able to concentrate on the paper. Sometimes, it felt as if Paris had been a dream. Looking back, it seemed unreal, like an incident from one of the novels she'd been reading.

She managed to avoid Binnie Appleby, and concentrated on studying for next day's paper, then the next. She also avoided, though not deliberately, doing anything for the election which took place in the second week of June.

'We're stuck with that woman till the end of the world,' Dot moaned when Mrs Thatcher was elected for a third time. The Conservatives had lost seats, but still won a majority of over a hundred. 'I thought we'd do it this time, Annie, with that nice Kinnock lad.'

'Never mind, Auntie Dot. There's an awful lot of people as upset as you are. Nearly sixty per cent of the country voted for someone else.'

'I know, luv,' Dot sighed. 'Democracy can be a pain in the arse.'

Dot wanted to die and give Bert some peace. She'd been hanging on by the skin of her teeth waiting for the election. Now it meant her old painful bones, her threadbare body, would have to hang on even longer.

8

Before leaving for the other side of the world, Annie wrestled with the problem of what to get Marie and Justin for a wedding present. In the end, she had a brainwave and rang the Labour Party for Ben Wainwright's address. She wrote, enclosing a cheque, and asked if he would kindly send one of his paintings directly to her sister.

He telephoned next morning. 'What's this about "something bright and cheerful"?' he demanded. 'I paint real life, not happy images.'

'You know what I mean,' Annie said. 'I don't want a picture that will make our Marie feel depressed.'

'How about "Sunset over the Slag Heap"?'

'You must be joking! Have you still got that one of the miners finishing their shift?'

'No. I had an exhibition in York a few months ago and it was sold. Don't worry. I'll find one that won't send your sister into a decline.'

He said he'd be in Liverpool shortly and could he take her out to dinner? Annie told him she was going away for at least three months.

'We seem fated never to meet again, you and I,' he said ruefully.

'Perhaps when I get back.' She was finding it impossible to get Euan Campbell out of her mind. If she still felt the same when she returned from Australia, another man, one so completely different, might help her to forget her tender young lover of Paris.

Chris Andrews offered to cut the grass and keep the weeds at bay during the summer, and Monica Vincent would come in once a week to make sure everything was all right – last year, number two had been completely ransacked when the occupants were away, and an expensive bike had been taken in broad daylight from outside number eleven. Two houses had burglar alarms on the front wall.

Annie asked Chris if he'd open the letter which had the result of her degree and let her know what it was, even if she'd failed. 'I'll leave Sara's number by the phone. The results are due mid-August.'

'You won't fail, Annie,' he said staunchly.

She kissed him warmly before she left. He'd always

been supportive of everything she'd done, even as far back as when she was at school.

Sara had warned her mother that it was winter in Australia. 'Bring warm clothes, not summer frocks,' she advised.

'Winter!' Annie expostulated after a few days, convinced she would melt in the heat. 'It's at least sixty degrees out there.' She put her thick coat in the wardrobe and never wore it again. She'd actually seen women walking round Sydney in fur coats and boots! Their blood must be awfully thick – or was it thin? She'd ask Nigel.

Since she'd last witnessed them together, the relationship between Sara and Nigel had completely reversed. It had been obvious from the moment they picked her up mid-morning from Kingsford-Smith Airport that things weren't merely rocky, there'd been a shipwreck.

Annie felt guilty when Sara threw herself into her arms, clinging to her, sobbing, 'Oh, Mum! I'm so pleased to see you. Oh, Mum!'

'There, luv.' Annie patted her daughter's shoulder. 'I should have come before,' she thought. 'I never realised she missed me this much.'

Nigel shook her hand. He'd grown a beard and his fringe was longer. There was little of his face to be seen behind the hair and heavy glasses. He didn't look as cocky as she remembered. 'Glad you could come,' he murmured.

She was introduced to Harry, three, a serious little boy with dark straight hair, and Anne-Marie, eighteen months, who had Annie's colouring, even down to the same blue-grey eyes. It wasn't until then that Annie herself felt tearful. These were her grandchildren, her own flesh and blood, they carried the same genes. She knelt down, not wanting to overwhelm them with hugs and kisses, something Sara and Daniel had hated from strangers when they were small.

'Hi,' she said. 'I'm your grandmother, but you can call me Annie.'

'Hello, Annie,' Harry said solemnly. Anne-Marie giggled and hid behind her father's legs.

'See to the luggage, Nigel,' Sara said sharply. 'Come on, Mum.' She picked up her daughter and made for the exit. Annie took Harry's hand and followed uncertainly. Nigel didn't look up to managing two large cases and a travelling bag on his own.

They reached the car, a long silver Peugeot estate with a red suede interior. Sara strapped the children in the back and climbed in with them. 'You sit in the front, Mum. It's a bit squashed here.'

Nigel turned up with the luggage in a trolley, and it was horrid the way Sara nagged him the whole way home. He drove too fast, he drove too slowly, and if he thought this was a short cut, then he was mistaken.

Annie felt too on edge to take in Sydney. She'd known Sara was unhappy, but hadn't realised things had sunk so low. She was thankful when, after about an hour, they turned into a large leafy drive. She had a photo of the bungalow, but it looked bigger than she had expected, a white stone square with floor-length sliding windows on every side.

'It's pretty,' she remarked. Everywhere was beautifully tended, with big exotic bushes and flowerbeds surrounding a vast lawn. A small, kidney swimming pool was covered with canvas at the far end.

Inside the house was light and airy, the rooms large. The oatmeal coloured walls were bare. Annie couldn't abide a bare wall. She itched to put up pictures.

'I'll make some tea,' said Sara.

Annie followed into the kitchen. Nigel's job in the laboratory must bring in a pretty penny, she thought, impressed. The automatic washing machine looked more like a computer with its range of dials and knobs. There was a dishwasher, a drier, and one of those split-level cookers she'd always fancied herself. In front of the window overlooking the rear of the house, four wickerwork chairs stood around a glass-topped table with cane legs. Sara put the kettle on, then slid the windows open. The children rushed outside.

Annie admired the view, so green and fresh and pleasant. It was hard to believe this was part of a big, noisy city.

'I can't tell you how glad I am you're here, Mum,' Sara sighed.

'I'm glad to be here, sweetheart. I would have come before, but I had me degree, and the fare to Australia's not exactly cheap.'

Sara blinked tearfully. 'No-one's called me "sweetheart" in years.'

'I'll drop a hint to Nigel,' Annie smiled.

'If he called me sweetheart, I'd be sick,' Sara said, in such a harsh, cracked voice, that Annie felt her scalp prickle.

Harry came in and asked for a drink and Sara said no more. She poured her mother a cup of tea and Annie asked mildly, 'Where is Nigel?'

'Gone to work. He took the morning off to collect you.'

He hadn't said goodbye! Things were even worse than she'd thought.

After a few days, Annie recovered from the jetlag and the tiredness of the long journey. From then on, each morning after breakfast, she and Sara and the children set off on a sightseeing tour.

Sydney was a city in a desperate hurry. Cars, pedestrians, shoppers, seemed to be possessed with an urgent desire to be somewhere other than the street, the pavement or the shop where they currently happened to be. The city centre throbbed with brash and exuberant energy. Although Sara could drive and had a car of her own, they mostly used public transport, which was cheap and quick and far less nerve-racking than trying to manoeuvre yourself through the horrendous traffic.

They had tea in the Sydney Opera House, a building that looked more like a magnificent yacht about to break loose from its moorings and float into the glorious blueness of Sydney Harbour; explored The Rocks where the first fleet had dropped anchor in 1788; and saw the statue of Captain Bligh, which didn't look a bit like Charles Laughton. Everywhere she went, Annie collected postcards for Auntie Dot.

Sara said, 'I hate the thought of her dying and me not being there.'

They'd climbed to the top of Observatory Hill, with its breathtaking view of the harbour. Annie nursed Anne-Marie, tired after scrambling up so many steps. Harry was searching for stones for his collection.

'It's what happens, luv, when you move far away.'

'I made a terrible mistake, Mum. I should never have married Nigel.'

Annie had no idea what to say in reply. It was obvious that every single thing that Nigel did or said drove her daughter to distraction. Her husband, so assertive back in Liverpool, was a shadow of his former self, scared to speak lest Sara lash out contemptuously at the most innocent remark. Nothing he did was right. If he put something down, it was in the wrong place and he would be told sharply to put it elsewhere. When he put his dirty dishes in the sink, Sara would take them out again. If he left them, he should have put them in the sink. He crept round like a mouse, and spent most of his time either tending the garden or in the little room that purported to be his study.

Sara was short-tempered with the children, particularly Harry. He was an intelligent little boy, obviously aware of the tension between his parents. Annie noticed his reluctance to go to his father if his mother was around, as if he knew it would upset her.

It was disconcerting to see the sneering, discontented way her daughter's mouth turned down, her hot angry eyes. She looked ugly, unpleasant. There were lines of strain round her jaw and a permanent furrow in her brow. She'd lost all interest in her appearance and lived in jeans and T-shirts which she didn't bother to iron. When they went out, she wore a navy donkey jacket.

'You look as if you're a member of a road gang,' Annie said once.

'What's the point of getting dressed up?' Sara answered listlessly.

Annie had been looking forward to a relaxing, carefree holiday, but found herself struggling to come to terms with the fact that the fresh-faced innocent girl who was once her daughter had turned into a sharp-faced harridan.

Why? Was it Australia? Was it Nigel? Would Sara have changed whatever the circumstances? Annie loved her daughter, but she didn't *like* her all that much. If only Sylvia were alive, and she could sneak a phone call in the middle of the night. 'Honestly, Syl. It's dead embarrassing when she's having a go at poor Nigel. I don't know where to put meself sometimes.' Some days she woke up feeling physically sick at the thought of the day ahead. Sydney was beautiful, she adored her grandchildren, but the atmosphere in the house made her stomach knot.

The couple had no social life. 'Haven't you made friends?' Annie asked one day. Nigel was at work.

'There's one or two girls I have coffee with sometimes. One's from Devon. She's as homesick as me.'

'Why don't you go out in a foursome? I'll babysit,' Annie offered.

Sara snorted. 'You must be joking, Mum. Dinah's husband wouldn't be seen dead with Nigel. No-one can stand him.' She kissed her mother's cheek. 'Anyroad, I don't want to go out and leave you.'

Annie couldn't disappear into her bedroom for a minute before Sara would come and root her out, or sit on the bed and ask questions about the Gallaghers or Heather Close or something else to do with Liverpool.

Some mornings, they strolled through picturesque Rushcutters Park, a stone's throw from the bungalow, or went to the beach, which wasn't far away. The smooth golden sands, washed clean by the white frothy waters of the Pacific, were virginal and untrodden so early in the day. It might be winter, but the sky was blue and cloudless from horizon to horizon, and the sun was warm.

On one particularly glorious day, Harry ran ahead, stamping his feet, fascinated by the sight of his own footsteps. Anne-Marie followed, shrieking happily.

'It's beautiful!' Annie breathed. 'You're so lucky, Sara. You've got a lovely house, two lovely children and you're not short of money. You're living in one of the most interesting cities in the world. God must have been in a really good mood when he made this beach. There's millions of women who'd give anything to be in your shoes.'

Sara's mouth twisted discontentedly. 'I'd prefer Liverpool any day.'

'You haven't given Australia a chance, luv. You didn't like it from the start. I'd have thought a lovely place like this would grow on you.'

'There's not much chance of that, Mum.'

'Mummy,' Harry called. 'Come and see the lovely stone I've found.'

'In a minute,' Sara said abruptly.

Harry came running up, his eyes alight with triumph, holding up a blue mottled stone. 'Look, Mummy. It's terribly pretty.'

'I said *in a minute*!' Sara swung her arm and slapped his face.

The little boy dropped the stone and stared at his mother in bewilderment, his bottom lip trembling. Annie felt a rush of pure anger. She picked the child up and could feel his heart pounding wildly against her own. She said hoarsely, 'If you do that again, Sara, I'm catching the next plane home.' She was conscious of the rage trembling in her voice.

'Mum!' Sara looked as bewildered as her son.

'How *dare* you hit him! No-one ever laid a finger on you.'

Harry buried his head in Annie's shoulder and began to cry. 'There, sweetheart,' she murmured softly, stroking his back. 'Mummy didn't mean it. Did you?' she said in a steely voice to Sara.

'No, no.' Sara burst into tears and reached for her son. Annie handed him over and picked up Anne-Marie, who'd decided to cry in sympathy with everyone else.

Later, as they walked along the flat sands, Harry having recovered his good humour and off in search of more stones, Annie said, 'The mistake you made by marrying Nigel, it's scarcely his fault, is it?'

Sara kicked at the sand. 'I suppose not,' she said sulkily.

'And the fact you don't like Australia isn't his fault, either.'

'Yes, but you see, Mum,' Sara began, but Annie wasn't prepared to listen to any excuses.

'So why take your unhappiness out on him? You knew exactly what you were doing when you married him. You knew where you'd be living. To be frank, I wasn't over-thrilled being married to your dad some of the time, but I didn't make his life a misery.'

Sara gaped. 'But you and Dad had the perfect marriage!'

'That's what you think, and the fact you do shows I kept me feelings hidden. It's sheer bloody selfishness to radiate your discontent onto innocent people, particularly the children.'

'Oh, Mum, please don't get cross and spoil the holiday!'

'I'm not cross,' Annie snapped. 'I'm as mad as hell, and as for spoiling the holiday, it's already spoilt. I've been here a month and I haven't enjoyed meself a bit. In fact, it's made me sick, and I mean properly sick. I'll have to sit down for a while before I fall over.'

That night, she knocked on Nigel's study door. He was listening to a jazz record. It was disgraceful the way he was forced to isolate himself from his family. His face was pathetically pleased when she went in.

'That's nice,' Annie said, sitting down and nodding at the hi-fi. 'It's New Orleans, isn't it?'

He looked surprised. 'You know something about jazz?'

'Not a thing, only that's what they played when we first went to the Cavern. We only went for the atmosphere, not the music. It wasn't until they played rock and roll that we began to listen.'

'The Cavern?' he said, impressed.

'We were there on the opening night,' Annie said proudly, 'and me and Sylvia saw the Beatles before hardly anyone else.'

'I always thought the Beatles rather pedestrian. I far prefer the Rolling Stones.'

'I find them too raucous, but how you can find the Beatles pedestrian is beyond me. What about "Eleanor Rigby" and "She's Leaving Home"?'

'"Twist and Shout" and "I Wanna Hold Your Hand" could hardly be termed musical.' His tone was abrasive, and Annie was about to take umbrage when she recalled the thin little figure sitting at the top of the stairs the morning Sara had changed her mind about coming to Australia. Behind the beard and the glasses and the hair, she sensed a lonely man trying to get out. Nigel was unable to communicate like normal people, and Sara had made no attempt to get to know him better.

'I suppose it's all a matter of taste,' she said. 'All I know is, I cried for days when John Lennon was shot.'

They talked about music for a while. Nigel said, 'I go to this jazz club sometimes, Jock's Café. Perhaps you'd like to come one night?'

'If you don't mind being seen in public with your mother-in-law!' Nigel was thirty-three. It was strange to think she'd slept with a man younger than her daughter's husband.

Next morning Annie was woken by the sound of an argument. Nigel couldn't find a clean shirt. As she listened to the row, she felt nauseous. The situation was playing havoc with her insides.

'I told you, they're in your wardrobe where they always are.'

'I've looked, Sara, and they're not.'

The voices got angrier and angrier. Then the front door slammed, a car started and drove away. Had Nigel gone to work in a dirty shirt? Her heart was racing and she was bathed in perspiration. She wondered if it was the menopause. Her May and June periods had been unusually scanty and the July one was late. Dawn Gallagher had suffered terrible nerves and palpitations with the change.

She tried to coax Sara into hiring a babysitter so she could come with them to the jazz club, but she refused. On Saturday night, she looked at her mother accusingly when she was about to leave, as if she were a traitor. 'You'd think there was a war on,' Annie thought.

Nigel looked painfully casual in a check shirt with the collar daringly turned up, jeans with knife-edge creases and polished shoes. Annie got dressed up for a change, in a chocolate brown crushed velvet suit which had a long loose top and a long, gently gathered skirt. She wore boots for the first time, as it did get rather chilly in the evenings. It was awful, but she was glad to be getting out of the house without Sara. Her body felt thick and heavy with tension. She was desperately in need of a lighthearted break.

As they drove towards the centre of Sydney, Nigel kept clearing his throat as if he were about to speak. Eventually, he managed to bark, 'I love her, you know, Mrs Me- . . . An- . . .'

'Please call me Annie.'

'I love her, Annie. I don't know what's got into her since we came home. When we met, I thought she was the girl of my dreams.'

'You mean she was willing to run round doing everything you wanted?'

'No, no' he said, hurt. 'I didn't feel uncomfortable with Sara the way I did with other women. I felt I could be myself. Not many people understand me,' he added humbly.

'I was wondering – it's what I came to see you about the other night, but we got talking about music –

perhaps it might help if Sara and the children came home for a holiday, Christmas, maybe.'

'Anything,' he said willingly. 'Anything's worth a try if it will sort this mess out.'

Jock's Café was beneath a camping equipment shop by St Mary's Cathedral, where Sara had taken Annie to Mass. The large cellar had tartan wallpaper and a tartan-shaded lamp on each table. It was like entering a Turkish bath; the air was thick with cigarette smoke and so warm she could scarcely breathe. The band were playing New Orleans jazz with a remarkable lack of enthusiasm.

To Annie's surprise, Nigel seemed to know quite a lot of people. They sat with a group from the laboratory where he worked.

'This is Rod, Mitch, Charles and Barbie. Barbie's Rod's wife.' He coughed awkwardly. 'This is . . . er, Annie, my mother-in-law.'

They shook hands. 'Mother-in-law!' Mitch said in astonishment. 'You lucky so-and-so, Nige. My ma-in-law resembles a rogue elephant.'

Charles was older than the others. He was English, an attractive man with deeply suntanned skin and prematurely silver hair. He bombarded Annie with questions about what it was like back home. 'I haven't been for years. You get all sorts of mixed stories in the press.'

'It's fine if you're in business,' she told him. 'There's a boom at the moment. The price of houses goes up every week and the estate agents are having a ball. If you're poor, it's another matter. I never thought I'd see beggars on the streets of Britain.' Her voice rose. 'There's what's called Cardboard City in London, whole acres of young people living in cardboard boxes. It makes you dead ashamed, yet we're told we should feel proud of our country.'

Charles looked slightly taken aback by her

vehemence. Mitch leaned over and said, 'What's it like having a genius for a son-in-law, Annie?'

'I don't know,' she smiled. 'I've not seen all that much of him.' A genius! She knew Nigel was clever, but a genius!

Listening to the subsequent conversation, she understood he was head of the laboratory. Rod actually called him 'Boss'. There was respect in the voices of the other men when they spoke to him, and she realised they looked upon Nigel as a brilliant scientist. His personality was of no concern to them.

'You know,' she said to Charles, who was beside her, 'I've no idea what you lot actually do.'

'Have you heard of President Reagan's Star Wars Initiative?'

'Yes.' The US president had some mad idea about waging war in space.

Charles was only too pleased to expand. 'We have a contract from the States to develop high-energy lasers using crystals. The lasers will be mounted on satellites orbiting the earth, capable of destroying incoming intercontinental ballistic missiles.' He went on about death rays, the speed of light, weapons entering the outer atmosphere . . .

'It sounds fascinating,' she said, awestruck.

'It's the most interesting work I've done.' He looked embarrassed. 'Annie, you obviously don't realise, but your nose is bleeding.'

'Jaysus!' She jammed a hanky over her nose and made for the Ladies, where two girls glanced at her sympathetically as she mopped her nose with toilet paper. The bleeding wouldn't stop. 'Have you got something cold to put down your back?' one asked. 'It's what my mum always does.'

Annie ran her metal powder compact under water, and the girl slid it down the back of her velvet top.

'Hold it between your shoulder blades for a while,' she advised. They both left.

'I'm fed up!' Annie said aloud to her miserable reflection. She was rarely ill, but since coming to Australia, she felt lousier by the day. She wriggled uncomfortably. The compact was no longer cold and her arm felt dead. She let it go and managed to catch it with her other hand.

Barbie came in, her face full of concern. She was a lovely young woman, tall and well-built, with shining, healthy hair and rosy cheeks. Her teeth were very large and very white. 'Are you all right? Charles said you had a nose-bleed.'

'I'm fine,' Annie said automatically. 'It's more or less stopped.'

'I used to have terrible nose-bleeds when I was pregnant.'

'Did you really!' Annie mopped her brow with tissues; her face suddenly felt as if it was on fire. 'Would you mind telling Nigel I've gone for a walk? I'm desperate for some fresh air.'

'Have you got a coat?' Barbie frowned.

'No, I came as I am.'

'Your son-in-law may be clever, but he's totally impractical. He should have told you how hot it gets in here.' She shook her head in despair. 'I'll lend you my cardy, otherwise you'll catch cold.'

The four men were too engrossed in conversation to notice their return. Barbie handed Annie her thick cardigan. 'Keep it to go home in. I've got a coat as well.'

She was glad of the cardigan when she got outside. The change from the steamy atmosphere of the jazz club to the cool night air of Sydney was pleasant, but she definitely needed the extra clothes.

Annie walked slowly along the unfamiliar streets of the unfamiliar city and everything fell into place. She knew the reason for the nausea in the mornings, the meagre periods followed by no period at all, the thick, heavy body. She paused in front of a shop selling bicycles. She'd yearned for a bike when she was a child, but not as much as she'd wanted skates. Closing her eyes, she imagined herself skating down the middle of Orlando Street, which seemed an incredibly stupid thought to have when she'd just realised she was carrying Euan Campbell's child!

Next morning after Mass, she bearded Nigel in his den and asked if he'd look through the medical emergency section of her travel insurance policy – Australia wasn't blessed with a National Health Service like Great Britain. She knew he would appreciate being asked for his advice. 'It says it doesn't cover anything I had back home. The thing is, I didn't know I was pregnant.'

'Pregnant!' His eyes widened in shock and his mouth fell open. After a few seconds, a grin appeared on his face. 'Have you told Sara?'

'No. I thought I'd wait to see a doctor and get it confirmed.'

He looked flattered that they were sharing a secret. After glancing through the policy, he declared it to be ambiguous. 'The firm I work for has comprehensive medical insurance for employees and their families. I'll have you added temporarily.'

'Will it be expensive?' If so, she'd have to return home.

'There's no need to worry about the expense.'

'But, Nigel . . . ' she began, but he dismissed her objection with a wave of the hand.

'We haven't seen much of each other in the four years since I married Sara, but you've been a great mother-in-law, Mrs . . . Annie.' The remark must have been an effort, because his face turned dark red.

*

514

The female doctor had a long, gaunt face and a thick East European accent. According to the tag on her white coat, her name was Nina Kowlowski. After an internal examination, she confirmed Annie was pregnant. 'What was the date of your last period?'

'April Fool's Day – I mean, the first of April,' Annie added quickly when the woman looked blank.

'That means you're carrying a sixteen-week-old foetus. You must make up your mind quickly if you want a termination.'

'You mean an abortion!' Annie gasped, horrified. 'I believe in abortion for other women, but not for meself. I've never been so delighted about anything in me life.'

'I merely thought, with your age.' The doctor shrugged. 'In that case, I'd like urine and blood samples, and you will require careful monitoring throughout.'

'Is everything all right?'

'Absolutely fine. You're a very healthy specimen, Mrs Menin, but way past the age when women normally bear children. Now, lie back and I'll listen to your heart and take your blood pressure.'

'What did you buy?' asked Sara.

'Nothing!'

'I thought you went out early with Nigel so you could do some shopping on your own?'

Annie grinned. 'I was lying. I've been to the doctor's. I didn't say anything, because I didn't want to worry you.'

Sara's hands flew to her cheeks and she cried frantically, 'Mum! Oh, Mum! Are you all right?'

'I'm absolutely tip-top,' Annie sang. She removed her daughter's hands from her face and held them tightly. 'I'm expecting a baby, Sara.'

Sara's expression was a mixture of disgust and shock. 'A baby! Mum, how could you?'

'Same way as everyone else does it, luv!' She wasn't

ashamed. She didn't give a damn about what people thought.

With an anguished cry, Sara broke away and disappeared into the lounge, where Harry and Anne-Marie were watching television. Annie hummed a tune as she went into the kitchen and made herself a cup of tea. She took it into her own room, where she sat on the bed and thought about the entirely unexpected situation she found herself in. She'd always been ultra-conventional. For the first time in her life, she was doing something out of the run.

Of course, things weren't ideal. She'd be sixty when her child was fourteen, and it wasn't much of a world to bring children into, but it would never become a better world if women stopped having babies. And the baby would never have a father. Even if she and Euan Campbell had a future, which they hadn't, he'd made it clear he didn't want children, which she completely understood. Losing two was enough to put you off for ever. She'd make sure she never saw him again, which meant the degree ceremony in November was out, that's if she'd passed. She chuckled.

'What's so funny?' Sara snapped from the door.

'I was just thinking about turning up for me degree when I'm seven or eight months pregnant!'

'You find that amusing?'

'Yes.'

Sara sidled into the room. 'Who's the father?' she asked curiously.

Annie sighed. 'A lovely young man called Euan Campbell. He lectures at the university and I happened to meet him in Paris. He's thirty-two.'

'Oh, Mum!' She sat on the bed. 'Have you seen him since?'

'No, luv. He wanted to very much, and I did, too, but I refused. It didn't seem right, me being so much older.'

'Age doesn't matter, surely, if you love each other?'

It seemed strange to be discussing such matters with her daughter. 'Euan said much the same thing, but you see, luv, it's not long since he lost his entire family in a car crash. I didn't think he was ready for a serious relationship yet.'

Sara looked dubious. 'He's the one to decide that, not you.'

'You sound as if you want to get me married off,' Annie said.

'I want you to be happy, Mum.'

Annie opened her arms and Sara collapsed into them. 'And I want you to be happy, sweetheart. I can't stand seeing the way things are between you and Nigel.'

'I wonder what he'll think about his mother-in-law being pregnant,' Sara sniffed.

'He already knows. Now, don't be hurt,' she said quickly when she felt her daughter's body stiffen. 'I only told him because I wanted advice on me medical insurance. It was him who arranged for the doctor.' She stroked her daughter's hair. 'He's a nice chap, and he loves you. You should be proud of him. The other night, someone said he's a genius. You can't expect him to be like everyone else, luv. He's different. I mean, you can't nag a genius for not putting his dishes in the sink.'

'I've been horrible to Nigel,' Sara sobbed. 'It's Australia. It's a lovely place, but it isn't Liverpool. I miss the streets and the people. I miss everything. When I drive into Sydney, I get this awful lump in my throat, and I wish, like I've never wished for anything, that I was driving into town, that I'd end up in Lord Street or London Road.' Sara looked at her mother, her face anguished. 'Christmas is unbearable, they have dinner in the garden. Imagine, Mum, having turkey and

Christmas pudding out of doors! I long for snow and hail and frost.'

'Have you never thought of coming home on holiday, Sara?'

'Loads of times, but I know this sounds stupid, I can't bear to leave Nigel. He adores the children and he'd miss them terribly. I hate to think of him being unhappy.'

Annie smiled wryly. 'And you think he's not unhappy now?'

Nina Kowlowski found Annie's blood pressure to be rather high. She returned fortnightly for a check-up and was told to rest and take things easy. Sightseeing stopped altogether, and most days they strolled to the beach or the park. Occasionally they went on gentle shopping trips and had lunch or tea in one of Sydney's lovely restaurants. The weather grew warmer as the Australian spring approached. She dreaded to think what it would be like in summer.

Barbie and Mitch came to see her several times, and Charles often arrived with flowers. 'Do you like Sydney enough to settle here?' he asked once.

'I love it, but me roots are in Liverpool. It would take an awful lot to make me leave.'

'That's a pity,' Charles sighed.

Annie felt totally content as her baby grew inside her, although she had several more nose-bleeds and if she walked too much her ankles swelled. Harry and Anne-Marie joined her in bed in the mornings and she told them tales about when their mam and Uncle Daniel had been little. Sara, buoyed up by the knowledge she was going home for Christmas, was being nicer to her husband. Nigel remained his boastful self, but Annie was aware of the decent, honourable man within and grew quite fond of her awkward son-in-law.

In the middle of August, Chris Andrews phoned. 'Congratulations, Annie. You got a Two-one. I always knew you had it in you.'

She hadn't thought about the degree for weeks. 'That's marvellous news,' she said excitedly. She asked how things were at his end.

'Good, in fact things are quite wonderful.' He sounded unusually cheerful and she wondered what had made her old friend so happy.

'Chris, I'll look a bit different when I get home.'

'Have you dyed your hair or something?'

'I've put on a bit of weight. I'm expecting a baby in January.' She hoped he wouldn't feel hurt – he still asked her to marry him occasionally – and was relieved when he laughed out loud. 'Trust you to do the unexpected, Annie!'

She thought that a rather odd remark, as she couldn't think of having done anything unexpected before. That night, she wrote to everyone she could think of and told them about the baby. She didn't want to encounter a series of incredulous faces when she got home.

Annie had been in Australia over three months, and September was drawing to an end, when she decided it was time to go home.

'Why not wait till Christmas and we'll go together?' Sara suggested.

'No, luv. I've got to book meself into hospital, and there's things to do, like get a cot, for instance. I sold the old one after your dad died and we were hard up. Anyroad, if I wait much longer, I'll never get on the plane. I'm already as big as a house.'

A few days before she was due to leave, she saw Nina Kowlowski for the final time. The two women had become friends. Annie lay on the examination table and could hardly see Nina for her bulging belly.

'You must promise to send me a card when the baby arrives.'

'I promise.'

Nina's head appeared. She was tapping Annie's stomach and listening hard. There was a puzzled look on her gaunt face.

Annie felt her blood run cold. 'Is something wrong?'

'No, nothing wrong,' Nina said absently. She continued to prod and listen, totally absorbed.

'Is there a radio in there and you can hear music?'

'No, no.'

'Then what the hell d'you find so interesting?'

Nina jerked upright. 'Are there twins in your or the father's family, Annie?'

'Twins! Why, yes, I told you about Euan, didn't I? The little girls who died were twins.'

'Well, Euan, bless his heart, has scored again. I don't know how you feel about this, Annie, but I can definitely hear a second heartbeat. You're expecting twins.'

9

Heather Close seemed narrow and cramped in the English autumn sunshine, the houses squashed too closely together. She noticed the paintwork was peeling on quite a few doors and windows, including her own. The Vincents had had a bright red burglar alarm fitted whilst she was away.

'Here you are, luv!' the taxi driver grunted. 'Bet'cha glad to get home after that long journey. Good job it's a nice day, else you'd feel dead miserable after Australia.' They'd had a long conversation during the drive from the station. He had a cousin in Darwin. He carried her cases into the house. 'Would you like me to take these upstairs?'

'No, ta, I'll unpack down here.' She paid him, closed the door and leaned against it, exhausted. As soon as she'd had a cup of tea, she'd go to bed. The house seemed dark and small and drained of colour. Beside the phone, she noticed a thick wad of post held together with an elastic band. She picked it up and took it into the breakfast room. It looked like mainly bills and circulars.

To her surprise, there were dirty dishes on the table. Annie felt a prickle of alarm. Had she acquired a squatter?

She crept into the lounge and saw records spread over the floor. The French windows were open. She went over and called, 'Who's there?'

The garden was neat and tidy and appeared to be empty. Then the branches of the willow tree parted and a young man with long plaited hair emerged. He was a bag of bones, thin to the point of emaciation, with hollow cheeks and deep-set, haunted eyes. He was either growing a beard or badly in need of a shave. The jeans he wore were filthy and full of tears, and his collarless shirt was little better.

They stared at each other for several seconds without speaking.

'Haven't you had a bath since you got home, Daniel?' said Annie.

'There's no hot water. The fairy in the boiler isn't working.'

'It should be switched on in the airing cupboard first.' It was a terrible anti-climax. She'd thought about him, prayed for him, worried, cried, longed for him for over four years, but now he was back and it was difficult to feel anything but mild irritation. 'Did you find yourself?' she asked.

'I'm not sure.' His voice was deep and mature and he'd lost some of his Liverpool accent.

'D'you want a cup of tea? I was just about to make one.'

'Please.' Inside, she could smell the dirt on him. She told him to go upstairs and switch on the water. 'I'd like a bath meself later.'

When he came down, he nodded at her stomach. 'The woman next door said you were in Australia, so I rang Sara. They'd just been to see you off, but she told me about the baby.'

'Babies,' said Annie.

'That's right, babies.' His smile was sweet and gentle. 'You don't do things by halves, Mum.'

Perhaps it was the smile, perhaps it was the 'Mum', but Annie felt a sudden rush of emotion. Daniel was back, her son was home. In two months, Sara would arrive and she would have all her family there. She patted his shoulder. 'It's nice to see you, son.'

'Same here, Mum.'

The post was mainly bills as expected, but there were a few personal letters, one from a solicitor informing her that the ten-year lease on Patchwork had expired. Annie blanched when she saw the cost of renewal. The sum had gone up fivefold. Patchwork would have to go.

Ben Wainwright had written to ask if he could borrow her painting.

I'm having an exhibition in London. If you're back before the end of October, please get in touch. He added that she'd made a good investment. *They went for five hundred pounds each at the last show.*

Annie recognised her sister's writing on the next envelope. *Just thought I'd let you know, sis,* Marie wrote, *that I'm ecstatically happy. Being a doctor's wife makes you feel very NECESSARY! Of course, I'm chuffed to hear your news. A baby! It makes me realise I might have managed it myself. Still, I feel as if Justin's patients are my family. I've been asked to make another series of* Lorelei *and I might, just might, agree. The money would be useful, as Justin would like to start an AIDS clinic, but can't raise the cash . . .*

She was relieved her sister was so happy and felt a lifetime's worry slip from her shoulders. 'I must write and tell her it's twins.'

The final letter bore a Turin postmark, so she knew it was from Cecy. *How delighted Sylvia would have been about the baby, Annie, dear. Her girls were over for the summer, Yasmin and Ingrid for three whole months, Dorothy and Lucia for just a fortnight with a nurse that Mike had hired. We hear nothing from him, but Bert wrote to say there's been a terrible row. Apparently Mike voted Conservative at the last election and Dot refuses to speak to him, so the Gallagher clan are split.*

'Jaysus' Annie gasped. 'I must get round to Dot's as soon as I can.' She turned to the final page of Cecy's letter.

I've left the worst news till last, my dear Annie. You'll be sorry to learn that my darling Bruno is dead. But trust him to go down with flying colours. You'll never believe this, but he got involved in a fight at some silly anti-Mafia demonstration. They're not sure if it was the blow to the head or the heart attack that killed him. It's curious, but I'm glad he went that way. Bruno hated growing old. He would sooner die upholding his beliefs than become a doddery old codger like me.

Annie had rarely seen her doctor since the children were young. Once contacted, he regarded her as a challenge. A twin pregnancy was risky at any age; with Annie, the risk was even greater. She was told to do nothing except lie on the settee and take things easy.

'If I'm lying on the settee, I won't have much choice, will I?' she said the first time he came to see her.

523

'I do hope you're not going to be an awkward patient, Mrs Menin.' He was a short, stout man with a friendly outgoing manner.

'Don't worry, doctor,' she said hastily. 'I'll do everything you say. There's no way I'll risk me babies by over-taxing meself.'

'I'd like you to attend the ante-natal clinic fortnightly. You mustn't hesitate to contact me if you have a problem.'

She felt rather like a precious object that had to be handled with extraordinary care. The Gallaghers came in their hordes, bearing gifts of babyclothes and toys, some new, some old, though there was no sign of Mike. He'd cut himself off from his family.

'It was losing Sylvia that did it,' Tommy claimed bitterly. He had a new, young family to support, but had just been made redundant by AC Delco. 'He's become as hard as nails, our Mike. He bought out Ray Walters, so now the whole lot's his. All he thinks of is the business. That's why he voted as he did. He doesn't give a damn about people any more, just business.'

Daniel took his mother in the car to see Dot and Bert regularly. Apart from the clinic, it was the only place she went. Dot's face twisted in pain the first time she spoke about her errant son. 'Me heart's shattered into a million little pieces, Annie,' she cried. She might be at death's door, but she'd not lost her taste for the dramatic. 'I never thought the day would come when a Gallagher would vote Tory.'

'Oh, Dot, you'd think he'd committed murder or something.'

'It's worse than murder,' Dot said chillingly. 'Anyroad, luv, how are you feeling? You look as if you're carrying a whole football team. Jaysus, the world's changed. Forty years ago, a woman would be ashamed to show her face if she was carrying a baby out of wedlock. Nowadays it's all the rage.'

Annie patted her stomach. 'I'm fine. Everyone's looking after me. People pop in all day long to ask if I want shopping done, or to make a cup of tea, and I don't know what I'd do without Daniel. He's a tremendous help, aren't you, luv?'

'I do my best,' said Daniel. 'I came home just in time.'

She would never have the same close, demonstrative relationship with her son as she had with Sara, but Annie and Daniel got on fine. They mostly kept out of each other's way. He more or less kept the house clean, ate like a horse, went for long walks by the river or sat in his room, reading. He never spoke about his travels and she never asked. He'd tell when he felt ready, if he ever did. Annie sensed that if she hadn't been pregnant, Daniel would have gone by now on another fruitless journey to find himself. She had no idea for what her wandering son was searching, perhaps he didn't know himself, but she desperately wished she could present him with the Holy Grail of his dreams. Daniel, alas, would have to find it for himself. He was part of a lost generation, completely disillusioned with the world and the way it was run. Still, he'd come back a better man than when he'd left. He was patient, even-tempered, and that sad, sweet smile was too mature for a man of twenty-two. It reminded her of Euan Campbell and made her want to weep.

Dot winked. 'Give your ould auntie a big kiss, lad. I live on kisses, they keep me going, otherwise I'd've been dead years ago.'

Daniel embraced her warmly, which he would have hated doing before.

Ben Wainwright looked flabbergasted when he arrived

525

to collect his painting. 'I didn't realise you had a partner!'

'I haven't,' said Annie.

He nodded at her bulging frame. 'You did that on your own?'

She blushed. 'No, it was . . . well, the affair was lovely when it happened, but it's all over.'

'I don't know why, but that news gives me great pleasure.'

Annie blushed again. 'Where's your exhibition being held?'

'A gallery in Hackney. It's not exactly Bond Street, but every little helps. I'll return your painting in January when the show's over.'

He stayed for dinner; salad, which was all Annie could eat. Hot food gave her heartburn, coffee made her sick, the least sip of wine and she was dizzy. She lived on fruit, raw vegetables and de-caffeinated tea.

After Ben left, Daniel said, 'I thought that was the father at first, but Sara said he was only thirty-two. What's his name?'

'Euan Campbell,' Annie said uncomfortably. It was parents who asked their children questions like that, not the other way round.

'Does he know about the babies?'

'No, and I'm not telling him, either.'

'He has a right to know.'

'Since when have you been such an expert on people's rights?' Annie demanded crossly.

'It's only fair. I'd have a fit if some woman had my baby and I knew nothing about it.'

'Well, you're you, and I'm me, and we're both different.'

'I can't argue with that, Mum.'

Annie remained fit, the babies were growing nicely in her womb, but in November she was visited with terrible depression. Everything seemed dark and bleak and the future held no promise. What was she supposed to live on? Dawn had taken over the lease of Patchwork. Annie had received two and a half thousand pounds for the stock and goodwill and the rights to her designs. She'd finished off the mortgage, but what was left wouldn't keep her for more than a few months. She hated the thought of being a burden on the State.

Even worse, it was cruel and irresponsible for a woman of her age to have children. She could die at any time – look at Sylvia! In the blackness of the night she imagined two tiny waifs being thrust into uncaring hands and placed in a Dickensian orphanage. In a blinding panic, she stumbled downstairs and telephoned Australia.

'Mum, what on earth's wrong?' Sara cried.

'If anything happens to me, will you have my babies, Sara?'

'Oh, Mum, of course we will. In fact . . .' Sara paused. 'Nigel and me have already talked about it. But nothing will happen to you, Mum.'

'I'm terrified, Sara.' Annie shivered on the stairs.

'Don't worry. I'll be there in a few weeks to look after you.'

Monica Vincent called every evening and said it was perfectly normal to feel depressed. 'Lots of pregnant women have depression, Annie.'

'It's worse at night. Everything seems so dark and it plays havoc with me blood pressure.' The doctor had been quite stern the other day, and asked if she'd been climbing mountains.

'You could take sleeping tablets.'

'Oh, no! I haven't taken a single tablet, except iron. I'm too scared it'll do the babies harm.'

'It'll pass, Annie.' Monica squeezed her hand. 'You know, I'm envious. I wish I was in your position.'

'It's not too late, luv. You're younger than me.'

Monica's cheeks turned pink. Annie had found a little gold pendant down the side of the settee which she immediately recognised as her neighbour's. At the time, she looked from the pendant to the neat grass outside, thought about the way Chris Andrews went round whistling his head off since she came back, and the shy but rapturous look on Monica Vincent's face, and realised something had happened between them whilst they'd been looking after her house. When she returned the pendant, the woman had almost collapsed with embarrassment. 'I wondered where it had gone,' she muttered.

So far, the affair seemed to be a secret. Perhaps they were waiting for the right moment to tell Mrs Vincent.

November passed and so did the depression. It was a shame, with Christmas so close, that she was unable to go out and choose little presents for the tree for Harry and Anne-Marie. Sara would do the Christmas shopping when she came home.

Annie half-lay, half-sat, on the settee, dozing a lot of the time. She felt extraordinarily relaxed, her head thick and dreamy. Sometimes she woke and wondered why on earth she was asleep during the day, then remembered the babies moving gently inside her. In a detached sort of way she watched television, read, listened to records. With the Beatles playing softly in the background, she would nod off and dream she was in the Cavern with Sylvia. One dark afternoon, she woke up with a start to see Sylvia sitting in the armchair watching her anxiously.

'Syl!' Annie's heart turned a somersault.

'It's Ingrid, Auntie Annie,' a small voice said. 'We didn't like to wake you. Daniel let us in. It was Mummy's birthday last week, and we still feel miserable, so asked if we could come and see you.'

'Oh, luv. Hello, Yasmin.' She held out her arms and the two girls knelt and buried their faces against her. 'Now as you're getting bigger, you can come and see your Auntie Annie more often – in fact, you can help with the babies.'

'We'd like that,' Ingrid said eagerly. 'Do you know if they're boys or girls?'

'I preferred to wait and see.' She could have had a test to discover the sex and ensure the foetuses were perfect, but what if they weren't? She would still have felt unable to go through with an abortion.

The girls spent the next hour trying to think up names for the twins, and ended up in fits of giggles as they outdid each other with outrageous suggestions; Mutt and Jeff, Tom and Jerry, Gert and Daisy. 'Granny Gallagher was always on about Gert and Daisy, but we haven't seen her for ages.'

One of Mike's employees turned up at six o'clock to collect them. Annie felt sad as she watched them go. Sylvia would do her nut if she thought her darling girls were unhappy.

The days merged, became muddled. Sometimes Annie wasn't sure whether it was morning or night. Visiting the clinic was a shock to the system; the cold, different people, loud voices, white, clinical surroundings. She blinked, confused by the strangeness of it all, relieved to get back home. Things were proceeding nicely, but she *must* take it easy, otherwise she might bring on a premature birth. More twin than single babies, she was told, died within the first few hours due to being premature.

It was nice to be ensconced on the settee and have everybody wait on her. Daniel fetched the decorations from the loft and all she had to do was lie there and give orders as he put them up, ready for when Sara and the children arrived the next day.

He reminisced over every ornament as he hung them on the tree. 'I remember this! Ah, this was Sara's favourite! And this was mine!' He held up a golden ball covered with red stars. 'There should be another somewhere. There used to be four. One year, I took them off and broke two. You didn't get cross.' He looked at her curiously. 'You *never* got cross. Why was that, Mum?'

'I dunno, luv. I don't suppose you meant to break them, did you?'

'No, but you took everything so calmly. I thought you didn't care. Sometimes, I wanted to do really shocking things, like draw on the walls, throw something at the television, just to see what you'd do, but I couldn't imagine anything that would make you lose your temper.'

'It doesn't do to lose your temper, luv,' Annie said. Her voice sounded odd, husky and far away, and it was an effort to speak. She felt dazed and lethargic, and made an effort to pull herself together. 'You say terrible things you don't mean. Afterwards, it might be too late to take them back.'

'I don't understand,' said Daniel.

'I lost me temper once and I've never stopped regretting it.'

'When was that, Mum?'

It all came back, as fresh as if it had happened yesterday. She watched the tickets for *Goldilocks* shrivel on the fire, heard her furious voice, shrieking at her parents that they were unfit to have children. She walked down the back entry, opened the door to the yard, tried to get in the kitchen, but couldn't because Dad's legs were in the way. The smell of gas was overpowering. She gagged . . .

'Mum, Mum, stop! Mum, it's all right!'

Annie opened her eyes. Daniel was shaking her by the

shoulders. 'That was awful. Why have you never said anything before?'

'You mean I told you? I thought I was just reliving the whole thing.' Her heart was racing. She felt hot and could still smell gas. 'Now you see why I vowed never to lose me temper. I only did it one other time. This chap at work got fresh and I nearly laid him out.'

'I'd like to know more about my grandparents,' Daniel said, 'but not now. Lie back and rest and I'll make some tea. You're all worked up and it's my fault. I'll have the doctor after me.'

Christmas Day, and Sara and Daniel were in the kitchen preparing the dinner. It was just like old times, Annie thought dreamily as she listened to them arguing, except her grandchildren were playing with their new toys on the hearth.

'Do you sleep all right in your bunk beds?' she asked. The beds were secondhand, but good as new.

'Yes.' Harry looked up from the Junior Science Kit that Monica had bought on Annie's behalf. 'I like being on top.'

'Why can't me sleep on top?' Anne-Marie queried.

' 'Cos you're too little,' Harry told her brusquely. He turned to Annie. 'When's my new auntie coming?'

'Marie? Any minute, luv.' Marie and Justin were on their way from London. They'd booked into the Blundellsands Hotel for two nights, as Annie's house was too full to put them up.

'Mum,' Sara shouted, 'do you want wine with your dinner?'

'I do,' Annie shouted back, 'but me stomach doesn't. Just give me fresh orange juice. It's in the fridge.'

Sara came in with a cup of tea. 'I thought you'd like this to keep you going. Is there the usual big do at Mike's today?'

'No.' For the first time in many years, the Gallaghers wouldn't be gathering for their Christmas dinner. 'Some of the lads are going to their mam and dad's.'

'Can I have orange juice, Mummy?' Harry tugged his mother's sleeve.

'Of course, sweetheart. Come in the kitchen and I'll get you some.'

Sara began to sing 'Away in a Manger', and Annie thought that never had anyone changed so swiftly as Sara had since she came home. The lines of tension on her face had disappeared. Her voice was softer, her eyes shone, she sang a lot, and there was colour in her cheeks. Annie was relieved to have her real daughter back, but dreaded what would happen when she had to return to Australia.

Marie arrived in a mink coat, with a weary Justin trailing behind. 'He was called out twice in the middle of the night,' Marie said, pulling a face. 'A patient, an old man he was very fond of, died.'

'I'll never get used to death,' Justin said tiredly. He wasn't at all the sort of man Annie had expected her glamorous sister to marry. Approaching sixty, his face bore an expression of perpetual worry, as if he carried the weight of the world on his shoulders. But he was a good man, who cared for his patients to the detriment of his own health.

'Can this really be Daniel!' Marie smothered an embarrassed Daniel with kisses. 'And Sara! I would never have recognised you. Where are the children? Look, darlings, I've brought loads of presents.' She turned to Annie in her usual prone position on the settee. 'My God, sis! You're *massive*! When are the babies due?'

'In a fortnight. I feel as if I've been pregnant for ever.'

Dinner was a noisy, chaotic affair. Except for Annie, who remained resentfully sober, the adults drank too much and laughed too loud and the conversation geared dizzily to a peak of utter ludicrousness.

'I'm so happy,' Annie whispered to herself. 'So, so happy. I never thought I'd have me family back again.' There was only one person missing, the father of her babies. She rested her hands on her stomach and wondered what Euan Campbell was doing right now.

After dinner, she went upstairs for a nap. The laughter downstairs sounded muffled and muted. She dozed off and dreamt she was in the hotel in Paris with Euan. His lithe brown body was bent over hers. There were strange noises coming from the boulangerie. 'The bread's exploding,' said Euan. He kissed her lips, kissed her breasts, buried his head in her flat belly. Then a poodle came leaping through the window and Euan laughed and chased it away. He got up and closed the window, and Annie held out her arms, her body aching for the feel of him, his touch, the oneness when they were making love. Their eyes locked together and the feeling, the yearning, was so strong that she gasped. Then Euan disappeared, literally vanished before her eyes, and she was alone.

'Euan!' she shouted in alarm.

'Who's Euan?' a voice said.

Annie woke and saw Justin Taylor sitting on the bed. For a moment, she forgot he was a doctor and was annoyed to find him there.

'A friend,' she said.

'I see.' He nodded briefly. 'I came to see if you were all right. You've been asleep for quite a while. There are more guests downstairs.'

Chris Andrews and Monica Vincent! Monica had an engagement ring on the third finger of her left hand. 'Mother's flaming mad,' she grimaced.

Annie kissed them both. 'I couldn't be more happy

for you. As for your mother, she'll get used to the idea.'

Annie felt increasingly as if she were drunk. Her head swam most of the time and she could hardly walk. She was asleep on the settee more often than she was awake. Marie and Justin returned to London, and on New Year's Eve, Daniel and Sara stayed in and watched television. She tried to persuade them to go for a drink. 'Why not try the Grand?' she suggested. 'See what it's like under new management.'

'The Grand wouldn't be the same without Bruno,' Sara said. 'Anyway, Mum, you're not fit to babysit. You'd fall asleep.'

Daniel woke her a few minutes before midnight. 'Come on, Mum. It'll be 1988 shortly.'

The telephone rang just as Big Ben finished chiming in the New Year. 'That'll probably be Sylvia,' Annie said groggily.

It was Marie, for the first time ever, ringing to wish Annie a Happy New Year.

She stayed in bed on New Year's Day, and the day after. On the third day, when she felt too exhausted to sit up, Sara called the doctor. He examined her thoroughly. 'Everything seems to be all right,' she heard him say. 'But I think we'd better get her to hospital.'

Annie was only vaguely aware of being helped downstairs and into the ambulance, where she promptly fell asleep. When she came to, she was lying in a high bright room and a dazzling neon tube on the ceiling above was hurting her eyes. She felt light-headed and her stomach hurt.

'Good, you're awake.' A nurse appeared, smiling, and mopped her brow. 'How do you feel?'

'Not so bad, but I'm dreading the labour,' Annie

groaned. 'I know it's going to be much longer with twins.'

'What labour? It's all over, Mrs Menin. You've got two lovely little boys. One four pounds ten ounces, the other a whopping five pounds.'

The boys were small but much fitter than their mother. All Annie's health and strength had drained into them in the weeks prior to their birth. Too weak to withstand the protracted labour, the babies had been removed by Caesarean section. Some women felt disappointed if they missed the experience of delivery, but Annie didn't care. Nor did it bother her that she had no milk to breastfeed. All she wanted was to feel well again and get her babies home.

Within twenty-four hours, she managed to make her way to the incubators where Andrew and Robert had automatically been placed.

'They're mine!' she whispered as she stared through the glass at the tiny sleeping bodies. 'Oh, Syl, if only you were here!' And what would Euan think if he knew he had two sons with Scottish names that she'd chosen specially in his honour!

Andrew was the biggest, not that you'd ever notice. His hair was possibly a darker shade of red than his brother's, but otherwise they were identical. The flesh lay loosely on their stick-thin limbs and their tiny hands were curled in fists. They were beautiful. She longed to hold them.

Two days later, Annie did. She felt almost giddy with happiness as she looked down at her babies, one in each arm. At the same time, she felt fearful. Her other children weren't particularly happy. What did fate have in store for Andy and Rob?

Scores of visitors, cards and flowers arrived; roses from Cecy, chrysanthemums from Marie and Justin. A basket of dried flowers came with a little handpainted card, 'From Yasmin and Ingrid (and Mummy)'.

To Annie's astonishment, Ben Wainwright appeared at her bedside one afternoon. 'I returned your picture and your daughter told me the news. Congratulations! I've seen the boys and they're a grand little pair.' He glanced round the ward. 'This takes me back! I remember going to see my wife each time our sons were born. It felt as if a miracle had happened, but at the same time, the world seemed a more frightening place. You knew you had this heavy responsibility for the rest of your life.'

'Where are your boys now?' Annie enquired.

'Vincent's in Leeds, married with two kids and a big mortgage. Gavin wants nothing to do with such nonsense. He's living in a squat in London without a clue what he wants to do.'

'He sounds a bit like my Daniel.'

'Annie, I want to tell you about my marriage.'

She glanced at him, perplexed. 'But it's nothing to do with me!'

'It's just that Janice and I were childhood sweethearts. We married in our teens, but outgrew each other. There was nothing sordid about the divorce. We're still friends.' His dark blue eyes danced in his grizzled face. 'You can say it's nothing to do with you, but I'd like to think it might be some day.'

Once home, Rob and Andy thrived and their weight increased. Their bodies filled out and gradually different personalities began to emerge. Although one was rarely awake without the other, Rob cried and demanded more attention than his brother. Andy was patient, but his legs were never still. The second a sheet or blanket touched him, he would contemptuously kick it off.

Daniel was fascinated by the twins. Annie often found him in her bedroom where they slept, staring. 'I always wanted a brother,' he said.

'I always wanted four children.'

The operation had taken a lot out of her and she tired easily. She'd lost weight and could zip up her jeans without a struggle. Her face was bloodless, and she could see her cheekbones for the first time in her life. Strangely, her fragile appearance made her look younger, almost girlish, and her red hair looked even redder against her white skin.

Annie didn't know what she would have done without Sara. In the middle of the night, it was more often Sara who got up to prepare the bottles, and mother and daughter would sit up in bed, each with a desperately hungry child in their arms. If they weren't fed together, poor Andy would be left as Rob was fed first to shut him up.

At half past three one morning, Annie said, 'Isn't it about time you went home, luv? I love having you, but what about Nigel?'

'Liverpool's home, Mum. I'm not going back to Australia.'

Sara's tone was so implacable that Annie knew it was no use arguing. It was an undeniable fact that Australia, that young, vibrant country, disagreed with her daughter. To return was to condemn herself and her family to a life of misery. Annie wasn't sure which was worse for Nigel: an unhappy, nagging wife, or no wife at all.

As the weeks passed, Ben Wainwright seemed to discover frequent reasons for visiting Liverpool, until it became clear the only reason he came was for Annie. They got on well, he was the right age, he adored the twins, and Daniel and Sara liked him. Annie knew one day he would ask her to marry him, and thought it would be sensible to accept.

In March, Nigel James turned up. Annie answered the door, and there he was, looking slightly ridiculous in a wide-brimmed felt hat and wrapped in several scarves against the searing wind that had been shaking the house all day.

'Am I pleased to see you!' she cried, thinking mainly of her phone bill. Sara spent hours in urgent, whispered calls to Australia. She told him his wife was out shopping with the children and made him coffee and a sandwich. 'Nigel, luv,' she said when he'd thawed out and looked as human as he was ever likely to, 'I know it's none of me business, but I hope you don't intend persuading Sara to go back with you. You wouldn't believe the difference the last few months have made. I think you'll find she's the girl you married back in Wivenhoe.'

'Don't worry, Mrs . . . Annie,' he said harshly. 'I've got a job in a laboratory in Chester. The pay is poor, and the work's way below my intellectual capacity, but I'd do anything to keep Sara.'

She patted his arm, smiling. 'That's my Nigel! Now, if you've finished your coffee, you can give one of your brothers-in-law his bottle. I heard a cry, which means Rob's about to bawl the house down.'

It meant Sara would leave soon, and Daniel was getting restless. She could tell he was itching to take off, but this time she wouldn't be left alone. Her daughter wouldn't be far away and she had Rob and Andy. One day they too would go, but it was so far in the future it wasn't worth thinking about. All she hoped was that fate would be kind and it wouldn't be *her* leaving *them*. That wasn't all. Ben had decided to take up painting full time, something he could do anywhere, including Liverpool. He had asked her to marry him. All she had to do was make up her mind. She knew she would be safe and comfortable with Ben Wainwright.

Tomorrow

It was the sort of day she loved; late autumn, crisp and brilliantly sunny, though not particularly warm.

The twins were sitting on the hearth, the soles of their feet planted firmly against each other. In the diamond formed by their chubby legs stood a wooden garage, and they were pushing Daniel's Matchbox cars up the sloping ramp onto the roof. When the roof was full, they pushed them down again, making engine noises the whole while. Their faces were intent, as if what they were doing was more important than anything in the world. They had no idea that history was being made that day.

The television had been on since early morning. In a week of political turmoil, Michael Heseltine had challenged Margaret Thatcher for the Conservative leadership. To everyone's astonishment, the support for her from Tory MPs was much less than expected. The imposition of the Poll Tax had done it, so grossly unfair. The whole country had been up in arms. Annie had taken the twins in their double pushchair on several protest marches. The leadership election had gone into a second round and rather than risk losing and be humiliated, Mrs Thatcher had announced her resignation. Annie was waiting for her to arrive in the House of Commons for her final appearance as Prime Minister.

She jumped when the French windows slid open and a couple stepped into the lounge, wiping their feet carefully on the mat, the way strangers did in someone else's house. The events unfurling on the screen before her were so gripping that she'd forgotten Mr and Mrs Loftus were looking round.

'I love the tree,' Mrs Loftus said, 'and the estate agent failed to mention the summer house in his details.'

'The summer house? Oh, you mean the shed!' Annie was trying to keep one eye on them, and the other on the television.

'Do you mind if we have another look upstairs?'

'Not at all. Look anywhere you like. After all, buying a house . . .' her voice trailed away when Mrs Thatcher was shown leaving Downing Street. The cameras switched to the packed benches of the House of Commons, where the atmosphere sizzled with excitement.

The couple came back down. 'We like your house very much.' Mr Loftus rubbed his hands together. He looked pleased, as if they'd been searching for a long time. 'Have you been here long?'

'Nearly thirty years.'

Mrs Loftus was staring at the boys, as if she'd love to pick them up. 'What are they called?'

'This is Andy,' Annie pointed to the slightly darker red head, 'and that's Rob.'

'Their hair's your colour, but they're not particularly like you.'

'They're the image of their father. They're nearly three,' Annie added to save the woman asking.

Mr Loftus was walking round the room, hands in pockets, as if he already felt at home. 'I'm surprised you can bring yourself to leave a place like this. It's got such a happy, lived-in feel about it.'

'Thirty years is a long time to be in the same house. We're moving to Sefton Park to be near my daughter.' Two years ago, Sara had started a playgroup in her home. Now Anne-Marie was ready for school and Sara wanted to finish her degree at Liverpool University, Annie would take over the playgroup and look after her grandchildren when necessary. At some time in the future, she intended making use of her own degree.

Mrs Loftus had become aware of the events occurring on television. 'She's resigned, hasn't she? I suppose it's the end of an era.' They stood watching as Mrs Thatcher took her seat in the Commons, then Mr Loftus shrugged. 'We'd better be on our way, dear.' He turned to Annie. 'We'll go straight to the estate agents. We definitely want to buy.' He shook hands. 'Well, goodbye Mrs . . . sorry, I've forgotten your name.'

'Campbell,' said Annie. 'Mrs Campbell.'

It was a bravura performance, full of defiance and gritty pride. In the rows behind, the politicians who had betrayed their leader hung their heads in shame. Annie had never witnessed a scene so full of drama and emotion, not even in all the films and plays she'd seen.

Mrs Thatcher had left the Commons, and the first of the interviews which would probably go on all day had begun, when the phone rang. It was probably the estate agent to say the house was sold.

'Annie!' Dot sounded as if she were speaking from the bottom of the world. Her voice was thick and deep. Her voice and a smattering of hearing was all she had left. 'Did you see her, luv? Oh, what a grand ould girl she was at the end! She's worth twenty of those men who voted against her. Jaysus, if only she'd been born a socialist!'

The voice faded and Uncle Bert came on. 'She's happy now, luv. I'll have to ring off and see to her.'

Annie replaced the receiver slowly, knowing that was the last time she would ever speak to her Auntie Dot.

Dot Gallagher died one minute after midnight, her

goal achieved. Despite the years of crippling pain and suffering, her indomitable spirit had kept her alive long enough to see the back of Margaret Thatcher.

The weather changed. The funeral was held on a bleak, cheerless November afternoon. The lads looked stunned, even though their mam had been on the verge of death for years – but this was no ordinary mam, this was Dot, interfering, opinionated, embarrassing, and much too loud. They were grown men in their forties and fifties, but almost to the end, their mam always had something to say, not always welcome, on almost every aspect of their daily lives. They had no idea how they would live without their best friend and closest confidante.

Mike Gallagher stood slightly apart, his body language such that no-one dared approach him. The effervescent young man with the long ginger curls whom Annie had seen in the Cavern, the man who'd married Sylvia, was no more. He had a new woman with him, as thin as a lath, with smooth black hair and a brittle face. Dot would never have taken to her. It was said the woman was an executive from an electronics firm that Michael Ray Security was about to take over.

Mike didn't come back to the house with the others and Annie didn't stay long. Dot would never have approved of such a miserable funeral. Perhaps, later, everyone would get drunk and sing her favourite songs. After a cup of tea, Annie approached Uncle Bert. 'I'll have to be going soon to catch the bus. Sara came over to look after Rob and Andy and she'll want to get home for Nigel's tea.' Daniel had the Mini. When she last heard, he was on his way to Dubrovnik. Although Euan had never said anything, she knew he hated the thought of her driving, particularly with the children. She apologised for his absence. 'He's in America for a month, on some sort of exchange visit with a university in Maine. He'll be back in December.'

Bert had aged a decade in the past week. Dot had been his wife for almost sixty years and his eyes were watery with grief. 'Just a minute, luv. There's something I want you to have.' Annie followed him into the front room, where he took a shoebox from under the bed. 'It's what Dot called her "things", just stuff she collected over the years. I can't bear to open it meself. The lads won't know what to do with it, and I don't fancy the wives rooting through. It probably just wants burning.'

'I'll see to it, Uncle Bert.'

He glanced at the bed, his old face bewildered. 'I can't get used to sleeping there without my Dot beside me.'

The box was falling to pieces and had been mended with Sellotape from time to time. Even that was coming off in places. According to the faded label at the end, the box had once contained 'Court Shoes, Black, size 6.' They'd cost seven and elevenpence halfpenny.

At first, it appeared to contain only papers. Dozens of letters from Bert to Dot posted during the war. Annie put them on the floor. She'd burn them later. There were postcards from all over the world, some dating back to the fifties. She found one she'd sent from the holiday camp in Pwllheli, one from her honeymoon with Lauri, cards from all the places where the Gallagher lads and various friends had gone on holiday over the years. She put them with the letters to burn.

Underneath the letters and the cards, she found the photo of her mam and dad's wedding, the pair of them looking so pleased with themselves, as if they shared a huge secret. 'Jaysus!' she muttered, and was about to rip it into shreds, when she remembered Daniel often asked about his grandparents. She'd show him what they looked like before Hitler put in an appearance and Johnny was killed.

A prayer book, well-used, the corners dog-eared; two pairs of rosary beads in worn leather purses. She used to love rosary beads when she was little, but although she still went to Mass, she hadn't said the rosary in years. Perhaps she could say one for Dot on Sunday.

Near the bottom of the box, she found a cameo brooch with the pin broken, and decided to get it fixed and wear it. There was more jewellery, none expensive; a few strings of beads and earrings. She'd give them to Yasmin and Ingrid next time they came to see the twins. They'd loved their Granny Gallagher.

Finally, she came to a brown paper bag with something flat inside. She pulled out the contents and found a Paisley scarf in her hand, a scarf identical to the one on the woman going into the pictures on a sunny December day a million years ago. What had the picture been? *The King and I*! She still hadn't seen it.

Annie sighed and thought of ringing Marie, but what did it matter after a million years? She took everything down to the compost heap at the bottom of the garden. It was bitterly cold and pitch dark, but the light from the lounge was enough to see by. She set fire to one letter, then another. The flames flickered eerily. One by one, she added the other letters and the cards. Finally, she put the scarf on top of the miniature inferno. The material melted to nothing in no time, and she thought she could see her mother's face in the red ash, which quickly turned grey, then black, until Annie could see nothing at all.

For a man of eighty-three, Bert Gallagher was in excellent health, but nine days after the death of his wife, he passed away peacefully in his sleep. There was no apparent cause, but everybody took it for granted that Bert had died of a broken heart.

That night, Annie telephoned Mike. His voice was stiff with grief and he sounded glad she'd rung. 'They won't talk to me, Annie,' he groaned. 'I found a note through the letterbox to say me dad was dead.'

Annie came straight to the point. 'I want you to do something, Mike. I want you to hold the usual dinner on Christmas Day.'

'But no-one will come, luv.' He was close to tears. 'No-one came near me at our mam's funeral.'

'Everyone was too scared. You looked very un-approachable. In fact,' she said bluntly, 'you've been unapproachable for a long while.'

'After Sylvia died, all I wanted to do was bury meself in work.'

'You shouldn't shut people out when they want to grieve with you,' she chided. 'The Gallaghers have always grieved together. If you hadn't cut yourself off, Dot wouldn't have got so worked up about you voting Tory.' He would just have been subjected to a non-stop earbashing.

'I suppose not,' he sighed. 'Mind you, Annie, a man's politics is his own affair.'

'I agree. Now about that dinner . . .'

'I'll do it, luv, though I can't see them being persuaded to come.'

'*I'll* persuade them,' she vowed. 'Every single Gallagher will be at your house on Christmas Day, or my name's not Annie Campbell.'

Mike actually chuckled. 'You sound just like our mam!'

Euan came home from America a week before Christmas. The tree stood in its old place in the corner, the lights reflected like little jewels in the dark windows behind. Number seven was sold, and Annie had brought the decorations down from the loft for the final time.

'Have you missed me?' he asked tenderly. The boys were clinging to his legs, demanding to be picked up. 'Not till I've kissed your mother,' he told them.

'Missed you!' Annie said shakily. 'It's been sheer torture.'

It was, as a character in Shakespeare said, the stuff that dreams are made of. A year after Paris, when Rob and Andy were three months old, Euan had arrived out of the blue. Sara, Nigel, and the children were out house-hunting, and the twins were taking their afternoon nap upstairs.

Annie had never ceased to think of Euan, to miss him, since their enchanted holiday, but had assumed she'd been right and things had seemed different in the cold light of Liverpool. Perhaps he'd taken her advice and found someone his own age. One glance at his thin dark face confirmed what she already knew. She loved him still. He was too young, she was too old, she didn't really know him all that well. Now there was something else, a family that he'd never wanted.

'Have you been ill?' was the first thing he said. 'You look much thinner and your face is pale.'

'I'm tired, that's all.' Annie already felt rejuvenated just seeing him. Quite unexpectedly, she felt a rush of desire and longed for him to take her in his arms.

'The last year's been hell,' he said slowly. 'Women haven't exactly jumped at me as you predicted, but I took out a few. I've just got back from Paris, but it was hopeless without you.' He looked at her defiantly. 'You were wrong, Annie, completely wrong. I wasn't fooling myself, I love you . . .' He paused, as if struggling for more words to emphasise the way he felt. Then he shrugged his shoulders and said simply, 'I love you and I want us to be married!'

'I know, luv.' Annie nodded. They were a mismatched pair, but so what? 'It's just that something's happened since Paris.'

'You've met someone else!' His face contorted with alarm.

'No, nothing like that.' She completely forgot that safe, comfortable Ben Wainwright was still waiting for an answer. 'It's . . .' At that moment, Rob set up a wail. She went upstairs without a word. How did you tell someone they'd acquired two sons since you last saw them?

She picked up Rob. 'You little tyrant,' she whispered. 'Look at your brother! There's not a word of complaint from him.' Andy was regarding her serenely whilst doing his utmost to kick away the blankets.

Suddenly, Euan was in the room, staring openmouthed from one baby to the other, dazed incomprehension on his face. Andy gurgled in triumph when his legs broke free, and he regarded his toes with delight.

'I told you something had happened,' Annie said, hastily returning a still complaining Rob to his cot because Euan had burst into tears. She took him in her arms, feeling as if her heart was about to explode with happiness, and thanked her lucky stars that Binnie Appleby had decided not to go to Paris.

'Are you ready?' said Euan. 'The taxi will be here soon.'

'I think so.' She glanced round the lounge. The removal van had just left and their furniture was on its way to the big Victorian semi in Sefton Park in the road next to Sara and Nigel. The Gallagher lads would be arriving en masse tonight, including Mike, to help them get sorted. Annie had wheedled, bullied, yelled, and had managed to get the entire clan together on Christmas

Day. 'Our mam will never be dead while you're alive, Annie,' Tommy said weakly. Cecy had flown over from Italy, and Marie and Justin had come. Only Daniel wasn't there, still wandering the face of the earth searching for a reason to be alive. The atmosphere had been frosty at first, but quickly mellowed, and the lads were again the best of friends. Of course it would never be like old times with Dot and Bert not there, but old times inevitably became new times. Mike had insisted Annie take Dot's place at the table.

'I'll keep an eye on the kids,' Euan said. 'Rob's upset because we can't take the willow tree.'

He blew a kiss and disappeared and Annie went upstairs. Much as she was looking forward to their spacious new house, it was a wrench leaving Heather Close, but she felt it was time to go.

The walls and carpets were full of pale patches where pictures used to hang and furniture had stood for nearly thirty years. She cleared her throat and the sound was ghostly in the empty rooms. She glanced briefly in Sara's room, Daniel's, then the bedroom she had shared with Lauri. Memories chased each other: Sylvia and Eric outside the bathroom at that Christmas party; Marie turning up when Lauri died; Lauri himself, so kind, so difficult – she was never quite sure whether they'd been mostly happy or not. Then there was the time Daniel left, when the house had seemed more like an enemy than a friend.

She sighed and returned downstairs, caressing briefly the smooth, cupola-shaped knob at the bottom, one of the first things she'd noticed when Lauri first brought her to the house. Through the front window, she saw a woman she didn't recognise coming out of number three. Apart from Mrs Vincent, there was hardly a soul in Heather Close she knew. She was the last of the original residents. Chris and Monica Andrews had moved to Crosby when Mrs Vincent refused to give them any peace.

The Close bristled with burglar alarms – no wonder Mike Gallagher had become a multi-millionaire. The red, blue, yellow boxes seemed to signal a warning, not just to prospective burglars, but to ordinary citizens, that the world was becoming a more evil and dangerous place. In fact now, at this very minute, in the first few days of 1991, Great Britain was poised on the brink of war in the Gulf. In a newspaper yesterday, it had been reported that eighteen-year-olds were to be mobilised ready for call up. The report had later been denied on television as scaremongering, but she couldn't help but think that if Daniel was younger or Andy and Rob were older, they could be killed.

She rushed to the other end of the room to make sure the twins were safe. Ready for the journey in their anoraks, jeans and boots, they were dodging in and out of the willow tree. Euan was clapping his hands and they were singing, *Here we go round the mulberry bush, the mulberry bush, the mulberry bush. Here we go . . .*

It was a picture of pure innocence, the total opposite of what she'd just been thinking. Perhaps, in the end, Annie thought hopefully, innocence would prevail. She felt sure it was what most people wanted.

A horn sounded. Euan looked up and caught her eye. He signalled he was going round to the front. Annie watched as the deceptively fragile branches of the willow fell into place. They shuddered momentarily, then were still. She felt a lump in her throat; the tree was the hardest thing of all to leave.

She closed the front door for the final time. Euan was trying to persuade Rob and Andy into the taxi, but they refused until she came.

'Mummy!' they shouted together.

'Coming,' she called. Euan held out his hand and

Annie thought she had never seen a sight more beautiful than her young, handsome husband waiting for her with their children.

MAUREEN LEE

MAUREEN LEE IS ONE OF THE BEST-LOVED SAGA WRITERS AROUND. All her novels are set in Liverpool and the world she evokes is always peopled with characters you'll never forget. Her familiarity with Liverpool and its people brings the terraced streets and tight-knit communities vividly to life in her books. Maureen is a born story-teller and her many fans love her for her powerful tales of love and life, tragedy and joy in Liverpool.

The Girl from Bootle

Born into a working-class family in Bootle, Liverpool, Maureen Lee spent her early years in a terraced house near the docks – an area that was relentlessly bombed during the Second World War. As a child she was bombed out of the house in Bootle and the family were forced to move.

Maureen left her convent school at 15 and wanted to become an actress. However, her shocked mother, who said that it was 'as bad as selling your body on the streets', put her foot down and Maureen had to give up her dreams and go to secretarial college instead.

As a child, Maureen
was bombed out of
her terraced house
in Bootle

Family Life

A regular theme in her books is the fact that apparently happy homes often conceal pain and resentment and she sometimes draws on her own early life for inspiration. 'My mother always seemed to disapprove of me – she never said "well done" to me. My brother was the favourite,' Maureen says.

> I know she would never have approved of my books

As she and her brother grew up they grew apart. 'We just see things differently in every way,' says Maureen. This, and a falling out during the difficult time when her mother was dying, led to an estrangement that has lasted 24 years. 'Despite the fact that I didn't see eye-to-eye with my mum, I loved her very much. I deserted my family and lived in her flat in Liverpool after she went into hospital for the final time. My brother, who she thought the world of, never went near. Towards the end when she was fading she kept asking where he was. To comfort her, I had to pretend that he'd been to see her the day before, which was awful. I found it hard to get past that.'

Freedom – Moving on to a Family of Her Own

Maureen is well known for writing with realism about subjects like motherhood: 'I had a painful time giving birth to my children – the middle one was born in the back of a two-door car. So I know things don't always go as planned.'

My middle son was born in the back of a car

The twists and turns of Maureen's life have been as interesting as the plots of her books. When she met her husband, Richard, he was getting divorced, and despite falling instantly in love and getting engaged after only two weeks, the pair couldn't marry. Keen that Maureen should escape her strict family home, they moved to London and lived together before marrying. 'Had she known, my mother would never have forgiven me. She never knew that Richard had been married before.' The Lees had to pretend they were married even to their landlord. Of course, they did marry as soon as possible and have had a very happy family life.

Success at Last

Despite leaving school at fifteen, Maureen was determined to succeed as a writer. Like Kitty in *Kitty and Her Sisters* and Millie in *Dancing in the Dark*, she went to night school and ended up getting two A levels. 'I think it's good to "better yourself". It gives you confidence,' she says. After her sons grew up she had the time to pursue her dream, but it took several years and a lot of disappointment before she was successful. 'I was *determined* to succeed. My husband was one hundred per cent supportive. I wrote

'I think it's good to "better yourself". It gives you confidence'

lots of articles and short stories. I also started a saga which was eventually called *Stepping Stones*. Then Orion commissioned me to finish it, it was published – and you know the rest.'

What are your memories of your early years in Bootle?

Of being poor, but not poverty-stricken. Of women wearing shawls instead of coats. Of knowing everybody in the street. Of crowds gathering outside houses in the case of a funeral or a wedding, or if an ambulance came to collect a patient, who was carried out in a red blanket. I longed to be such a patient, but when I had diptheria and an ambulance came for me, I was too sick to be aware of the crowds. There were street parties, swings on lamp-posts, hardly any traffic, loads of children playing in the street, dogs without leads. Even though we didn't have much money, Christmas as a child was fun. I'm sure we appreciated our few presents more than children do now.

What was it like being young in Liverpool in the 1950s?

The late fifties were a wonderful time for my friends and me. We had so many places to go: numerous dance halls, The Philharmonic Hall, The Cavern Club, theatres, including The Playhouse where you could buy tickets for ninepence. We were crushed together on benches at the very back. As a teenager I loved the theatre – I was in a dramatic society. I also used to make my own clothes, which meant I could have the latest fashions in just the right sizes, which I loved. Sometimes we'd go on boat trips across the water to New Brighton or on the train to Southport. We'd go for the day and visit the fairground and then go to the dance hall in the evening.

We clicked instantly and got engaged two weeks later

I met Richard at a dance when he asked my friend Margaret up. When she came back she said 'Oh, he was nice.' And then somebody else asked her to dance – she was very glamorous, with blonde hair – still is, as it happens. So Richard asked me to dance because she had gone! We clicked instantly and got engaged two weeks later. I'm not impulsive generally, but I just knew that he was the one.

Do you consider yourself independent and adventurous like Annemarie in The Leaving of Liverpool *or Kitty* in Kitty and her Sisters?

In some ways. In the late fifties, when I was 16, Margaret and I hitchhiked to the Continent. It was really, really exciting. We got a lift from London to Dover on the back of a lorry. We sat on top of stacks of beer crates – we didn't half get cold! We ended up sleeping on the side of the road in Calais because we hadn't found a hotel. We travelled on to Switzerland and got jobs in the United Nations in Geneva as secretaries. It was a great way to see the world. I've no idea what inspired us to go. I think we just wanted some adventure, like lots of my heroines.

Your books often look at the difficult side of family relationships. What experiences do you draw on when you write about that?

I didn't always find it easy to get on with my mother because she held very rigid views. She was terribly ashamed when I went to Europe. She said 'If you leave this house you're not coming back!' But when we got to Switzerland we got fantastic wages at the United Nations – about four times as much as we got at home. When I wrote and told her she suddenly forgave me and went around telling everybody, 'Our Maureen's working at the United Nations in Geneva.'

> 'If you leave this house you're not coming back!'

She was very much the kind of woman who worried what the neighbours would think. When we moved to Kirby, our neighbours were a bit posher than us and at first she even hung our curtains round the wrong way, so it was the neighbours who would see the pattern and we just had the inside to look at. It seems unbelievable now, but it wasn't unusual then – my mother-in-law was even worse. When she bought a new three-piece she covered every bit of it with odd bits of curtaining so it wouldn't wear out – it looked horrible.

My mother-in-law was a strange woman. She hated the world and everyone in it. We had a wary sort of relationship. She gave Richard's brother an awful life – she was very controlling and he never left home. She died in the early nineties and for the next few years my kind, gentle brother-in-law had a relationship with a wonderful woman who ran an animal sanctuary. People tend to keep their family problems private but you don't have to look further than your immediate neighbours to see how things really are and I try to reflect that in my books.

You don't have to look further than your immediate neighbours to see how things really are

Is there anything you'd change about your life?

I don't feel nostalgic for my youth, but I do feel nostalgic for the years when I was a young mum. I didn't anticipate how I'd feel when the boys left home. I just couldn't believe they'd gone and I still miss them being around although I'm very happy that they're happy.

Are friendships important to you?

Vastly important. I always stay with Margaret when I visit Liverpool and we email each other two or three times a week. Old friends are the best sort as you have shared with them the ups and downs of your life. I have other friends in Liverpool that I have known all my adult life. I have also made many new ones who send me things that they think will be useful when I write my books.

Have you ever shared an experience with one of your characters?

Richard's son from his first marriage recently got in touch with us. It was quite a shock as he's been in Australia for most of his life and we've never known him. He turned out to be a charming person with a lovely family. I've written about long-lost family members returning in *Kitty and Her Sisters* and *The Leaving of Liverpool* so it was strange for me to find my life reflecting the plot of one of my books.

Q & A

....

Describe an average writing day for you.

Wake up, Richard brings me tea in bed and I watch breakfast television for a bit. Go downstairs at around 8 a.m. with the intention of doing housework. Sit and argue with Richard about politics until it's midday and time to go to my shed and start writing. Come in from time to time to make drinks and do the crossword. If I'm stuck, we might drive to Sainsbury's for a coffee and read all the newspapers we refuse to have in the house. Back in my shed, I stay till about half seven and return to the house in time to see *EastEnders*.

Have you read them all?
Curl up with a

Maureen Lee

STEPPING STONES

Lizzie O'Brien escapes her dark Liverpool childhood when she runs away to London – towards freedom and a new life. But the past is catching up with her, threatening to destroy her dreams . . .

LIGHTS OUT LIVERPOOL

There's a party on Pearl Street, but a shadow hangs over the festivities: Britain is on the brink of war. The community must face hardship and heartbreak with courage and humour.

PUT OUT THE FIRES

1940 – the cruellest year of war for Britain's civilians. In Pearl Street, near Liverpool's docks, families struggle to cope the best they can.

THROUGH THE STORM

War has taken a terrible toll on Pearl Street, and changed the lives of all who live there. The German bombers have left rubble in their wake and everyone pulls together to come to terms with the loss of loved ones.

LIVERPOOL ANNIE

Just as Annie Harrison settles down to marriage and motherhood, fate deals an unexpected blow. As she struggles to cope, a chance meeting leads to events she has no control over. Could this be Annie's shot at happiness?

DANCING IN THE DARK

When Millie Cameron is asked to sort through her late aunt's possessions, she finds, buried among the photographs, letters and newspaper clippings, a shocking secret . . .

THE GIRL FROM BAREFOOT HOUSE

War tears Josie Flynn from all she knows. Life takes her to Barefoot House as the companion of an elderly woman, and to New York with a new love. But she's soon back in Liverpool, and embarks upon an unlikely career . . .

LACEYS OF LIVERPOOL

Sisters-in-law Alice and Cora Lacey both give birth to boys on one chaotic night in 1940. But Cora's jealousy and resentment prompt her to commit a terrible act with devastating consequences . . .

THE HOUSE BY PRINCES PARK

Ruby O'Hagan's life is transformed when she's asked to look after a large house. It becomes a refuge – not just for Ruby and her family, but for many others, as loves, triumphs, sorrows and friendships are played out.

LIME STREET BLUES

1960s Liverpool, and three families are linked by music. The girls form a successful group, only to split up soon after: Rita to find success as a singer; Marcia to become a mother; and Jeannie to deceive her husband, with far-reaching consequences . . .

QUEEN OF THE MERSEY

Queenie Todd is evacuated to a small town on the Welsh coast with two others when the war begins. At first, the girls have a wonderful time until something happens, so terrifying that it will haunt them for the rest of their lives . . .

THE OLD HOUSE ON THE CORNER

Victoria lives in the old house on the corner. When the land is sold, she finds herself surrounded by new properties. Soon Victoria is drawn into the lives of her neighbours – their loves, lies and secrets.

THE SEPTEMBER GIRLS

Cara and Sybil are both born in the same house on one rainy September night. Years later, at the outbreak of war, they are thrown together when they enlist and are stationed in Malta. It's a time of live-changing repercussions for them both . . .

KITTY AND HER SISTERS

Kitty McCarthy wants a life less ordinary – she doesn't want to get married and raise children in Liverpool like her sisters. An impetuous decision and a chance meeting twenty years later are to have momentous repercussions that will stay with her for ever . . .

THE LEAVING OF LIVERPOOL

Escaping their abusive home in Ireland, sisters Mollie and Annemarie head to Liverpool – and a ship bound for New York. But fate deals a cruel blow and they are separated. Soon, World War II looms – with surprising consequences for the sisters.

MOTHER OF PEARL

Amy Curran was sent to prison for killing her husband. Twenty years later, she's released and reunited with her daughter, Pearl. But Amy is hiding a terrible secret — a tragedy that could tear the family apart . . .

NOTHING LASTS FOREVER

Her marriage failing, Brodie Logan returns to her childhood home, letting out the spare rooms to women with nowhere else to go. Their lives intertwine and friendships develop but then tragedy strikes and the women find that nothing lasts forever . . .

MARTHA'S JOURNEY

1914. To Martha Rossi's horror her underage son has enlisted and is promptly despatched to France, with devastating consequences. Martha embarks on a journey that will give voice to every mother who ever sacrificed a son, taking her right to No. 10's door.